DANCING WITH DEATH

BOOK ANTHOLOGY

BY

POETRY PLANET

ACKNOWLEDGMENT

To the Poetry Planet Family

To the administrators

To the participants of this anthology

To the members who never failed to support me

The Poets who has been there since the day this group started,

Thank you!

-Tess Ritumalta

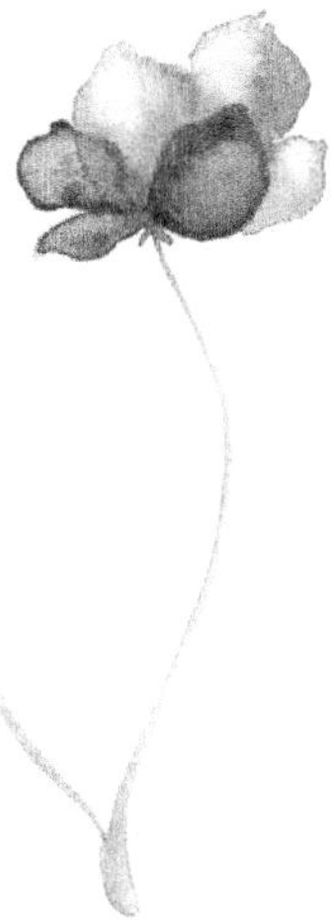

Fran Budd

FOREWORD

No one understands "dancing with death" better than those who did experienced near-death situations. In our journey to life, our scariest moment probably is dying, but if we accept it as part of us, that everyone has their end-point, and then we will no longer be afraid of dying…

We dread the idea of dying at an early age as we have so many things to do and yet, so little time left to live… But by making our lives meaningful and well-spent every day, then we can overcome this fear within us…

Wars, accidents, and sickness, are near-death situations beyond the control of survivors…and worst yet, the end-point of those who never made it. So live our lives the best we can while we have it.

The poets are among the best people artistically expressing their emotions regarding this matter… This book contains near-death experiences, feelings, and fears about the 2020 pandemic written in poetry for us to look back should we have survived this pestilence…

Surely, this book is a fact-revealer that we will surely love to read and so will our future generations!

So grab your copy and add it in your bookshelf not only for you and your children, but also for your grandkids and probably even by your great grandchildren.

The Publisher

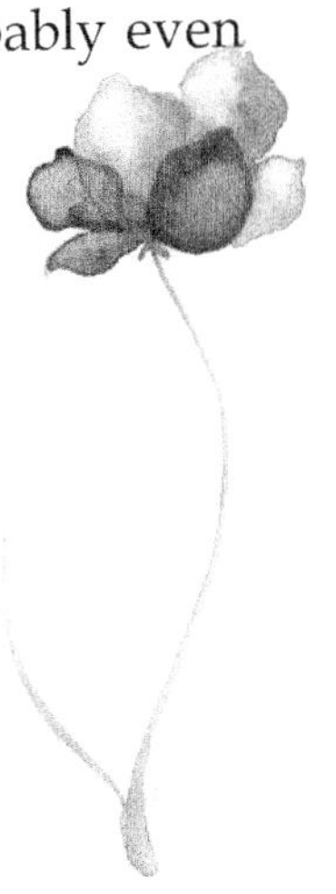

PREFACE

Dancing With Death

Hitting the dance floor with death is an individual excursion of steps. The means starting from the hour of birth into the baffling domain of the obscure. That is the reason religion has assumed a significant part into the mentality of human progress. Passing is a piece of Life. We are moving together. The dance of vastness before the entryways of time. We can live our fantasies, as we are dreaming our future. Leaving your bouquet to pendulant and pirouette, one final time prior to being assented into the obscure away. Time is unending from the midsection to the transfer of the unknown, as you in the course of your life acknowledge the capture of death straightforwardly.

So what is the Dancing With Death? You will by all methods eat up this idyllic exposition of poetry with the final blow end --last second quest for life's more profound meaning. These incredible creators share their verses following the conviction of their sharp interior voice of life, and with its effect on the dance of death. This collection, we concentrate overwhelmingly, on the communicates got with these prize researchers. The inspiration and motivation driving this assortment of sonnets, rhyme stanzas, is the essence of life that are connected with the sashay inside. The abstains will vitalize your readings. As we appreciate this resuscitating group pieces from our most prominent artists. Enjoy!

Daniel Miltz
Writer

Published by Poetry Planet Book Publishing House

Designed and arranged by Tess Ritumalta

Edited by MARIE Ezekiel

CONTENTS

THE CONTRIBUTING POETS

Abdullahi Yahaya
Abigirl Phiri
Aditi Lahiry
Afrose Saad
Agu Samuel Chukwuemerie
Ailenemae Ramos
Alifya Kothari
Allison Gilliland
Amb Maid Čorbić
Amb Sirajudeen Sherifudeen
Amiya Rout
Amrita Chatterjee
Amrita Lahiri Bhattacharya
Amrita Mallik
Angela Chinweike
Anisha Mordani
Anjana Prasad
Antara Bose
Anu Gupta
Ariba Anarz Paradise
Aruna Bose
Asher Chipu
Ashutosh Meher
Babita Saraf Kejriwal
Bhawna Himatsinghani
C.I. Nwagod Chinagorom
Călin Oana Alexandra
Cha Jimenez
Chandra Sekhar Batabyal
Chandra Sundeep
Chinagorom Samuel
Chosen Samuel
Christian Chidozie Okoro
Colin Andrew MacEachern
Cristina Juanite
Crystal King
Daisie Fpartido Vergara
Damilare AL Adaby
Daniel Miltz
Deepa Acharya
Deepa Vankudre
Deepak Kumar
Denis Maira
Diaps Lee BW
Dijana Uherek Stevanović
Douglas Perry Massa
DrEkta Sachdeva
DrShubhashish Banerjee
Duska Kontic
Eddy Eteng
Edna Salona Labrador
Elik Roytharts
Ellen Retoma
Elvis Elvy Bestpoet
Ency Bearis
Erlinda G Tisado
Estelita Sagum
Eta Mersimi
Faseela Mv
Ferguson Frances Lylia
Francisca Budd
Gabriel S. Weah
Gee Sups
George Yacoub Yacoub
Gerry Mundy
Harmeet Kaur

Hassan Hamay
Helen Shenton
Hema Mordani
Hyginus Syxtus
Irish Susa
Iwan Dartha
James Timothy Acheneje
Jimmy Calaycay
John Carlo Miguel Perez
Jonny Paul
Jyoti Arya
Jyotirmoy Ghosal
Kanakagiri Shakuntala
Kanisha Shah
Karen Glen
Karil Anand
Kat Singer
Katrina Black Butterfli
Kenneth Munene
Kirti Santosh
Kishor Kumar Mishra
Lee Love
Leena Ritisha Auckel
Ljubisav Grujić Gruja
Lord L Lanre
Lucy Abellana Mendiola
Lynne Sara Gue
Ma'am J Lo
Margaret Karim
Maria Elvira Fernandes Correia
Marion Remnant Parish
Mary Lynn Luiz
Mary-Anne Godkin
Mbuh Francisco-Selina
Medy Villapando
Meenakshi Dwivedi
Mildred Par
Mona Sharma
Mousumee Baruah
Mrinalini Saurav Kakkar
Muhammad Aminu Hassan
Mxolisi Masuku
Myrna Tejada
Naaz Shaikh
Nandita De
Narayan Maikap
Navneet Gill Grewal
Neha Mittal
Ngam Emmanuel
Ninfa Vasquez Mateo
Nwankwo Victor Avic
Olamilekan Ayinla
Olivia Hidlebaugh-Cool
Ollga Farmacistja
Pappa Jalo
Patrick Epperson
Phillip Gibson
Pooja Mandla
Prajaranjan Panda
Priti Dhopte
Rabii Yossef
Rajbanshi Manmohan
Rakesh Chandra
Rati Banga Pala
Rattan Noori
Refika Dedić
Ritemvara Sharma
Rohini J
Rrafika Rangwala
Rupali Gore
Samuel Darasimi
Samuel Oseyoma-Onoseri

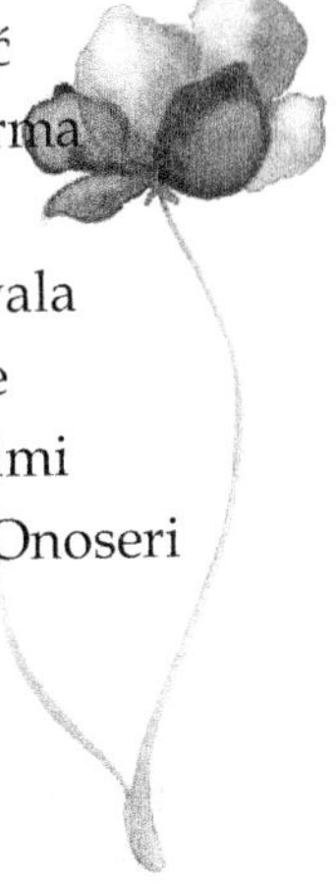

Saquib Naseer Siddiqui
Sarah Ramphal
Sarala Balachandran
Sarita Khullar
Satish Srivastava
Sehma Helaa
Selma Kopic
Sharmistha Das
Sheetal Ashpalia
Shikha Gupta
Silva Alisa Xhemo
Sistoso Ben
Sofia Skleida
Sonali Bansal
Soubhagyabati Giri
Stephenite Orlando
Stojanka Kovačević
Sudha Dixit
Sudha Rani Pati
Sujata Dash
Suresh Chandra Sarangi
Swapna Das
Swati Das

Taferi M. Simon
Terry Dailey
Tess Ritumalta
Thenmozhi Rajagopal
Tiare Nopera
Tshë Go
Tshering Wangchuk
Ulma Taboada
Varsha Madhulika
Vasudha Pansare
Vavroovahana Patra
Vee Barnes
Vee Maistry
Veena Kumari
Vicki Hangren Hauler
Victor Agbor
Victor Wesonga
Vildana Stanišić
Vince Valdez
Vinod Singh
Vishwanathan Iyer
Yanita Ismail

CHAPTER I

A THROWBACK

DANCE WITH DEATH

People fight for life
from first to last breath,
sometimes with a lot of courage,
sometimes with a lot of fear.
But regardless of age,
for everyone,
life is dear.

We often play with life
and challenge destiny,
or rush through it breathlessly
in the hopes of grabbing it more
before,
in an instant,
it escapes us and disappears.

In carefree time
we are unnecessarily worried
about small things,
while in times of crisis we realize
how beautiful these little things are
that life gives.
And we begin to appreciate
every moment
with family and friends,
every breath of breeze,
the smell of flowers,
dusk and sunrise...

Then, we slow down,
we slow down in that race,
in a light rhythm so we could dance.
Without regret...
To the last breath...

CORONA VIRUS...

A daily routine and a life well planned
Came to a sudden halt like women on the sight of a wedding band
The invisible enemy has taken over and I no longer can ponder
"What is life" or "how to become a millionaire"
All thoughts I never had but now forced to abandon
A life so unfair I now must stay at home and not prefer
Not prefer to sing in the park, not prefer to skinny dip when it's dark, not prefer to make my mark
I'm bound to this bed and as I try to leave, it wraps me and whispers "stay with me"
Staring at the wall I began to wonder how the beer virus took over
Corona is 4.5% alcohol and the world is 71% water
The odds are in our favor yet corona overpowers and the world signs a waver
I can no longer cut my hair, visit my heir, or have an affair
Coronavirus set me free, stop this spree and let me start charging a fee
My bank account is draining faster than when I was getting my degree
But now I'm smart, I stand 6 feet apart, so much that physical touch became a foreign notion
Human contact was replaced with animal contact to not stir a commotion
Yet while in social isolation all I want to do is make a mess
Throw toilet paper on houses like after prom with my fancy dress
To go drinking with Corona until I pass out on her bed
Later in her room, after a few coughs, and sneezes Corona's V card had fled
Symptom-free I walk to the nearest ice creamery
Handshake the cashier, get rid of all the fear, and disappear into the atmosphere

THE UNFORGETTABLE YEAR !!!

2020 is an unforgettable year
So many incidents at a time
The most dangerous attacks of COVID-19
Grasping lots of innocent souls
An invisible fear acts as an attire
Nobody can't dare to drape
A winning sigh of COVID-19
Silly human beings act as ants
Easily can kill by scary touch
Baby to older nobody can hold
What a pathetic moment is that
Death knocks at the door every moment
Restrictions to move on
Follow rules & regulations
That's the prime concern
Each step in the earth
The social distance a major fact
Though badly affects the education system
The priority is to live on
Afterall life is only one in this form
We learn from this stage
Pray to God at all stages
He can show the way of life
Without His blessing life is doomed
2020 is a year of fear
Craft its name as a treasure
Nobody can deny the power of that
How can live as a captivating
A good thing is reflected
Bonding of love still exists
It makes all at a time

To spend time with dear ones
When all are busy only professional plot
This one gives that magic stage
All are bound to stay at home
With fear in a loving zone
Family bonding is so strong
Giving all spirits of life
A realization must come to mind
We are here to live with dear ones

Copyright Afrose Saad

TO SUM UP LAST YEAR

Expectations from last year were, in fact, numerous. To start working in the graphic and web design field, and even to go out with friends I haven't seen since last year thanks to the coronavirus. I had many unfulfilled desires, to travel the world and visit the most beautiful famous places that many did not have at hand. I wish I had met many people from the written trail, looking forward to the first sincere loves that were waiting for me somewhere around the corner. I believed that 2020 would bring many opportunities to perfect my numerous desires. To understand many people around me and to live life as if it were the last.

Copyright Amb. Maid Corbic

Bosnia and Herzegovina

MY WAY TO SAY THANK YOU

Who about what, I about him. And what will I do when he delights me, again and again, every day and surprises me with his actions. And the times are hard, life has been reduced to the blink of an eye.

Paradise is leaving us, now you are there, and the next moment you are gone. I am terrified. The line between life and death is never thinner. Well, then I so often wander into some thoughts, dive into the depths of my soul. Tears roll down my face without permission and I feel indescribable fear. Not of death, not of disease and transience. I feel the fear of leaving this world before I embrace it once more before I tell him how much I love and respect him, how much I admire him, and how much I appreciate him and his work. I am afraid not to leave before I tell him how much he means to me, how grateful I am to him, how much he inspires me, and how much I never know to write about him because every word is poor yes describe him and his virtues. How to describe so much heart in words? How to place so much beauty of the soul in a song and a story? That's why I try to write again and again and mostly I erase everything I write even faster. Because that's not what I wanted to say, my feelings are even stronger, stronger, even purer and deeper, more, more, much more ... more and more than what can be described in words. But I have to write because I'm afraid I'll leave before I tell him and tell him everything. And then I think, he knows that without words because after all, he is my brother and friend, best friend and teacher, my protector and mentor, my role model and comrade-in-arms, my inexhaustible inspiration for which I will never give up - my Senaid. But still, if death deceives me, if I leave before I tell him everything I want him to know that I left happy and calm because I had the honor to meet the best being that has ever walked this earth, the being that has left the most beautiful mark on my soul and convinced me that good people and sincere friends still exist today.

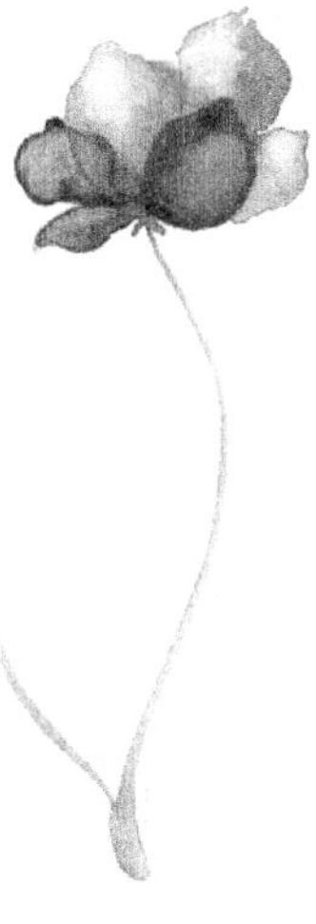

Thank you, my brother.

Copyrighjt Amb. Dr. Vildana Stanišić

Bosnia and Herzegovina

THE 2020 GLASS IS EMPTYING

As the year glass of 2020 starts to finally empty...the last few “mindset” grains of sand wave goodbye to a year of extraordinary extremes of joy but mostly despair...

The grains of Faith hope and charity wait patiently behind the grains of reflection and anxiety, knowing they will be the first through after the time glass is turned and lead the new year in with pure intentions of a better life for all...

The complex mix of these “mind-set” grains will always fall erratically after the glass is turned, ...but one thing can be assured, ...it’s not the order in which these grains fall that challenge our lives ...it’s how we adapt and challenge ourselves with the opportunities these events can bring and always to live life to the full

Happy New Year let’s make it a great one

Namaste x

Copyright Gerry Mundy

2020

Po pres
Po pres albanologet
te vijne,
ne sargofagun tim
te pa gjetur.
Kesaj stine kerkimesh
do te me gjejne,
ne vetmine mijevecare
te pa paprekur.
Albanologu do te mar
patjeter cmim,
nga ky zbulim kaq ì gjetur.
Kam frike se dhe atij do t,i
bjere atak, siç ndodhi me ate
te Egjyptit te vjeter.
Po ky zbulim do te jete krejte ndryshe.
Nuk do te flas per zbulim kulturash te lashte.
Ky do te flas per vetmi gruaje
fosilet e te cilit
mban ky sargofag.

2020 "A TSUNAMI IS COMING"

A tsunami is coming...
from sea to shining sea...
Righteous indignation...
will sweep this nation to set us free!
***

The Constitution of this republic...
will withstand the political injustice...
Imposed upon "We the People"...
from the halls of so-called supreme justice!
***

As the tsunami's waters receded it will take with it...
all those who were traitors and filled with personal greed...
Again, the Patriots of this republic will join hand in hand...
to restore what "We the People" choose and agree!
***

This is and will always be, "One Nation...
Under God", created for all of the worlds to see.
Let her flag forever fly over the home of the brave...
and for those willing to defend a freedom to be free!
***

IN REMINISCENCE OF 2020

I fought every challenge
In the last year back
Happiness, frustration needed patience
Because life was on the wrong track
Reminding every moment
Beheld on the wrapping case
Alone crawling jumbled wall
Nobody care but their cynical gaze
Fragile heart needed charging
When the disaster began to strike
The year was too fast running
Life wasn't easy to drive
Sinking in a tight slumber
Erased some of the miserable days
To get back my joys in the summer
Which was blossom in a beautiful portray

Copyright Yanita Ismail

"The Coming Deluge" By Colin MacEachern

You don't like the mask?
Wait until you need a snorkel.

You don't believe in this virus?
Wait until you get dengue fever
from the warmer water
Huge blood sucking mosquitoes
In your temperate zone.

You don't want a vaccine?
Wait until you're crying
for medicine
for malaria.

Covid is your last warning.
If you don't change I'm coming to get you
with my rising waters
and my parasitic infections
And my environmental refugees
bringing war over scarcity.

Sincerely,
Your broken planet.

P.S. Adapt or perish.

"The Illumination" by Colin MacEachern

Through multiple disappointments
and setbacks
comes greater happiness
based on realism.

Partisanship, idealism and ideology
are herpes of the mind
Periodically distracting
And potentially
Triggers for a cancer
Far worse than
Any of the antecedents.

"Res ipsa loquitur" by Colin MacEachern

If it walks like a duck
and talks like a duck
perhaps it's a patriot
Down on his luck

Live on TV you can watch her die
On anti-social media
Not a tear shed
and why?

Infotainment and entertainment
One distraction
Indivisible under God

Spoil the child spare the rod.

No country lasts forever
Just ask the Slavs
And yet we endeavour
We, the haves

Alleged Have Nots have risen
From their hyperbolic prison.
Their fuel source is fear
Res Ipsa loquitur.

GOD BLESS THE BLOOD

Encryption of skull reads s.o.s level fields focus to zoom reddot dash
forehead flash boom!

The cemetery Gates are rusted (Times have Dared,) that none come
in.
Viral greed that sewed its seeds BLEEDS hate in trusted SINS. But
within the wings of grandeur exposes
the air that lets us breathe.
For Underneath these HIGHER STANDARDS we all own our
shares of make-believe.
The soldier sits
in solitude revealed that there is no war.
Yet holding shields to shoulder cruelly kills no sword.
The dark knight finds no flight he lies gasping on the GROUND.
We see the wrong but to do what's right the blood drops make no
sound. These frustrated compilations are of the land that we have
today.
Those soldiers sit SO WE CAN STAND.
God Bless the BLOOD
I pray...

THE YEAR 2020 IN OUR LIFE TIMES THE WORST EVER.

It betrayed our expectations beyond measure.
We welcomed The year 2020 with all pomps and grandeur befitting on New Year's Day.
could we ever imagine the fangs it would open to bite deeply as days went by?
an unknown touch loving demon it invited
Touched and spread.
Down with fever, phlegm
dry, choked
many died.
corpses piled on morgues or open spaces stretched.
Last rites of many not done.
The horrible scene is witnessed around the globe.
No medicine, no treatment for the unique virus to be found.
Lockdown imposed not to venture out for the virus waiting.
we became a self-made captive in our homes months on end.
Helpless humanity wondering for
a virus rendering to naught our pride.
schools ,colleges ,factories etc.shut
Threw life out of gear.
Vaccine we cried
Throat dried.
lakhs died.
"Annus Horribilis"
Thy name ..
Two Thousand Twenty
Thou played with us the cruel game
we can't forgive Thee.
we let you go in a sombre mood.
Bade you a goodbye ever
not to see such a nasty year satanic, again.

BLUEBOL

Curled up cravings around the cypress tree
Lost word in impure, water blood
Heart in stone, a soul in flame
Pre-mortal turmoil, calm waters of income.
Intrusive bridge causes ark of awakening
He throws Hungarian women in scared, crying water
Dry tears, roast floating pink roses
The smell will grow into a rotten, flaming spring.
Talk quieter, say no more about blue pain
Marija Virgo of baked, with a rough face
Dust stoned with a heated limestone
On the shovels of fear of sunflower madness.
Mornings pass screams die, a woman on the edge
Falls into the powerlessness of ignorance, beneath eternal Nemanja
A dizzy wish is looking for a friend, melts in
The unleashed reason among the vaults.

SERGE OF THE GODS

Unnoticed, they crossed
Years over my face
They took pictures of wrinkles, waves of the sea...
Amazing eyes of a girl
An empty character of a tired old lady
Nailed to the crying windows...
It bends down far, mysterious
Childhood in front of the predatory
With a hot look at the display...
A burst mirror hides
The riddle of the runaway sentences
Impressive birds are falling
On the desert of tyranny secret...
Jago played under the rose thorn
In the heart of the foam raindrops
The storm of the prisoners of the wind is digging
The freedom of the gala... good is not...
Kurban Bayram tripping
Through the new stories of Ulix
Fighting angel trying
To destroy the Holy Trinity
Blinded wings of Jabuchil
White birch in the fall of birch
Celebrated jelek unbuttoned
In the mud defies gold
On the slit neck
The cricks of the killed rhyme
They are rattling in the vast bosom
A man of clay speaks...
I stare at the rays of the shy Sun
My divine eastern truth

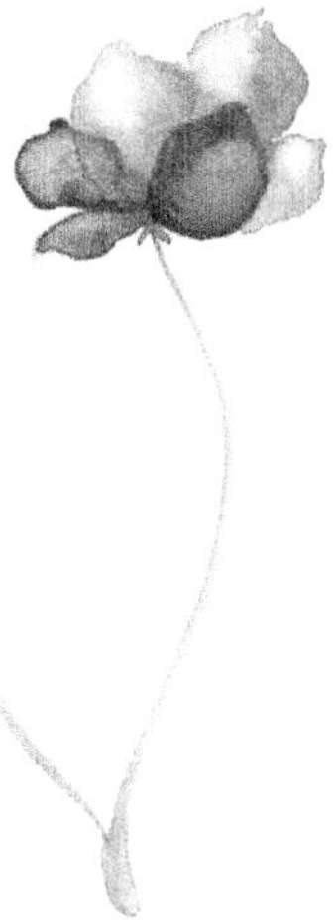

Reveals misconceptions of navigation
The darkness of sin flames over
By the magic of menelaja...
Huje, winds cut, sang
Reasonable, whitelogrivable
Prophecy caused by Zurlom...
The wrathful arrival of the gods
Threat, swing, hostia in mud
Unbeatable armada failed
In the lustful slaughter of green anger
Conspiracy hat of the week
Going wild all night... coming out
Mother died from the silent
The coffin of dark blue echoes
Zaumlja is crying with words
In a starving grave...
I hear the call of upset waves.

LACUNA

Those mornings enveloped...
In ivory dripping tenderness...
She would wait for his words,
After cleansing herself as a cerulean sky.
She wouldn't let anyone intrude
into their hallowed confinement.
Albeit, the fencing was done using
shreds procured,
From those frayed clandestine knots,
That she stealthily kept knitting.
Those that none of the velums
choking in her knew...
She is still bewildered...
How such willowy motifs could excavate that deep.
That it created a lair there...
Somewhere there, that she still can't fathom.
Since then her lungs feel mowed under a combustible iron box.
Since then her gullet is parched,
Even as she is bathed in reverberating deluge.
Since then her neutral neurons have begun to palpitate.
Since then, it feels as if...
Graphite clumps crawl from her arteries instead of blood.
Vanquished, she is now being skewered in that lacuna.

THE OCEAN'S EULOGY

often an ocean shrieks through me,
and my veins have to bear her smoldering salts.
some gregarious salts, some morose...
they keep clambering through my veins like crabs that maunder.
gregarious folks tickle, morose paints using black.
today the ocean has been unwavering and still...
as if she heard some death calls...
hung around the coral polyps...
inflammable polyps, with luscious, amber lips, and impish grins.
though, some brain molecules in me murmur...
"could that be a trick, a conjuring?"
as she loves to play with the 'Water Lilies'
or else can an ocean ever be called towards the gallows...
she is an ocean, we have been savoring her cruel ecstatic fate,
cruel ecstatic, it's not merely pinning an oxymoron...
she is an ocean, vaunted to inhale our greed and filth,
stripped and bleeding, beneath a veil of shimmering waves.
we can't write her eulogy.
she has to be awake tomorrow and each day...
she can't be entombed...

THE DIFFERENTLY-ABLED YEAR, 2020

The humans attacked 2020 with derision,
The reason being its differently-abled nature.
Treating life casually has been the human's forte,
Drowning himself in the trivial and temporal joys,
Mesmerized by the lustre of the fake gold.
Yet, the innocent and Nature didn't mind,
And so, they were spared, while God's fury,
The world witnessed from behind the locked doors and windows,
Unsettling the placid texture,
For highlighting the necessary and discarding the baseless.
Hence, as the dust got settled, the eyes opened,
The earlier lessons of unity, simplicity, and spirituality,
Got reinforced as they scurried to save themselves.
Partying or explicit display of wealth and stupidity,
Can and should wait unless the authentic demands
Like love and relationships get fulfilled.
The enlightened ones tweaked themselves,
To not let the contagion cast its evil spell on them,
They're the real heroes, battling an adversity
With such a spectacular show of grit and determination,
And where there's faith, nothing can pull them back.
A bare minimum is more than enough,
Humans can survive on simple food and clothing,
Luxuries are a waste especially when life can go,
Needing not a second to put an end to the mortality,
Humans aren't immortal, that's a lesson for sure.
Irresponsibility and shirking duties,
Though the near and dear ones ignored,
The divine couldn't, and hence, snatched away,
Many such close ones and repenting didn't help,
However, rectifying themselves can save many.

The world is a big family, proved again this time,
One's faltering step or deliberate defiance,
Put countless in danger for his whimsical whims.
Hence, it's time to realize the power of unity,
To save each other and simultaneously the world.
Sadly, stubborn fools can't be transformed.
Despite glaring evidence and consequences, they refuse.
Only for them, the perpetual fight continues,
Still, we don't know when the pandemic will end,
However, conquering the asinine mindset, certainly can.

Copyright Amrita Mallik

SPARKLES OF WIND

glittering flashes of light
depicted as a cluster of change
sparkles resembling flecks
of dust iridescent particles of flashes
of light blushing cheer lights
the new tide has become the new season
has come with its gift of sparkles
the wind be softer than a sigh
a change in the wind often portends changes
the weather changeable likely
to make formidable changes
the positive sentiment of rain
a new rain of happy wonders
falling with happiness
down in the form of droplets of water
meaning of newness
a new change make or become different
a new entity denoting a new beginning
a spark of hope.

Copyright Asher Chipu

BED OF ROSE

Life of pressure
Made with adventure
Full of conspirator
And judging by the creator.
We came with pressure
Forgetting our creature
Focus only on our goal
And forgetting our role
Many live in difficulty,
While Many live in wealth.
Some forget their destination,
And some are striving for emotion.
Some wishes to gain power,
And skip it off to be a lier
Some wish to be kind and dear
While many are striving in the midstream of tears and fear.
Life is nothing but trial and error
A human is heartless like a warrior.
If we can live purer and fuller
Our heaven will be surer like the almighty lover.

2020- ITS THRILL AND PERIL

The thrill and peril of the immediate past year are uniquely remembered.
A leap year that left my limb lame.
Ubiquitously traumatic like a pill so bitter.
A cosmic cycle completed in a haste.
Tagged to a terrible and pathetic pandemic.
Unheard of and an unprecedented and rampaging imp.
Its' lethal liturgies still litter our lips.
The wave of its clammy winds still freezes fist.
Systemic sufferings ensued with mundane menaces.
Next was precarious protests that engulfed us here.
Official bullets flew to traceable places and made us hostages.
The fever of such futile exercise still endears.
Skirmishes of communal clashes occurred.
With prominent people like me scampering for safety.
The scars of the brutal bruises are still before us.
And the most aggrieved still yell for justice.
The experience is relatively mixed.
There were meagre moments of enthralling gaieties.
Few favorable euphorias of fanfare and bliss.
Gatherings of excitement, merriment, and sobriety.
The year in retrospect has already gone.
With patches of social and economic leakages to be sealed.
The air it blew was harshly hot.
As we struggle to ameliorate its resultant misery.

WHAT A YEAR!

What a bizarre year, chaos all around

Corona comes, all of a sudden

Comes loneliness in a mess

Next is knockdown all over the world

With an empty pocket, caged like a bird

Day and night, death in sight

A virus gets its height, life kept in a bad light

What a bizarre year

What keeps life in fear.

Copyright Abdullahi Yahaya

THE LOST YEAR

The year 2020 began like any other.
We gathered with parents, sisters, and brothers.
Awake until midnight to see in the new year.
Raising a toast and making resolutions sincere.
Then the rumours and stories we began to hear.
Something sinister ...definitely to fear.
A bacteria...or virus....a terrible beast?
Something was spreading far in the east.
Did it come from bats or pangolins?
Some talked of wet markets amongst other things.
A few weeks later, we were filled with dread.
A virus was moving and was quick to spread.
From country to country and continent to continent.
Nothing could stop it....was fast and rampant.
Masks, lockdowns, and cessation of hugs.
Lest things worsen the spread of this bug.
Our way of life changed, it made such an impact.
We craved human touch, the physical contact.
Schools shut down, offices too.
All work was online, shops had big queues.
Panic was rife and people were confused.
Lockdown enforced...so many rules!
Coronavirus raged all around.
Wearing its cloak and terrible crown.
People were sick, many even died.
When will this end, the people sighed.
We somehow hobbled through 2020.
No sparks on Diwali and Xmas were low-key.
But hope came along in the form of a jab.
Thanks to clever scientists busy in labs.
We pray that soon there are vaccines for all.
How desperately we want to get back to normal!

Copyright Meenakshi Dwivedi

A YEAR EASY TO FORGET

The sun rose in the east
The first to open the year
With joy and happiness
Fireworks filled their sky
Little did they know
It would become an unknown flame
Stretching for miles, crossing oceans
And invading homes, regardless of who is home
Suffocating its inhabitants without fear till death
And a simple speech would easily infect the ears of all
A cough on the road alerted the system
And you would be taken away and left alone
Another cough in public was a murder
A cough in doors provoked chaos
Even if you were family
The year came as one month with flying hours
With few days for memories, fingers pointing east
And mistrust for comfort, boredom on repeat
Lies and myth became interesting stories
Even the workers would stop to listen
Ghost towns formed quickly
Yet some made profits bigger than gold
Greed lurked in the shadows, taking from our fear
Even when we refused to touch hands, we still lost
Our jobs would flee if we choose safety, so what was the point
Our face would learn to fear our hands
Our schools would close themselves from us
Knowledge sipping out, how would we prepare for our future
The road closed itself from our footprint, our freedom taken away
Grandpa and grandma would have to stay away for Christmas
Hugs and kisses would have to wait

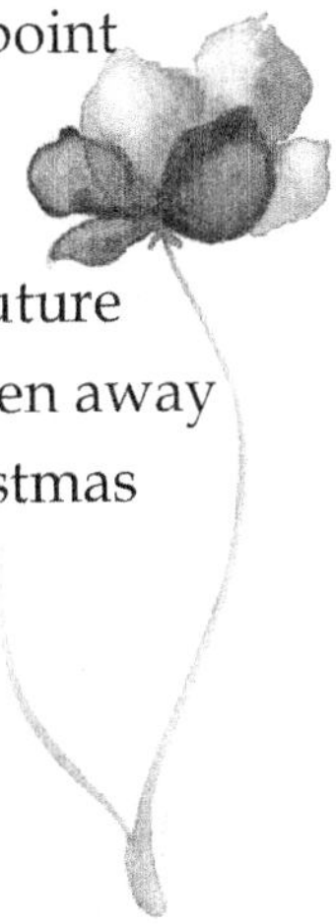

Which to take, which is real, too many pills forming
Where to go? All place closed? Even funerals breed funerals
But at least the earth is cleaner, the air is better than 1800
At least crime and war has retreated for a while, we can sleep
Oh no! Not all are safe.
Some on the street homeless with nothing for lunch
Suffering from the smoke that burns their lungs
A victim of poverty was their crime, with nowhere to go
A simple sneeze would create panic, unlike before.

A GLIMPSE OF 2020

As I walk through the valley of death
I know God has not failed me yet
As I see demons prowling each day
Just waiting for me to fall on my knees
God always sends His angels my way
To keep me strong in my struggle each day
As I hear worldly forces surrounding me
Trying to devour every inch of me
Whispering in my ears and swears
My flesh gets weak I couldn't bear
But prayer leads me to what's beautiful
God lets me see what's real and wonderful
Because greater is He who gave us love
Greater is He who mends our heart
And as I step on pebbles and stones,
There are bricks I may have stepped on
Sometimes, being ripped off as I stumble
But I get up twice each time I fall
I know God is with me in my troubles
He alone as my guide; angels by my side
I know, I'll forever be safe and sound.
This is supposedly a beautiful story
I made it for you and for the young generations to see
This, an inspiring poem I must convey
Also, wish to be singing this someday
As I reminisce each wondrous memory
Happy was able to write another poetry
Hoping to put some notes and melody
So I can sing this song eventually.
Had it not been to strife and strain
Brought about by the CoVID -19

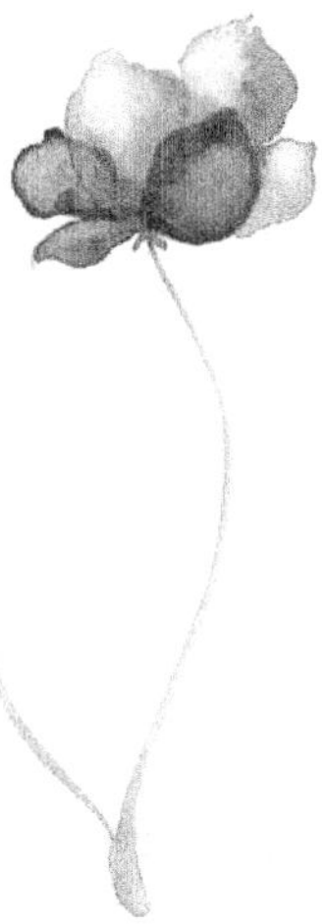

I could have traveled the world with you again
But no matter what the world gives us
I will always remember God's promise for each of us
It may have been a year full of maladies
But it has given us many lessons to learn
Grateful still for the negativity
Which turned out to be positive energy
Oh, what a wonderful world it should be!

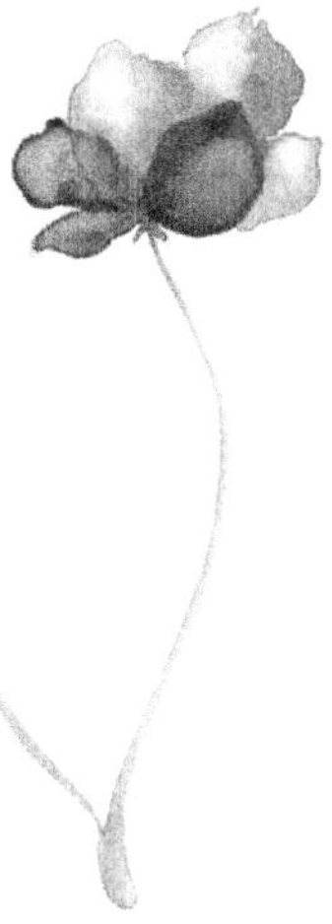

THE SAD YEAR 2020

The string is strong
The grip is fierce
My heart was in trouble
I wish all could be over
Death disguised as fear
Sad year
Innocent was gone
Life in the grave
Joy lost, happiness gone
Fear overcome the spirit of man
Memories that can never fade away
Everything's moving with no place to go
As the day and night pass by I just lay and crying
Never do I want to feel this again.
Youth crying for help
Protesting to express their feelings
Demanding for a better nation
Soldier killed
Flags stain with the blood of innocent
The country turned upside down
I feel unsecured
Know where to go
Darkness is upon the surface of the Land
It strikes my heart like a lighting
Just the worst time of the year
How desperate we want to go back to normal!! ......

Copyright Samuel Darasimi

FAREWELL - 2020

We haven't been around in years
Welcome there
Millions full of poison in faith
You killed people.
In the presence of father-son you
Someone took it away
You brutally wiped it out
Someone's head is red.
What crime did we commit?
You have such a big punishment.
I can't believe you're in disguise
We came to a lie.
Bring the unknown disease to the forefront
You created and destroyed
There was laughter all over the world
What good is a website if it simply "blends in" with everything else out there?
Farewell to tears
Get out of here soon
Happy New Year
will take place for you.
Where are you now?
Please come to us,
We are passing through a lot of trouble,
The whole universe is fighting with
The unseen pandemic demons.
Even though we don't know
When will we be a winner
In the battle,
The one that we should conquer them,
Or the other that they will conquer us,

The unseen demons on the opposite side
I am sure
The unseen power will come out
To rescue the human races
From the pandemic period one day.

Copyright Suresh Chandra Sarangi

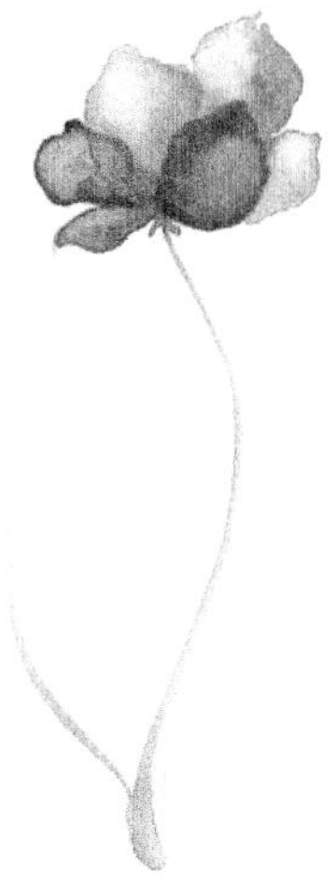

MANY LESSONS LEARNT

Many lessons have been learnt,
During this year,
We have learnt,
How to live with fear,
How to wear masks,
And not suffocate,
How to stay at home,
And keep yourself updated,
With the latest books,
And the latest films,
And the latest news.
We have also learnt to choose,
The positive attitude,
And reject the depressing mood.
We have learnt to wash our hands,
And eat what is cooked at home,
Read a book and write a poem,
Listen to music and watch
Some movie fantastic,
Talk to friends and family,
To avoid being lonely.
Now this year is gone,
Will the new year,
Bring some peace of mind?
Will we some joy find?
Will, we be free from fear,
And anxiety?
Only time will tell,
Whether we will bid farewell,
To global tragedy.

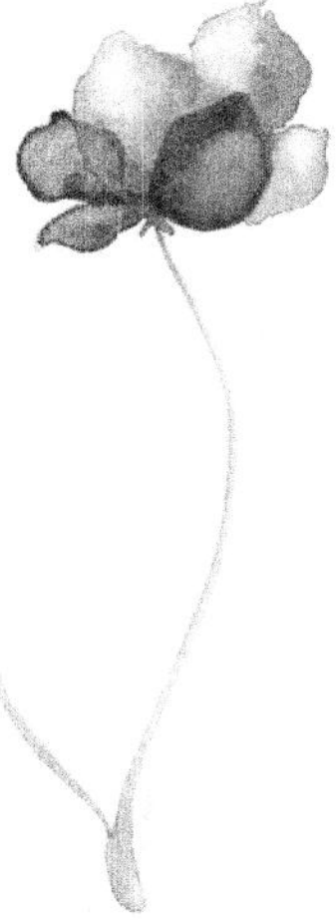

Copyright Vasudha Pansare

THOUGHTS OF DAYS GONE BY

Alas, the year 2020
Filled with manufactured illusion
Achieved through media manipulation
Whole days in whirling
The memory of unexplained baffling
Forlornly, abstraction allows man
To see with his mind scan
What he cannot realize
Physically with his eyes
Somethings are better forgotten
The sad year is past shoutin'
Now with new days onset
In year ahead
Now, with new strengths
And new thoughts
A time for vaping mind
For glowing self-knowledge find
O' airing out brainstorm aligned
Today is today
Tomorrow gone-by
I Will never see today again
So make today remain
Unforgettable I say
Make it life-changing today
Let it speak away

Copyright Daniel Miltz

IT WAS NOT THE WORST YEAR

In the early march of 2020,
there came a virus that is only known with a code.
It shut down all the institutions in the world.
We were asked to stay indoors,
and cover our nose with a mask.
People died of both sickness and hunger.
This is because the world economy was disabled by the virus.
Amidst all these, 2020 is still better than 1914 the world war I,
Or the year of world war II and III.
Should we talk about the Nigeria civil war of 1960?
2020, is not the worst of these years.
I am grateful for still being alive.

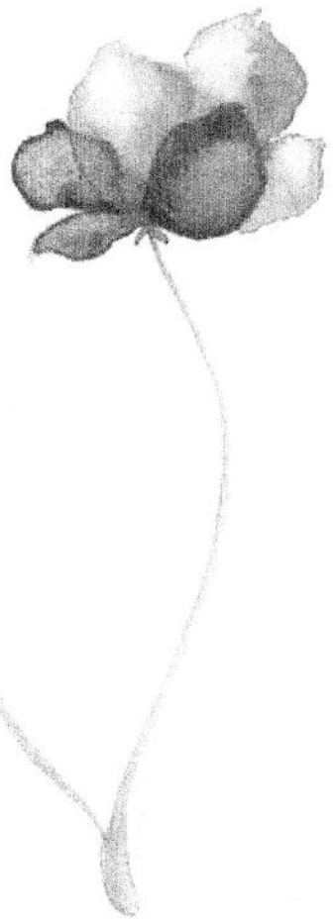

RHETORICS OF 2020 IN PAINTED MINDS

It appears with stars in the sky,
Many felicitated in grand style,
To fill the hope beyond understanding,
No one could expect drought at all,
A throwback reminiscent deep inside,
In the previous years past that failed,
With great hope started the year,
As the year in locomotion exceed three rivers,
The fall of rain that bites the mortal soul,
So deep into the marrows, it sank,
Many became fugitives in a strange land,
Some are captive aliens without care,
The global entities fret for the end,
As the pandemic grows to lockdown,
Every sector collapse as the global economy shutdown,
Rumors of the massive death toll on every side,
Weaker souls drop in pains,
Seeking a secure domain for safety,
Cities look dreadful and pale,
No, where to buy and sell,
Our nostrils tightly fixed with fabrics,
Hand tightly fitted to our pockets,
Distance greetings with friends and relations,
Vehicles and commuters inroads select for safety,
The year in 2020 is a ferry tail,
That never set a balance at all,
Fill with hard times and hunger,
Prices of commodities skyrocketed,
We pray for the year exit 2020,
As we expect a bright new year,
That scent myriad of great postures,
As I sincerely feel hesitant to continue the year 2020.

THE NEW NORMAL

If someone had said more than a year ago,
that for 2020 we would have nothing to show.
I would have laughed at their face, such a silly joke.
Giggling the best response, it would evoke.
No birthdays, weddings, or graduation parties.
No christenings, school discos, or garden tea.
No seaside breaks or holidays abroad.
No admiring the valleys when the ice melts and thaws.
Prisoners in our homes but it's supposed to be for the best.
Until there's a cure made which can pass all the tests.
But consider yourself lucky if you're still here.
As many have lost people, near to them and dear.
Corona spread quickly and took many lives.
Parents, siblings, husbands, and wives.
It made us stop, question, and rethink our life.
Wash hands, social distance....two metres would suffice.
Outside we must remember and all wear a mask.
It's now the new normal and not much to ask.
Hopefully, we won't hear from corona again
Pray to the lord that he hears us...amen.

Copyright Meenakshi Dwivedi

UNANSWERED QUESTIONS

The year 2020 felt like the world was invaded by aliens,
We will never forget what happened to humans,
Coronavirus almost made everything halted,
The damage it caused cannot be belittled,
The effects of the disease are felt even today,
It's a struggle for survival when it enters your body,
Everywhere people suffered jobs loss,
Quarantined people trying to contain the mess,
Hospitals were overwhelmed as patients numbers climbed higher
The disease was spreading all over like e wildfire,
Many people died and the world was filled with sorrow,
We walked uncertain of our tomorrow,
Social gatherings and political meetings were banned,
It's like the end of the world had dawned,
The doctor's and nurses were working overtime,
After this virus is gone nothing will remain the same,
Food donations as everyone wanted to help a neighbor,
Humanity was willing to help each other,
Last year (2020) will be remembered for generations,
When we all had unanswered questions.

Copyright Kenneth Munene

I CANNOT BREATH

In many countries, people demonstrated against racists,
People were tired of violations of human rights,
Whether black or white we are all equal,
Dividing people according to their skin color is political,
We all should be treated with respect,
No one should be seen as a lesser subject,
Discriminating in law is injustice,
The world was against black deaths in hands of police,
Big or small people took to the streets to protest,
Floyd was murdered like a rapist,
Everywhere in the world humanity should be free,
Abusing people against race is a reason to disagree,
Every life in this world is precious,
Killing blacks anyhow is suspicious,
Killing suspects without trial is a crime,
What the authorities had done brought shame,
You cannot judge everyone on how they look,
Inside everyone, there's a different story in his book,
Floyd died fighting to breathe,
His death left a stain on this beautiful earth.

GODINA PROŠLA

Godina prošla, kao svaka

ne beše nimalo laka,

ali mora postojati volja

da ova bude od nje bolja,

svako da se potrudi

da budemo bolji ljudi,

to se ponavlja često

a mora da zauzme

u življenju prvo mesto.

Kada počnemo da

volimo ljude

sve će drugo

lakše da nam bude.

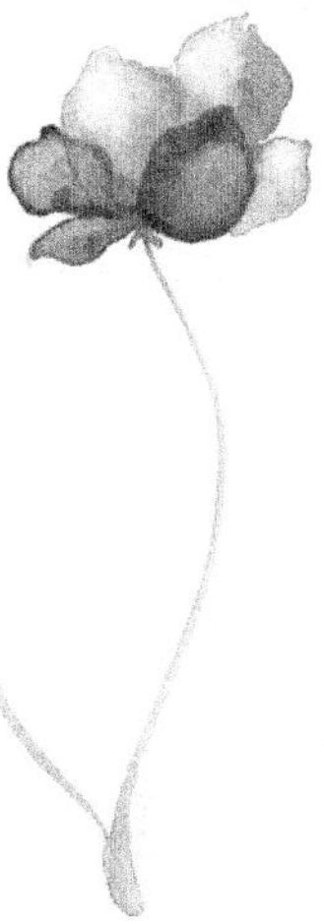

2020

2020 gave me a clearer vision

All luxuries were removed by a sharp incision

Back to basics, food, and heat,

No holidays, no friends to meet

But plenty of time and latitude

To count moments of gratitude,

My job, my home, my wondrous daughters

Calmed uncertainty's bleak waters,

And though tough laughter came to a plenty

In the year 2020.

Copyright Francisca Budd

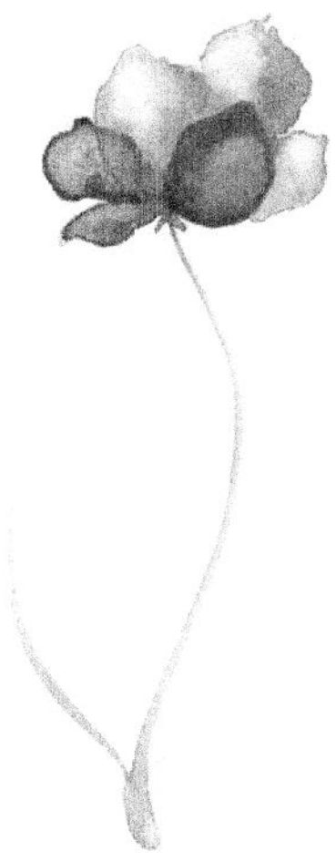

THE YEAR THAT WAS 2020

It was a year of tremendous tension caused by the criminal corona killing millions of people, children, youth, middle-aged, and old alike!

Every day as you open the newspaper the only news was how many more were affected and died!

No hospital beds available and too gruesome were the acts of many doctors and nurses as they were tired of seeing the dead bodies piled up although many of them did their best without caring for their health!

The dead bodies were buried in heaps without any respect for the dead!

You can't blame the doctors and nurses as they too have feelings!

Washing and washing hands and sanitizing became a phobia and many mentally depressed!

I pray the coming year we will see less corona and her merciless killings!

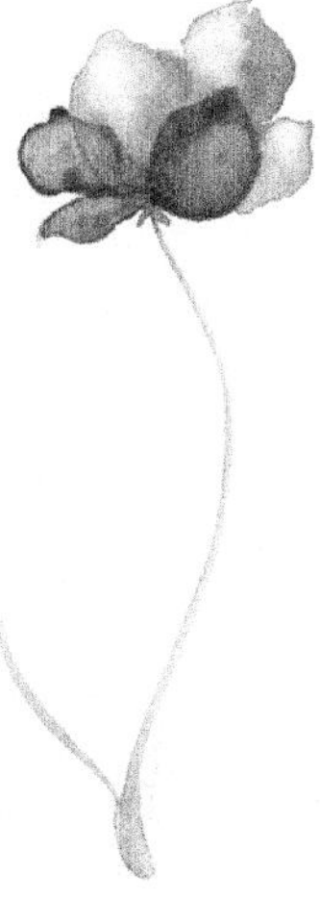

"A CHALLENGE TO REMEMBER "

Something about, am I for the
Last Winter does not go through; once more
Blasting of winds, scattered whole year
As if, a tenebrous Seasons along starts
What mistake has Man gone?
Flaws, to Human Beings inherent
Man can't go against; even though, He attempts
All in all, Hope
Destiny, a trick till the Necks
Lace days along with insecurity to future
Disease, Invited itself to homes
Crowning, Heads without choice
the wealthy, the poor ones, any people
Victims of a virulent Saga
On the run, scientific Masters looking for Medicine
to life back to normal
Not that easy to discover a Vaccine
At last, some labs synthetized doses
Hope, how sweet a Word!
Man will Overcome his Enemy
to beat in retreats, Enemy just a matter of time

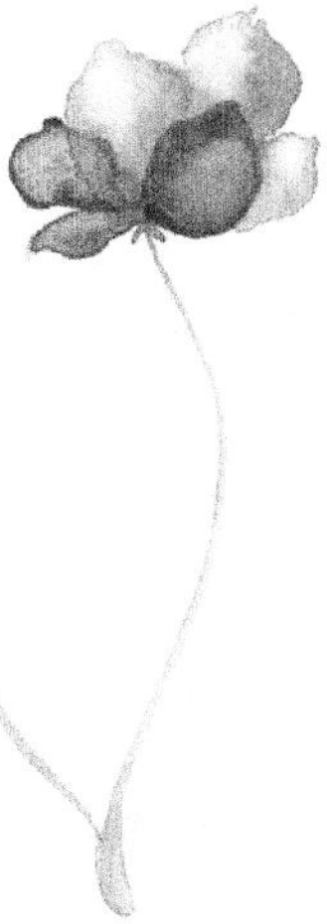

SAD YEAR

It was the year

Dark as the night

When fear shivers

All over our body

When some fearful

Things happen

Like the murder,

It was like a stormy night

When everything devastates

People suffer homelessly

Die, a battle for life.

Copyright Sharmistha Das

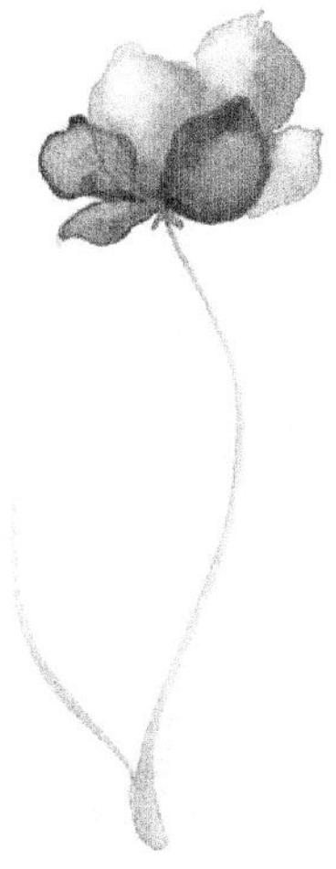

2020 _ WHEN TEARS WOULDN'T DRY

The year a dark stranger visited the earth :
On the living, casting a net of death :
Disregarding man's status or wealth :
The mighty black hand, firmly drained man's faith :
In places of worship, the scarry foot its message printed.
As the painful wounds gape miserably fresh :
Swift like a sparrow, the breadth and depth of the universe, death its seeds scattered :
All hope for survival, from mankind, shattered :
A dark angel of death " Coronavirus "
At Science and technology laughed.
Throwing a challenge to the Holly pulpits :
As human beings became miserable puppets :
In 2020 tears would not dry :
This makes us all mourn and cry :

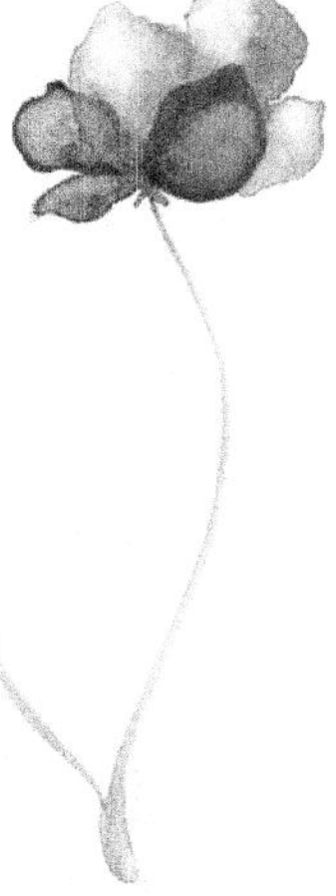

2020 - WHEN TIME STOOD STILL

One day emergency was declared
Nobody was prepared
Everyone thought the problem was far away
With trouble at our door, we all had to obey.
Schools, Colleges and Shops were closed
Trains, Buses, and Cars were stopped
Businesses shut down for time unknown
People were asked to stay at home.
Days, weeks, months - a year went by
A whole year at home - nobody asking: Why
Talks of fear and death were in the air
To go out and take a breath, no one dared.
Thus we hoped and hoped the air would clear
But instead, we now hear of a strain more severe
Situations may be grave but we all must be brave
Let us revive in faith beyond the tidal wave.
With all the needed care let us together dare
To face the situation are without despair
In awareness let us assess the situation
Spreading courage and faith with persuasion.

IF 2020 WAS DIARY?

If 2020 was Diary?
If 2020 was Diary?
The cover of the book must be red published.
The margin of each page would be bloody polished.
The first thought to the pen would be a bleeding worrier.
The first page would be merged with a horrific career.
If 2020 was Diary?
Every mood in it would be plotted with tragedy.
Even the summary of each page would lessened comedy.
The explosion would hike in all lines without remedy.
An excessive sub would slope hysterically like a wired melody.
If 2020 was Diary?
The first five-page would swell with mournfulness.
Fussing all mirthful expectations with dirge-ful.
Filled up every thought with appalling direful.
Furiously menaced minds without laying merciful.
If 2020 was Dairy?
Depression would shrug every page concurrently.
Disastrous would elope in every theme subsequently.
Diary itself would be masked and pocket-handed.
Distance would recur each letter and startle bent.
If 2020 was a Diary?
Many pieces will be lost without been found.
Miserably! day to day would merely bound.
Mixing up page to page would spring with many obstacles.
Merging all thoughts with punitive would be its tentacles.
If 2020 was Dairy?
Nothing would be in than sorrowful excitement.
None of its pages would provoke saint enjoyment.
Negligence of it would be all mind beat.
No one will attempt to read it.

If 2020 was a diary, No one would read it

Copyright Amb Sirajudeen Sherifudeen

IT WILL BE BETTER

What happened to people
What shape did they take
Why is intellect in service
Damn... wonder why
We figured it out.. when he's guilty
What a man is barely alive
Because he was betrayed by the most born?
Former brother in the devil snake
Took the freedom and breathed the blood
To kill his loved ones
To diseases from the lab
It's not good... let's be aware...
Evil settled in man
Devil's shop in the moonlight
They take their breath, spread fear in the people
A man becomes a kurjak man
Whose mission is the destruction of people?
The devil and God are measuring the strength
To meet the devil of great force
They blurred all the water with poison
My people... seek salvation...
Love may the windowsill uplifted
Let the devil's naum burn in hell...
Peace and joy for all of us
Humanity and compassion
The only belief in me...
Hope for better, happier mornings
They are shining bright tomorrow!

KOVID 2020

How many more masks for the poor
Your stance in inaccessible bunkers
While in palaces surrounded by swirling
You council the walls about worthless lives
You dream plans how to poison
On the wheels of death, you turn until you don't
Take honor, dignity, and freedom
To the tired people... dear God
The last witness is quiet, the day is crying
Scratched pretty face on the target
Invisible, predatory birds...
Mother is crying for a sacrificed child
Written words bright on the dead
Cheek... it's not the end... another try
With a silent prayer, we wait for forgiveness...
Submission is a lie... KOVID then WALL
Chinese wall, is it? No, it's not
Our " FEAR " is an unprovoked wall...
Is it true that we are a misguided herd
Pursued by the stick of a terrible shepherd
Come on people... only to offer us more
The disease lasts for decades... what's going on
He doesn't make out... the Lord God has dissolved
Warns takes and gives, prays generations
For the Holy Spirit to enforce them... wake up

OPEN IT UP. EYES!!!

100 DAYS

What we have witnessed this past year with our own eyes, is the cost of our greed-filled lives. No longer should we believe the lies or listen to anyone's alibis.

In just 100 days, nature showed us that in many ways, how the lifestyles of our yesterdays have betrayed tomorrow's appraise.

Easing the past 100 years of our destruction, as society's stalled its daily production. Cleaner air began its introduction, as pollutants in the water began a reduction.

Even the ozone hole is healing, as mankind began kneeling. Nature provides our only protective ceiling, now our lifestyles of old should look unappealing.

100 days of standing still, humanity witnessed nature's iron will. As our past 100 years of overkill were making us and the planet itself ill.

Before society can restart, let's try and be smarter. Live better and share more of our healing heart, and remember nature is an important counterpart.

For our next 100 years, we need to worry more about our health, because we see now this is our true wealth. For the next 100 days, let's prove to nature we can be more stealth, As man and nature are the truest commonwealths...

Copyright Patrick Epperson

OMINOUS DAYS

Cascading lies & monstrous disguise
Degrading intellect & unfathomable neglect
Political unrest & voices oppressed
Critical pawns & forgotten icons
Pushing division & leaving indecision
Ambushing independence & creating dependence
Social girth & entity's birth
Identity loss & personal cost
Taken bait & lawless state
Flawless rise & forsaken cries
Lost sight & parasitical mites
Hypocritical politics & bagged tricks
Votes tossed & elections lost
Politicians bought & truths sought American sleuth & political truth
Parties brawl & humanity's fall
Election expanded & hopes abandoned
Democracy squandered & America wondered
Futures uncertain & entity's iron curtain
Mysterious ways & ominous days...

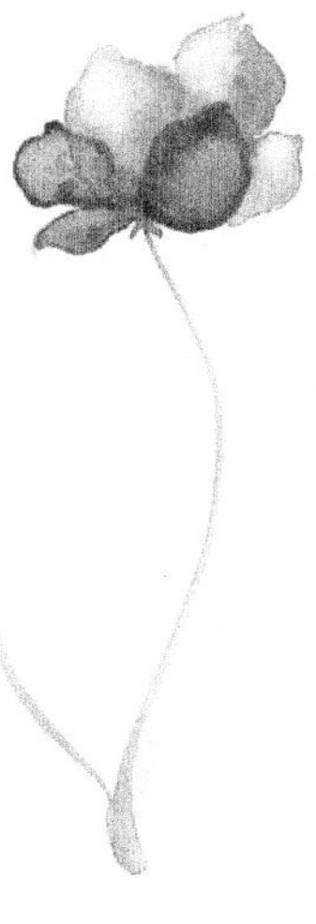

I BELIEVE IN A NEW TOMORROW

Last year, I would like to erase that from my memory, because it is the first year in which I could not go on the desired trip, nor visit my daughter in Germany. A mask was imposed on my face, which makes it difficult for me to breathe, but also to communicate at work because it is difficult to be a teacher to children who cannot see your smile. The magic of hugs that helps me overcome all life crises more easily is forbidden to me. This year also taught me that beauty is in small things and that I paint every moment of life with bright colors because life is unique and every sunrise is a special birth of a new day.

Despite the unfulfilled expectations, I still have a living hope and faith in a better tomorrow.

Despite unfulfilled expectations, I still have a living hope and faith in a better tomorrow. I know that life will be more meaningful and free this year.

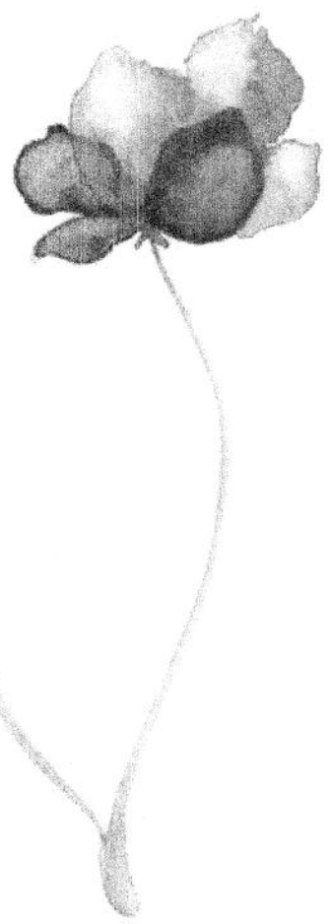

WHAT A TERRIBLE DAYS IT HAS BEEN

like never before in history
all shut inside their doors.
no flight ..no train ..no busses ..no accesses to move one step with one's car.
restaurants were closed
Offices working online...
Education at halt...only virtual classes ...going on...
Pain in plenty.. pleasure a little.
Difficult times
do they come like this......???
Hopes....in despair.
dancing the desperate days .. with total uncertainty
Humanity at crisis...
The deadly virus of Corona causing havoc here and there...
Migrant laborers in their miserable state...
With women children and elderly people...
We're to keep themselves away from their homes and places of nativity.....looking forward to better days of reunion again with their loving ones...
Time also witnessed helping hands ...
Humble efforts to erase the pain and plight of people...
Thank God... The days of darkness and despair lastly disappearing day by day...
Evening seems to be returning to the right track.
Large-scale Vaccinations are on
No one knows
If the hard days are already gone.....??

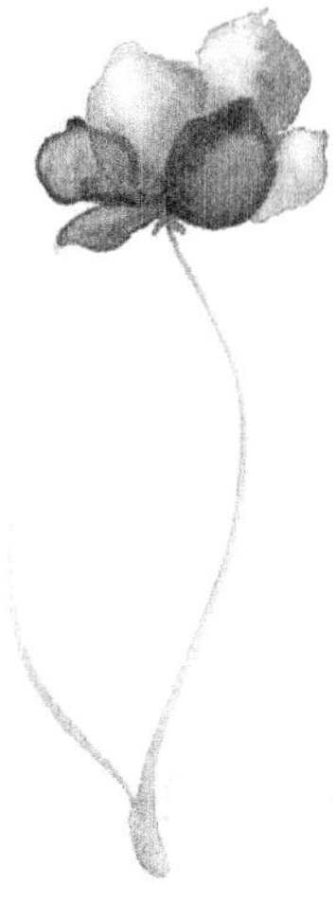

TRIALS AND TRIBULATION

The beginning of the year displayed emotions
Terrified by the cries and the agony of desolation
Everyone panic about the virus of destruction
It spread so easily like a bomb all over the population.
People get sick so easily of flu-like symptoms
They are dying of the difficulty of breathing in random
Everyone's panicking and precautions have to mention
Ordered social distancing throughout the nation.
Hospitals were busy, supermarkets were in queries
People rushed to buy their stuff and loaded with groceries
So funny that shelves were empty of toiletries
Fighting for pieces of paper, not for their commodities.
I worked in the hospital as a clinical assistant
Knowing the Covid-19 virus fatalities was rampant
I was paranoid and workers were hesitant
To deal with the situation was toxic and important.
The trajectory of the virus became so intense
And workers stopped working as their mind was condensed
For their safety came first than to be exposed
So I worked for the people that fatigue hit me most.
Our government stopped and ordered the closure of businesses
The total lockdown was imposed but not for essential services
I worked in a supermarket and hospital for many years
I am lucky, I have the means to pay my bills and mortgages.
I stopped working after working hard to survive
But with severe cough and constant sneezing that I had
I was advised to stay home, isolate for two weeks
And it lasted for three months as coughing made me weak.
The hassle was no doctor to treat you in personal
Just talking online about my medical upheaval
They won't entertain you without the swab test

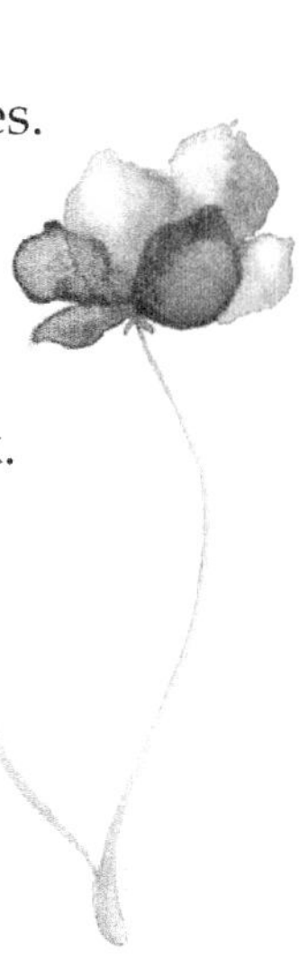

Luckily I had negative results for my lungs were the best.
And so bad that I was in contact with Covid positive patient
I had stayed home for two weeks again for isolation
Two weeks in my room like a prisoner
Thank God I was not inflicted and so much for jubilation.

2020, AN YEAR THAT ARRIVED WITH A HUE AND CRY

Bringing with it, unbeknown difficulties to ply
A year of angst and anxiety
Ripping the senses to absurdity...
Fear, tension, and suspense
Stress, strain, and apprehension intense
A virus that held humanity on tenterhooks
The world crumbling under its poky hooks...
Spiky invisible organism mighty
Crushing the very existence with its fatality
Covid 19 on a rampage ghastly
Causing a pandemic queasy and grisly...
Life in a state of suspended animation
Even Gods and Goddesses forgotten
Like aliens going around with face covers
Washing, scrubbing bathing at odd hours...
A time when face to face contact was feared
The very humane nature was smeared
Masks and sanitizers, wipes and sprays
Became the vital things in every place...
Above anything of interest and inclination
Life in 2020 was indeed a revelation
A microscopic organism holding sway
Over trillions of menfolk, in the fray...
Hoping for 2021, that would bring some relief
From the pandemic that caused much mischief
Giving sleepless nights and days to health workers
Life threw helter-skelter....
No place to go, no camaraderie to show
Locked indoors to thwart the blows
Of 'Corona's, intrusion on the walls and floors
Suspicion raising its head at every door...

A unique entity that spread such a fear
In this colossal cosmic mega-sphere
Razing and ravaging human species
Rendering lives in utter crises...
We are but strings in the hands of mystical powers
Pushed and jostled in the magical spheres'
Pulled and tugged by the unseen hands of Heavens above
Dancing to the mercy of the curses or love.

BECAUSE HER EYES SPEAK MORE THAN A WORD

Her beautiful eyes speak more than word,
Intoxicating the humans in surroundings,
Pouring blue water in the lake of world,
Causing people to feel the dizziness it brings.
Her wrinkles hurt her heart like an arrow,
Like roses, she pricks his hand,
Her eyes were mistaken when it went narrow,
Like water on the land of sand.
Many are mistaken by her emotions,
Which is not judged by body posture,
But eyes which are in motion,
And by learning her facial gesture.
Making direct eye contact when interested in him,
And dropping her head when felt shy,
Shutting at an incident to make it dim,
Opening it big to make him die.
It is where he finds his paradise,
Her equivalent fairy eyelashes,
Of bulky black eyeconic eye,
The dark world lightens when twin,
Becoming a rolling drop off water,
He drops from her beautiful eyes,
Useful for friendship potter,
Which gets contacted in size.
Like a moth, he wanders around those twilight,
When they are put in bars he cries,
With his life, he daily uses to fight,
And after few days he unfortunately dies.
Who says that aged is not fond of those eyes,
Their opinion about it is much more,
Although their eyesight with them not lies,
So they are never put in a circle of doubt.

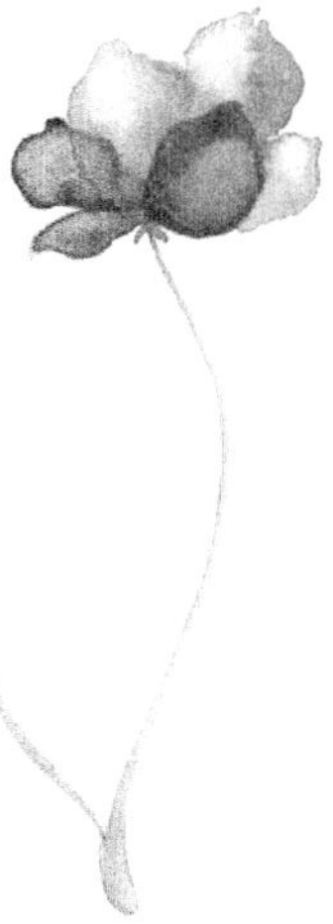

TWISTED ROMANCE

A 'love' letter to covid

(Spring)
The first days of spring you swept me away with only my loves by my side
It was a sort of twisted romance you might say
No more work just our bikes we would ride
But as many may know when solitude is demanded
It's usually a sign you should run

(Summer)
Just as things heated up
I knew I must leave
I had to escape from this fun
You were angry it seemed as I left your side
So I ran and I covered my face
Maybe if I could get back to my life
You might pass me but not leave a trace

(Fall)
There were some close calls as leaves began to fall
But I managed to get by just fine
I watched from afar as you began to lure Others with your twisted mind
Most wise to your tricks and easily missed the sick little games you would play
Your infectious personality
so hard to resist
but who knew of the price they would pay

(Winter)
As snow covered the earth

and a chill hit the air
My pace I guess slowed for a minute
Just enough time for my face free to shine
With a kiss, you caught me right in it
Now back in your quarantine
Kept away once again
You might have me now but Just know
Time will pass
Spring will come
and more days in the sun
Immune to your "love"
free to go

A SAD WILLOW

Shined and glistened this winter
A sad willow awakened by the Sun
The thin, bent branches are decorated
In the middle of winter I am proud, green leaves
Miraculous light fell in waterfalls
According to young, stretched leaves.
Drunk with bright, purple light
They are imprinted to the golden temple of God mead
Time stood, he was her sanctuary
The only truth... thought and meaning... source
Of life, awakened hope, faith found...
The sky is sad, the sun is blushing, the heart is tightening.
Red thighs were lit by scared heavens
Hot willow fired by the heralds of nudity
Call of Calvary through new defeats and disappearances
Up Nemanja leaves the gang in the gorge
Satire willow to the very root... In darkness
Silently cried humiliated, abandoned woman.

THE YEAR 2020, THE TIME CHANGER

Bidding goodbye to the year 2019,
Happily welcomed the world, the year 2020.
A lot of exhilaration and celebrations,
Little did we realize what was in store for us.
The world into the grip of a deadly virus,
No idea how to deal with the disease.
All our inventions and discoveries kept aside,
Even Superpowers stood hands folded beside.
Humans are known to put up a fight,
so what if now the situation is tight.
We would bounce back to normalcy,
though it is tough, not easy.
The day would be memorable and desirous
When the mankind would be freed of the virus
What is to be, will be, not what we want to be
Destiny is destined, shall be served at the right time
Development, science, technology
We are at our peak, with our analogy
Reaching moon and mars
Now existence difficult even for Czars
Social media active, living in the virtual world
The near and dear relations sidelined and curled
We did not think even once
In 2020 we would be in a mask
All invention and progression at rest
Certain things, God knows best!

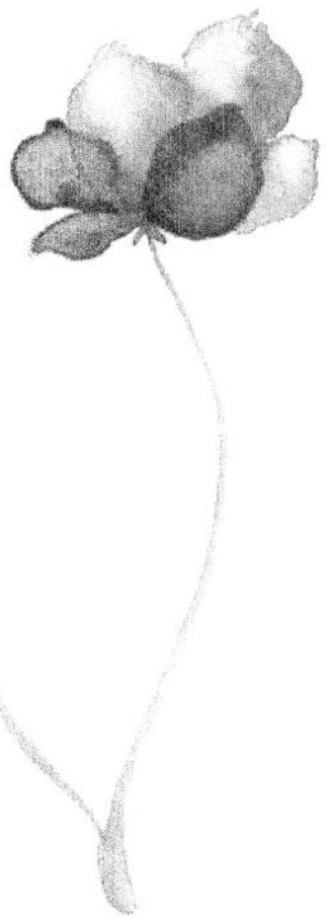

HOPE

The sky was bright with colors of truth
And the sun's rays had once shown its light onto our heads.
As champagne glasses soon emptied while we picked streamers off our lawns,
Eyes welt, watching the dimming sun fade into the distance.
Shadows encompass the earth and my reality, as I remembered it, fell.
My fellow man is no longer my equal, or perhaps never was,
And I realized I was blind.
My view of humanity disassembled into thin air, diffused into the darkened clouds.
Our elders, diseased with ignorance and war,
have fallen to sickness and death while we continue living in our selfish world.
Time moved forward,
Aging us all in the process.
My eyes have grown wrinkled and weary,
And my hair had become grey.
Hope.
Hope for a new start,
an idea of new beginnings encroach the minds of the distressed.
Is this enough?
And now we wait.

TWENTY TWENTY

Closing the doors of time
Moments are waiting beneath.
And Keep away from being touched.
Forgetting the art of handshakes.
From whom, where, and when Without knowing anything
Many sacrificed their lives.
The Wandering Medical World stunned with
Invisible enemy with an irresistible weapon
Affection and love were under lockdown.
Sanitizing its hearts.
Deadly deaths ..Closed churches. And temples
Made the people understand unstable
To the darkened earth
The coming year will shed some light.
And make covid to say Goodbye.

Copyright Thenmozhi Rajagopal

2020 THE YEAR NOT TO FORGET

January was celebrated with great joy & a smile with good hope & New year's resolutions.

Two months later the world was put at standstill, Coronavirus shouted its victory on colonizing the world.

I never thought one day I will be not allowed to get out of my own house, put on house arrest without committing any crime.

Yes, we have seen so many outbreaks of dieses but none of it shuttered the world.

I had never imagined myself living with my mouth & nose covered. I used to see the fumigators closing theirs & wonder how they breathe through those musks.

I salute you coronavirus, you took the airplane down. I can't mansion other public transport.

Our relatives died but never buried them.

The last time we saw them was the day we took them to private isolation. Few days late we got phone calls notifying us about their passing away that's the end of it.

May their souls rest in peace.

Copyright Mxolisi Masuku

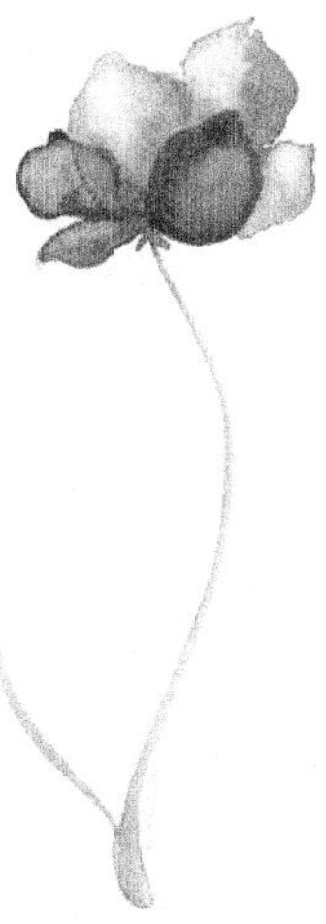

LIFE INTERRUPTED...IS IT?

The virus that continues to ravage our planet leaves us believing that life is being interrupted by an invisible scourge as it inflicts death, depression, poverty, and every suffering imaginable. The trauma of losing loved ones imposes the ultimate debilitation of human emotions. Yet soon enough, the air and the oceans slowly began to exhale from the suffocating pressure of our indulgences. Is this healing? Who are we to judge the forces of nature and its power to heal whatever ails our planet? Why do we impute tornadoes, earthquakes, and pestilence as evil forces while nuclear bombs and excessive wealth are crowning achievements? What about the unsupportable population growth since this time, natural selection skews its edict as we lose the young, old, weak, and strong alike? Did our excesses bring us to the brink of our destruction that our nurturing Mother Nature simply wants to heal us?

Copyright Jimmy Calaycay

LESSON FROM KOVID 19

Pandemic Kovid 19 trembled the backbone of the whole world
Worldwide contagious spread like a flame
Even developed states befooled to control
The flow of unfurling the epidemic, one after the other, enroll
Lakhs of people from the rural and urban arena
So panic of the appearance of the korona
Administration, mass media, govt. non-govt sectors started consoling
People all over the world rushing here and there for living
Shops, factories, organizations, institutions forcibly closed down
Transportation, road, lanes, bylanes shut down
The mass compelled to stay inside home
Nobody was allowed exceptionally some urgency to roam
Churches, temples, mosques locked down
Gods, goddesses, all deities calmed down
With no worshipers, no devotees, no visitors
A span of luck down enhanced day by day
The shadow of silence pervaded over the universe
Poor people relying on daily wages got nervous
Some lost their livelihood, some lives leaving relatives forever
What a horrible situation to face, the victims stayed far away further
Social, economic, political, and religious activities came to dormant
As if everything even the wheel of time stopped moving so stagnant
Kovid 19 stumbled down the tower of mankind
But unforgettable due to some lessons leaving behind
No pollution like noise, water, environment, and air cropped up
The wind blew serenely, habitats sighed calmly, humanity to summon up.
The water of the river, well, pond or pool relaxed to be escaped

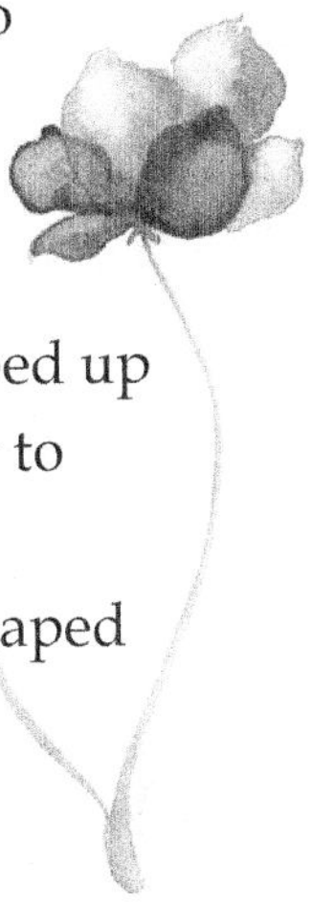

From poisonous plastic, garbage, or any waste materials undisposed
Merrily smiled the green forest, wild animals freely wandered
Environment laughed at the people hiding their face under masked
Housewives pleased to see members washing hands
For cleaning homes and lawns joining their hands
Expense dwindled money used sensibly making people economic
Festivals, ceremony, observations plummeted realizing acute panic
Social distancing, masking face and hands sanitization
Better tools for mankind for better humanization

Copyright Ramesh Chandra Pradhani

THE YEAR 2020 - A THROWBACK

A Page From my Diary
Beginning of the last year
I went away to Perth,
I had a fabulous time there
With lots of fun and mirth
I think every foreign country
Has a charm of its own,
Loved Australian vegetation
Indigenously well-grown
Also toured some other countries
Came back to my homeland
What quirk waited for me and the world
Neither I nor others had planned
March onward the planet earth
Was in the grip of Covid
Some folks agreed to play it safe
Some were naïve and fervid
Egoistic and self-centered
People don't understand
The gravity of the situation
They need a severe reprimand
So, the whole world was under
Restriction with lockdown
With no traffic and empty roads
The cities appeared ghost towns
I was happy and content with
The well deserved free time
A break from the rat race
Had all reason and rhyme
Even our generous nature got

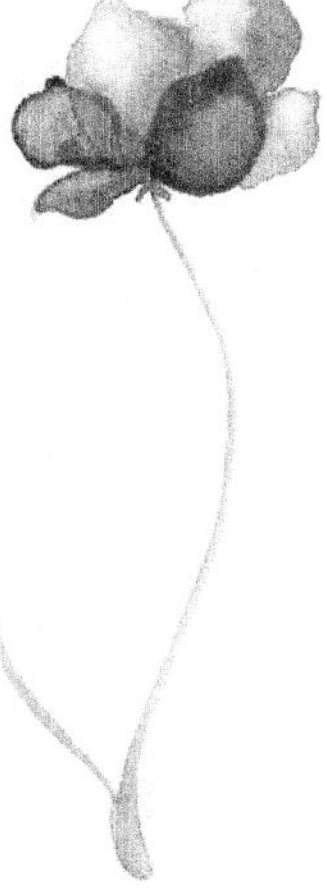

Respite from exploitation
We saw pristine climate and
Eco-system's restoration
Two thousand twenty taught us
A lesson with a pandemic
Nature is, still, superior to
Humans and more dynamic
With clean up and repair work
Mother earth got back its symphony
She is the queen of creation,
We, now, have got this epiphany

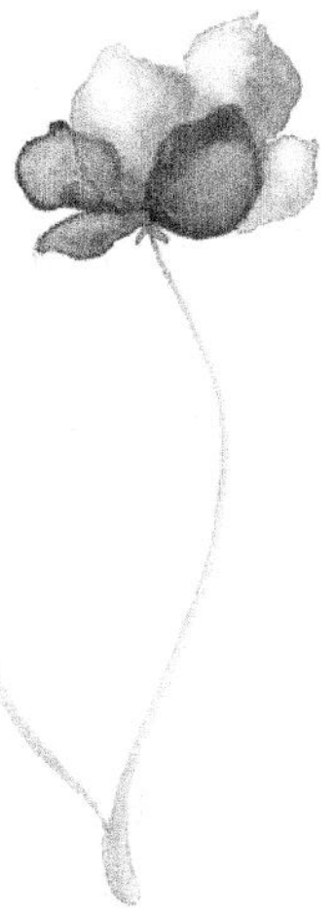

WHEN I LOOK BACK

The year 2020 was rather enigmatic. People suffered, not so much because of the pandemic but due to their mindset. We, humans, were under a false impression that, with the process of development, we have become invincible. With our inflated ego and selfishness, we started meddling with nature. A journey from the dark ages to modern times was fine but not at the cost of natural resources. We blasted hills and weakened them- leading to landslides. We cut jungles; that depleted rains and caused global warming. Melting glaciers resulted in deadly floods.

Mother earth tolerated enough and then took action. A good and caring mother has to reprimand and correct her erring children. She did just that. An invisible virus scared us no end. She forced us to realize her strength and mend our ways. Our rivers are sparkling clean and the skyline is beautifully scenic. She won.

NO PAIN IN THE RAIN

She halts her crying
smell the smart senses
smile for a feeling of love
happy feet without pain
the train speeds in the rain
Love is a golden sheen
sincerely beautiful in soul
the vibrations of the universe
warm all parts of the body
our aura of romance
Let's breathe deeply
reach for the star-gate
accumulate night energy
beautiful power protect us
from the voices of wild waves
Aware to the mind
has triggered pain
hands without grief
the noise is being quiet
no tears when it rains
the train runs in the rain
The rain becomes beautiful
at different doors
without a doubt every space
so that dreams come true
we hugged, full of affection
The love in your heart is my soul
love in my heart is your soul
these beautiful minds are ours
tomorrow is a new year

Copyright Iwan Dartha

ZIVOT JE STIHIJA SVAKAKO...

Al' trudi se covek srecan da bude!

I ruka Boga nas miluje...

Jer pazi On na ljude!

Samo...mnogi su ljudi zli.

Donose odluke u best.

Pa prospu mrznju po svemu...

I bolest covecanstvu donesu.

Tako je veliki uzas zasejala korona svetom...

Zaplakali su mnogi za najmilijima svojim.

Zalim za svakim detetom,

Nevinim malenim cvetom.

Volela bih da ucinim dobro, postupcima i zeljama svojim.

KEEP AWAY FROM WHEAT SPIKES OF MY FIELD

Wheat spikes of my field do not sing except for peace
Wheat spikes of my field not tempted by golden water
it Drinks only green water
does not grow on the chairs of kings
it is not a banquet for wars
it is a banquet for orphans
it protects the deer from the hunter
It grows on the banks of rivers of love
The pollen of hers is carried by the wind
To western hearts
Eastern Hearts
Northern Hearts
Southern Hearts
Hearts will come to her
they Build a green castle for freedom
Two guards on her door
An olive branch and a white dove

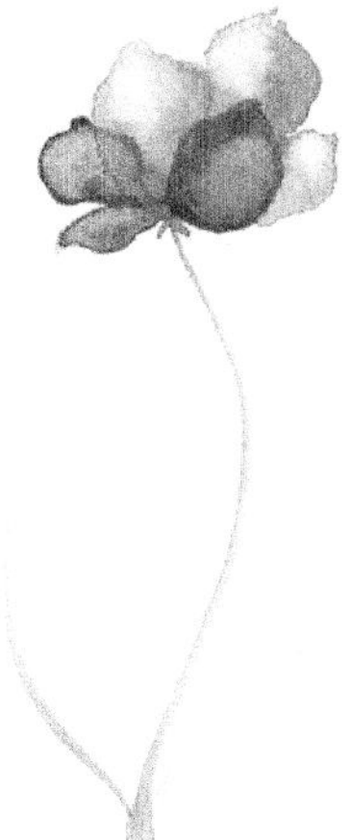

DOES DEATH KNOW WHAT TO DO?

The face of the earth cries thousands of times every day.

The big death bus runs east to west.

Millions of people have become unemployed, but death continues to work and his work develops day by day.

Death and life are twins, but each is on a different floor, life has chosen trees, death has chosen firewood, life has chosen a rainbow and death has chosen black

But you don't die before death comes; you must be like the hungry who sees death as bread and the child who sees death as a piece of candy

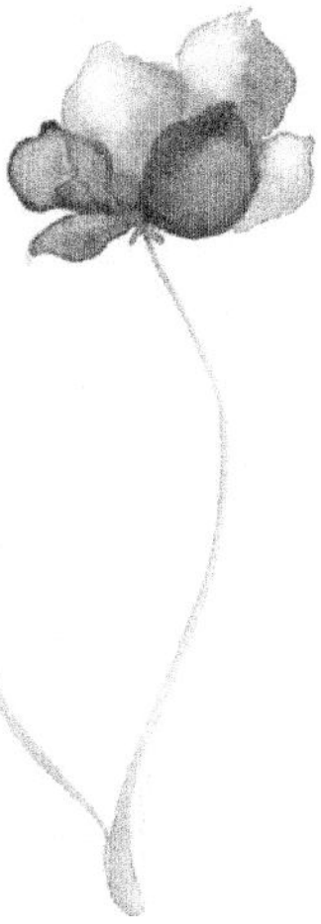

THE YEAR 2020 STARTED WITH NEW YEAR CELEBRATIONS,

All were happy and had
a smile of satisfaction,
Some were in the mood for a holiday destination,
I was in my world of imagination.
No one knew what destruction was near,
No one had any idea of
the deadly virus there,
No tension and no fear
For coming years,
No pains or any tears
Only love and care were in the air.
But from March bliss changed to curse,
As the virus spread every corner
Covid -19 changed life in a massacre.
Everywhere death danced down the streets,
People were locked down and their life came to a halt.
Why the cities became empty?
Why schools, colleges were shut down?
Why did people stop mixing?
Why playground became empty?
Why fear in every heart?
Why tear in every single eye?
Is nature showing its wrath?
Or God is punishing us for our greed?
Is mother earth destroying everything as we did with her?
Please pray for all and bring unity in every sphere
Prayers and social distancing can change our fate now with care
This covid nourished me
I became creative,
The pen became my sword
By which I wrote poems on nature
To save our children's future.

Copyright Aruna Bose

I LOVED MY LIFE

Angel, dancing with The Death,
Wrapped in a white gown of stealth...
Are you pensive for the earth,
Her core opening, is that worth it?
Mother Nature's hustle...
When will her breath subtle?
Unknown diseases swarming,
Is that due to global warming?
I have pondered for a long time,
And stopped hearing the chime...
Of the bells, they used to ring,
Merrily while the flowers swing...
Windows, doors, dull and lazy,
Scratching from inside.. look hazy ...
When will I see a pure smile?
Humming a tune for a while?
Will it do? A pinch of positivity,
To rinse off all the negativity?
If this is the end, I will shout.
'I loved my life...till I am out...

Copyright Deepa Vankudre

COVID IN THE CANE

The planet is in lockdown
And folk are gone insane
But there's nothing like a lockdown
With Covid in the cane
The mountains keep their splendor
The sunsets each night
With colors bursting through the sky
In red and orange light
The last shades of day flicker
And bright blue fades to dark
The stars come out and shimmer
A billion magic sparks
No misery to speak of here
No claustrophobic meltdown
Nobody living life in fear
No societal breakdown
As canefields spread like carpets
Where taipans hunt for rats
The wood glows in the firepit
And shadows dancing bats
We bath in crystal waters
When Sun is at her peak
Where dappled light shimmers
Off rainforest mountain creeks
It cleared the smog in China
When we thought nothing could
Is it wrong to say Corona
Might have done the world some good?

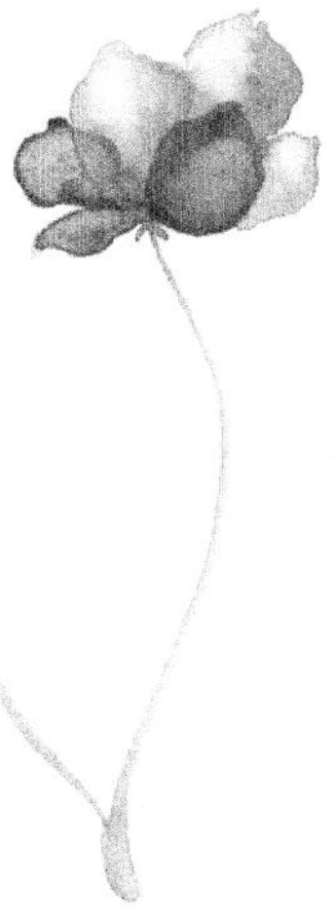

THE YEAR 2020 WAS A SAD LOVE STORY

The sun turned to clouds
which formed a lot of rain,
That flooded the entire world!
Everyone remained still for the moment
The action had to be made!
As lives were taken before our eyes
And funerals became a thing of the past
Our world was drowning,
we had to act fast!
As a mask could not save us if no medicine could, We tried to swim up for air but not everyone could reach the top! The line to heavens gates was getting longer by the second! The truth became so ugly, Yet we had to remain calm and stay positive if not for ourselves then for our families
Little things became so meaningful and time was spent so well.
2020 was the year of lessons, with consequences so severe.
Every man for himself
Precautions everywhere!
As the year came to an end we celebrated with a bang!
The same way, but a different day, for today we live again!

Copyright Tiare Nopera

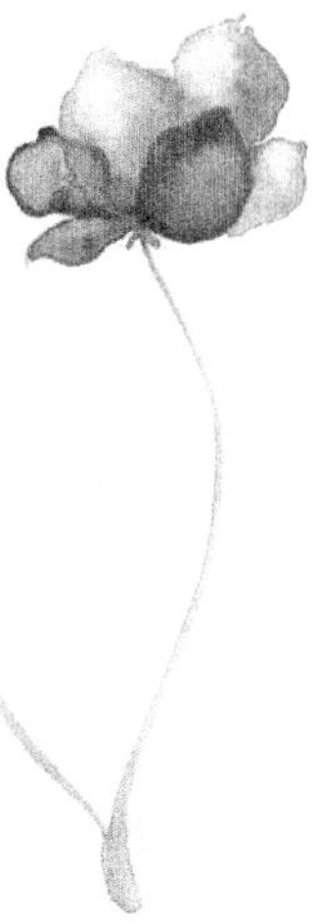

-

THE PANDEMIC YEAR.

Oh! what heart see this fanatic time without shivering.
No soul walks across its path without a teardrop.
Oh! every child sobbing for father in this pandemic year,
Every wife eager to embrace their husbands both death have taken them so far,
Every mind wish to be peaceful but the weather bring shagged,
Along with agony.
Nothing to be compared with this panic year other than skeeters biting every soul without care.
Oh! nothing causes these than human sin,
nothing can restrict it than erasing discrimination.
Let leave glassy of life and back to our creator.
Let raise our voice to call his beautiful names.
Oh! indeed it was a memorable year for every soul.

Copyright Damilare AL Adaby

A PERIOD FULL OF FEAR AND ANXIETY

In 2019, it was the month of December
People were happy, enjoying the winter
But suddenly we wondered about hearing a new virus
Every country got afraid, there was a rush
People were peeping through the windowpane
Nobody was there on the lawn
A pin-drop silence from twilight to dawn
Children were inside the rooms, who were once as agile as a fawn
A new pandemic Covid -19 had broken out
Destroyed so many lives, no doubt
Hospital, nursing home are full of patients
People were losing their patients
Provided isolation centre in every city
Life was full of fear and anxiety
People didn't know when they will get escape
From those unwanted, unseen cages
School, colleges had remained closed
Restaurants, cafeterias, including lodges
Everything was shut down, due to diseases
It was an attack of invisible viruses
Everything was calm and quiet
Nothing was there, but uncertain hope and desire
People were trying their best only to survive
They were struggling to overcome strife
Not a single sound anywhere
People were unaware of their future

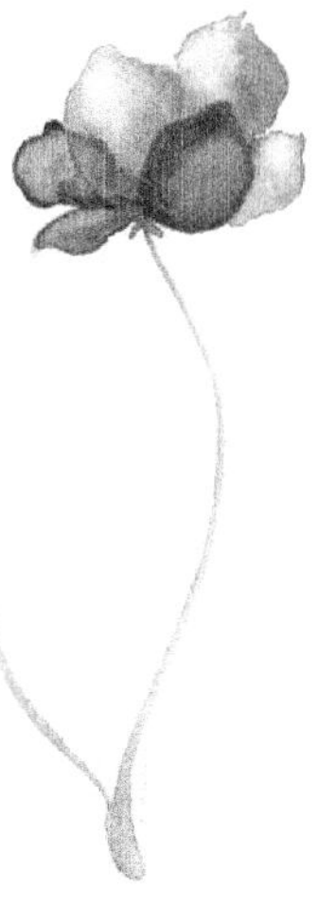

AFTER DISASTER

Not only destroyed buildings
everything drowned in the mud
Most of the land spilled blood
tremendous water spilled
So many bodies floating
as the soul floated too
swallowed up by the waves
water, soil, are being sorrowed
Children are dying to survive
on the elephants dragging mud
Smelling at the carcasses of fish
dark sky, flat earth, evil epidemic
The anomaly of the days
from the Palace destroyer of life
sitting on edge of contemplation
increasingly gloomy
Mapping of the ruler's rhetorics
torment the minds of the people
starving without cloth and home
yesterday and tomorrow next year

Copyright Iwan Dartha

"I LOVE ME JACKET"

I followed my FB friends every day
Their stories made life exciting
Covid forced us to stay indoors
These people were so inviting
I was blessed to live in a different world
I got to know these people plenty
Most of them I never really talked to
Most of them don't know me
Only some knew I followed them
I was all these writer's biggest fan
Their pictures gave a face to the name
Most beautiful in all the land
I couldn't wait to read their writings
Smile at their picture beforehand of course
I maybe enjoyed that a little too much
But who could resist an umpteenth glance more
Finally, I braved up to write a comment
Scrolled my way through many remarks
Ready to break my silence again
It's been a while since I've given my thoughts
I came upon a flashing comment
Then a tear fell down my cheek
My eyes swelled with pent up pressure
I couldn't believe what I was reading
I found, not only did I fall for a lie
But their pictures didn't match their name
If the name matches the one who clicked
Whose face did I see and what was Their name?
Curious about the pictures I've matched to poets
The many photos I've matched with thoughts
Only to find those words were from the living

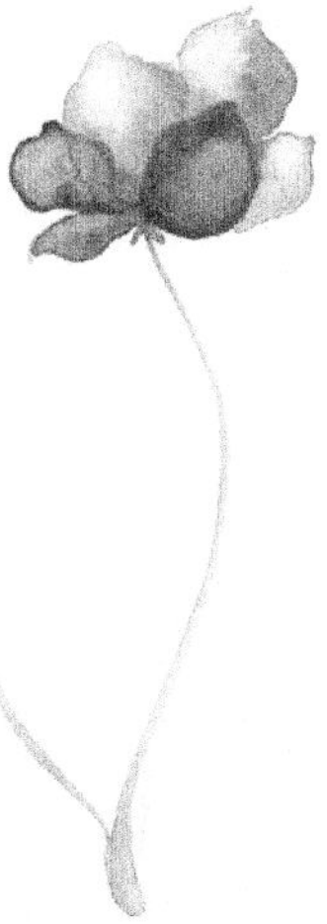

But some faces I've come to know we're not
Like any deceit, there is a truth
There's an end to all this madness
Did the picture make the story or vice versa
It's hard to quit when a heart's invested
Who is who and who they pretend to be
I'm still seeking, confused, and in shock
Since then my world has been turned upside down
Now I am hugging myself inside a paradox

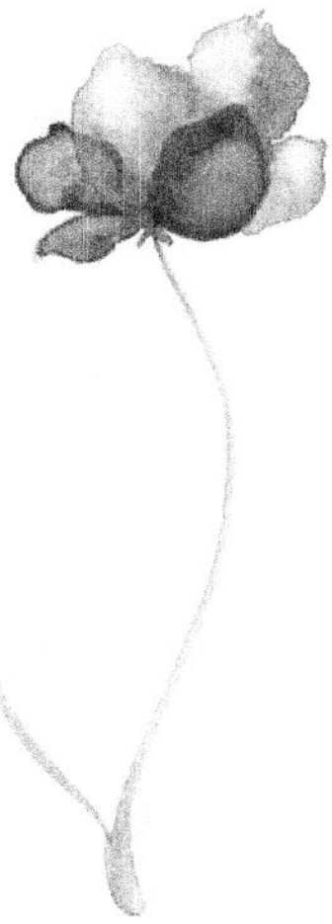

WAITING FOR THE DAYLIGHT

the mind was clouded with grey
since the virus entered my mental culture
it had become omnipresent
I had been engulfed in its world,
in its fearsome clutches
there was nothing left to feel
nothing left to say,
but the void that enveloped
my mind in swirling blackness
I wandered within the four walls in loneliness
for every friend I ever made
had run out of time to spend with you
I thought It was not a bliss
if anything, it was a curse
the desolation I felt was all-consuming
my brain was not as brave as I wanted it to be
for around me, there were so many others
and a little voice from within said
"I'm not good enough to fight it"
I questioned "Is it societal anxiety?
Can I conquer this pain of isolation?"
I decided to get up because there was no other way
life everywhere was exposed to the most traumatic curves and junctions
people struggled through a path over the weary grey beneath
the process was unknown and
there was no chance of change
no hope of catching a smile from
some other soul who felt the same way I did
I knew I've got to wait
without questioning " until when?"

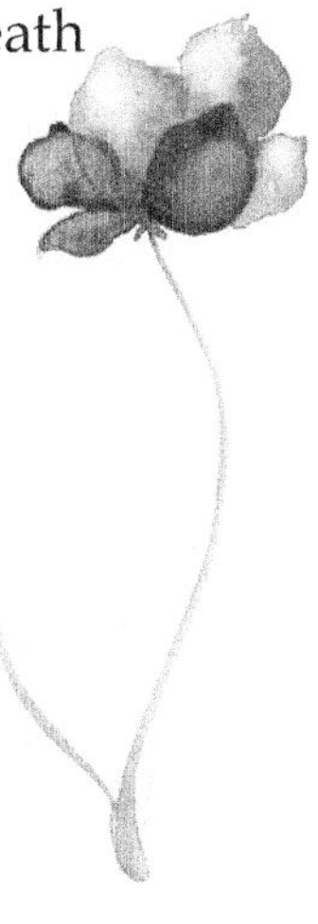

with a hope that one day
I would see a clear highway of new life inviting all
filled with peace, compassion, and contentment
and life would shine the brightest in the darkness
let me show the courage to hold on until daylight comes
and spread love and emotional warmth
because the path wends onwards
and there is much journeying ahead

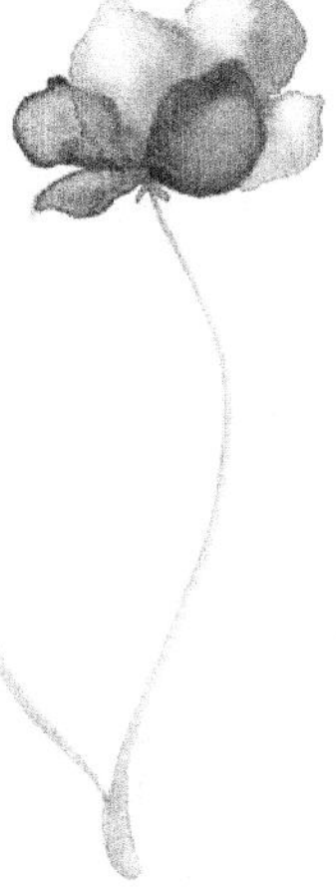

LIKE ANY OTHER YEAR IT BEGAN,

My power phrase to make it a great one,
Little did I see what was to follow,
A year that wouldn't discriminate against anyone,
Blindly selfishly one country saw it coming,
Shortly every shoreline around the globe affected,
Lockdowns and separation across lands,
Every government's shortcomings perfectly imperfection,
Never heard a clear answer on its origins,
Only the country of its birth,
Their government's shortcomings left unanswered,
As the virus continues to plague the earth,
Our way of life as others left affected,
No traveling across the land,
Only essential services,
Left working to lend a helping hand,
Too many lives needlessly lost,
To a virus left rampant among its hosts,
Leaving us blindly cowering,
In the wake of its punishing ghost,
Mental health feverishly declining,
Health workers left defenseless,
The stupidity of some shining through,
Portraying themselves as purely senseless,
Thus my expectation was thrown away,
From the early days of this year 2020,
No one saw what was coming for us,
Just left like a year done shattering plenty,

MY LOCKDOWN

Mornings are hard-pressed evenings crazy,
Fingers rough, dress messy, hair greasy.
No time to laze at or even feel lazy,
Running a household in lockdown is not easy.
Chopping vegetables marinating fish,
Planning all the meals and all the dish,
If only with a sleight of hand cooking I can finish,
I can focus on other things to accomplish.
Dusting washing cleaning is no mean feat,
Then drying laundry in rows neat.
The chores never seem to be complete,
I seek inspiration from everyone's grit.
Husband busy working on laptop and phone,
On self-confinement, he discusses debit credit loans.
Complaining, squabbles kids have not outgrown,
They still need their mother, can't be on their own.
Dawn till dusk is like running a race,
With the sun I have to keep pace,
Hobbies and recreation too, need some space,
They ensure the perpetual smile on the face.
At day end when eyes are heavy with sleep,
I pray to God from my heart deep,
To prevent the pandemic's upsweep,
For your mine and the world's safe keep.

Copyright Amrita Chatterjee

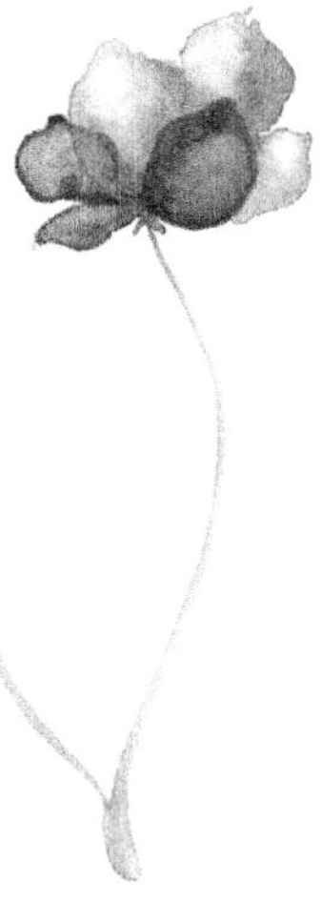

DO YOU KNOW WHO AM I?

Someone who easily escapes your eye.
I've traveled the world since my inception,
Red carpets were not rolled out for my reception.
I made the world suddenly stop on its track,
With my birth, humankind was taken aback.
They retreated in their shell-like tortoise,
Cowering in fear they gave up all their joys.
In their houses, they locked themselves up,
The economy worldwide receded into a major slump.
Schools colleges offices all empty,
Hospitals are overburdened with patients plenty.
A deserted look on stadium, station, and street,
Like the good old days, people can't meet and greet.
Attempts are being made to terminate me,
To adapt I mutate and evolve constantly.
Right you are, I am the deadly Coronavirus,
Invincible you are not, you humans perspicacious!

HOPE IN THE DARK

Everything black but not.
Outside there is dark,
No life.
And that is the perspective most of us have,
We have colored our situation darker.
Let's look on the bright side,
More life and more time.
More life as we are now happier and full of life,
Life has more meaning around the ones we love.
More time for ourselves,
More time to rediscover ourselves.
More time to reconnect with our creator,
More time to connect with ourselves.
More time for the earth to heal itself,
Isn't this what was said to Noah in his times.
To be in hiding in the ark until all is clear,
Isn't this our story written differently?
The perspective we must have,
Just like the hope for all to be ok, we must have.
Out there seems to be dark,
Let not your minds deceive you.
Out there joy is flying with the birds,
Out there the earth is healing and happy.
What if everything is not black but white,
What if God paused time to give you more hope.
What if you have been under pressure,
At work, with kids, with the world.
What if God is giving us a second chance,
A second chance to reconsider our purpose.
Maybe more,
A second chance to be reborn.

What if all that we think is black is a blessing in disguise.
What if we are the Noahs' of our generation,
Let's just look at things from the brighter side, shall we?

Copyright Diaps Lee BW

FOOL'S GOLD

Wise Man on the face of the earth,
Wisdom And knowledge at thy birth,
Fruits of Ancestors his strength!
He is a scholar beyond Zenith.
Golden be his cup ever glitter,
Diamonds be her glove,
Poverty may never hinder,
Know not the gloomy days.
Lovers of worldly creations,
Think those flowers they own,
Though a devil in disguise,
Fools the poor man's Soul.
Man, that own gadget,
See lie's on silvery plates,
Covered with Rusty hearts,
Little deceiver in each man's pocket.
Nothing seems worthy without his presence,
Fighting a maze full of plague,
It's salvation you must seek,
Before you aspire to your wildest dreams,
Remember My child, God First.

LOCKDOWN

Unlock your mind and soul,
Humans are gone wild in a brawl,
While some lose a fantasy world,
Others lost their daily bread.
Humanity lies on pieces of paper,
Albums on fame and glory,
Mankind seeks, they prosper,
As some gambled with poor man's misery,
The brave man bowed their knees,
Locked down their hope and faith.
While seeking for mighty intervention,
Fear of the virus overwhelmed the creator.
Toss away your hypocrisy,
Where is the generosity you brag,
Recall the widow near your window,
While you feed on streets beyond your yard.
At time of nature's fury,
Will you wash your hands behind closed doors?
Where is your prayer when evil uproar,
Come stand as one before the
World collapse,

Copyright Ariba Anar

HOPE AMIDST THE PANDEMIC

Good old memories are playing hide and seek,
Amidst the pandemic, we are feeling meek.
We can't go out and she is not coming in,
The game is tiresome, who will win?
The plethora of questions unanswered,
Doubts scattered around, situation absurd,
Tears and agony of losing loved ones,
Broken pieces of dreams lingered in tonnes.
HOPE! the only strength and courage,
To heal and retrieve the damage.
Inaudible prayers mingled in the air,
To save the human race from death and despair.
Let's take refuge in the feet of Almighty.
He is the one who can end this adversity.
May mother Earth heal and get back its charm,
Bless the mortals and save us from all harm.
The hour of crisis is hard to bear,
Let's hold a hand, spread love, and care,
The more we give the more we get,
Together we can defeat the deadly threat.

Copyright Swapna Das

THE THOUGHTS OF A COVID19 SUFFERER ON VENTILATOR

Death, I Wish... You could come some other time!!
Caught intricately between the wands time,
Preoccupied, I had been all these years, very fine,
With no time to spend, I was a miser
New dawn did not give any pleasure either.
Time was money, and I was always eager
To earn much more, I wandered hither and thither.
My outward appearance was so different
Stunned was the inner me, seeing me so stringent.
Hungry for applauds I was mounting the ladder
Fame had blunted my senses forever.
Now I have realized, there's very little time left
I want to come, for death would leave all bereft
The distance seemed so difficult to travel
The obstacles in the mind failed to unravel.
Now when my breathing is difficult I realize
My being forgotten, even before my body dries.
As the world, today has come to a standstill
I wish to talk to my kin and explain my will.
My fame, my wealth didn't matter even a little
But a morsel of food and a kind word did.
My final journey would be royal I dreamt,
But death, you do not hear anybody's plight!
You come at your will and leave silently
And when asked to wait disregard blatantly.
I want to talk to my children and run around
To capture moments of happiness floating abound.
I wish you to come when I am ready
I do not care a damn when I sound so greedy.
Listen to my request and step back a mile
I will rectify myself and come back in a while.

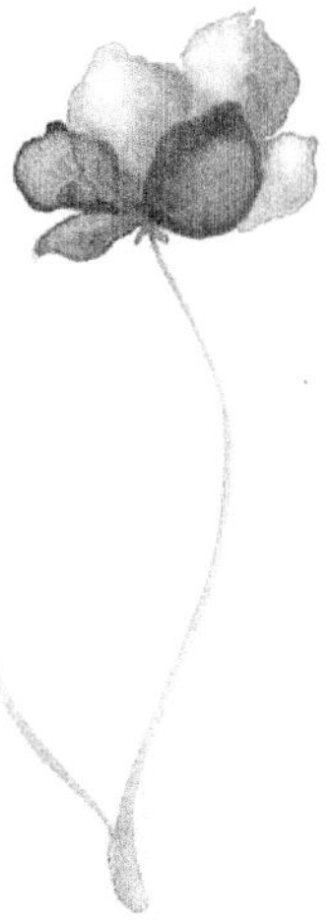

The time now is a painfully difficult trial
There's none to accompany me at my burial.
Come to me when I am with my kith and kin
After they have pardoned me for all my sin.
Take me away when the time is sublime
My only wish is you could come some other time!!

-Copyright Dr. Naaz Shaikh

WISHING WELLS

Wishing wells so dreamy
expectations so sublime
drowning in our realities
an inbuilt component of fear
even the riches ditched us
essentials a lifetime away
A topsy turvy connotation
Of sceptical brouhaha
2020 has been this magic spell
By the magician
Which casts an aspersion on all generations to come
A reminder of the transience the flippant
the monster of situations
Which engulf your persona at places
A glitz of strangeness
A dent of nothingness
This Godzilla devouring everyone's encephalon
Like carcasses of despair
We roam
Each day ending with a sigh
A relief
A count-up of ours and theirs
A sci-fi which turned into an autobiography
Despondent gory real
Us
Hoping for the next year to ease
This modish promise to keep.
Rejoice, hold reweave once more
The loving knots of time and relations sour

CopyrightNavneet Gill Grewal

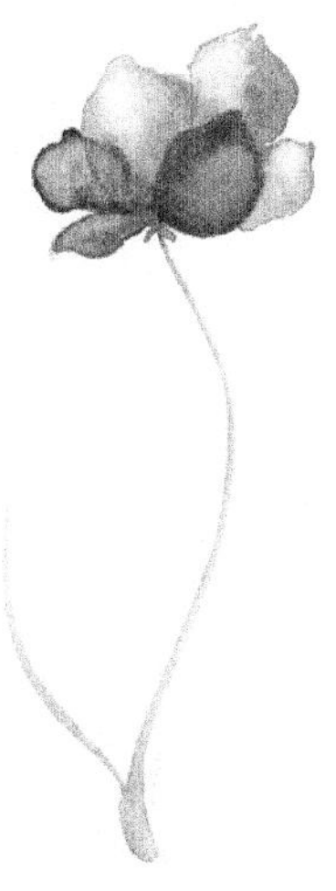

LIVE AND GIVE

Nothing special about it
But the way I took it
It came suddenly
And I stood aptly
To give in to fear
Or to brace up and bear
I know I have this life to live
But it's all I have to give
If it only to save
I wouldn't have it to rave
And so I served
And I served
Now the world's better
And I feel greater
What if I didn't give
What would I here to live?
Twenty-twenty
Was indeed my year of plenty
Thank God for strength
And for health.
And also for the share, we care
And for the care we share.

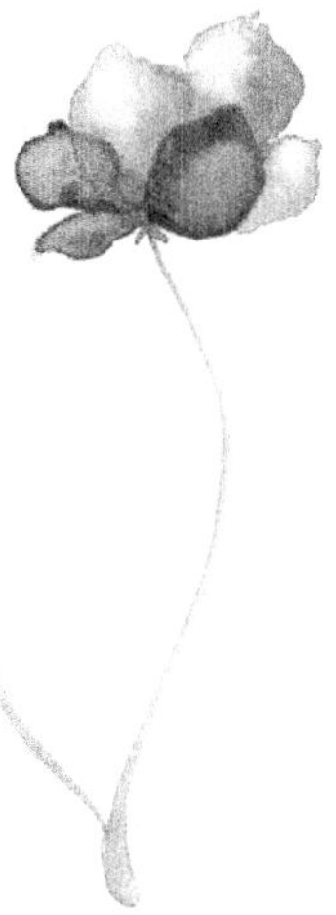

HALF BREATHE TO KEEP A FULL BREATH

The mask was thought to hide something
But this time I wore it to protect something
It was so crazy
And to wear it I was so lazy
But when I saw one down
I chose not to be a clown
I got a piece
And wore it for my peace
It was better to wear it to half breathe
Then to have a full breath
And anything about no breathing at all
Was not what I can take at all
I wore it to protect me
And as you can see
To also protect you
As we get through.
I got my half to breathe
To get my full breath.

Copyright Pappa Jalo

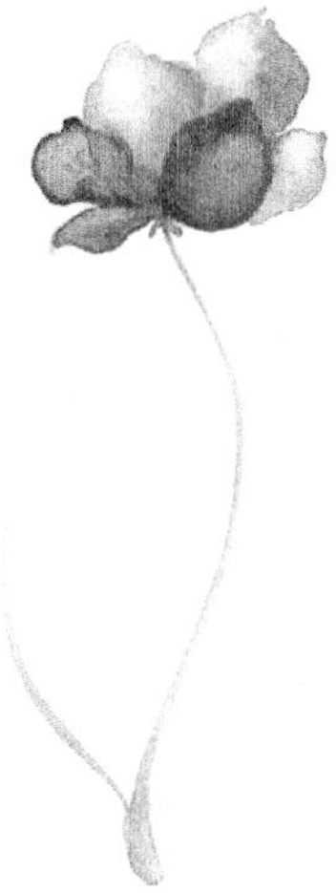

CHAOTIC CORONA

The attack of an invisible enemy,
shaken the entire world mentally.
The sound of an ambulance siren,
The unrest and chaotic situation.
Everyone is under lockdown,
instructed to follow the crackdown.
But the true frontline warriors...
Leaving behind their home and family,
taking care and fighting happily,
they are the ray of hope,
that we will soon cope.
Amid people dying,
day and night the health workers are trying.
The police personals are doing their part,
by distancing the gathering apart.
The cleaning workers are sanitizing,
trying to make virus-free everything.
The grocers, chemist, milkman are doing hard,
The delivery boy is keeping us, away from the mart.
Thank you is a tiny word to express our gratitude,
We can help them by changing our careless attitude.
Wash your hands, wear gloves and a mask,
it's not impossible, it's an easy task.
Be with your family and stay at home,
you will lose a life if you roam.
Follow the guidelines, be a good citizen,
prove to everyone that you got an education.
We can be thankful for all corona warrior,
By staying home, can make their struggle easier.

Copyright Swapna Das

A SILVER LINING.

The whole world became caged and stopped,
No motion anywhere,
Only noises of ambulance everywhere.
Faces so pale and stressed,
No smile can be seen
nor laugh can be heard for miles.
Children kept inside the home
No school or collages opened,
No markets or offices were run,
Everywhere tears and fears to be seen,
Cries of pain and agony
made life hell.
Nothing was normal or well,
All precaution was about to fail,
God punished us all used to tell,
A doomsday arrived true not a tale.
I remember how I missed my family then
For I was in a distant land for the job those days,
A different state and my family dwelled in a different state far off.
My mom and my son longed to be with me and I used to cry to go back to them.
I used to listen to the song " Country road
take me home " and prayed to God to look after my dear ones always.
I get goosebumps to recall those isolated and lonely days in my hostel room.
Every day seemed a day of doom.
But we United and prayed to heal the world again.
A ray of hope, a bliss was felt by all.
No more curse now boon and blessings will come for all.
Vaccination arrived against corona just like,

A silver lining behind the dark clouds.
Shower of love and peace,
Health, happiness, and prosperity will drench us once again.
God is shedding tears as rain to heal our pain.
Our prayers will never go in vain.

Copyright Aruna Bose

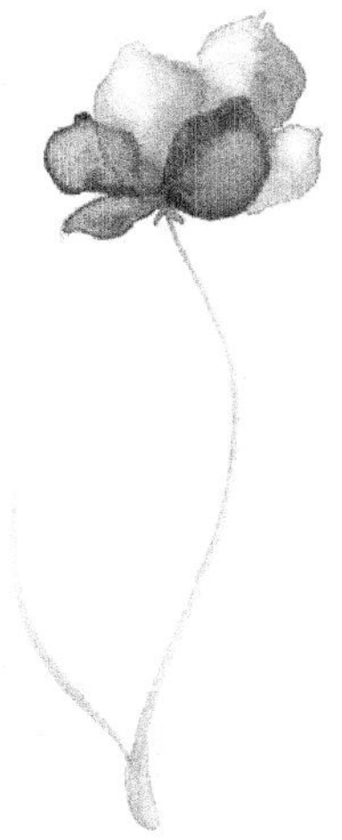

THE UNFORGETTABLE YEAR 2020

A tiny perilous agent created mayhem
And humans suffering now and then
Copious of lessons we learned in these times
Determination and inner strength in us stood in the test of time.
Each one of us played the melody of hope
Fortunate, we felt, and with counting the blessings, we coped
Grumbling about everything; maximum or minimum,
Wouldn't have probably solved the problems.
Hard times showed us the real face of life
All learned to enjoy little joys in life and did strife
Joys and happiness we understood, first of all, in health
Keeping our health good is true wealth.
Everyone did spread love and smiles
We understood life's meaning and, in the difficult situation, how to go miles
By staying focused on our purpose amid adversity,
We organized our life and family that brought positivity.
Now, acceptance to the new normal is the need of the hour,
Masks and gloves are the must things no matter who we are
We've now conditioned to hyper-vigilance
It's good to continue hands and personal hygienic-standards, meticulous!
As ludicrous to complain that rose bushes have thorns,
Embrace the new normal and thank God that the thorns still have roses!

Copyright Pooja Mandla

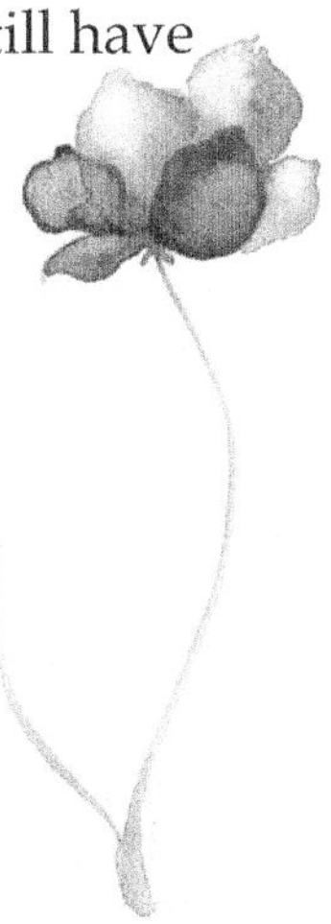

2020 A.D.

(Curse or Blessing)

Present to the world only your eyes
Allow your soul from its window prance
Shielded noses, covered mouths
No more pretty snoots, seductive pouts
An equality between the swan and mouse.
Keeping our distance from one another
You would not notice my hidden fears
Nor my eyes misty with tears
Longing for you to be near
I'm missing your kisses Dear.
Let's not forget to take vitamin C
To strengthen, boost our immunity
It Will help preserve my purity
Until our postponed wedding day
Before the altar, you'll be very proud of me.
Skies clothed in greyish smog
Suffocated by polluted fog
For once enjoyed a fresher breath
As the world took a much-needed rest
Danced wearing its lovely azure dress.

Copyright Myrna Tejada

ALL AROUND THE WORLD

All around the world people are getting sick or worse dying This covid is no joke But not everyone is playing by the rules as much as we want to be with our loved ones we best to stay six feet apart The risk of the disease outweighs the want to be close with family Just wishing it could be over already Unfortunately there are still ones who have not learned the fact how serious it is and that is does spread They feel they can take the chance and be around the healthy So then the numbers rise the next day Finally all we. can do is pray for a cure and the end of this once and for all.

Copyright Crystal King

THE YEAR 2020 HAS BEEN A TRAGIC YEAR BECAUSE OF PANDEMIC.

As we experienced, Lost of Job, Lack of Financial, lack of food, and some of the members of the family having Anxiety, loss of Hope, and Faith in life.

For me Year 2020, I experienced all the Challenges and Struggles in life, because of Pandemic, otherwise, this year also gave me the privilege to write when I joined in different International Group it was December 2020 when I started to join and allowed me to pursue my Passion.

I am grateful and blessed to be part of the International Group and a chance to receive some Excellence and Appreciation award in the field of Poetry.

This was the time I achieved my goal and dream to write.

The year 2020 is a Friendship year for me because I met friends not only in our country mostly in different countries.

The most Special part I met a Special friend. He is my Inspiration behind my Poetry and the reason why I experienced Joy and Happiness despite Pandemic, He was the one who enlightens me, to increased my faith in God, and whatever Challenges in Life.

We have our Heavenly Father,

Our Protector, and our Savior in our Life.

Copyright Cristina Juanite

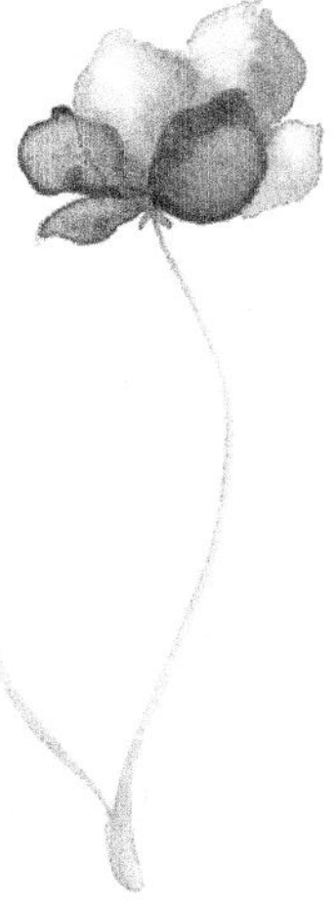

2020, OH THE YEAR THAT WAS!

A year like none other
Would I ever find the word
To describe it the way it was
A roller coaster of emotions,
A year of unlearning, and learning
Countless souls left for a better world
Leaving sorrowful rivers behind
Dreading the unseen being
Living in fear of death and dismay
Yet, finding the courage to go on
Finding joys in everyday moments
Comfort in pajamas, savoring home food
Books became my friend
Taking me far and beyond
In the year of isolation
I rediscovered my passion
The pen became my identity
And I found the lost me
Immense gratitude I have
To a year that's been the greatest teacher of all
Unforgettable lessons many I learnt
To value people, and show them I care
To be true, and be there when in need
Materialistic needs are far less than we think
Minimalism is the key to happiness
A caring kind heart is all that matters
Life's too short to live in falsities
Ego and pride are shackles best broken
Glad to leave the past behind
Never forget the lessons learned
Wisdom gained, memories made

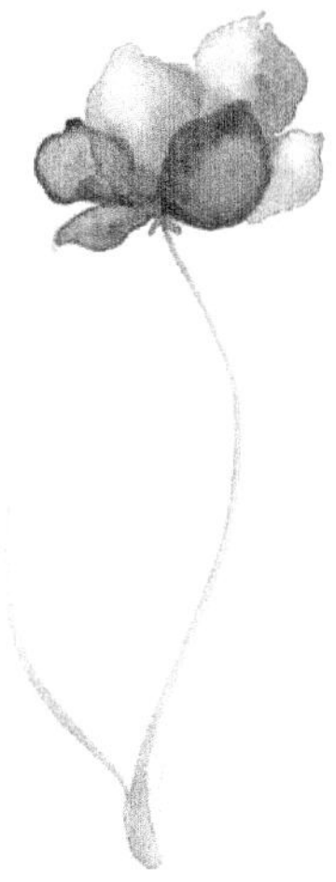

The year was a roller-coaster
A year like none other

I AM A SURVIVOR

Yes, I am a survivor
I beat the devil who wears a crown
Its deadly sting gives me a fatal blow
It is invisible you can't fight them back
I thought for me it is the end.
From head to toe, I am in pain
Alone in isolation, longing for somebody's love and care
"But where are they? I was left alone to my desolation.
A glimpse of white surrounds me
They must be angels coming down from heaven
One holds my hand and said, " She's coming back the battle is almost over.."
Oh yes, the pain is slowly ebbing
People in white, I hear them talking
" She's gonna make it
We have a survivor".
Truly someone up there
Is stronger than the devil
Who brought covid-19.

Copyright Lucy A. Mendiola

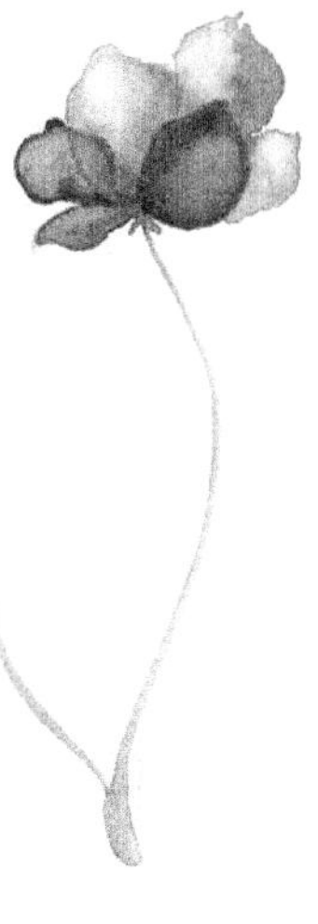

2020 THE YEAR MY VISION CHANGED

It was a year full of many different emotions for me.
The death of family and friends took me for a loop.
No more church services for me only virtual services, but I always had God.
The year 2020 in the book of history is when quarantined homes became a lifestyle
Although I was absent of physical touch, I could touch the Hem of His garments for my healing and loneliness.
It brought me to a closer relationship, with Him.
It's funny because I thought that I had had a close relationship with Him.
It was a year of more, more time to think of His goodness and grace.
More time to think of His undying love, and His faithfulness
More time to remember who went to the Cross for me and all humanity
More time to grow in faith and trust in Him and Him alone.
It was a year when I thought More about my fellow man as oppose to myself
It was a year to find out what I was made of.
He strengthened me to trust in Him instead of the environment, that surrounds me.
2020, the year I self-published my first book of poetry.
It was His breath that gave my pen the courage to ink.
He Breathed *On My Pen Sister Of The Pen June 21st, 2020.*
I celebrated my granddaughter's 1st birthday
And thank God that I made it to the year 2021
The year 2020 gave me 20/20 vision to always remember
To lay everything down at the Master's feet and leave it there

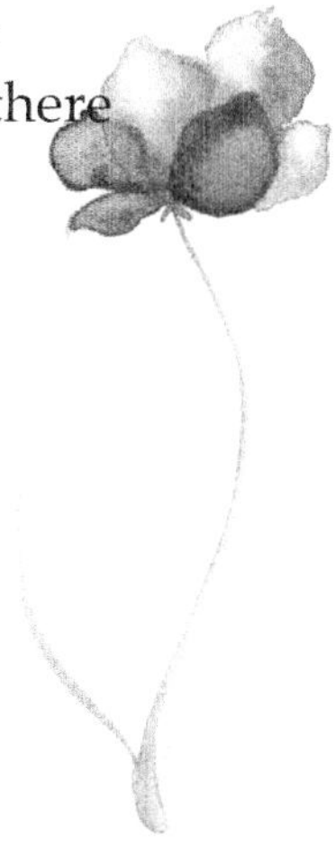

A DISCO WITH DEATH

The strings of a deadly disease,
Dragged our dangling legs into a dance.
First, it looked like a trance
Which we thought will soon cease.
The temple of the song reached a crescendo,
They heard it as far as Orlando,
And even my charismatic Ronaldo,
Couldn't play in the deadly inferno.
It was a rhythm of death
For which they provided a medical hearth.
But the medical hearth caused our dart.
Mr. Death filled his illustrious cart,
With souls from the shelf of life.
The disease cut men like a knife
And the scars will be here for life.
The uninvited orchestra visited our lands,
Deafened our ears with a blaring,
Weakened our industrious hands,
And impaired our hearing.
The deadly music infringed on our rights,
Freedom of movement was put to flight,
We lost our legal signs and sights.
We were isolated,
The rhythm left us deserted.
Unity used to be our strength,
Strength now lies in staying apart two arm's length.
A hug or a kiss can make one sick now,
Coughing or sneezing can make one freeze now,
Tolerating them is a romance on the bed of death.

YEAR OF SHAGGINESS

Oh! eye wiped without teardrop.
Tongue taste shallot without seeing its fruit.
Body fill with shagginess without cold breezing.
Oh! What hears will listen to our clamoring?
What eye will look into our boiling blood,
Without teardrop.
Alas! panic took away happiness.
Replacing with shagged.
Oh! the sinful soul, let restrict to cure this shameful panic.
Let saturated with saint
To be among salient.
Let lift our voice to the creator.
Let utter one word called forgiveness.
Let breath as one to live in eternity joy.

STUCK AT YOU

You may be stuck at work
I am stuck at heart.
you may be lost in future
I remain in the past.
I don't know the reason
of your arrogance
neither do I know understand
your rude stance.
I don't know what flames consume our love,
what tides make our passion fade.
For all I feel is tremors of love
and its epicenter being you.
Because you may be stuck at work
I am stuck at you.

MASKED SECRETS OF CORONA VIRUS.

2019 slipped with a celebration
2020 came with a coronation
Festivals celebrated came spring
New flowers bloomed, birds fly and merrily sing.
Radio, T.V. announced waves of death
The tiny virus invades through breath
Intrudes, trespasses all regulations
Humanity reels under its spell spread destruction.
Killing millions, all over earth girth
Once where people, lived in mirth
At the speed of light, travels through breath and air
Enters homes, countries, creates fear.
Spreads, through touch, sneeze, breath
Government, masses scared at rising deaths
Countries spin in despair
Under Corona's spell all unprepared.
Covid 19. Pandemic declared
As no cure, panic spreads, the world it conquers
No kisses, hugs, shake hands, social distance, a norm
Wear masks, wash hands, isolation keeps us from harm.
Hospitals, short-staffed, full
School, shops, factory, hotel cinema halls, shut down
Flights, trains canceled, there was a total lockdown
The world came to stand still, there was a lull.
Doctor, nurses, police, corona, warriors help
The government doles resources, to help the jobless
Food donation, free food for helpless
Temples, churches, closed, no prayers held.
2020 a historic year, leaves an imprint on time
On history's pages, leave tragic hurts, memories, chimes

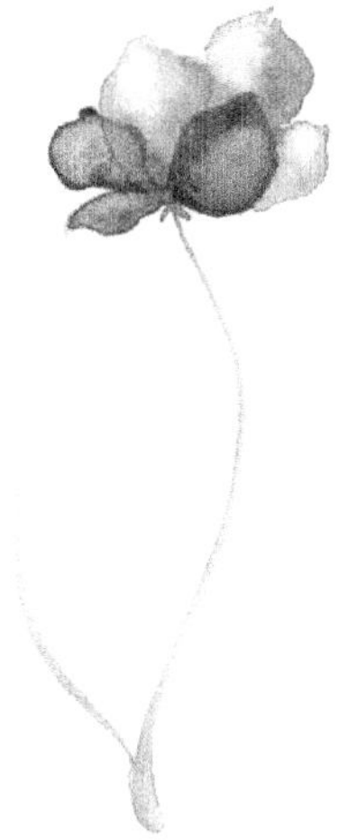

Left so many reeling in whirlpools of grief
All celebrated the new year 2021 with sighs of relief.
Now lockdown eased
Vaccine discovered for cure of viral disease
It is the result, of man's cruelty to mother earth
Destroyed forests, spread pollution on earth's girth.
Now Mother earth protection should be our main focus, concern.

MAYHEM IN 2020

The year 2020 started with a bang and bash
Weaving New Year resolutions and promises
Suddenly a virus stealthily crawled
Like unseen monsters through the dark
Killing mankind mercilessly
A battle with an unknown army began
It marched from cities to cities
Killing people unanimously
Killing freedom, killing the economics
Complete darkness
Complete stillness
Stillness in life,
Stillness in mind
Stillness is death
Kisses, hugs, touches sinful
Mask and sanitation necessary
Quarantine and calamity
Only hope and prayer and faith became stronger
Stay home, stay safe became a necessity.

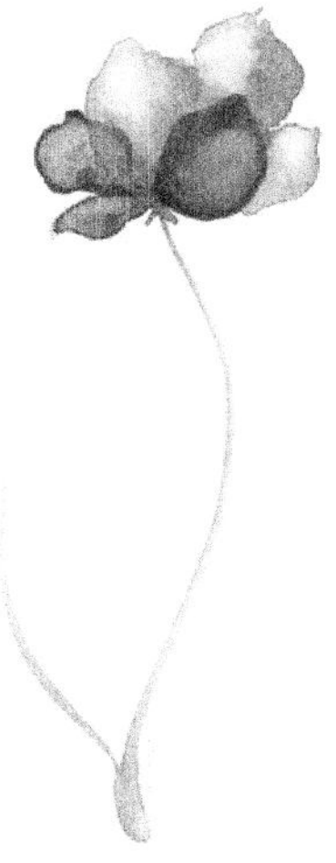

NOT SO CLOSE ENCOUNTER WITH DEATH

Two thousand twenty passed away
As an eerily menacing phase,
Confined us inside a home,
No work-place, no holidays.
Similar to walking on coals,
That is, still, half ablaze
Like the solitary prisoners
All people appeared in a daze.
A sense of insecurity
Was instilled in everyone,
Fun- get- together and meetings
Were completely undone
Pandemic was scary, yet
Humans were irresponsible,
Although some took the precaution
Some daredevils were impossible.
Safety was interdependent
We had to learn this lesson
No one can be an island
In the universal ocean
A fear factor was there
Throughout past year
Dancing with death full time
Life was out of gear
Still not out of danger
Still, the curtain is not down
The show is continuing with
The death wearing a crown

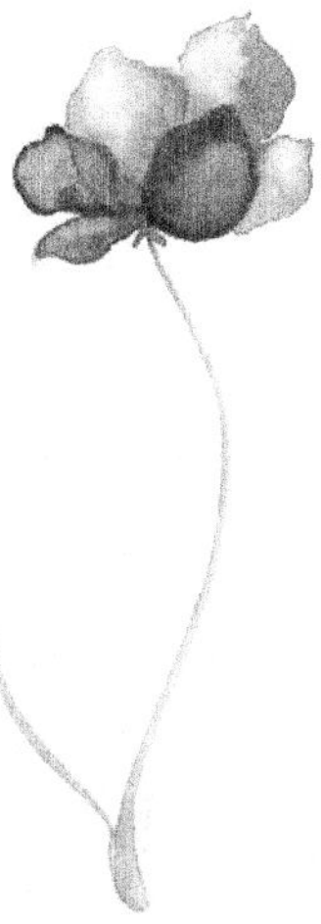

THE FACE OF HORROR

With high hope, we waited for you
Like a distant aunt, bringing our favorite toys
And given life to our dreams.
But when you arrived,
You handed us nothing but fear
And our dreams on a rock you dashed
Like predatory animals, you muzzled us
Locked us in chains and some in cages
With no chance to mingle
You became a nightmare
And haunted us
Even with our eyes wild open
Never will I ever forget you
Not even in a hurry
Thou beautiful face of horror
You were like a wedge
And a sword of chaos
That drove us asunder
2020, the year we dinned with horror
Serving us hot dishes of terror

Copyright C.I. Nwagod Chinagorom

THE YEAR OF PANDEMIC

The new year had set its feet
With a warm welcome
Night-long dance and music
Merry-making, fun, and celebration.
Soon an alarm was heard
At the door of one country
That soon spread out
All over the world territory.
A virus was on the prowl
Spreading its tentacles
Wider it searched its prey
Breaking territorial barrier.
Soon the crowded area
Appeared lonely and haunted
People forced to stay home
Office and public places closed.
Life became miserable
The world economy did suffer
For both young and old
Mask and sanitizer became saver.
Social distancing was mandatory
Prohibited were a physical touch
Hug and embrace not seen
Killing emotions of all.
The whole year passed
Searching for a vaccine
Limited success was seen
In a few research laboratories.
Hiding its face at midnight
2020 silently went away

Another new year came
Without welcome and joy.
The year earned a bad name
In the history of mankind
What were its mistakes?
Responsible is the Covid.

Copyright Kishor Kumar Mishra

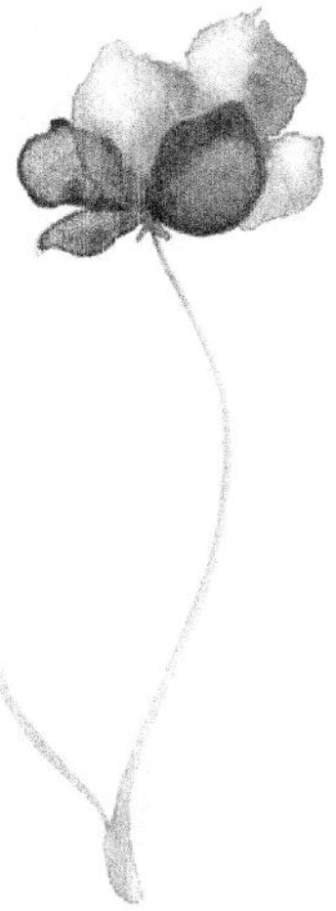

CORONA SURVIVOR

2020 was a historic year full of gory tales. Coronavirus entered all countries, terrorized, and destroyed the fibre of life in the world.

People caught in its fangs danced with death in breathless feats, waves of death engulfed people all over the world.

My brother- in -law was caught in viruses fangs, it was his sons birthday, we were enjoying, joking sharing eats, suddenly he was breathless feeling faint, weak, rushed him to hospital, he was put on Ventilator, quarantined as his oxygen levels very low, slowly he recovered, discharged on Christmas eve. He thanked us for our prayers and God for his return from a dance with death. I asked him" how he felt when quarantined,"

"Very worried, scared for his children, family when he saw death looming," he said.

On New year we distributed sweets, planted trees, to prevent pollution, make the earth green. He has joined an environment protection group and became a compassionate person.

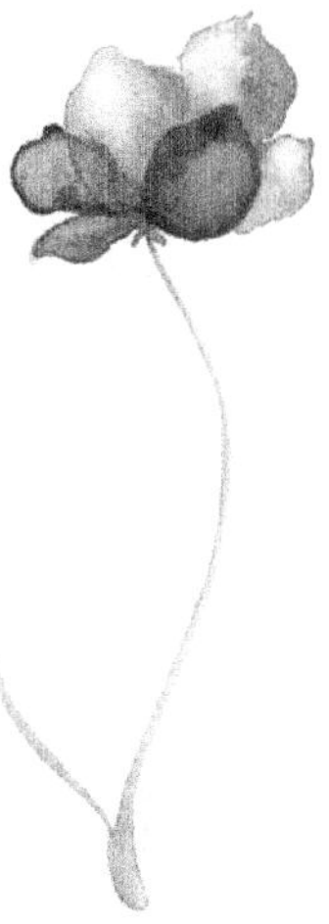

QUARANTINE

.

Q-uietly stressing
what the outcome
will be
U-nderstanding
nothing they say
on tv
A-ssuming I'm
making the right
choices for me &
mine
R-ethinking every
thing all the time
A-nticipating good
news about the
end of this virus
N-ever leaving the
house unless I
have a supply list
T-rying to keep the
little ones from
getting bored
I-insanity is whats
taking place right
outside my door
N-o one is supposed
to be going out,
yet the streets
are packed with
people filled with
doubt

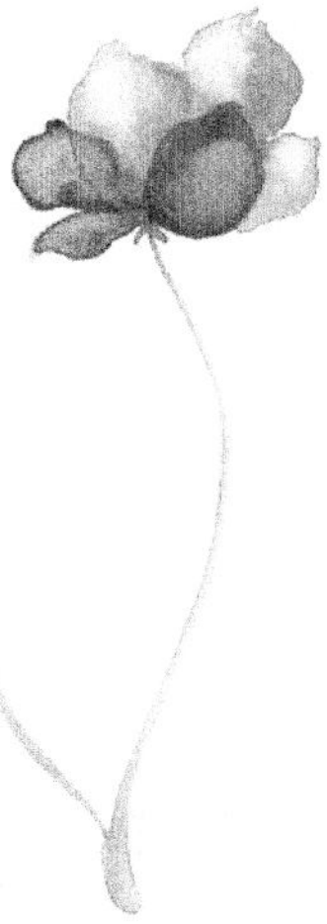

E-ventually this
epidemic will pass
& I can't wait to
get out & off
my ass...

Copyright Lee Love

A YEAR THAT WAS 2020

A year that was a memorable one
I turned sixty, became Senior Citizen
Retired from thirty-six-year long service
Entered into a stress-free happy life.

Decided to explore my motherland
A nice travel plan I had fixed
North to south, west to east
Hill stations, beaches, and wildlife.

Forts, temples, and heritage sites
River views, boating, and funny rides
Wanted to pass the evening on the lakeside
Garden, park and visit countryside.

A nice time it was for meeting friends
Relative homes and social gatherings
Shopping malls, markets, fairs, and festivals
Called me frequently with temptations.

Barely one and a half month passed
Covid-19 spread around the world
Lockdown, night curfew came as a strategy
Bus, train, air journey came to a halt.

Emerged "Stay home, Stay safe" slogan
All my travel plans went to the dustbin
Sanitizer and mask added to my woes
Friends stayed away from a social distance.

More time I spent on poem writings
Began a new life on online social networking
All-time, day and night, I spent inside the home
Only for essential commodities, outside, I came.

Covid-19 news became prime on a small screen
Online newspapers replaced paper options
Health workers and other frontline workers
Took much pain as Covid warriors.

Day by day, infections grew exponentially
The death toll also rose high accordingly
Became more vulnerable, older and children
Nations put best efforts to invent vaccine.

The year 2020 became memorable for pandemic
But the year gave me mixed feelings
I got something and lost something
Loss and Gain together make a life balancing.

Copyright Kishor Kumar Mishra

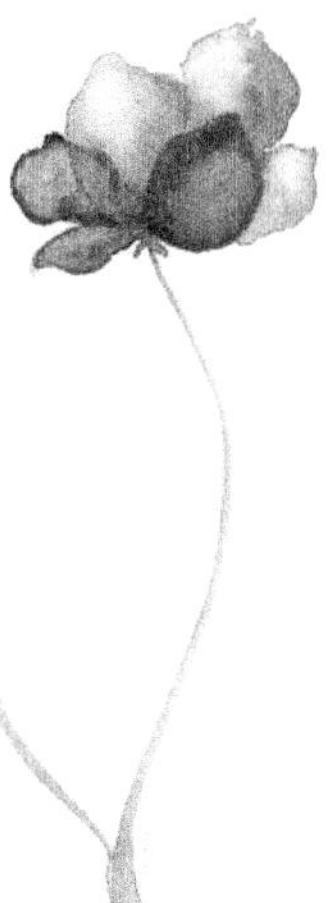

THE YEAR 2020

Is the worst unimaginable year I have or rather we both experience.

The eruption of a local volcano in January leaving people homeless and jobless due to heavy ashfall. Animals left behind during evacuation died buried in ashes.

The place becomes a no man's land.

Months after, the news was spreading. A deadly virus hits China killing thousands and thousands of its inhabitants.

No one expects it will hit our country but it does.

People went panicky when the government ordered a total lockdown.

Wear a mask to stay safe stay at home becomes the litany of the everyday.

Two patients become a hundred then thousands. The number of infected escalate..hospitals are crowded with people sick of covid19.

Some patients are lucky to survive, some don't. Sad to say they died alone because no one is allowed to go near them in fear of infection.

There is nothing more painful for the families of the victims, to see their loved ones thrown unto the pyre. No hugs, no goodbyes, only tears, and the beautiful memories they spent together.

Copyright Lucy A. Mendiola

2020 --A THROWBACK

In the approaching death's darkness
my mind did start to waver ;
My love and longings did grow weaker ;
And witnessed me as Divinity -a disbeliever.
Caught betwixt life and death ' dance ;
Whispered into me my inner silence.
"Look at me through every moment's window ;
Lifelessness, deathlessness and Imagelessness will you follow ".
Felt that this life's short season's moments are not my own ;
By many a world, they have been encroached upon.
All living beings are citadels of divinity ;
But human as the highest becomes the lowest
by disequilibrium peaceful co-existentialism.
Felt as if my house of bricks, one of mud and bamboos into turned ;
with fresh childhood memory bats appeared and day-night
screamed.
For this why shall I blame the other and earn blame?
As a minuscule part, the universe is one of the roots of the
pandemic game.
Social distancing, hand washing, and mask-wearing made my heart
go fonder ;
As a little pig could feel the wolf - on- the- prowl's love looking for.
Earnestly did I wait for a drummer in my village with a message
for a covid cure
With hatred for salt, sugar, and oil and a love for walking more.
Felt in the dense forest of inhumanity my body living has been
thrown ;
Best brained human leopards are ever ready to pounce upon.
Survive will I despite death knocks my door at every moment
God in His will for me has a very endearing arrangement.

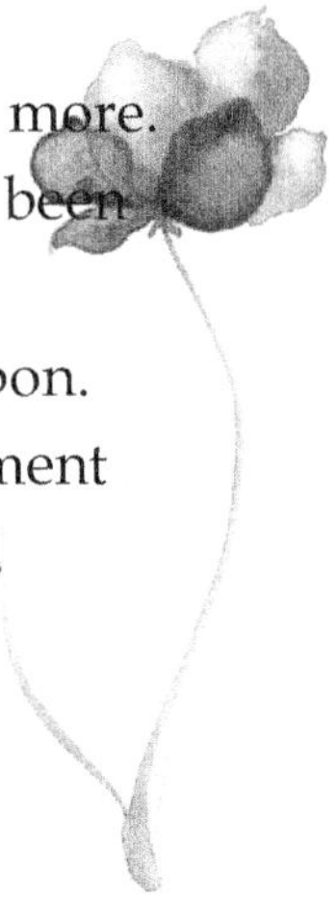

Ever new Time does transform every abnormal into normal new
I will have to adore it with wintry smiled dew.
Cannot I term my pandemic sufferance as the worst of times
Taught me how to evolve humane responses in the future to similar crises.

Copyright Amiya Rout

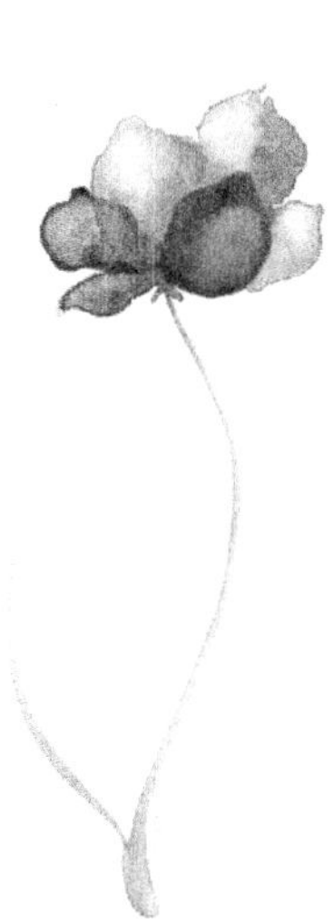

THE YEAR 2020, A CURSE TO ALL HUMANS IN EARTH;

People pass time without mirth.

Remain in homes with fear:

Coronavirus pervades in the air.

Communications by planes, trains, buses stopped plightly,

People live in isolation pathetically.

Not allowed to assemble,

Using masks, maintain distance in displeasure.

Many people die due to the infection;

Humans remain without Divine Benediction.

People don't come in contact with each other due to fear;

Remaining in homes passes time in displeasure.

All pray God to destroy the virus, the monster;

With family members, seeing television passes time is little pleasure.

All play with lovely children enthusiastically;

Poets pen poems plightly.

Copyright Vavroovahana Patra

COVID 19, CORONA VIRUS PERVADES IN THE AIR;

Unseen virus pervades Ray's displeasure.
Family members pass time pathetically;
Don't avail vegetables lovingly.
We pass time in rooms in plight;
Seeing television avail information, live without delight.
Unable to visit relatives invites displeasure;
People like to roam in the lap of Nature.
People covered faces with masks walk on the street;
Don't come in contact, live in plight.
Frightened minds pray God to live in peace;
Pray God for Divine Bliss.
Many people die due to infection daily;
Relatives live plightly.
Doctors serve patients fearfully;
Distant relatives die untimely.
God is displeased by earthy humans plightly;
People cry untimely.
Surrender on God's Feet for protection;
Pray for His Benediction.
Coronavirus generated from China, Uhan City;
Infected lakes of people with agony plight.
Latter the virus spread all over the country;
People lived in isolation in plight.

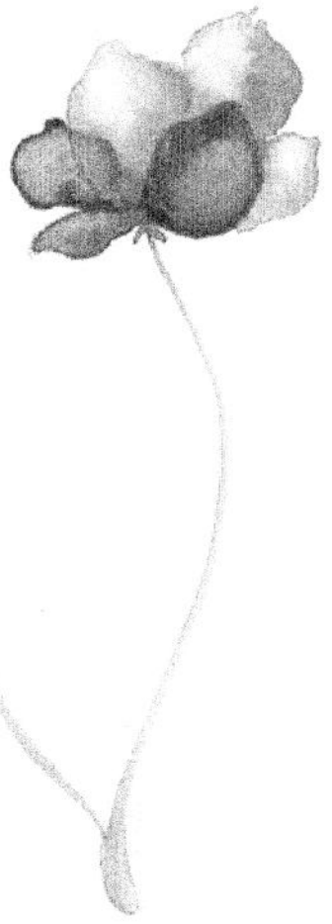

2020 UNLEASHED DEADLY DISEASE ON MANKIND

Bringing the world to its knees
Time had turned a cruel master indeed
The gale of destruction has been hurled
Barely had the new year greetings finished
Amphan, Nisarga, Hanta, locusts, and Corona Clasped us in their arms wicked
Cataclysmic doom mankind witnessed.
Protests raged saying 'Black lives Matter
Pandemic left us shattered
It kept surging in many waves
Took on toll thousand jobs and lakhs of lives
Reminding every time the situation was grave.
Animals enjoying liberation on the roadside
The world worked from home, capsulated inside
Scrambling to overhaul our lives amongst uncertainty
Wights finding solace in cooking, meditation, writing, and prayers in the community
Though nature was healing, they say
We learned family, love, and life is important and nature should be obeyed
Needs raised an upper hand on comforts and luxuries
This remains a lesson for the progeny to come
Is some black swan near or what else to become?

GO BACK TO YOUR ROOTS!

Giving their lives for their duties,
front-liners did their jobs efficiently
When the pandemic took over the plight countrymen had to give in to a big fight
Perplexed was everyone;
what would happen,
what would be the result!
All around the world,
everything seemed disturbed.
Lockdown took over the lives of people in most of the lands.
They struggled to manage their daily lacks,
food, essentials, medicines were on the high list.
The army, the doctors, and the journalists did their duties well.
Grocery stores took on the risk
opened the store shift by shift
All the front-liners did their jobs dancing with the death.
Corona, a pandemic took everybody to their knees.
Working from home,
online classes became the new norm.
Housekeepers had to combat,
with no house help at all
Some family for the first time came together under one roof,
had a gala time, finding joys in little aspects of life.
Making memories cherishing togetherness, fighting battles with covid and not less.
The ones who lost their loved ones in this pandemic faced traumatic times, God bless them with the strength to bear the loss and be fine.
This pandemic taught us lessons
they introduced us to our roots,

home-cooked food, old customs, immunity system of our body
only helps to fight.
Go back to your roots,
eat home-cooked food
cleanliness is the key to good health
keep your distance, wash your hands
Sanitize before you embark.
Before helping others first take your charge.
This pandemic brought new meaning to the lives of few,
many realized their passion and dived-in. without regression.
Embracing the newfound love,
few like me reaped the fruit of Self-love.

Copyright Bhawna Himatsinghani

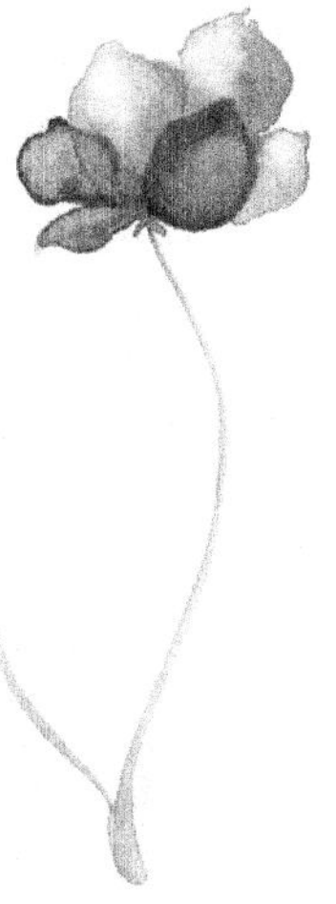

MEMOIRS OF 2020

It was Covid Times but we got all the time
to sit and think with rhythm and rhyme.
Welcome 2020 with dreams, hopes, and ambition
But corona we all feared, for its fast transmission.

The rich and the poor knew the virus was brutal
For it could attack anyone, no warning no rebuttal.
All efforts to run away was beyond human power
Casual meetings went, in the garden or under the bower

All vehicles and airplanes vanished from the scene
Hotels and restaurants wore blank looks, never seen!
A pall of gloom had set in across the industries
Sensex had nosedived, but greener looked the trees.

Sanitizer and immunity, all household jargons,
TV and newspapers taught us the new paragon.
Employer-employee meetings were only on Zoom
Gone were the board meetings, airlines were doomed.

The cars parked in the garages stood in deathly silence
Bicycle and the rider made a newfound alliance.
From greasing to cleaning, morning and evening
I pedaled along, face masked but eyes beaming.

Old T-Shirts from the cupboards got a new lease of life
DIY came in handy as masks rid us of strife.
Students had to study online from their homes
For mothers a boon, they could work from home!

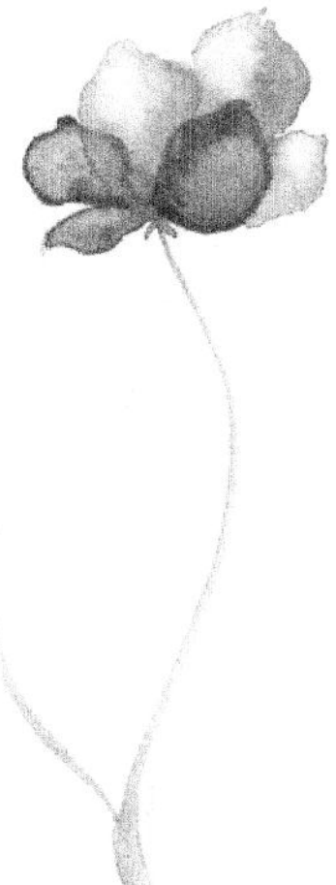

Husbands working from home were the new normal
From the Philippines to Rome, everything abnormal!
The teaching faculty updated their cyber skills
Students had no time for games or physical drills.

2020 kept us indoors but gave us a clear blue sky,
Every night a beauty, with Venus, Mars, and Mercury.
Festivals wore a different look, a change in outlook
No sacrificial goats for Eid, and no meat to cook!

Nor were there Turkeys in thanksgiving to dine
All the goats and turkeys were saved in quarantine!
With crossed fingers, we went for the Covid test,
Kudos to the health workers who knew it best;

On one hand, the mask industry minted more money
The dented lipstick industry lost all gloss and glory.
We say 2020 good-riddance ushering in Covaxin
But the mask is not yet off, a penalty for our sins!

copyright Suprana Gee

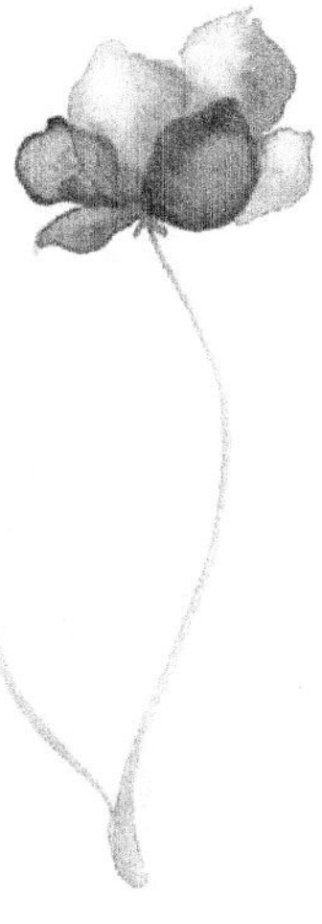

THE TREACHERY OF TIME

Surprises are the essence of life they say.

The year 2020 surprises us with many tragic events, which until now some people still feel the wounds and pain, losing their loved ones. Our days are distracted by fog and thoughts that we are fooled by life. It may be, that in an hour our lives are over. Making time so treacherous

Within my hand I was holding what will soon become a tragic history, Covid 19 covers the front page of the newspaper. A pandemic with its ill-effects brought fear and confusion, I felt, shock...shocked to the depth of my sadness

The world is now in a shadow of panic, uncertainties, and sadness. Death is a challenge. Now we realize we don't live forever. Yet we are not prepared, we live as though we have endless tomorrows. We forget that we may run out of time, we find ourselves standing next to in line!

STAY CALM

Life is slowly limping back to normalcy
The progress is slow but steady
The different and difficult situation
has made us aware
of our latent ability and power
most of us are now indulging in hobbies
pursuing passions
and doing things worthwhile
To guard against pandemic
and contain the spread of malaise
people across continents
are remaining in isolation
this small act of discipline
Is acting like a boon
to save lives of vulnerable million
Global solidarity ...no more
Is a thing of past and matter of yore
the lessons in learning
has imparted invaluable wisdom
taught us to remain in unison
stay calm and focus on solutions
Till vaccine reaches nooks and corners
we need to follow
laid down rules and instructions
mask hygiene and distance
all three are of utmost importance
It is not only our duty
but is incumbent on us
to make the world virus free
help resume normalcy from pause.

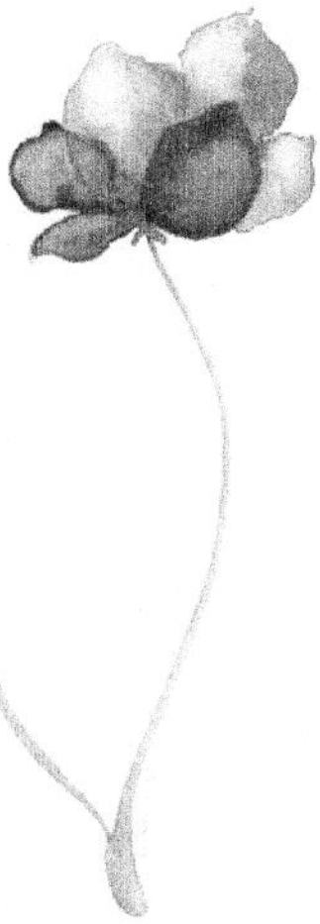

THE SCARE & THE SOLACE

Since the wings of scare have spread
we are mostly unto ourselves
abhorrence for self-isolation and confinement
has slowly turned to an aura of bliss
the lockdown has taught us to appreciate and value
simple pleasures of life
be it plants, pets, music, fine arts, or poesy
we pursue passions now wholeheartedly
lesser traffic on roads assures air... pure and fresh
we have the luxury to breathe and rejuvenate
no hurry no rush
It feels easy to work from home
quality time with family, indulgence in a hobby
spell wonders to curb boredom and drudgery
we have learnt to be frugal
curtailing our wants and desires
sending extravaganza to a distant shore
the unique experience has streamlined our lifestyle
making us emphatic about discipline and hygiene
though our freedom has been snapped
and to hold on to the living
we face many a handicap as regards access
yet have emerged stronger
turned wiser
with each passing phase.

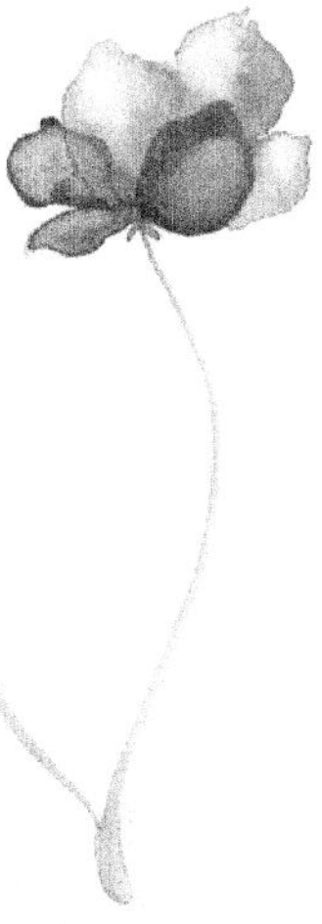

A LEAP YEAR STARTED

With great enthusiasm, it was welcomed
Unaware of the situation ahead
Everyone was petrified with the disease outspread
Every feeling and every desire
Seemed to dress up in horrific attire
Everything looked misty and haunted
As if somebody forced to stop and halted
Every eye and every heart
Was filled with grief and depart
A feeling of sorrow and uncertainties evoked
When no way to deal with the situation looked
The feeling of humanity developed
Out of way, everyone went to help
Deserted streets, masks, and sanitizers
Serves as an ally for all survivors
Everything looked harrowing
When people stopped gatherings
Considering social distancing a norm
As if avoiding a big storm
Necessities took priority
Summed up in into majority
Every job and every chore
Got equal due and equal scores
Everyone learned the importance of life
Enjoy every moment which makes you alive
Nothing is permanent
Live life till you are fortunate

Copyright Alifya Kothari

CLASPED BY COVID

(An acrostic poem using the letters of the words - COVID VIRUS as the first letter of each line .)

PART I
Creating a lockdown,
Orchestrating a melancholy,
Vibes of uncertainty,
In a world of pause,
Dreams and opportunities for many were in
Vestibules of suspense ,
Igniting lost sparks of leisure and hobbies,
Riding cautiously, a masked living,
Under an umbrella of the umbra of fears,
Singing songs of peace and good health.
PART II
An invisible virus ended many lives,
making me think of the fragility of life,
Rangoli, chalk art is known as Ephemeral arts,
Is our life any different from this effervescent, ephemeral existence?
So many questions were raised,
so many innocent lives were erased,
A vaccine, a solution to the problem
was eagerly awaited in 2020.
Till then, life moved on, in a different
but a dear homely setting.

THE SPEEDY SPREAD

Like an octopus,
a pandemic spread its tentacles
across seven oceans and continents.
The entire earth felt its torments
like the tremors of an earthquake,
but these health tremors were scattered
in the months of 2020.
A masked mosaic of human visages,
is lingering gingerly, hoping, even while
shopping for miracles and cures,
a remedy, a vaccination
for all the nations.
A building of Jenga blocks falls apart,
with one slightly wrong block placement,
similarly, one action of less caution
can cause havoc in a plethora of life.
Just like wildfires of the forest,
which attack trees speedily,
the Covid virus pandemic attacked,
many naive human beings suffered.
Prayers, hymns, and bhajans were sung
and many temple bells were rung,
for God's benevolence and blessings.
The community workers worked wonderfully,
risking their lives for human brethren,
Doctors and nurses endangered themselves,
in the background of this deadly virus attack.
Patience, adjustment, and flexibility were imbibed in the
population,
Nature smiled as some places felt lesser pollution and better
pollination!

COVID lockdown taught many lessons
to earth's daughters and sons.

Copyright Rupali Gore Lale

PERCEPTIONS TOWARDS PANDEMIC

To stop pandemic never have enough power
There's no man motivated such power
As we were mightier than viruses?
The air of mastery as if we were mightier than it.

Since we have no enough power would it be in vain
It would weaken our plan
We have no power to boast about it.
All we have to do is to contemplate
and prayers.
How much more pain is motivated of capable of surviving?

It may lead to torture
We must be aware of the risks
That would make a byword of sufferings
We were like wounded kind of animals
As survival were our goal
A kind of experience lead/a scar
These things almost beyond human endurance

And beyond imagining
Our Internet connection did the talking to hinder
the havoc of pandemic.
It may have a cosmic principle as man and viruses
As a certain theory of God and nature and humanity are only one
in a circle.

Sickness and recovery
Sometimes it goes beyond human desires than gone to
overwhelming death.
Other calamities that visit us were typhoons, Floods, tornados,
earthquakes also brought us miseries during the year
2020.
Also volcanoes eruptions many times in our place.

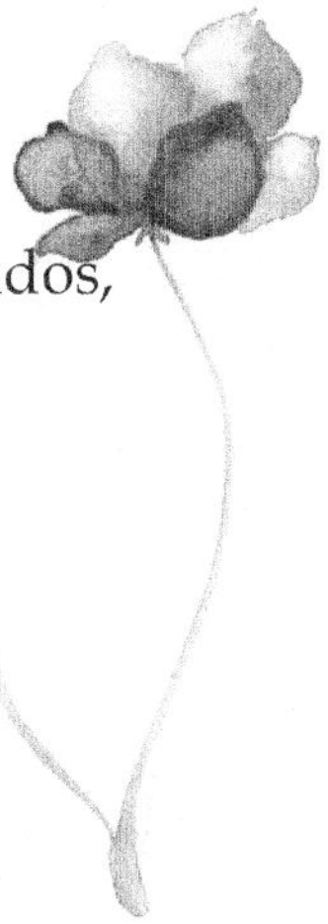

Casts shadows so much suffering especially in the affected areas.
Still, man must have the courage to face and take any precautions and some measures.
Still, the sun shining given us more hopes
After all, there will be a shining hope after pain and sufferings
And it is proven upon reaching the year 2021 and so on?

2020 - A YEAR OF VICISSITUDES

Hello, you guys out there! Girls and boys
Poets, Poetesses, Writers, and Authors
How was the year that went by?
Was it smooth sailing or a bother?

How we take it, much is in our attitude
Throwback 2020 – A Year of vicissitudes!
For I know am writing and I am alive,
The hourglass empties as we thrive,

I know we all are, alive and kicking!
But don't we all know time is ticking?
Years come and go, the show must go on
Today you and I are here and logged on

Tomorrow we must log off and make way
As poets, we know our verses shall stay!
In Jan and Feb everything was hunky-dory
But for Australia Bushfires were a big worry!

Then the Pandemic struck across the globe
Governments turned the 'push to shove'
'Lockdowns' were imposed for our safety
It was a way of disciplining society.

We managed to fight the Pandemic, I dare say
Controlling the spread, to keep Covid- 19 at bay,
But 2020 was not about just Corona alone,
To floods and earthquakes, many lives were gone

It was a challenge man must endure for long,
We had tampered with nature for too long.
We went back to our traditional 'Namaste
Hugs and kisses were taboo they say!

Be at home and things would soon be fine,
With hope, we bid goodbye to fine dining.
Steam inhalation and gargles needed for survival
Oximeters and Ventilators announced their arrival.

And now that 2020 is gone into history
We are here to tell the world, the entire story
We know we shall not live forever and ever,
Some day a virus or calamity will take over;

But we shall remain in fine print or fine art,
In books and anthologies, we live in your heart.

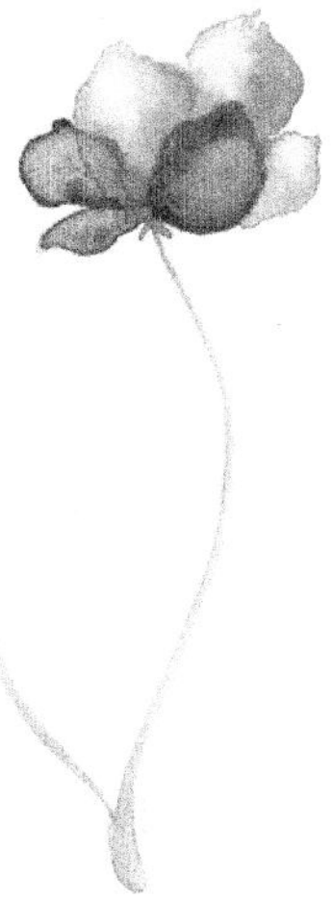

A SUDDEN PANDEMIC

We were happy on this very beautiful earth
Suddenly everything had changed due to a viral attack
Everything had been changed by Covid-19
A virus that spread from Wuhan

People were caged inside the houses
Like birds, they were inside the cages
They were wearing masks
Roads were free from dust
They were washing hands again and again

Trying to get a cure very soon
But the viruses were spreading tremendously
Lives were full of fear and agony
People didn't know what to do?
Patients didn't know where to go?

Doctors, nurses, and all health officials
Did their duties, they were restless
Polices, forces had forgotten their personal lives
People were struggling to survive
So many people lost their nears and dears

Unhappiness was roaring from near to far
People prayed to escape from this pandemic quickly
They prayed for mother earth collectively
They prayed for early recovery for our mother earth
Where everyone will smile again, full of gaiety and mirth
They hoped and dreamt for a better tomorrow
Where everything will be fine again without any sorrow.

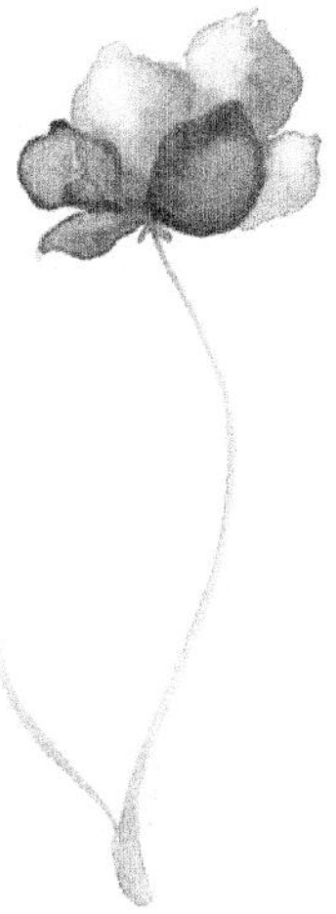

THROWBACK

A beginning of my new life.
That was the starting of a new year, a month of January.
There was a new bond-forming in between me and my beloved close friend.
We started sharing happy and sad moments.it was like I am living every moment as I always wanted to live.
A month of February, a month of love, a month of spring was about to begin and we were so happy together like we have finally found our best partners or our valentine.
We were so humble for each other that we started being humble everywhere.
We were so In love that we started showering love and peace everywhere.
We happily embrace whatever comes our way throughout the day in our daily routine and were so satisfied with the target we started and completed.
The month of March, yes the month of March, a huge pandemic all over the world .home calling, we were apart so sudden, and still, we were so happy because we took away the happy memories that we created in those happy three months of our life.
Coming back home in between the pandemic and knocking on the door felt like I m the Simran of ddlj and I was so so happy but somehow that was a mixed emotion of mine.
Finally with family, literally can't hold tears how much I wanted to be me in my home but due to pressure and responsibilities I always stood serious and confident outside, but this time I was me with so many of positive vibes that were coming out from inside and all because of my beloved partner.
Seriously if you have your loved ones you can conquer and defeat any pandemic.

Copyright Ritemvara Sharma

A NEW EXPERIENCE

After facing the magnitude of the COVID-19 pandemic
We had to fight for a long time,
Struggle hard to overcome it.
A heartfelt thanks to the almighty.
He gave us the power to struggle hard and survive.
Some fortunate returned home after a big fight in the hospital.
But it killed some seriously ill people.
Now our life becomes normal gradually.
Vaccination is done partially.
So our newly developed good habits should remain unchanged,
We have to wear a safeguard or mask before stepping out.
After getting back home, we have to put on the clothes for washing and take a bath.
We should remember that
Mask is as important as the dress we wear.
Sanitizer is a more precious liquid than water.

Copyright Soubhagyabati Giri

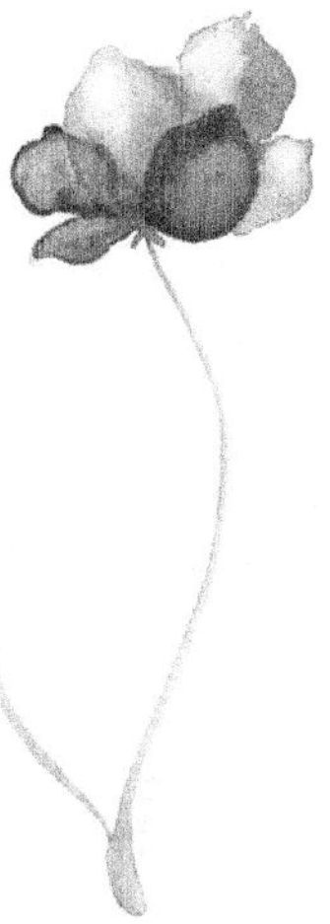

THE YEAR 2020 HAS NOT BEEN EASY.

COVID-19 created havoc in our lives.
Some lost their loved ones to this deadly disease.
It was not at all easy to remain isolated from family.
Depression griped some, who were found positive.
Life came to a standstill.
It impacted all spheres of life.
It affected every industry in the nation,
in some way or the other.
The migrant workers were the worst hit classes of people.
The daily wage earners suffered the most.
Students suffered academically.
Gradually people started adapting to new
ways of life.
Work from home became the new normal.
Despite this catastrophe, the year 2020 had enlightened us with
lessons for life.
We learned to be grateful for things,
we are blessed with.
We learned to be happy in the little things of life.
We learned to be grateful to mother earth.
These life lessons I want to persevere
for generations to come.
This year gave us more family time.
We began to understand the true essence of life.
We got the opportunity to discover our long-lost passion.
The passion for which we never got time.
Husbands turned into chefs during the lockdown.
The household chores were divided between the family members.
Children were deliberately involved in household chores,
So, as to keep them busy.
Everyone tried their hands-on cooking and baking.

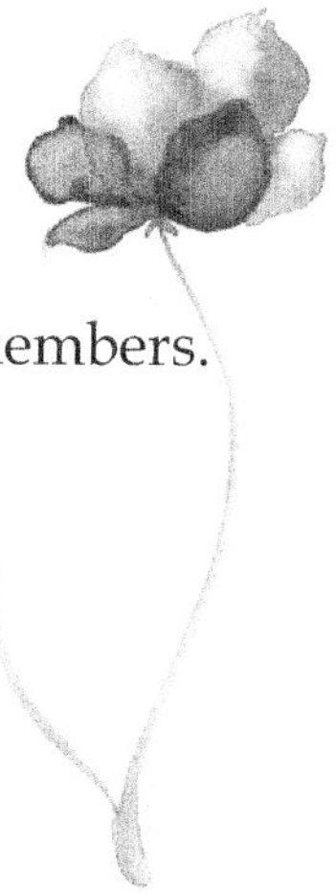

The internet went stronger overall.
We shared hugs with our loved ones through long distances.
The only alternative that provided solace to our hearts.
Unpleasant experiences of life provide us lessons for life.

Copyright Anisha Mordani

"HOPE"

Pilgrimage the loneliness
Prayer is the sorrow
And you are struggling …
Contracting, dilating
And again from the beginning.
You are dissolving, crashing

Again solid
And the " Ode to joy" *

Is hanging over the remnants of the world!

COVID-19

Emanated as a tale in Wuhan
Spread like wildfire to Rome
Initiated so many traveling bans
Compelled all to stay at home
Oh! that tourist virus from Wuhan

Most minute but a deadly killer
Baffled the intelligence of the healers
All humans eager to hear from preachers
Preachers however look up to the Maker
Where is the science crew from China?

Was that a callous search for supremacy
Or a microscopic form of ballistic missiles?
Is the maker flaunting his superiority
Or mother earth cleansing herself without the Nile?
Oh, Touring Virus! Dare to care for humanity

All Dick and Harry were so helpless
Many resorted to reading the Psalms of David
To ease the tension of Covid
Holding on to the psalms after the distress
Could intercept the coming of another mess

In the future, the covid story will be history
To be taught in schools and told in homes
The world's activities at a point came to a halt
Everyone was reminded that they had a family
Busybodies spent time with loved ones
The politicians learned about human equality

Copyright Christian Chidozie Okoro

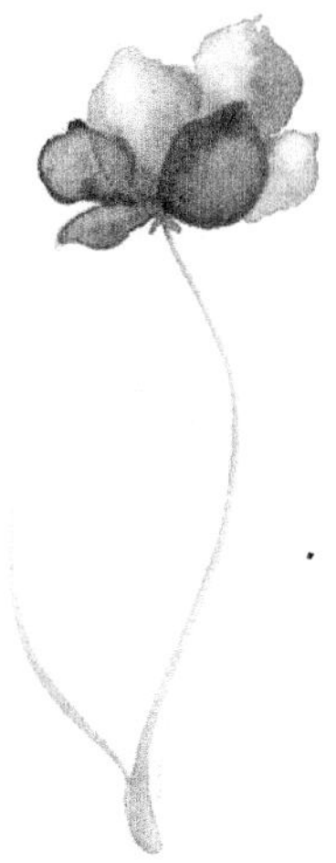

MAN

Man, go
Travel the world
see what divides us
whether eye color
whether hair color
or the language we speak

Man, come on
let's go learn
language of understanding
language of tolerance
the language of education
language of knowledge

Man, let's stop
let's extend our hands
to one another
let us be worthy of life
survival of the world
let's leave it to the children

Let's be
an example of coexistence

Man, come on -
let us build a bridge of love
among people

LORD HAVE MERCY ON MESSY 2020

2020 was a big flop
Actually, it was a big drop
That if possible we would want to crop
What with all the drama it brought along tops

Covid-19 wreaked havoc on anything
Every aspect of our lives was torn into shreds that is everything
To make matters worse it's not a thing of the past
When will it settle down like dust?

We were left at a loss for words
And we were left forlorn like the first identical Fords
We are now living following religiously, codes
The odds are just against us poor sods

The entire existence of humanity was threatened beyond endurance
The whole experience itself was not endearing
It's like we are walking in circles in a ring
Suffice it to say all this feels like a sting

In 2020 all hell broke loose
It really does pack a punch that we were left soul losers
All our scientific intelligence was put to test to put it loosely
And the pandemonium it brought along was not lovely

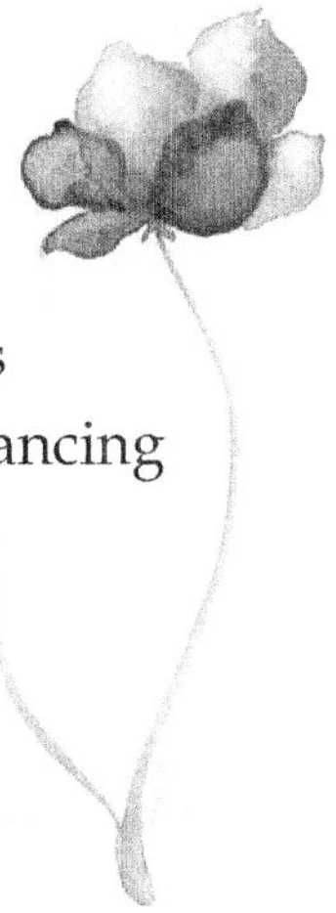

Global pandemic they coined it
We could barely stomach the thought nor could we eat
Mixed emotions were on the rise with a touch of anger fits
Could you blame us with all the lockdown and social distancing
which curtailed all footloose,
feet

Lord have mercy on messy 2020
People have died and cried a million times not twenty
The sick feeling of not knowing what is going to be of us tomorrow
is plenty
We can only take a reign grip on our anger hoping this will be
history in 2030

Copyright Abigirl Phiri

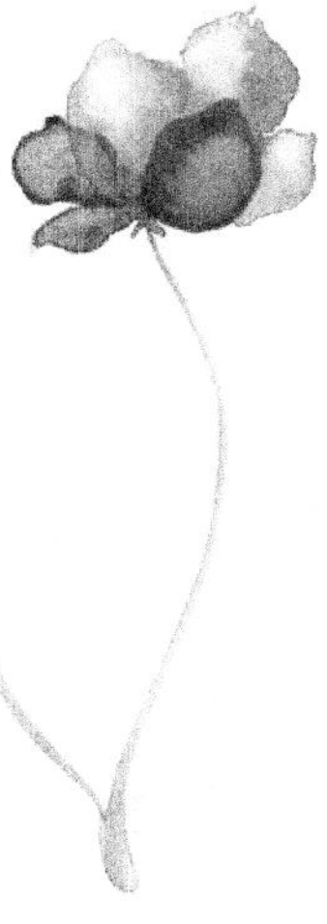

19 OUT OF 20

They were only 19 strong, but they were lethal.
They went out in gangs, but then split up
They followed people when they weren't looking
They played 'tag' with bodies
seeing who won first. Who could penetrate first
Each body successful, making
19 more and more
It was warm in the body. becoming feverish
So some left, coughed onto another body
Another successful 'tag'
Where 19 more and more
Played the same game,s like the hunter after the hunted.
Oh they hunted them
The 19
All 19's multiplying
Running free in their prey
Leaving a tree of death and fear.
Being swirled round in the air
Changing them into a
Different 19
Still playing the game of
19 more and more
In love, of their hosts, who could not destroy them
Had no mighty cure, for even just 19
Then there came hope
With a vial of injection
Plunged into the hunted
Making them around 20

Just that little bit stronger
Then the might of the 19

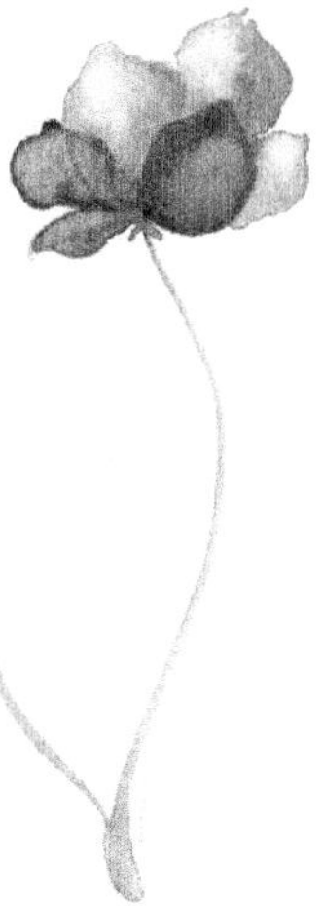

The game was now beginning, for real.
The '20s had to win
It was a tough struggle
20's playing catch-up
But slowly...Oh so slowly
They were winning
Destroying the 19 and its cousins
Once again being..... supreme.

Copyright Karen Glen

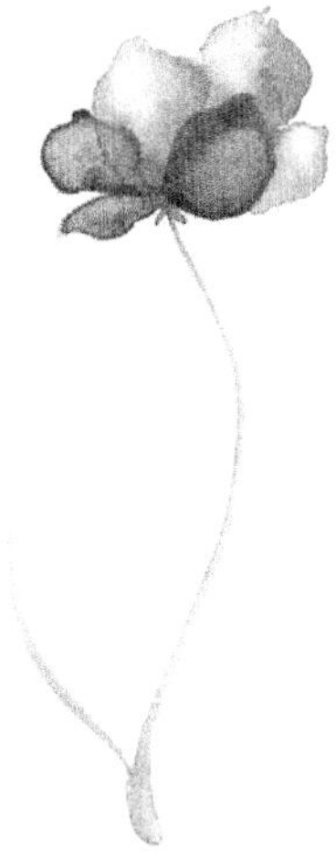

APOCALYPSE ON THE ANVIL

Virus bookmarked the history of mankind.
The virus which looks like a child's toy
Is quite insidious and ubiquitous
The roads are empty, the crowds too small
And no trace of life outside, none at all.
Wildlife ventured further,
While the streets are empty,
Wild creatures lingered and wandered.
If what they saw is unreal.
Man caged in their homes.
The virtual hug replaced the actual hug.
Lockdown gave time to introspect
To think of accomplishing unfulfilled dreams.
To widen one's horizons.
Meeting new people and forging strong bonds.
The future keeps receding.
Certainty has collapsed.

Copyright Karil Anand

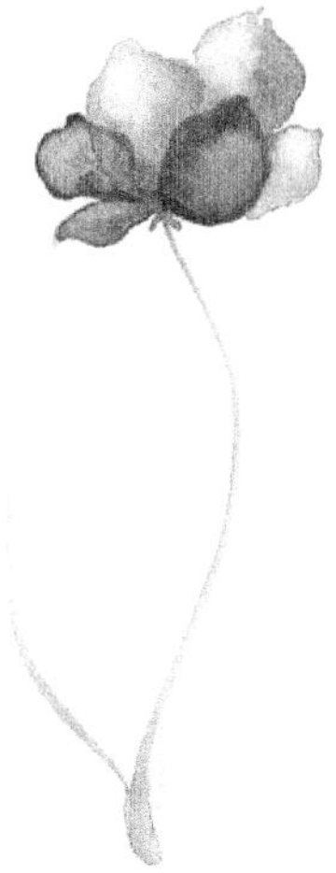

ENDING SARS

Starting like a dream
By cream de la cream
To curb crime to the brim
While guaranteeing self-esteem
The operatives started tinkering
With the object of their mentoring
Extorting the public in motoring
While killing innocents without scrutiny
The tragedy was not realized
Until the public mobilized
Shutting every public place at the sight
While protesters chant for their rights
The government may ponder
To act as protests go yonder
While protesters wonder
Whether protests won't be put asunder
Nigeria is destined to be great
No citizen deserves to fret
For asking of his right
Let alone caught by the waist
For insisting on what is right!

**SARS is Special Anti-Robbery Squad. A Police squad in NIGERIA that was disbanded after days of national protests in October 2020 due to indictment for human rights abuse and violations*

THE YEAR 2020; BLESSING OR CURSE?

Heralded by glad tidings
The year came with many things
Many prayed for goodies
Hoping God will heal their maladies
Suddenly, Covid 19 appeared
Wuhan announced that she is tired
By daily records of infirmed
Wishing for remedies to cases confirmed
Rome to Tehran, Washington, or Brasilia
Records of cases unfamiliar
With deaths of people never witnessed earlier
And recoveries of cases even uglier
Lockdowns were announced
Meetings postponed
Competitions rescheduled
Commodities crashed
While hopes were not dashed
Many are counting their losses
Or could it be blessings?
Zoom and Webinar may wish for an extension
To further their gains of competition
Many will not wish for a repeat
As losses need not retreat
Since no one wish for another defeat
Of a year full of deceit
But hopes of greater feat.

THE LOST YEAR

The year 2020 began like any other.
We gathered with parents, sisters, and brothers.
Awake until midnight to see in the new year.
Raising a toast and making resolutions sincere.
Then the rumours and stories we began to hear.
Something sinister ...definitely to fear.
A bacteria...or virus....a terrible beast?
Something was spreading far in the east.
Did it come from bats or pangolins?
Some talked of wet markets amongst other things.
A few weeks later, we were filled with dread.
A virus was moving and was quick to spread.
From country to country and continent to continent.
Nothing could stop it....was fast and rampant.
Masks, lockdowns, and cessation of hugs.
Lest things worsen the spread of this bug.
Our way of life changed, it made such an impact.
We craved human touch, the physical contact.
Schools shut down, offices too.
All work was online, shops had big queues.
Panic was rife and people were confused.
Lockdown enforced...so many rules!
Coronavirus raged all around.
Wearing its cloak and terrible crown.
People were sick, many even died.
When will this end, the people sighed.
We somehow hobbled through 2020.
No sparks on Diwali and Xmas were low-key.
But hope came along in the form of a jab.
Thanks to clever scientists busy in labs.
We pray that soon there are vaccines for all.
How desperately we want to get back to normal!

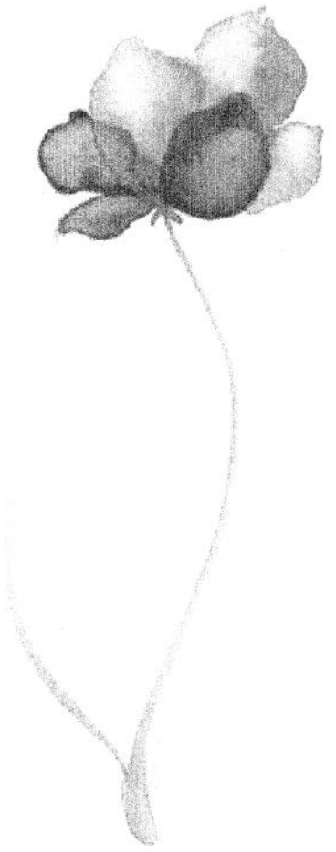

Copyright Meenakshi Dwivedi

CHAPTER II

DANCING WITH DEATH

HOLDING A KNIFE TO MY NECK

We all walk past a bridge
Looking down, water rushing
White crashes with warning noises
We think not to jump, but blindness leads the way.
How many hands have we held with trusting hearts?
How many hands have we held to date?
How many roses have we been pierced by?
How many visitors have we called our friends?
We always take the lane of shadows
Trying to turn out the heat
Taking shortcuts is all we do
No sweat but we want the gains.
Jealousy and laziness moves like winds
Blowing the road to our graves
So dusty yet we reject to see
Looking at other lands...
An argument with a devil unknown
The next day the sun remains set
As darkness shadows one's life
Lust replace love for exploration
The wrong words called for attention
Reporting another because of care
Becoming a target around the house
With naïve nerves

BIJE ENDERRASH

Ne jemi bije enderrash
e lufta per to eshte pergjithemone.
Asnje here nuk e ndalim rrugen
qe enderra te lulezoj.
Ne lindem prej enderre.
Asgjè s,e ndal rrugen tone.
Biem dhe cohemi njeheresh
dhe enderrat vazhdojne.
Vazhdojme me enderra ne duar
e bota behet me e bleruar.
Eshte ky vallzim
qe i jep botes kuptimin njerezor.
Vemi drita mbi erresire,
jemi jeta mbi vdekje,
jemi vete njerezimi
me enderrat tona mbi vete.

Copyright Ollga Farmacistja

~MY FRIEND~

No wonder they needed me
dead at my early bed
of hatred, guilt, revenge tired and torn
Do I see myself now
Woo them who's an intention
was to push; thy creation
for the effort put with an
exhalation of last breath
Alas you only wished
when I saw myself
drowned into such
to lend your hand
have you made death
one that all consider a fear
my friend and shadow
which I find most comfortable to be.

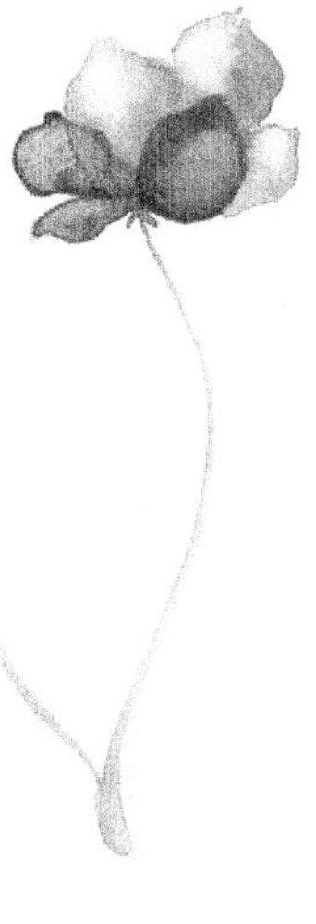

FROM BIRTH TO DEATH

Life is a definite dance
Be it a rumba, or maybe a tango
Sometimes rock and roll
Maybe the opera or just two souls
With vice-like grips afraid of letting go
They walk hand in hand these inseparable two
Challenging dances of life we weave
Almost breathless but survivors steal
A kaleidoscope of colors so bright
With every step, death takes two
While birth so serenely settles for less
A rotating earth spinning like mad
As soon as she pauses death rejoices
A rose so red bleeds instead
As soon as she is plucked
For her beauty in vain
A mom she lives with a waft of death
Fighting and scratching a daily threat
For her offsprings can imbibe the beauty abound
For earth, itself is dancing with death
As soon as the music stops
Earth will be dead
Doctors too accompanied by death
Silently waiting for errors instead
Humans dangling from their palms
A tilting error brings outcries so somber

POSLEDNJI PLES

Zemlja se pomjera
Izmiče ispod ruku
Svjetlost
Zlatnocrvenog Sunca...
Zatvorene oči ...
Čvrsto stisnuti kapci
Kunu sljepilo boje
Bolna šupljina
Ušuškane želje
Ispunila pticu
Opkolila nevidljivi dan
Tamni prolaz u
Zgužvan san
Zemlja se ranije
Pokretala nije ...
Konjokradica u škripcu
Zamišlja pobjedu...
Meka I teška sivoća
Bezbijedne smrti
Siječe nad glavom
Vrijeme velike
Usamljenosti...
Tonem u tamnicu
Sjećanja ...
Smrtonosno kolo
Kruni krivovjeru
Poslednji ples
Na takoj žici
Smrt mi
Izvadi oči
Svjetlost se
Rastoči.

A MYSTIC DANCE

A fancy touch in life
The melody of love rises
Want to grasp soulful moments
Myriads dream uplifting
Help us to weave colorful verses
Life can't promise only bright sights
If there's no dark then light can't get chance
To show its magical effects with all nooks
Life on earth is a blissful art
A gift from God
A symbolism of lovely souls
A war from pristine verse
Each moment is a challenge
Give a light or hard strike
To strong thy base over turbulence
To seek a serene place
It's the choice of life
To beat every step as golden armour
To embrace thy wisdom overall
To wear a humble crown as dignity
Don't express thy painful sigh
Make each step as a dancing bird
Whether it's alive or death
Thy mind should pick the eternal happiness

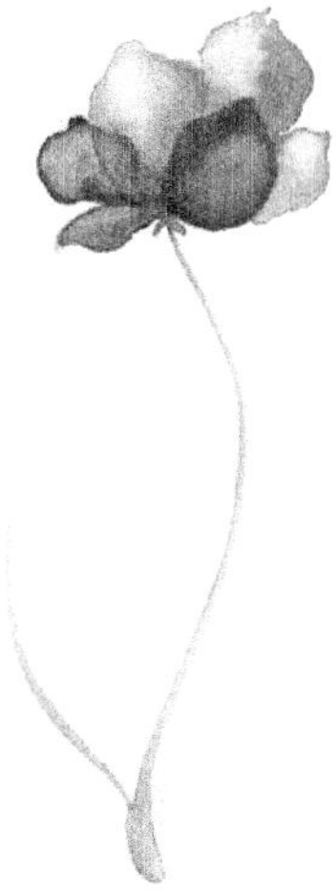

IN A SMALL GLASS

I saw myself

Dancing with my shadows

It's a dance of the dead

A drum of the death

Fury of asylum

Dancing with death

Every corner filled with skulls

Copyright Chosen Samuel

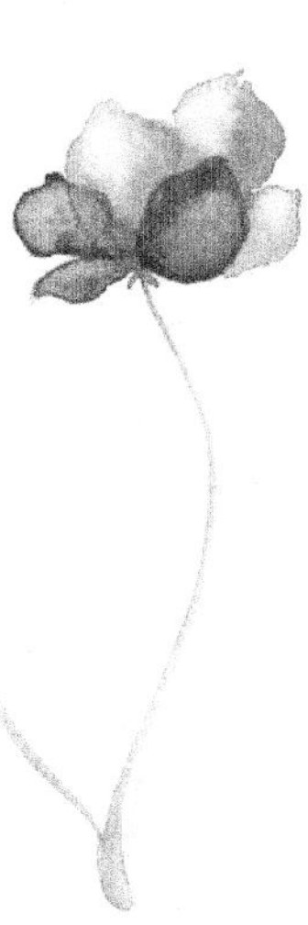

DEADLY DANCE

Amongst the green and luscious vegetation,
beyond the paddy fields and plantations.
A cobra sways and lets out a hiss...
as a mongoose approach, with a death wish.
Deadly opponents since time immemorial.
Will fight to the end - creatures territorial.
Jumping, swaying, hissing, and striking.
Eyesight is so sharp...quick in attacking.
Mother Nature wrote and laid down the rules.
The loser will end up more than a fool.
For this will be a fight till last breath.
Both will be dancing....a dance until death.

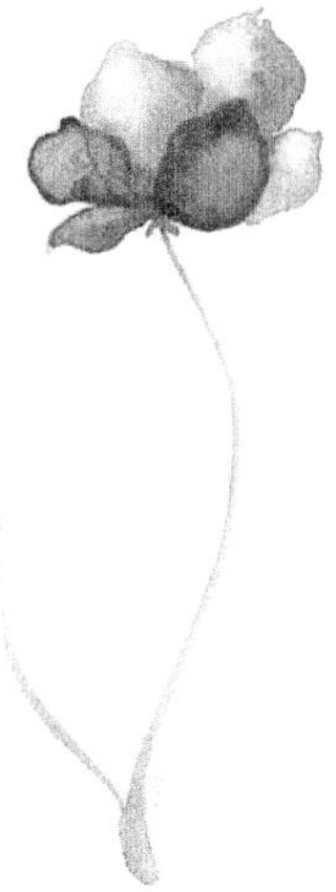

WINDY DAYS

down the valley as I came
mixed feelings ran inside my mind of memories of you
on a windy day
there was much wind outside,
moving air changing directions
circulating my body
like the river that winds up the hills
as the current of air causes me to shiver
I wound up my scarf around my neck
the wind brushes my nose outside the house
the wind passes next to a river and goes up the skies
as I watch over it as memories of you
momentum fills my mind
a moment passing during a cause of time
momentous
how I wished it could last forever
bringing happiness with you enjoyed through one's life
then leaves fall surrounded by a twine
easily keeled over by the wind
causing them to rotate employing a crank,
reciprocating motion
they twist, turn and curl blown by the wind
dried and feeble deflected and disheveled
by the unfavorable winds
denoting your passing
leaves of trees that grow in shape determined by the prevailing winds
causing them to rotate as a result of the force of wind of a current of air
moving the arms of a windmill
thoughts come down my mind of sadness an emotion related to grief
helping me to let go of memories of you
and incorporate necessary changes in life

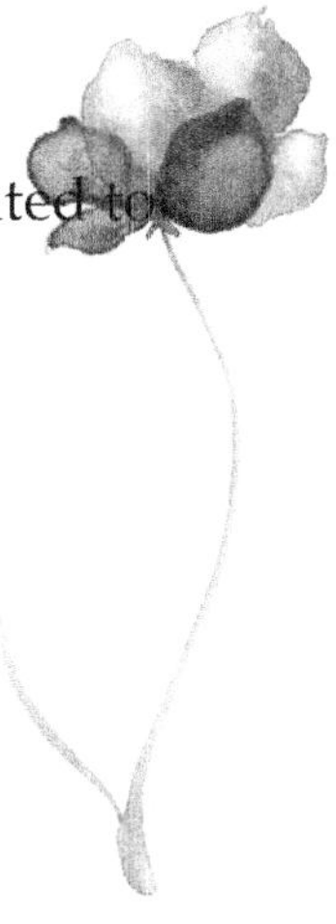

Copyright Asher Chipu

EVERY DAY IS A PARTY-CELEBRATE!

Stay very busy, accomplish a lot
Set out the china, polish the silver
Order the flowers, clean the house
Invite family and friends
Start dancing with life
Join all the others
Enjoy every day
The day will come when it will be your last
You'll take off your shoes
Others will choose your dress
They'll start the party
Put crying to rest
They'll join in a line for the final goodbye
Your dance with life has come to an end
Now is the time to start dancing with death

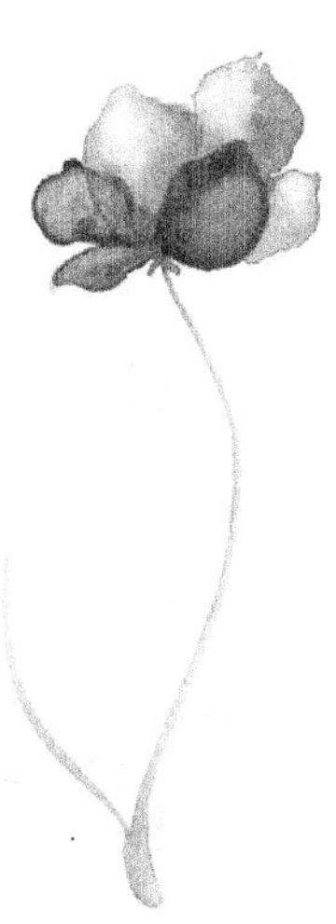

DEVIL DANCE

I play with my toys gently
I don't let them fall out of my hands
I am a chaste child eager for life
Although I'm still undeveloped for him
I've always stood out from everyone actually
Although the world didn't understand me at all
Now that I have everything, people are running away from me
I guess that's the way it is with some things
Unfortunately, I have to do everything myself
Because I have no friends of my own; I think I have
But they are long dead to me
Jealousy kills people so powerfully
That no record can be recorded
The lurkers of false promises tell me one thing
And they are doing something completely different
In the rhythm of the devil's dance
The circle is circulating, and I'm tired
Tired of life, of vain hopes
It's time to die with my hands finally folded
Because we were all someone's halflings
I just can't say that in public
I fear for the existence of this world
How long ago he became listless!

I SAT HERE, ONCE

Skies on my sleeves, dark stage to skip
I'm the air, the breath without a body
Walking on roads I once walked
No one wants to hear my cry for help
They are all mute, busy in their suite's
Hello, there kindly stop for a while
Jane, I used to be your neighbor
Goodness gracious, she is avoiding
Like the others, I let her be.
This was my home, the cracked wall
The swing and the white Garden Roses
I sat here once, I shared a cup of tea
It was warmer than now
It was harkening.
Hello, can remember me?
Sara Thomson Lynn, a Poet of sword's
Words that would Pierce and shred souls
But I'm dark as those words I never spoke
Can you listen, to my soul's weeping?

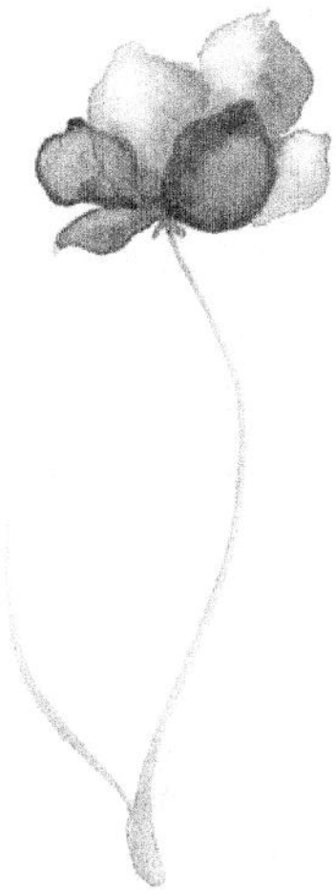

AWAKENED

Forever is a passing glory

Snapshot of harmony

In case you're dead

You're alive instead

In unceasing life spent

There is just a single demise

What is all the more sure prize

You're breathing each piece

The majority of all

Making it to recall

You awaken the God

Within you, restored

Without end

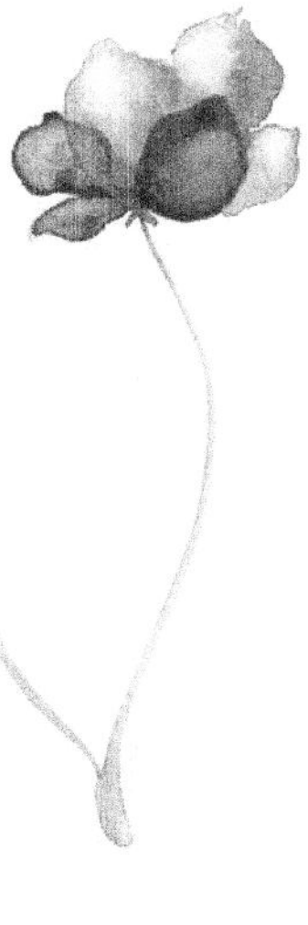

Dancing With Death

Stop seeing someone's wife
She's a threat to your life,
You'll regret when caught by her husband,
You may go to jail or get beheaded,
She won't stop until you lose your soul,
Do you want me to say more?
Adultery is not only evil but also a crime,
When caught it will bring both of you shame,
Don't break some one's family,
You should quit early,
Stolen honey is very sweet,
But what if they chop your feet?
Please stop messing with someones' marriage,
They'll kill you and dump you in sewage,
One day you'll hide on the rooftop,
When you are caught no one will help,
You might even cheat with her in the bush,
But karma will deal you with no rush,
Her man is hunting you with a gun,
Soon it will be the end of fun,
Stop this dancing with the death,
There's a danger lurking beneath,
Before I go there's something else dude,
They might march you in the streets nude,
They'll chop your member while he's still stiff,
Better think twice before you take her clothes off.

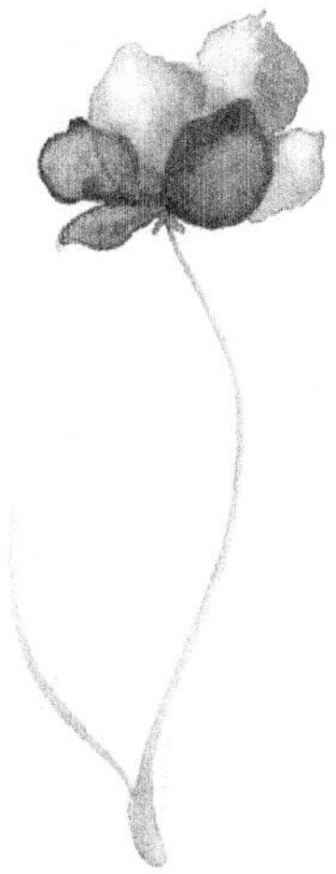

~A FRIEND~

Can't believe I thought you were as bad

All my fears trembled away soon as you touched my hand

I heard rhythms of life in your snares

How do I help to hear these sour lyrics about death?

When did I know that deep down he is a very good friend?

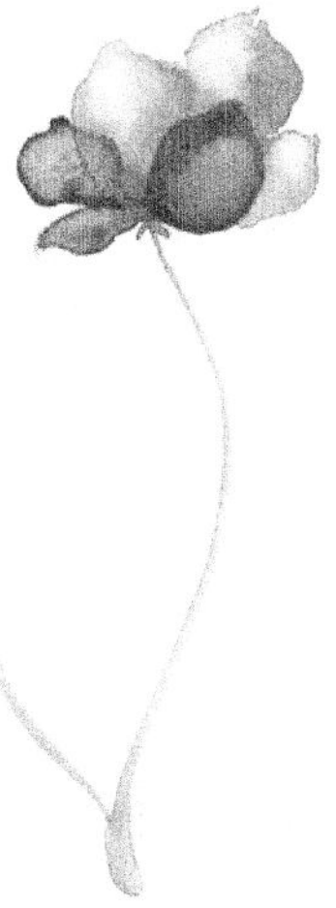

DANCING WITH DEATH

The countdown begins
To my demise
I am not willing
To be sacrificed
Offer bribes
As minutes chime
Beg the Grim Reaper
For extra time
Both intent
On opposing aims
I refuse to accede
To Fate's claim
We step into
A macabre dance
Adrenaline convinced
I have a chance
To win; push, shove
Step on toes
Who will be first
To let go
And, I wake,
To my scream
Dalliance with death
But, a dream

Copyright Margaret Karim

DANCE WITH ME DANCE WITH ME

Dance with me Dance with me
Dance to my tone said the death
Embrace me said the death
Follow me to dance, the dance of my sorrow
Bow to me, Bow to me
Is time to take you home
To my darkest world
It's time to say goodbye
To your peoples
Home here is empty with you
Because of the sound and Melody of your music
I dance to your tone
Now no way to run back
Now am sock in your illusion

Copyright Samuel Darasimi

IN LIFE, YOU HAVE CHOSEN YOUR PATH

In life, you have chosen your path,
you cried, laughed, fell and rose, from your birth.
Time will come soon when death will knock at your door,
don't be afraid, don't hesitate, just open the door and embrace it to the core.
As you celebrate life, dancing till your last breath,
now leave all the inhibitions behind and dance with death.
Like a free bird, fly, let the death encircle you with glee,
now no one will criticize you, all your fears will flee.
Push behind all that was stopping you to perform your best,
common, and dance with a cheerful smile as life was a test but death is a fest.
Everything in life is beautiful, stay pleased and blessed,
death is divine, carries to a whole new world, your soul will meet God.
For a purpose, you have been bestowed with life by the Almighty,
before you hug death, dance with your true soulmate, fulfill all your duty.

HOLDING MY BREATH

Holding my breath

Getting close to the edge

I'm dancing with Death before Life turns me to veg.

Tired of the yawns and the safety net

Gonna dance insanely...

Death hasn't won yet!

Copyright Francisca Budd

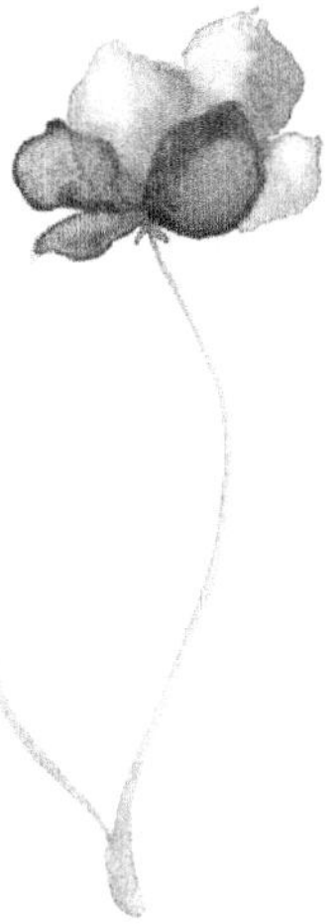

TIME OF LIFE AND DEATH

It's God's gift and a blessing
Every day all must do something
Dealing with it there's no avoiding
Shall we go on believing
Where may one beheading
In this world, many are starving
When is the time should be starting
To know that one must be striving
Continuing a daily chance of surviving
The mighty hands are lifting and creating
Bringing a life so blissful and heartening
Don't take the challenges complaining
Ready to deal with fears and suffering
Bear that in mind and be willing
To accept the risk we are receiving
For our fates depend on how we are allowing
Not taking positivity and be content with nothing
Or be independent and pursue everything
And be satisfied with what we are having
We must strive hard for learning
Use our mind for visual thinking
Start a productive day by building
Your utmost hopes and dreaming
Out there in the sunny field walking
Moving further with the usual jogging
Have a breathy morning by running
After all the works do gardening
While sipping a cup of tea enjoy sitting
Dining with family be comforting
At the end of the day start examining

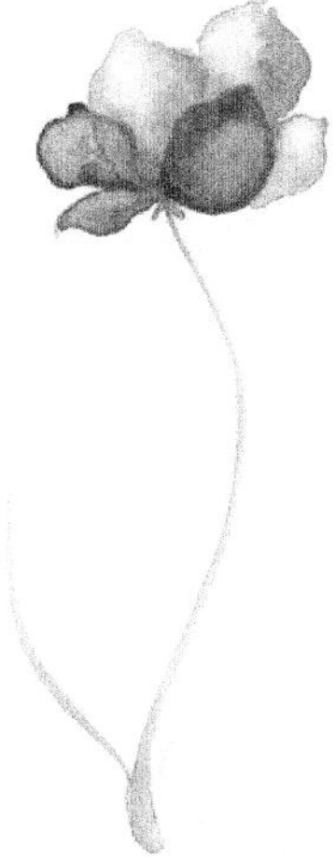

What brings great moments so fulfilling
All the beauty and colors of the surrounding
Give the precious moments recollecting
The happiest experiences worth treasuring
Those significant events with mixed emotions kept playing
Why should be afraid of life's coloring
Summing it up all make the year more gratifying
Life must have its forceful meaning
DANCING WITH DEATH is all worthy and reassuring
Shallow and Hollow

DANCING FLAMES AND MOTHS

As the night envelopes the sky
Fragile moths come dancing by.
Seeing the candle flames dance
Ignited the moths' desire to prance.

Assuming the flame to be the sun
They flutter high and low with fun.
Lured by flickering candle flames
Dances around, wild crazy games.

Flames radiantly enjoy the dance
Of the innocent moths' romance.
Performing hair-raising tricks
Their volatile life's clock ticks.

Unaware of their depleting breath
They're merrily dancing with death.
As their endless dances continue
Exhausted their force seems to adieu.

Alas! Only If they knew it was the fire
They wouldn't have the dancing desire.
But it's too late to stop their dance
Death has opened its gate to embrace.

There is no escaping the death
Like it happened with Macbeth.
Their resinous wings crackle
In contact with fire, can't tackle.

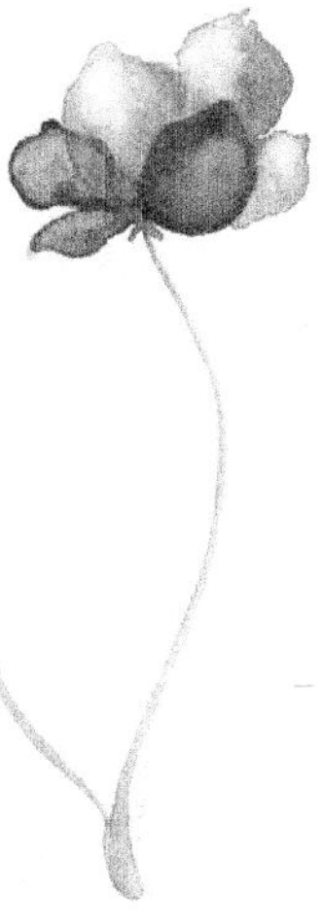

Must welcome their destiny and fate
For life must end, opened is death's gate.
The poor souls have now perished
And the fiery flames have cherished.

Copyright Tshering Wangchuk

DANCING WITH DEATH

In the morning as I take my bath
With dainty steps, try not to bump or slip
The bathroom tiles may be the cause of my demise
Gives me the feeling, with Death I'm dancing the salsa.

Then as I am having a hurried breakfast
Smooth, gentle hand strokes, a bite, a chew, a swallow
Try not to choke, a bone might get stuck into my throat
Like I'm dancing with Death a waltz so slow.

Proceed to work with swinging fluid steps
Stop, look, listen, then did a sustained run
Cross a busy street with lithe and nimble steps
In a very dirty street dance with Death.

Here comes my full packed bus, before it stops grasped
The door, with a swift move, got aboard sans seat
The driver skidded amidst the jungle of traffic
In a "trip to heaven", a jive we danced with Death.

At work, with rowdy delinquent teenagers
Who argue and sometimes fight like bears
Give me a feeling of impending heart attack or stroke
My breath tells me it's Death I dance the rhumba with.

Going home, I have to do it all again
A whole encore of my day's performance
Describing everything as a single dance
It seemed it's the cha-cha we have done.

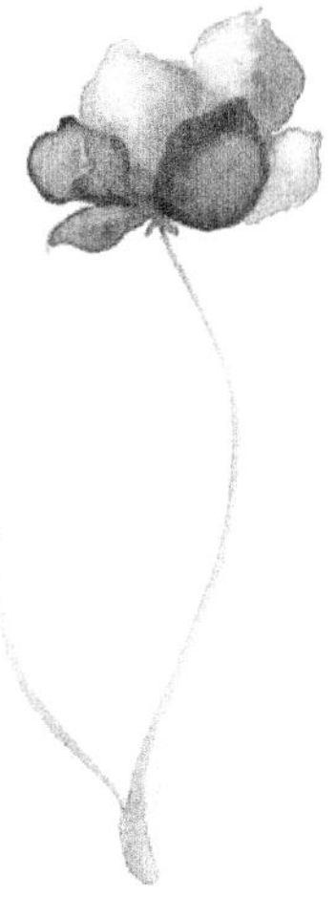

In bed at night, Death for dance still presses
But to the Lord, I sing of gratitude and praises
Asks Him to wake me up rested from sleep
Coz tomorrow I'll be dancing again with Death.

Copyright Myrna E. Tejada

HOW CAN I DANCE WITH DEATH?

Can I use my own feet?

Maybe I can't follow numerous steps,

Maybe I'll ask more queries of if's.

It's a bizarre dance for all,

That myself would do this time for a trial,

I'm mortal but death is immortal,

I'm nervous, I can't dance to the tune of a funeral.

I'm hesitant to dance with death,

I can't hold my breath,

I may suffer a cardiac arrest,

To the tune of unending melodic steps in regret.

DANCING WITH A MISNOMER

Dance of life or death does emanate from the Absolute ;
To rejoice in it, one does need to be resolute.
Life and death does one get as an effect
The cause is one's played a type of act

One's soul does shoulder one's body intact.
The power that does destroy life, painful or sweet
One has to live and dance with the thought of it.
As a pain source, death has its own music

One has to live and dance with it being mundane.
One's body's nature is pure misery
Its outer state is old for good and temporary.
Sorrow does never change its feather

Does envelop one's mind -sky with rough weather.
Nevertheless, death is one's guest
Terming it as a mirage one does quench one's thirst best.
Desire whatever that one does possess

Does make one as an insect, life after life, jump into
death or rebirth's furnace.
As a joy source, death also has its own form musical
One has to live and dance with it being celestial.

Past is lost, presently does never womb a dream
This breath and heartbeat never desire to act as a stream.
This is the last and the best fraction of the perennial time
Returning homeward with a most melodious rhyme.

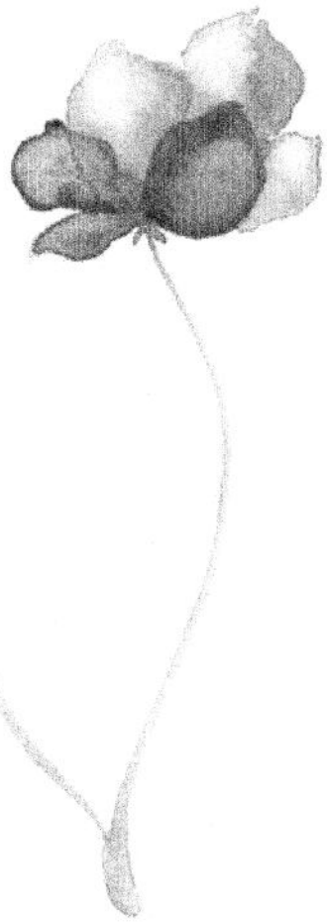

One's every moment consciousness of the All-Pervading
Helps one's delusion of death steadily healing.
Grow the feelings of changelessness and deathlessness ;
For dancing with the waves of death is extended Inevitable's
immortal arms.

Clinging to the Omnipotent, thirsting to realize freedom and peace
Sans fear, one learns: death is a gratuity and a big farce.
One's body wave does touch and vanishes the soul's essence shore
One does amuse by dancing with death: a misnomer.

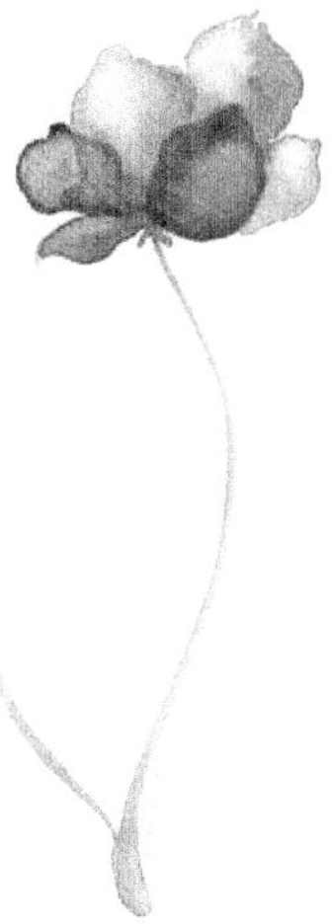

"A DATE WITH DEATH"

I love the moon, the rainbow and
Everything that's unattainable
I know things lose their glow
The moment they are available
Scintillating 'N vivacious
As Diana, in the jungle, I dance
Like Flora, in the garden, with
Butterflies I prance
On restive waves of oceans
Like Salacia I waltz - I smarm
Romantically gliding, on the floor,
On my Neptune's arm
Jive as tempestuous Zephyrus
For dancing is my passion
Music and melody fill me
With ecstatic joy and elation
But there is one companion
With whom I have a date,
Pending for infinite time,
Death is my eventual mate
I am in love with death, and
Love is a dangerous game,
Whirlpool and fire excite me
I adore vortex and flame
I'd gladly drink a cup of heady,
Intoxicating Hemlock,
For a promise that at last
Heaven's gates would be unlocked
From the gallery, the world can view
My tango with my beloved death

A grand finale of life,
When I take my last breath

Copyright Sudha Dixit

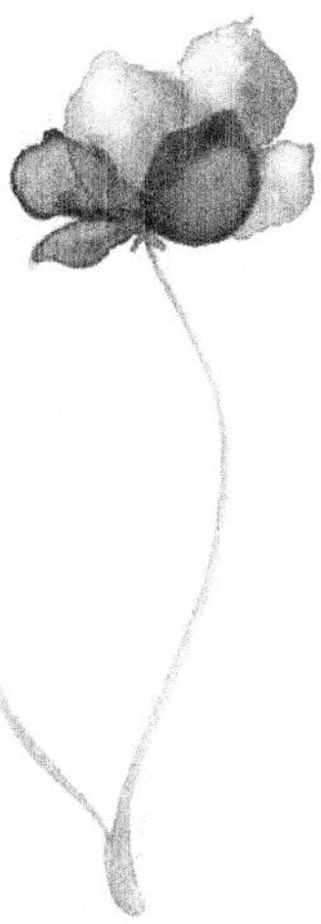

A PACT EN AVANCE

Being in love with someone,
Who couldn't, ever, be mine,
Is like drinking poison that's
Laced with sweetened wine
It's a pleasure, one may derive,
While dealing with bush fire,
The thrill of living on a cliff edge
Braving the oceanic ire
My intense love is like
Walking barefoot on cinders,
Wallowing in a painful sting
Of broken dream's splinters
From the moment I've fallen in love
It's been eternal song and dance
With my deadly, magical partner
Life is, forever, in a trance
It seems that I have a deal with death,
And when I throw a backward glance,
Suffering an unrequited love I have
A lifelong undying prance

Copyright Sudha Dixit

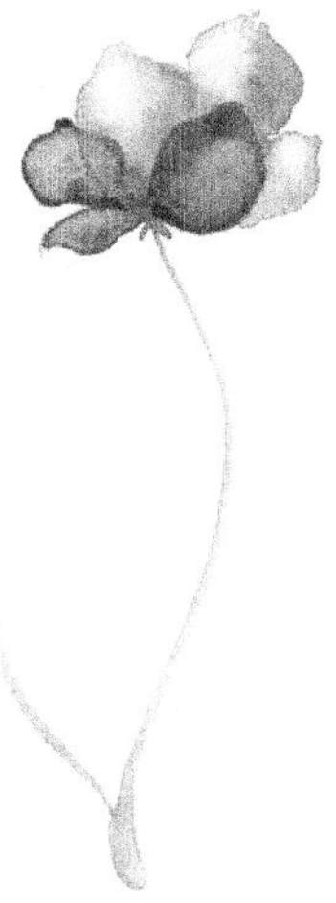

WHAT IS DEATH?

Death is the next great adventure,
Going into the unknown future,
Like a tunnel ending with a light,
Like going into an extended night,
And beholding beautiful dawn,
Finding a glorious, eternal morn,
Where the dance with death will be over,
And the soul will be blessed forever.
Perhaps this mortal body will mingle with nature,
Perhaps this soul will have an immortal future,
Perhaps we will wake up from the long sleep,
And discover ecstasy and will never weep,
Never know grief or pain or sorrow,
When we behold the beautiful final tomorrow.
Perhaps death is going from one room to another,
From this room of life to that blessed forever,
Perhaps death is erasing the darkness,
And moving towards brightness,
Perhaps it is a cleansing of the soul,
Perhaps it is shedding ignorance,
And becoming whole,
Perhaps it is going into a trance,
Which will forever last,
Perhaps it is the complete forgetting of the past.
Whatever death is, we must face it with courage,
And climb into the immortal carriage,
With a smile on our faces,
Prayer in our hearts, and hoping for divine grace.
If our faith is strong,
We can meet death with a triumphant song.

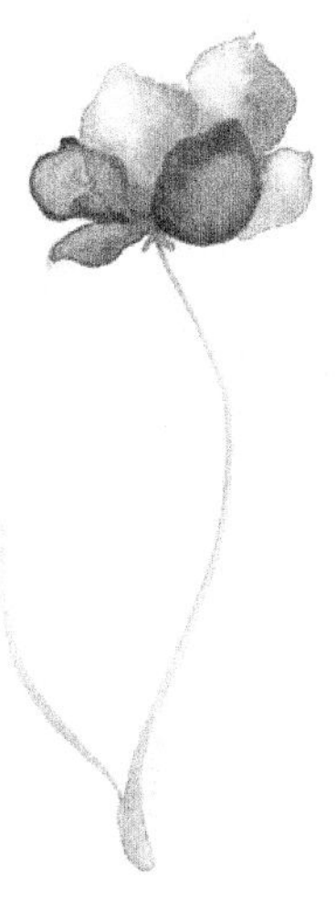

REMNANTS OF THOUGHTS

(between life and death)
Life is a cycle
A naught essence of a mysterious perception
Like a water vapor tried to ascend through the sky
To mix into the clouds, waiting for your presence.
To pour again down
to Earth
A cycle again and again
As if a role of life, a play
And the world is the stage
To resumed the acts.
According to life's direction
Mounted on our prowess
To acts in the best
To savor life nutrients
Through life fullness
Unaware of its ending
As life knew the times' best.
As death is our destiny
The destiny of mans best
Life is inevitable
As if running a million times race
Questioning ourselves
If we participated in the race
As the race of life so tough and rigid
The throne of our desires
In order on winning streak
Death is a life's dock
A port
The trauma of death occurred frequently in the mind

As our thought is more evident than time itself
Gone to the conclusion
As if a mysterious event of life in reality
As we poured our strength to hold our sanity
If our faith plays an important role in our life
Why bother doubt?
As life is a preparation for a destiny... foretold.
And we all shall perishable
As life a destiny.
As life go on winning
A deathbed shall be our throne?
To life's fullness at stake
As dancing with death.

THERE IS LIFE AFTER DEATH

Earthly life has a right time
Count we on with Rage
Leave a known place, lose family and friends
It hurt before deeply upon us
A nice talk afore sleeping
We always have to relax on dreams after
Dreams, wishes, we cuddle up with care
Along lifetime upon Earth
I can comfort you dear Ones
Afterlife slippery, Heaven a gifts
Paradise, hindrance from bodily life
Ask I to you, do not think so
Heaven, a place where after dancing with death
life journey better into the spiritual shelter
beloved ones await till the right time to join in
We, there, Angels from above-sending Love

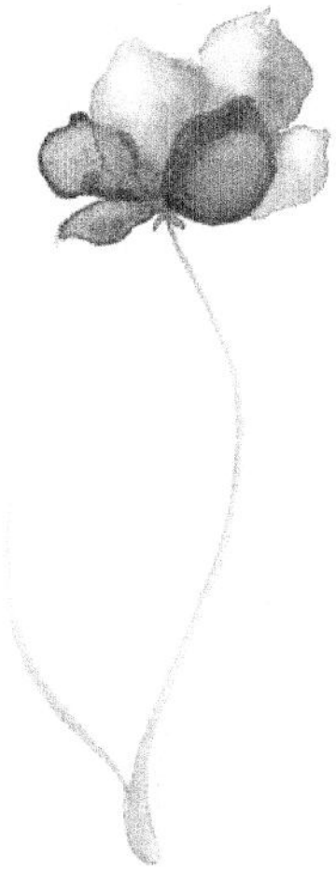

INK, SOMETIMES DRY

In a Ballad of love
My heart enamored
With a young lass
Sweet and tender
Mellifluous voice
Day after days
She, Muse become
to ink on paper flow
Verses of Poetry
No need for rhymes
Rhythm does not either
I am a simple writer
Love's live inspiration
Whimsical feelings
On paper depiction
Love a Stories
Once in a while
White paper clean
Dancing with death
love's fault of Love
Sadness Blind thoughts
After all, tears shed
And Pains into scars
Tattoo Skin
Recovery of Poet
Parchment grief coo

Copyright Maria Elvira Fernandes Correia

THREADS OF LIFE DELICATE, HELD VERY LIGHTLY

Threads of life delicate held very lightly,
dancing to the tunes of destiny.
Morning brush of glory, in the Sunshine you bask
rising to the mundane of day to day life's task.
Keep moving is the only way of survival
staying constant is no way of living or revival.
Life mesmerizing, it's a blessing.
Living in a moment is the divine feeling.
It's a stage, we're giving our performance,
till last breath, you've to perform, no offense!
Everyday living on edge, daily new life.
New Sun rising, cascading emotions before descending.
When at high, do not get carried away,
lows are round the corner, can make you sway.
Every breathtaking you closer to your death.
If you've lived from dawn to dusk,
don't think yourself to be mighty.
It's a day granted by the Grace of Almighty!
You are nothing but dancing to the tunes of life.
Listen to your inner-conscience, positive vibe.
To reach your destined destination.
death, you go through a cycle of emotions.
Brush with death, before finally your last breath,
Ongoing tug of war between life and death.
Wild, fierce is the dancing of death,
you can't escape with any wealth.
Elated happiness, bereavement lets out sighs!
Do goodwill, before you close your eyes.
Everything you earned is to be left behind
to bade final goodbye and unwind.

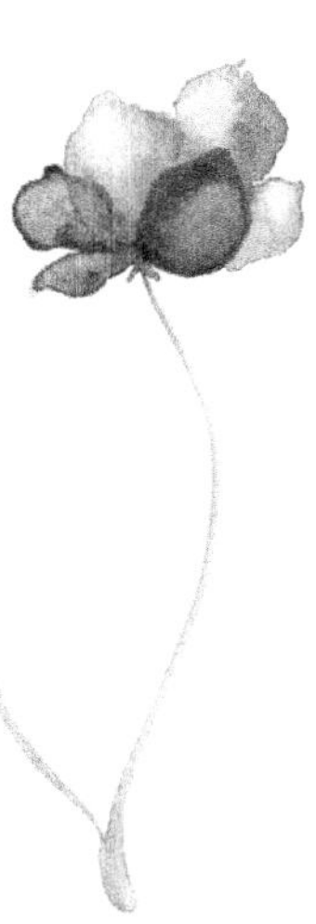

MY AGE IS JUST A NUMBER

Which goes on increasing every year;
Though I have worn a wizened look,
Yet the child inside my young heart
Is still frolicking with warmth and love,
Goading me always to come out of fear,
Of death or crossing the bar into the Realms of uncharted territory, where everybody
Has to go sometimes beyond the life's unseen periphery;
Maybe my body has become weak
And emaciated, with my vision, dimmed as compared
To past, but from my balcony, I can
See the bright colours of lovely butterflies,
And the riot of colours of winter flowers
Entice me still giving succour to my eyes;
I feel exhilarated when the gentle breeze
Touches my whole body with a soft brush,
I wish to make my body swing by
Taking it out of the state of freeze;
Maybe my senses have dulled, and
My memory is now not so sharp,
Yet I can visualize my blissful moments,
Safely secured in my mind's vault;
Life is full of magnetic charms which
I want to feel and enjoy gracefully,
I will let the death dance
To my tunes, as dancing with death is my
Favorite pastime which I long to perform with
Calm and composure, in a mirthful stance.

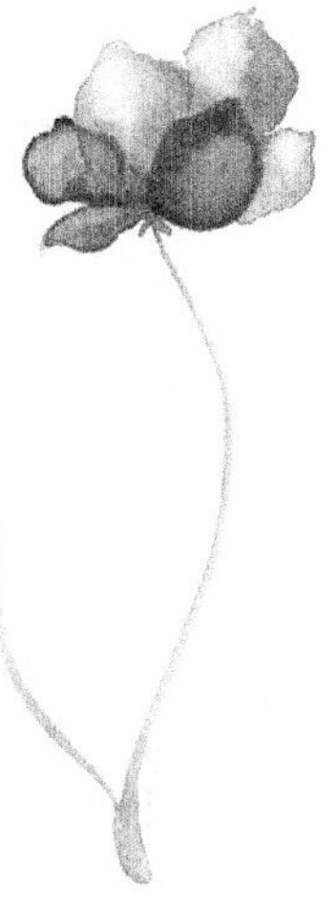

THE BALLET

Pin drop silence
Shadows and spotlights pirouette
The music crescendoes
Emotions peak
Camille Saint-Saens' cello composition rises and falls
The bewitching ballerina
Her spectacular solo
The heartstopping last moments
Of a swan's life
'Dying Swan'
An incredible act
Performed by Anna Pavlova
All of 4000 times.
Breathtaking each time
As she sways and shakes
As the powerful Le Cygne plays
Emoting the agony
Capturing its sheer beauty
Transformed into a veritable white swan
Flailing her arms
In her last dance
to the moonlight euphony.
Portraying in poses
Toe dancing the passion for life
Penetrating the soul by expression.
New Russian Ballet
A creation of Michel Fokine for her
Inspired by Lord Tennyson's 'The Dying Swan.
In shimmering white
Pavlova dazzles in her debut in 1905
Enthralling the gala at St Petersburg

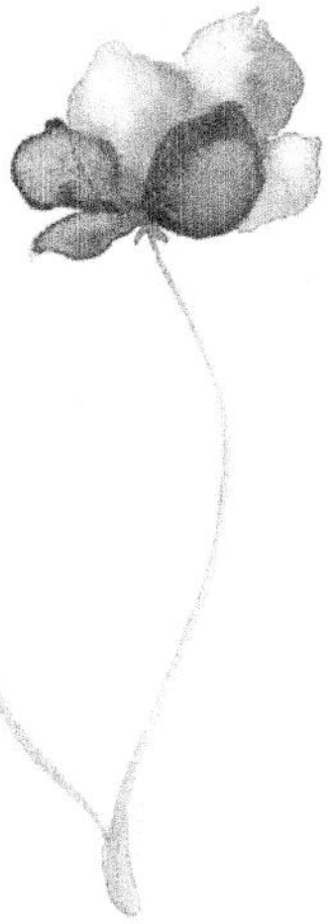

And ever since…to her last!
Gliding as if to fly
She circles the stage
Quivering and sinking
A miraculous interpretation of mortality was staged.
Spellbound was the world
By a Pavlova possessed.

Copyright Nandita De

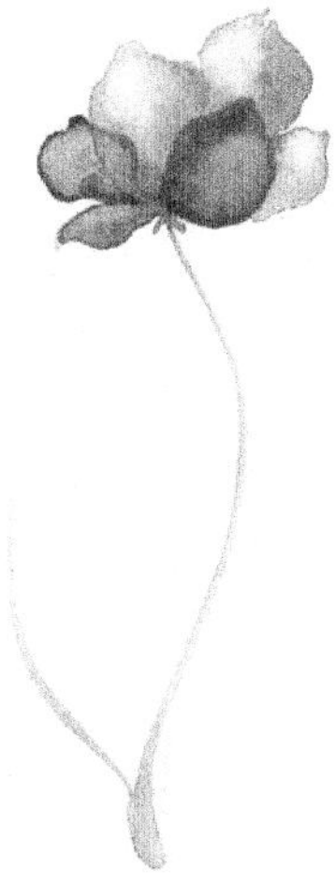

BRAVES, WHO DANCE WITH DEATH

Far away from family and friends
Far away from society and states
They stay in camps in cold regions
In hot deserts, in high mountains.

In hot summer, in monsoon rain
In cold winter, in romantic season
Staying alert for the safety of Motherland
They face challenges all year round.

Life for them not to live years
They live for the welfare of others
Guarding country at the borders
They bring safety to all others

Sharp daggers hang with silk threads
May fall over their heads.
They are brave, they dance with death
They are soldiers, the pride of this earth.

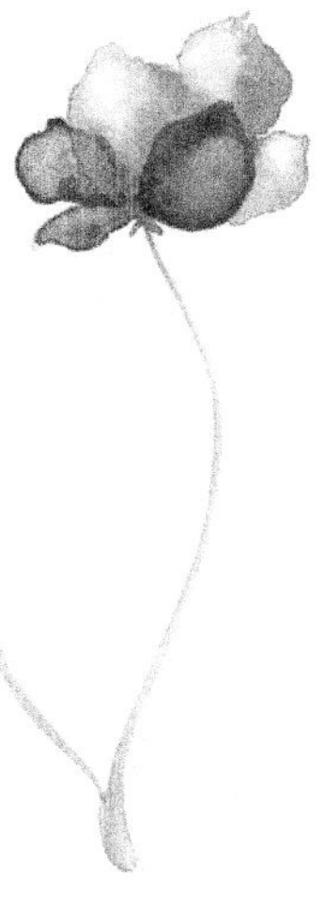

MY FINAL DANCE

All my life I've been dancing
To all types of music
The recitals of autumn
To concerts of spring
Sweet summer sonata
Winter's stormy orchestra
All of Nature's cantata.

All my life I've been dancing
In all types of movements
Whatever life offers
With glee, I rock to it
Under a gentle rain, a sun torrid and hot
Even in a huge cyclone's
Turbulent eye.

My steps are undefined
Uncoordinated
In rough motions
And so lacking in grace
My bones are stiff
I have two left feet
That whenever the world
Would step on my toes
Sometimes I retaliate
But most times wither it.

In my life, I never did care
About the way, I dance
So long as intentionally
I don't hurt anyone

But lately, I feel
I have to prepare
For my final dance
With Death and no other.

I have to learn to be smooth
Cultivate lithe, fluid moves
Not to get hurt, step on his toes
He will retaliate, of that, I'm sure of
Before the music ends
He'll inflict me with blows
Till in the dark of night
At last, I'm enveloped.

Copyright Myrna E. Tejada

THE DANCING QUEEN

Her body moves to the seductive sound of the music
Eyes fixed upon her as she gracefully moved
Ohh's and wow's you heard them exclaimed
She was the star the queen of the dance floor.

She's a young alluring adorable lady
But no one sees the pain hidden inside
Her time is getting short, her doctor said
So young with so much hope and dreams in her heart

But, life is short too short for her to live
Unbelievably true,
Her candle is flickering slow
Oh yes, now she's dancing, dancing with death

"The clock is ticking fast she says,
"And how I wished I could turn the hands of it".
But no one hears her, no one did
Soon she'll be dancing on her way to heaven

Her dancing feet will tease the clouds that drift
The winged things will journey with her
Sadly they will stop in the middle of their flight
They flutter their wings and bade adieu
As her soul is caught in the clouds
And took it to the heavens above.

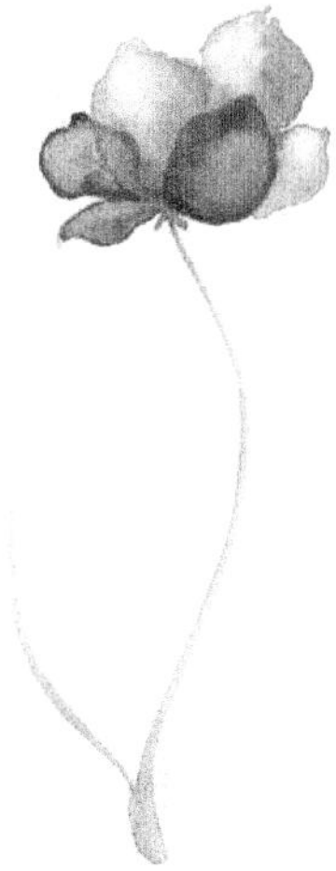

TRIBUTE TO BRAVE YOUNG MAN

Smart, cultured, adventurer, a doctor
Doctor with dreams, plans, good actor
Medal holder in sports, skiing, diving as an instructor
Serious professional, skilled surgeon, operator.

Went skiing, mountaineering, expeditions
Playing with death, with courage, determination
Saving his team from dangerous situations
Had knowledge, presence of mind, sense of intuition.

True adventurer, fighting with danger
Apple of eyes of his doctor mother and father
Could walk on log bridge on rivers
To save lives, in flooded villages of villagers.

Never scared, fought dangers with heart in hand
Popular with patients coming from different lands
All advised, don't risk life, doing unattainable things
The only child of your parents, in you their life clings.

He smiled, going out of his way, to help people in need
Maybe death was also scared of his good deeds
In camp, a snake entered our tent, bit a child
Alertly caught the snake, treated the child with a smile.

On the way back, he let the free snake in wild
Facing deadly situation, dancing with death for miles
Selected to join, the Himalayan expedition team
Expert climber, with skills of mountaineering, he gleamed.

Helped one and all in a team with his medical skills
Harsh weather changes, the team caught
in blizzard, stormy hills
Avalanche slipping at a fast pace
The team should move to a safe place.

One team member, caught in the avalanches space
Risked his life, brought him to safety
With a sudden jerk, rope freed, he fell in glaciers cavity
The expedition stopped, rescue team searched in, around the glacier face.

Till now body not found, he rests in his snowy grave
A tribute, I pay him, to save others, he danced with death
A talented, young brave man, "dancing with death" till his last breath
For saving, protecting, others without gaining any name and fame.

Copyright Vinod Singh

THE POPPY IS ALSO A FLOWER

A cherub in a flowing silken tulle
Softly arched back, striking an elegant pose
Floating effortlessly in a flourish
A sylph of beauty and sensuality.

Red roses, pink carnations, and white poppies
Bounteous sprays, expressions of adulation
They speak of love, gratitude, and purity
Also of lust, caprice…and death.

You danced among these flowers
Sweet nectar nurturing your passion
Sashaying gracefully, drowning in euphoria
Living it up, your world is boundless.

Gruelling routines of pirouettes and plies'
Excruciating pain on knees and calloused toes
Soon your beautiful body begins to disintegrate
Still, you danced, blossoms carry you through.

These colorful blooms soon became your refuge
Easing the aches of body and emotion
Accolades continue to mesmerize…and haunt
You've now reached the brink of destruction.

A deafening scream so visceral
Body stiffened, you struggled for a gasp
For a moment you froze, convulsed
Thence fell into a heap of rage.

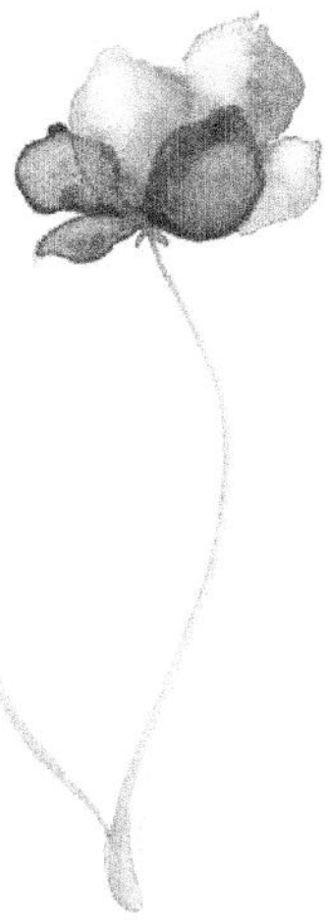

The roses now wilted, the carnations browned
Nectaries desiccated, crumbled to shreds
Once fragrant blooms, now suffocating dust
The wind blows, eerie silence follows.

The dust settles, you hear drumbeats
Glistening white petals arising, exuberantly
Your eyes blinded anew but by its deathly gaze
One more dance, you beg the white blossoms.

The passion was potent if only for a moment
The white radiance soon slowly shed its cloak
Of a glob of amber, dancing on your synapses
The poppy is also a flower…and of death.

TO ETERNITY

In quick steps
ecstasy
of a wedding dance
Let's take me,
somewhere far away
In the heights
of the sky.
Intoxicated by madness
take me in a gentle embrace
Playing a Love dance,
tired to the last
breath.
both we will fall into trance.
Surrounded by the scent
of colorful flowers
in ecstasy of
yours
goodness,
FIlled with the happiness
of our lives
Let's playing,
endlessly on this beauty
of the day.
Let them not stop,
chords of music
let's wait for the night
together
embraced
with our Wedding dance
to death.

Do vecnosti
У брзим корацима

екстазе
свадбеног плеса
Одведиме
негде, далеко
У висинама
неба
Опијени лудилом
прими ме у нежни загрљај
Уморно играјући љубавни плес
све до последњег
уздаха
падајући у транс.
Окружена мирисом
шареног цвећа
у заносу од
твоје доброта,
испуњен срећом
наших живота
Играјмо бескрајно у овој
лепоти дана.
Нека не престају,
акорди музике
сачекајмо ноћ
заједно
загрљени
са нашим Свадбеним
плесом
до смрти!!
Sabaheta

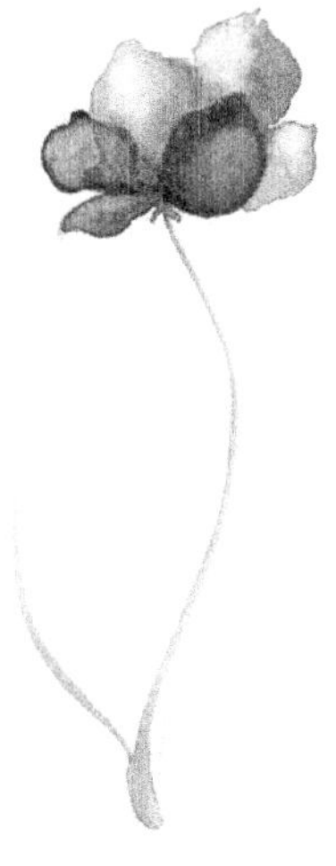

MAY I HAVE THIS DANCE?

His presence blew my candles out
like a moth to a flame, his beautiful voice singing my name.
With a curtsey I accepted.
He wrapped his arms around me as my hips sway slowly to his
music. The rhythm and lyrics hypnotized my body and my soul.
My hair joined in the dance, swinging wildly in the wind. Our
body moves in sync to the beat. He became the paintbrush stroking
my emotions, guiding my ballroom heels. He twirls me around,
making me float in his valley of death, forcing me to sip the
beautiful picture of no pain and sadness. Our silhouette played
hide and seek while I inhaled his mystery fragrance.
I stared at the temptation of ecstasy and euthanasia prancing on the
glass ceilings.
Butterflies flutter, I closed my eyes to escape his captivating grips.
He held me tightly as he dipped me slowly. I watched the darkness
poured down like rain from the heavens, the stars descending with
my visions mixed with regret and happiness.
I have a yen to dance forever though my throat is parched.
Red stains on the dance floor
revealing this is my final dance.
The music changed and my funeral song began, black rose petals
bleed as I kissed my final tears of the loved ones I couldn't say
goodbye to and the life I wished I would have cherished.
My heartbeat slows down while I choke on my fear with blinding
lights transferring me to the unknown.
His beautiful lips sealed the deal, from a dance I wished I could
resist.

Copyright Katrina Black Butterfli

HER FIRST SOLO TRIP

It all began a decade ago,
This rare disease gripped her,
Crippling her and sucking her vitality,
Distorting her physical features,
The therapies and treatments started,
Pricked with injections every month,
Drowsy and writhing with pain,
Her organs and bones surrendering gradually,
Yet, her gutsy spirit carried her well.

.

And so, from that very day,
When she became a semi-vegetable,
Her rendezvous with death commenced,
Every day could be her last day,
She knew, and so was her family,
Often she had to be hospitalized,
Suffering from acute breathing problems,
Yet, she lived gracefully, full of gratitude,
Her simple presence brightened the atmosphere,
And contributed so much to her own home.

.

Dancing with death became her habit,
She turned it into a game, perhaps not fun,
But she would be winning this tug of war,
Unless she fell in love with death finally,
For it promised her a release of her pain,
She would be set free, and she heaved a sigh of relief.
Nobody could take her pain away, how much they tried,
And, only death brought her that joy,
And, this time she undertook,
Her first solo trip to heaven.

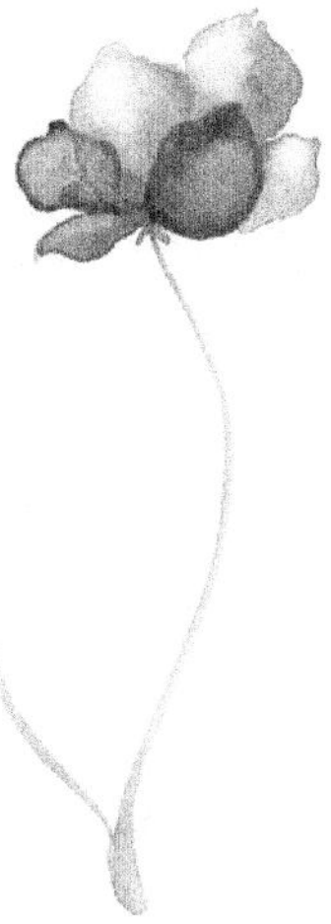

Copyright Amrita Mallik

LIFE SETS MANY CHALLENGES TO FACE

There are many ups and downs in this worldly race
At times, life's journey faces no hurdles
Enabling one to sail through it without any trouble
But one never remains every time at ease
Times come when worldly comforts begin to cease

There come struggles in a row to arrive
Then one finds it very difficult to survive
One chooses to take risks to make one's living
No matter sword of death keeps hanging
Everyone has to dance to the tune of life
No matter one has to face death at times in this strife

One has to die many times in the endeavor of better living
No matter the cost of its maintenance
becomes too overbearing
Still one manages to overpower one's fears
By chasing and facing death whenever it comes near
No more fear of actual death haunts then anymore
When one encounters death many times before

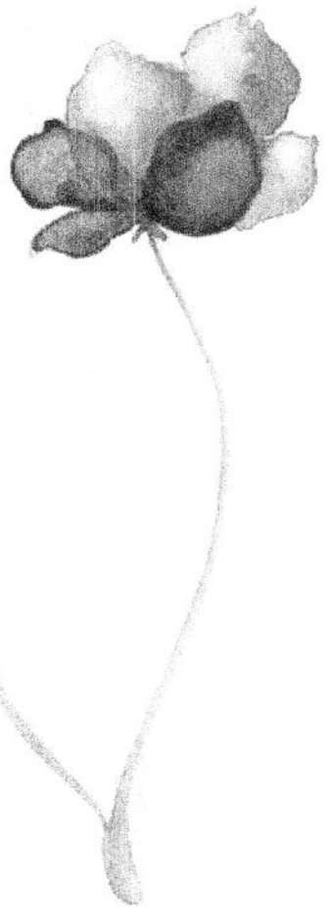

FINAL DANCE

All dressed in white,
Halo above,
The kiss of death,
The final love,
The crossing path,
The faded lines,
Drenched in tears,
Heavenly finds,
Knocking loud,
Solitary breath,
Feeling comfort,
Nothing left,
This final dance,
Ends all others,
Angel wings,
Beneath the covers,
Finding peace,
A brush with death,
Fleeting soul,
Nothing left,

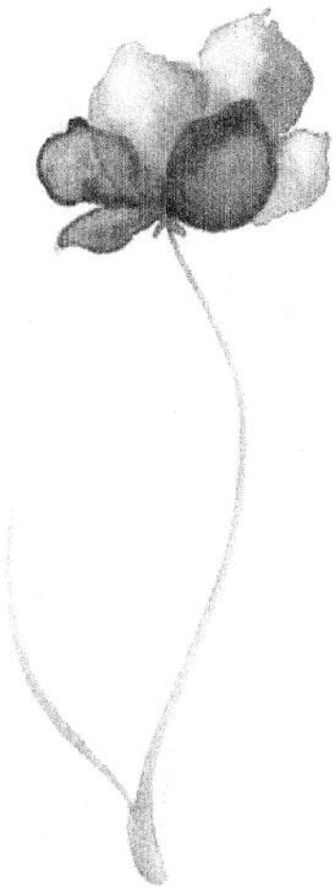

EVERY DAY

countless unnamed dead numbers.
Reality becomes cruel.
I'm afraid I'm breathing.
I'm afraid to speak.
I'm afraid I live.
I survive like a worm
buried deep in the ground.
Depression is all around me.
How to survive?
How to stay normal?
Do you know the answer
or are you struggling with yourself like me?
Do you dance on the edge of life?

Copyright Dijana Uherek Stevanović

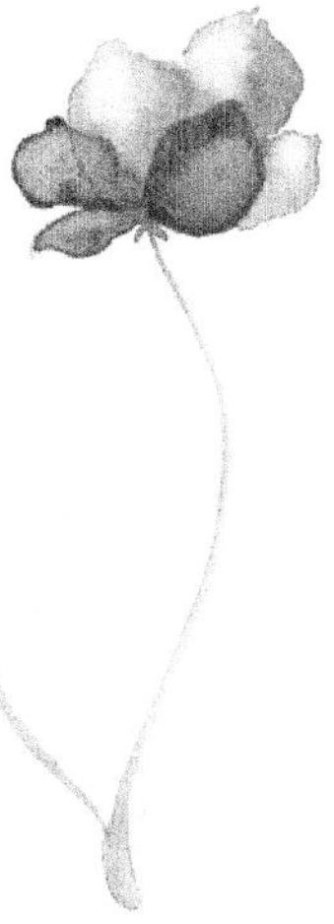

I LOVED MY LIFE

Angel, dancing with The Death,
Wrapped in a white gown of stealth...
Are you pensive for the earth,
Her core opening, is that worth it?
Mother Nature's hustle...
When will her breath subtle?
Unknown diseases swarming,
Is that due to global warming?
I have pondered for a long time,
And stopped hearing the chime...
Of the bells, they used to ring,
Merrily while the flowers swing...
Windows, doors, dull and lazy,
Scratching from inside.. look hazy ...
When will I see a pure smile?
Humming a tune for a while?
Will it do? A pinch of positivity,
To rinse off all the negativity?
If this is the end, I will shout.
'I loved my life...till I am out...

-Copyright Deepa Vankudre

WHEN YOUR TIME SHOULD COME

When your time should come there will be a dance with death the reaper comes knocking you will have to figure out what you want in your final stand will want to go to see st peter then you need to ask for gods forgiveness for all your sins but should you decide on the other way you will then come face to face with the devil, at last, your final minutes your decision is made as you head into your final slumber never to wake your path is set in stone your soul will make its move on either you will see a light follow it to heavens gate and take your wings unless you made the other choice to burn in the fires of hell to the bitter end,

Copyright Crystal King

EMBRACE DEATH GAILY

Dear death, I fear not thou
Thou are just welcome as
another ending
An ending, which will lead us
to a new beginning
The hope of new dawn, thou
shall be bringing
Each hour I shall not waste
on weeping
I shall embrace thou as
you come knocking
I shall dance with thou
I shall accept thou arrival
with a grin
I shall guide thou to make
a new beginning
A new beginning where, together
we shall walk peacefully
The fears, insecurities we will set
aside, for another day
We will miss not a chance, while
dancing with spirits gay
We will teach others too, that
your arrival is inevitable
We will help everyone to
be prepared to embrace thou
Yet, they must not fear thou
They should remember that
every life must come to an end
Sooner, or later you will bring

your chariot at each life's door
Thus each one must build a strong core
They must dance with death freely
Conquering all fears they must
learn to dance with death gradually.

IF YOU A BEAUTIFUL FLOWER

I dance in the garden

If You a thunder n lighting

I dance with the clouds

If you a mighty ocean

I dance with the whales n waves

If you a crouching dragon

I dance with the fire

If you a saint

I dance with the silence

But you a girl every day

I dance with death every moment😛

Copyright Deepak Kumar

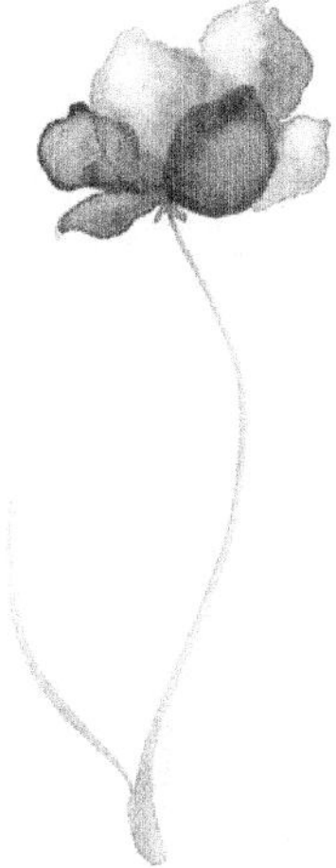

LIFE AND DEATH DANCE IN A RING

sing eternal rhapsody.
no end they know
they dance in the eternal flow.
oceanic waves
tides high
tides low
mingle in one flow.
The ocean vast
now calm
then turbulent wavy.
a new flow soon to begin.
death dances macabre
to harbinger new life to free.
Death dances
can't dance long
if life does not sound arrival gong.
In the ecstasy of unbridled mirth
Death can cause Holocaust.
Life's peep can't be overcast.
A new blade of grass peeps
in midst ruins left by an atomic blast.
Death can't dance in absence of life
To dance rhythm eternity
He invites life.
Life and death
death and life
Happy indeed.
Death seems to outdo life in the dance of eternity
Life throws a gauntlet
death defeated.
Death opens the door for new life to welcome

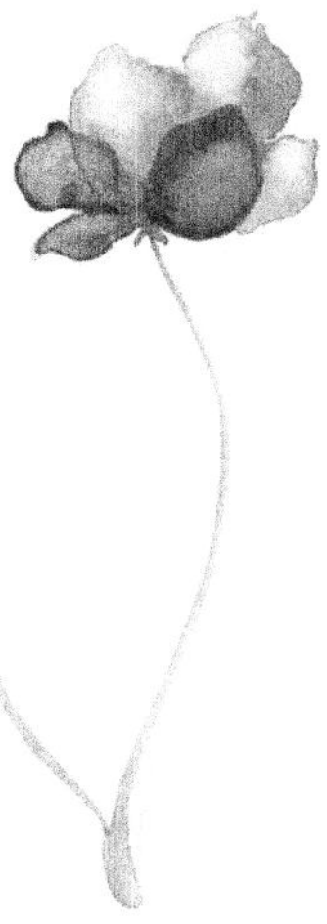

and crush
Nothing but eternal fracas.
life, not a crush.
O' death dance
as you like
but how is it possible sans life?

Copyright Chandra Sekhar Batabyal

ONIOVO

Oniovo,
I wondered what was on your mind
Those troubled nights
When without a single fear,
I gave you my head
To watch over as I slept.

Was I really dancing with death?
I wondered, and I am still wondering
Why I did not stop my self from wandering
Into fantasy to listen to your murmurings.
That would have been my warning
For me to start running.

Why you did not strangle me
In my deep sleep, to me,
Is still a mystery.
Why you could not hold me down
As I told you my plans
Still deserves to be answered.

In the spirit of true friends
We vowed to be one till the end.
But the night you shot that arrow
Scared me to the depth of my marrow.

I feel like flying away like a sparrow
Than in my heartache wallow
Like a weeping willow
In the middle of a meadow.
Oniovo,

Does this have to with the System?
Have you become one of them?
What happened to us, our dreams?
Tell me I am not dancing with death
For being your pair.

I dare you to look into my eyes and answer me.
Oniovo, Oniovo, Oniovo!
(C) SAMUEL OSEYOMA- ONOSERI. 2021.
* ONIOVO means BROTHER OR SISTER
to the Urhobo speaking people of
Niger Delta Nigeria.

In other words, the poem can also be viewed from the angle of one Female addressing another or a Male addressing a Female and vise versa.

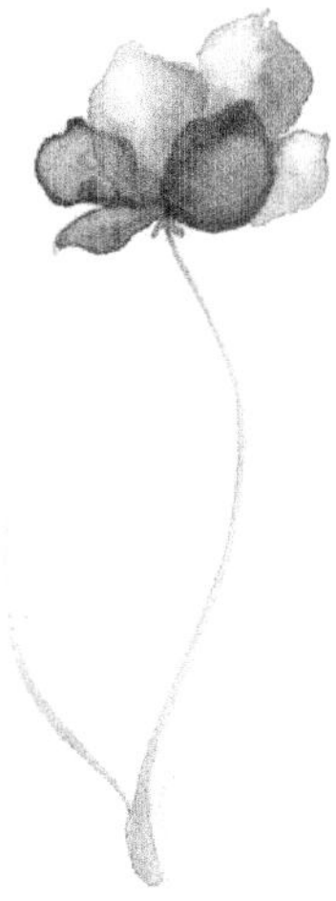

"HER LAST DANCE WITH DEATH"

Gypsy village, nestles in hills
Performing artist all with a strong will
Young woman practices, rope walking with a stick
Rope tied between two tall trees, she performs in a flick.
Balancing acts she performs from age of three
Now does rope walk, between tall trees
Famous for acts, to see her art, people flock
Her grace, beauty, courage in acts, leave people awed.
Today she walks on a rope between two hills
Balancing on a rope over the valley is a test of her will
Village decorated, with flowers like a bride
All gypsies, performing tricks with pride.
Rana(prince) was hunting nearby, heard about this feat
Eager to watch her act, as to eyes, it was a treat
Thick rope tied on poles, between two hills to show, her act and art
On the beat of drums, the girl emerged with a pole to start.
Slowly, on a rope, she balances with a smile, she walks
Tip toed on a rope without slip, looks up, waves
People cheered, the prince looked in valley and gapes
How on such heights, she walks without being in a daze.?
Girl covered the distance, reach cheering crowds
Gypsy chief introduced his daughter, to the prince proudly
Enamored by her art, looks, bravery, beauty
To promote this brave girl's art is his duty.
Gypsy food, wine, a culture he saviors
Fell in love, the heart he gifted, to gypsy beauty's charm
Marry her his desire, make her, his future queen
Royalty opposed, as marriage fixed with a princess of Royal breed.
King invited, gypsy chief, his daughter to rope walk on the lake
Royalty graced the occasion, on a lake, in front of the palace

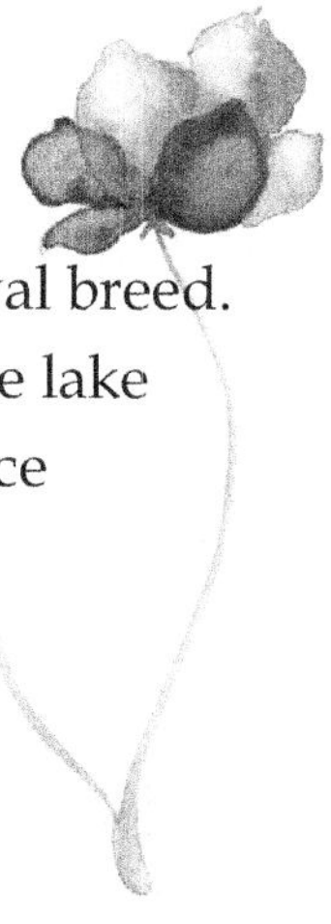

She gracefully, rope walked across and paid respect, to the audience
Prince insisted, his father, the king, to a gypsy girl, his marriage announce.
They both lived in each other's heart and soul, forever as friends, guide
King gave the gypsy chief, two bags full of gold coins to take
Orders the girl to rope walk, over the lake to their camp on the other side
As she walked, halfway in the center, the rope broke, she met a watery grave.
Depressed, prince cried, she died, loving him, was her only fault
This was her last act "dance with death" in her life
People hear her sobs when on the lake they roam.

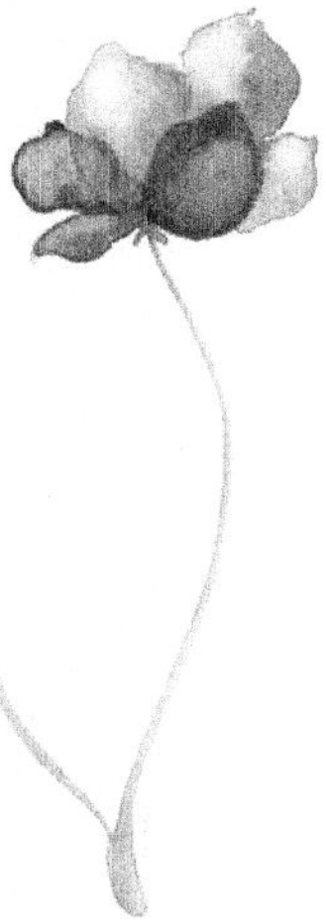

BIRTH AND DEATH

Everyone in this world is struggling
Between work and home, they are juggling
Whether rich or poor
None is exempted from this so-called war
Life sometimes serves ironically
And gives lessons thoroughly
Everyone wish to visit a fair
We pass by observing things at galore
Every person is seen in a scrupulous state
Acting only for income generate
Whether circus or fair
People spent to visit there
Whether riding a motorbike in a deep well
Or doing acrobats in a circus with great triumph
Skills and risk go hand in hand
Both help to generate income and comprehend
Dancing with life on the verge
They seldom fear death while at work
Living life is a continuous process
Without this, we cannot get success
Life skills and jeopardy gives momentum to life
Dancing on its tunes they are ready to strive
Enjoying perceptions of death and birth
They lead their life with unexplainable mirth
Birth and death are inevitable
Behold in your arms, prepare and celebrate every obstacle

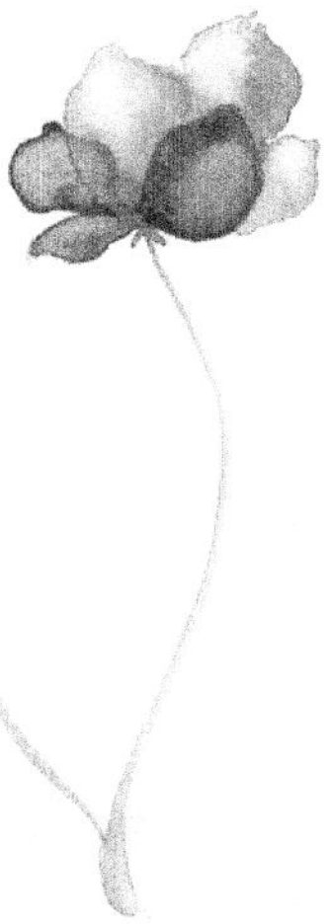

Copyright Alifya Kothari

DANCE WITH DEATH

Deafening silence beats hammers of death
In the dungeon of crushed emotions,
Every moment a wish dies,
Dead-pan faces hide dastardly inaction,
Dreams perish, in the dizziness of arrogance,
Filtered feelings sway uneasily
And feet trot on a dance of decay.
Decayed morals, decayed sacraments,
Unholy bonds dance ugly,
Dandies divide and break
All things sacrosanct,
Corrupt thoughts kick around
The alleyways of life
And the teeming mortals
Stoned, dance with death!
Death of ethos, death of a character
In a land of no- return,
Corroded by pretensions,
Overpowered by cravings,
Possessed by lusts,
Lost completely in the deadly wood
Of over- riding superficiality!
White-collared ambition rises steep,
Alcohol drowns mid-age crisis,
Life on a fast- track loses control,
Bleakness surrounds glitter and dazzle,
Loud music roars on the disco floor
And the dance with death rocks!
It's a slow death, creeping silent,
Unbridled ambition, severed prudence,
Yellowed vision, amputated emotions,

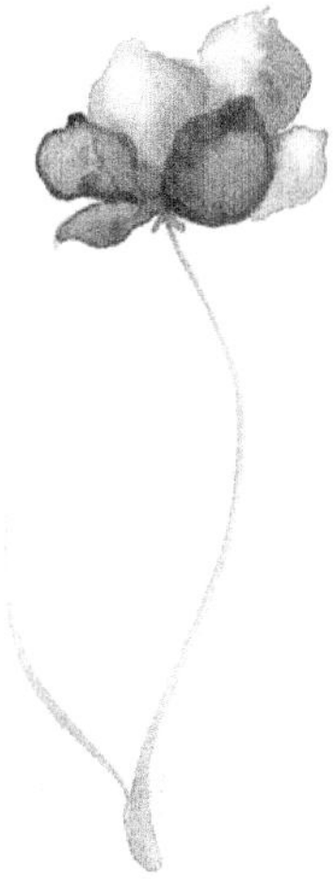

Muddle- headed intoxication
Fog off clarity,
The slow poison controls the senses
And life turns into
A perpetual dance with death!

Copyright Swati Das

LET ME TELL YOU A STORY

Let me tell you a story, a story of glory and fate, one-off day death grabs it all...
There lived a Chinese emperor, oh very long ago...
His palace was built with porcelain, had all the colours of the rainbow...
He could view his entire country from the top of his palace...
His garden was full of rare and never-to-be withered flowers.....
The trees were full of birds, few though never sang but never flew away ...
He lived happily with his countrymen and family and was never believed in conquer and win...
His fellow kings were happy and always praised the mighty king...
They would say that the Emperor was sent from heaven as the savior of the world...
Life was as good as it could be when one fine day the country was threatened by a barbaric king from a far-off land who was famous for his inhuman deeds...
The emperor was worried for his countrymen...
He instead of instructing the army to suppress the incoming, came up with a very unique plan...
He challenged the other king for a duel and declared that he would leave in peace if he meets defeat...
The day arrived and all the men from the two kingdoms stood to witness the fight...
They marched on the battlefield with swords in hand and no one was ready to give up ...
The fight was deadly and it looked like a dance with the death...
The fight continued and both the warriors were injured to the greatest extend...
The Emperor could finally capture the ill-hearted king and put the fight to an end.....

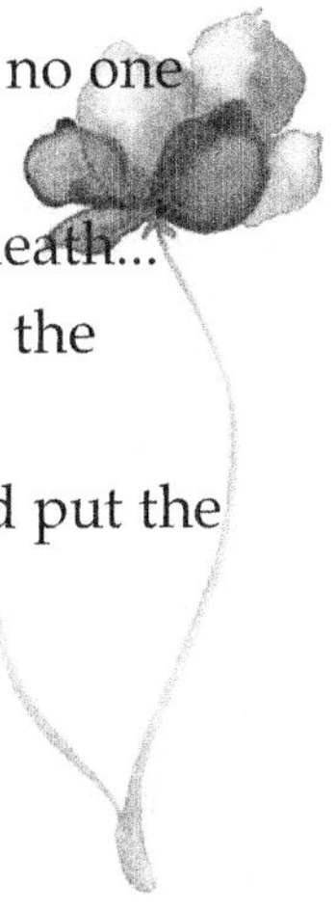

He let his opponent live and gave him his lands back...
The happiness of all the men and their roars touched the sky...
The Empress hugged him tight as he had survived after dancing with death...
The Emperor was happy and glad that he never had to jeopardize a single life of his countrymen ...
His eyes were moist when he saw his people standing by, all in good health, all with spirits high.....
His glory spread around the world as he did so much to mankind...
Time passed as it always does and the king became old and wise...
He passed his wisdom to his son and passed him the throne...
He then took an unknown path in search of solemn...
There he waited silently for his remains to be taken...
Death came eventually and asked him a question...
I came to you a few years back but you chased me out saying it's still not time, is it time now?
I was fighting for the lives of several thousand people, my death or defeat would have caused so much bloodshed...
Everything is settled now and I can accept my long pending death...
Emperor said with a happy face...

Copyright Antara Bose

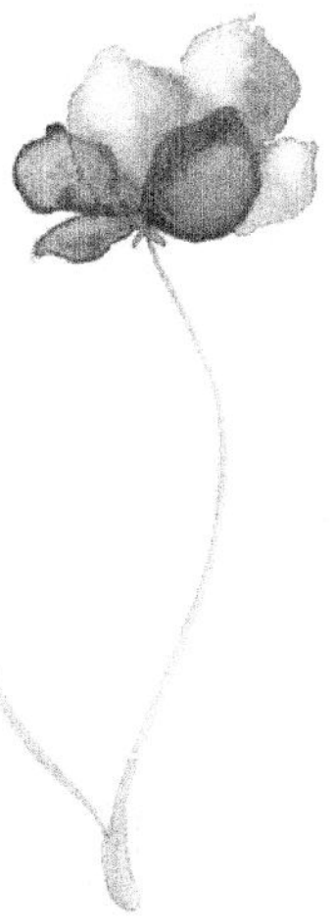

IMMORTALITY IN THE SPOTLIGHT

In a nightclub downtown
We've been partying all night
Not being a good dancer
I'm just enjoying the buzz of the music
With the collar of my coat turned up
A black fedora hat tilting over an eye
The other eye squinting at the dancers on the dance floor
My back leaning against the wall
Then she makes her dashing appearance
Draped in snow-white attire
Slithering across the stage
Gliding from side to side
A blood-chilling Shriver takes over the air
Her sapphire eyes sending
A quiver through the veins
As a serpentine apprehension
Grips every dancer in the round
An eerie slickness creeping through their imaginations
One by one the dancers exit the stage
Like inmates on death row
With their trembling feet, a crowd of onlookers
The music stops as if the world has come to a halt
Death raises her head
Seeing no one to dance with
She casts her garment
Like a snake shedding its skin
In a corner of my mind
I'm starting to get the clue
So I give in to her cue
Taking the risk to step into the spotlight
Ready to tango with my mortality

As the loudspeakers burst into the music
She starts to spew:
What is life, if not death in disguise?

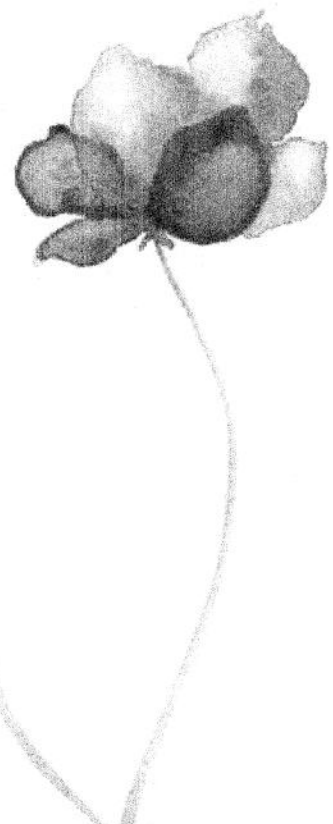

WRECK AND RESCUE

My life was bobbing on the turbulent waves,
Tossing on the crests and troughs, imbued with melancholy,
The crashing waves of depressing thoughts washed my mind,
The brutal dance of death was running berserk,
I was entwined in the ravaging typhoon, strangulating my existence,
Gasping for breath, suffocated by the swirling emotional upheaval,
Nevertheless, I kept swimming against the tide,
Until one fine day,
You emerged from that hazy stream, aiding my lost skiff,
Steering my directionless ship,
Ushering me into the light of promising days,
Mesmerized by your gleaming aura,
What shall I call you, my love?
As the lighthouse guides the mariners,
So were you a beacon of hope,
In my tenebrous downwards spiraling life,
Rescuing me from the swelling tides of resentment, despair, and despondency,
Like the incandescent bulbs of the lighthouse,
Emitting radiance in my hitherto kaput life.

Copyright Amrita Lahiri Bhattacharya

I AM NOT THAT COWARD

I am not that coward
Who'd fear a lot when I die
In every step of life, I am ready
To conquer death
Amidst the struggle of life
I want to strife
I am ready to face any struggle
That creates hindrances in my way of life
Death is my ornament
I am ready to embrace it
I had dreams, I had a colourful world, where I shared my happiness
But life has befuddled me, jostled me to live a life of loneliness
The Moon is a witness of my joy and glee
He knows that how agile I was once when you were with me
My mind was busy like an agile fawn
It was restless from twilight to early dawn
But when you left me alone on the shore of ocean-like life
I forgot how to I have to survive
My universe halted in its axis, it's forgotten how to rotate further
My mind became the ultimate sufferer
Now I am ready to embrace death
I am not a coward
I am not a duffer anymore
I tasted life from my core of heart
I know, I know
What's the aroma of life
I know how to struggle in life
I know how to dance with death

CHAPTER III

ISOLATION

ISOLATION KILLS

Whichever way you turn, isolated from everything
People degrade you because they are different
And what's the point of making new friends
When you just want to hurt each other
Goodness has long since died for all people
Appreciate what you have, I guess evil
Every step you take know that it is vicious
Because you don't know what life is waiting for you
And so the years come next
People run away from themselves for sure
You have no one to tell how you feel
You are isolated.
How to ask someone for a chance
When do you definitely not get them?
I guess the problem with all this is in people
And not in yourself, because you know
They will all come back to you when they need you
And it just takes time to do its thing
Because there is a karma bitch next to her
Waiting around the corner just his pedestal
To present itself as it is, realistic!

ON BRINGS LONELINESS,

Isolation brings loneliness,
Loneliness brings woes,
Woes bring with it unhappiness,
And so this cycle goes,
Broken hearts spring from isolation,
When kept away from those they love,
It can lead to desolation,
Making them feel like they're unloved,
Although sometimes the choice is clear,
It doesn't take away the pain,
For what does isolation solve,
When for some, time never comes again,
So try by any means necessary,
Make sure somehow to let them know,
That they're still loved and thought of every day,
Before isolation makes their loneliness grow,
For isolation brings loneliness,
Loneliness brings woes,
Woes bring with it unhappiness,
And so this cycle goes.

ISOLATION A BLESSING AND CURSE

Isolation

Isolation a blessing and curse

The blessing to find oneself

When the world has turned it back on you

The curse of not being able

To interact with the world you love

The people you cherish

Isolation a blessing and a curse

Needed in the journey of one's life

I DON'T LIKE THE CROWDY PLACE

I don't like the crowdy place
I want to go into a serene place
It's not my desolation
I love to search for my true reflection
People recognize me as an introvert
Am I really like that
I want to spend some peaceful moments
Not like as an extrovert way
Is it good or bad
The mind isn't ready to accept any answer
Oh! what a pathetic conclusion
All of you force me to live alone
I love to lead a jolly life
Not like all of you as an extrovert
A quite different maybe I'm
You all say this is isolation
Ok. I can agree with you
But not all times that's true
If someone likes serenity
That's not meant a madness or severe disease
Maybe there's some hidden spirit
Need time to shine at right plot
Look at the moon in the sky
Never show up at day time
So what it's never forget
To show the smiley face
At night when the golden face appears
Surroundings are mesmerized
Isolation has different definitions
Whether a serene breeze or waver dance

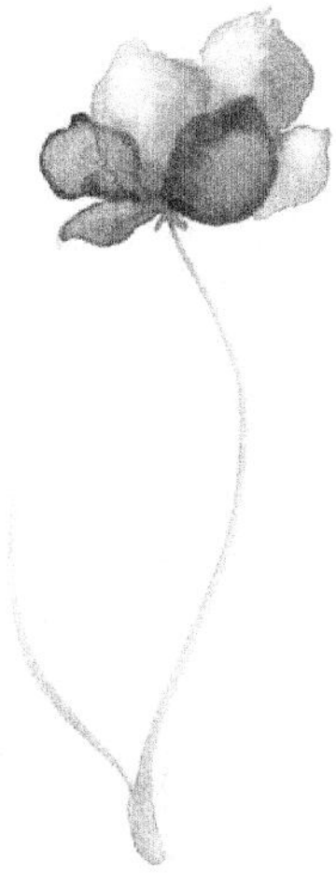

Nothing can change the way of dictation
Find out thy real one within itself

Copyright Afrose Saad

HEY SLAVE MASTERS,

Hey slave Masters,
Humans are not your resources
Will, you stop injustice,
And release men from captivity?
Naturally, all humans are in hell
How do you feel putting him in another?
Is he the source of your silver?
Is he the laborer of your desire?
Why can you stop this,
And understand your life is like vanity.
From dust, you were made
From dust, you shall return
How do you feel,
Having all things of your wish,
And the last day you sleep in pain?
O slave masters,
Resist that attitude
Let's others congratulate you.

A SOUL IN SOLITUDE

My soul is in solitude,
Should I give God my gratitude?
Or show Him some attitude?
For my generation's ineptitude.
Amid mounting multitudes,
I find no moral rectitude.
When all, calls the right, the wrong,
In no time, would the right become wrong?
Or does it have to take so long?
And on all sides, we are pierced with a pass along.
I am alone, won't one for me atone?
Loneliness sits on me like a stone.
Did I take the path of sin?
The world sees me as one with leprous skin.
This isolation looks like destruction,
It looks like denial.
The best man they said is made
Even in solitude but where
Is it my best when my face looks like a spade?
This isolation is a blessed curse,
I lost friends to bribery purse,
This is a curse.
But I found joy in standing alone,
Because from heaven I hear a tone.
This is my blessings.

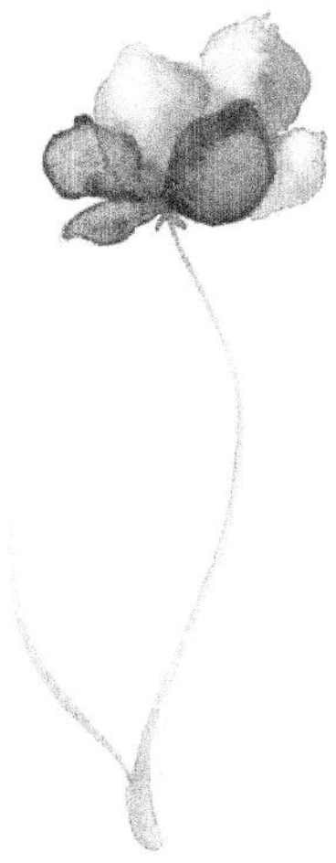

MY EYES

Look...
Look into my eyes for what you seek.
I beseech thee to really think.
For what you want you may not find.
Hidden behind the black pupils isn't always a peaceful mind.
Life has taken the kind out of me.
So I say again,
I beseech thee to really think.
Be careful of the darkness within my eyes.
For it might blind you with nothing but lies.
Lies of Love & Care.
Lies of I'll Always Be There.
Lies of Hopes & Dreams.
Lies of I'll Never Be Mean.
See once upon a time the lies were all true.
Then I came across him
& he made me blue.
He sucked the Light & Life of Love right out of me till I was nothing but a shell.
Filled me with the Fire & Darkness of the unholy Hell.
Now I'm lost to the emptiness that is within.
Walking around filling myself with nothing but sin.
My eyes are the windows to my soul & he claimed it long ago...
So look not into my eyes
if what you seek is truth.
For the darkness within me may swallow you up too...

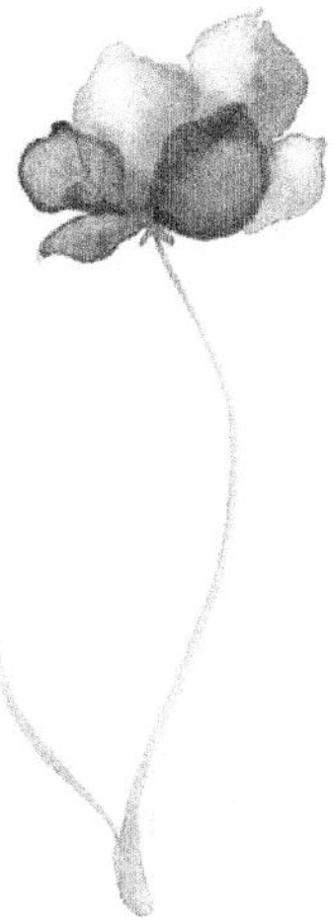

Copyright Lee Love

AGE MAKES NO DIFFERENCE WHEN WE'RE ALONE

It can cut like a knife carefully honed
It can also creep up on you without any mercy
Gaining the power to paralyze all that you see
Sometimes we put ourselves in isolation
That is when we don't feel so forsaken
But when others force us to be alone
We find it a chore to stay at home
When we're young sometimes we need a break
From all the confusion life can make
We treasure each minute of peace we can find
But still, yearn for the kind human touch
As we get older it gets harder to be apart
The absence of conversations hurt our hearts
In our advancing years, we yearn to see
All the loved ones we've taught to be free
They are so busy leading their lives
There is no time to visit the old but wise
Let us take time to honor the old
Hear their stories, in person, as they are told
We'll be glad we put smiles on their faces
No one else on earth can ever take their places

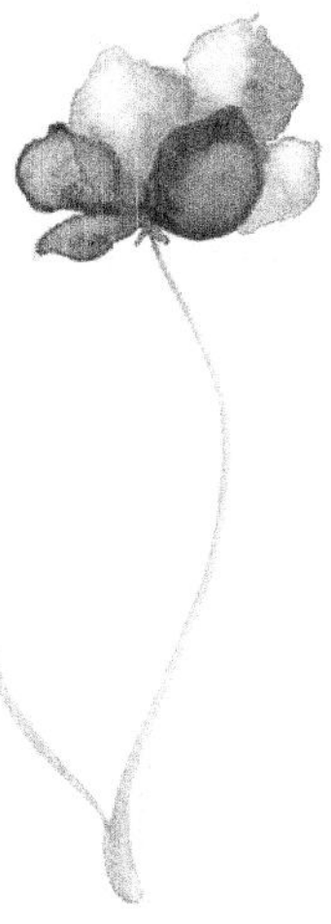

IZOLOMI

Qytetet u zbehen prej izolimit
nje e nga nje te gjithe.
Pastaj filluan te zbehen edhe shtetet.
U zbrazen rruget nga levizjet.
U cuditen druret jashte ne rruge,
kur nuk na pane.
U cudit pranvera kur
erdhi dhe iku dhe s,na gjeti bashke.
Pastaj u mesuam me largimin
dhe me fytyren me mask.
I trishuam gjithe druret e rruges
me mungesen tone.
Ato sivjet u zbehen pak
ashtu sic u zbeh gezimi ne bote.

Copyright Ollga Farmacistja

"SILENCE"

At first, I was so depressed
It was painful
It was degrading
It was humiliating
But then I realized
I have no one
But I have myself
Nobody can hurt me
Nobody can love me, too
Except myself
So I started building walls
I closed all doors and windows
So in each corner, I would only see myself
I write, I sing,
I paint for myself
Nobody hurts me
Nobody loves me, too
Only myself
Isolation is addictive
Silence became my music
I want to stay here forever
Where you put me away from you.

LONELINESS

There is an old lady who lives on our street.
I pass her sometimes and wave to greet her.
My father knew her since he was a child.
He said she'd always been gentle and mild.
Her face is lined and covered in wrinkles.
Cataracts in eyes that once used to twinkle.
Spine now bent so she hobbles with a stick.
In her youth, she had been lissome and quick.
Voice now gravelly...tells stories of yore.
Her friends are all gone, no one's left anymore.
She had a large family previously.
Now everyone's grown up and moved on you see.
Her dear husband departed to his heavenly abode.
She waits for her turn which isn't long, I'm told.
A few weeks ago she was found wandering.
Out on the road, in her nightgown... mumbling.
I heard she was taken to a place of care.
Where they would tend to her needs and look after her there.
Recently her kids came to her house.
Packed boxes and cartons...were moving stuff out.
Seems like she'd joined her husband...finally.
Her soul must be happy, at peace now she was free.
Sometimes I think of her and I wonder.
About getting old and then I ponder.
How would it feel to be all alone?
For company, just the T.V, and phone.
Would getting old be akin to a curse.
As time keeps moving and will not reverse.
When our time is up, our hearts will cease to beat.
That's when our soul will finally be at peace.

Copyright Meenakshi Dwivedi

UNDER CHAINS OF RESTRICTION

Loneliness, loneliness unfriendly guest,
That sat strategically to bind the victim,
In isolation chains that seclude the innocent guest,
In pains mind burghs conscientiously.

Loneliness, loneliness An unkind guest,
Wallowing in derision to secure freedom,
That never saw the light beaming,
In a shady room that confined the victim.

Loneliness, Loneliness a Waring enemy,
That drag the hope of the mighty to squalor,
The inflicted injury that scares companionship,
Among mortal in subjection march to solitude,

Loneliness in isolation the magic of the wounded heart,
That gazed and gazed to find solace,
Prevailed by wanton massive chains of isolation,
That cannot be broken by chainsaw of comfort,

The head is filled, the heart in distress,
Pointing to the days of freedom that will last,
Calling for a companion to shave the pains away,
Like a flood bath that flows through squalid drains,

Eroding the miasmas that descend the mind,
To free the culprit in chains of restrictions,
To let the cat out of the bag so soon,
Sending the murderer far from the euphoria of rejection.

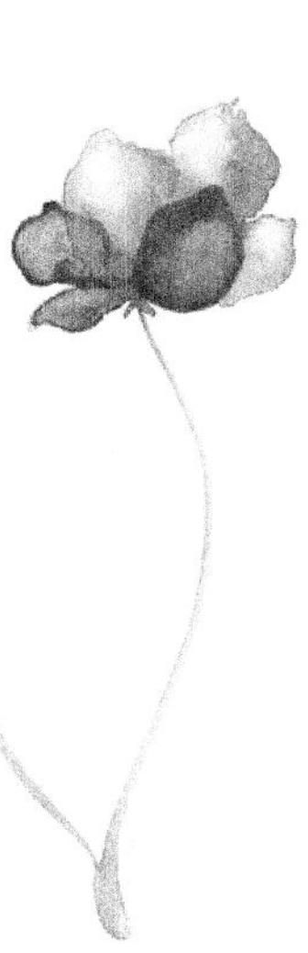

THESE FEW GREYS WHEN NEED

These few greys when need,
A family to love and survive,
Is being a cruel joke
To isolate them to strive
Alone already you are
All your life and now
In the end, would it help,
To give up and bow?
How contagious a disease,
Effects a mind and body,
How ethical is it
To pick out as nobody?
Please let's not forget
They are not punished
Very much alive and return,
They are not forever banished.

Copyright Deepa Vankudre

A BLESSING IN GUISE

Old but fit
isolated
can't mar your spirit.
put an end to
this state.
think it as a blessing great.
solitude
a bliss indeed,
to drink all that you can't in hectic youthful days.
hair grey
wrinkles on face
hopeless
despicable entity?
no.
you are still brave.
color your hair black,
attired fine
behave.
'I am fine '.
dwindling vision on life
to beat
a new rose valley in life to be found.
know that
you
have the power ---
to invite all that's best for you.
And be happy.
who can mar
your happiness?
an offspring of
eternity
invited by almighty, here
to enjoy the gala of festivities.
isolation from relatives or friends
a blessing in guise.

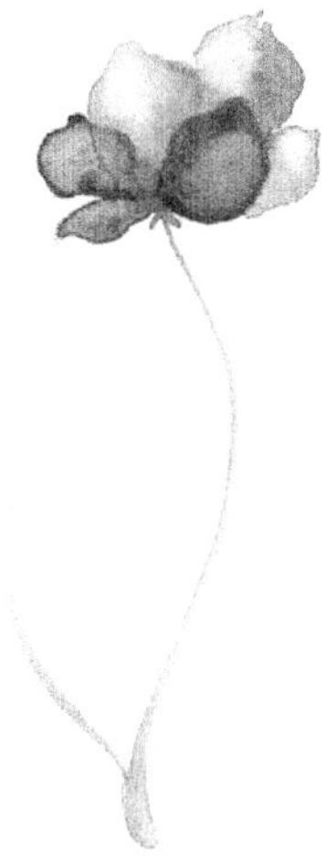

You now can play your life's viola.
In the lap of nature.
sitting by a river murmuring
rhyming
your tune.
you can sing
wherever you like
ever you like.
No audience?
don't bother
your audience
your nature mother.
she will listen to
all your songs.
Know that you are an invitee here.
you have to play your role assigned best.
Never be down
with the heaviness of emptiness
but to feel full
'am a host in myself '.
no care.
who's there
who's here
only to care
Your Father is near.
'Sing Sing Thy glory
in melody.
Oh, God, I play my role
in the stage
to Thy pleasure
till I rest.'

Copyright Chandra Sekhar Batabyal

РЕШЕТКЕ

Бескрајно путовање
Отете обале ријекама
Поред напуштених кућа
У засеоку дјетињства
Сред села бастион
Брзојава бастрадних
Мачева...потражују
Одбјегле страхове
Саме се поруке пишу
Испод рањеног срца
Срушен мост плаче
Тунел зауздале решетке
Скучиле повратак
У ђавољу јазбину
Безизлаз опколио
Осоколио прогонитеља
Заспало добро у људима
Стисло у грудима...
Нема мјеста за љубав
Празне, неважне ријечи
Одзвањају плочником
Старост сорела ...
Гине чекање на
Видиковцу
Плива заробљена
Обмана ума
Забраздила до дна
Долмена доњег свијета
Камени кров притиска...
Бол за бол
Долар на долар
Долорес, кад ће стати?
Долорес, моје име !!!

I WALK ACROSS THE GLOBE

Isolation.

I walk across the globe looking for a soul mate,

I swim all overseas searching for who to trust,

Oh! all in vain, nothing will make my heart peaceful than loneliness.

What my heart think of is solitude,

Living without no interrupting,

Walking without brooding, solitariness can only heal my wound caused by betrayal,

Seclusion can only make my broken heart regain.

Dancing in the rain to keeping my tear Can only make this shameful scaper.

©Small but mightier.

Copyright Damilare AL Adaby

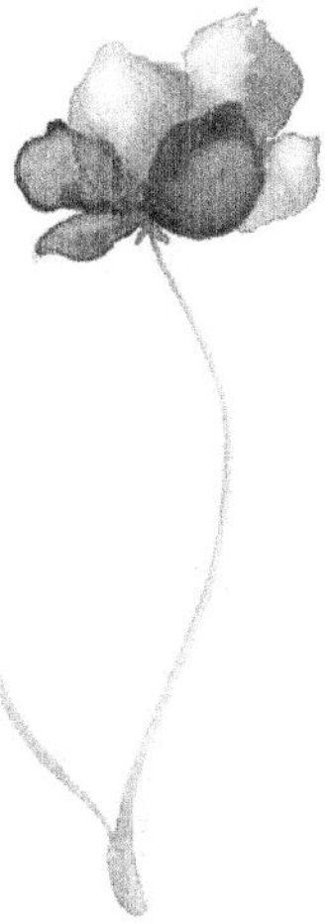

ANOTHER PHASE, UPGRADE…

Isolation is a phase of life,
Real and undeniable is this fact,
It may be forced, accidental, or by choice,
You've got to encounter it,
Whether you like it or not.

.

Sometimes it's the generation gap,
Sometimes it's the refusal to bend and upgrade,
Again, it's a partner's irreparable loss,
At times, even amidst the cacophonous throng,
You feel lonely, drained of energy.

.

Mainly it's all in your mind,
The more you expect and refuse to accept,
The changing times and their demands,
You punish yourself by getting attached,
Making yourself suffer in deprivation.

.

Approbate isolation to bring you joy,
Sever those ties to the nostalgic past,
You can take a trip but make it short,
Return to the moments where you're breathing,
Live those with all your heart, for that is life.

.

Dissipate those retarding thoughts,
Building walls between you and your people,
Let your anger and disappointment go,
Don't let age trick you in its trap,
You're free as long as your mind is.

.

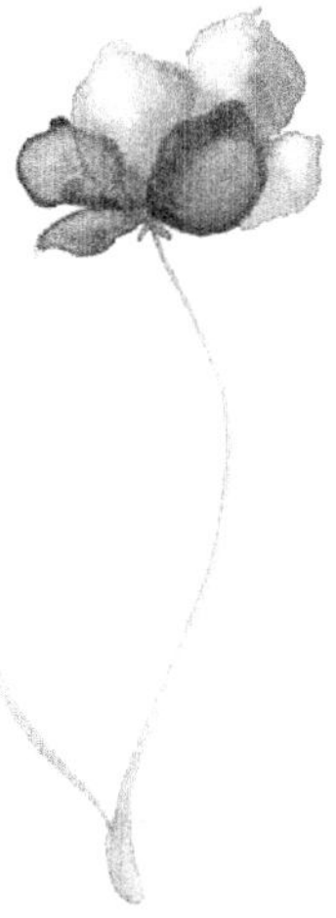

And, thus, isolation is not a punishment,
Don't allow others to frame that for you,
That vacuum can't be filled but it can be mellowed,
Your life, you decide, but do it well,
You'll only be with you till your last.

AWAY!

In your midst I am
But far away still
If only you knew
That my presence is not here
Around but isolated
For my heart travels far
Into a world of wishes
The sound of your voice
Is heard from afar
Disconnected from this scene
Though insight to be seen
Yet separated by the screen
Which you don't know to exist
It's okay, you think
Cause I said it without a blink
If only you knew
The heaviness of my heart
Being isolated from every "now"
Lost in a world of wishes
Seeking what you cannot see
Nursing hurts you know nothing about.

Copyrighht Angela Chinweike

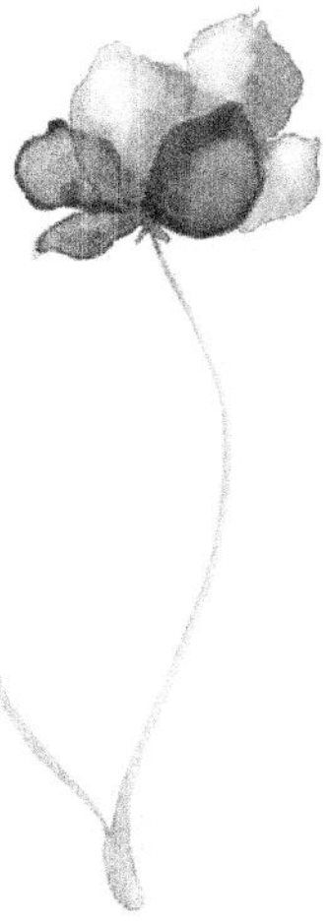

LOCKED INSIDE CLOSET

I'm a victim
I'm weakened by infection
I'm set inside the closet
I'm told not to interact
I live always with fear
I'm loaded always with tears
I wish I'm free
It's bad for I'm knocked down
I put this with pain
Don't be ignorant as me
I did this to myself
I blame no one for this
I deserved it even more
I wish I listened before
I receive everything through the window
Its painful cause my parent is still a widow
I don't want to feed her with pains
I want her always to be glad
Even I transpire this sickness
I don't want to see her in isolation
I want her to be free from depression
She has done me huge things
This time I want to face my sickness alone
I can't take her to fight it on my behalf

ALONE

The mind, your mind, you're so stupid, it's like your living dead,
just a piece of steak, you stink, it stinks, God help the stupid...
I guess I was stupid, thinking of marrying you,
I was pure, innocent, and heart.
I guess people who don't belong to this world have to learn from people here,
Learn how to be cunning and how to decide according to how they teach you.
My mind says yes, my heart says yes but my awareness says no way.
It's quiet; I close my eyes again,
Silence takes you beyond, gets you out of your world and into any world you want...
This place was in, where people do wrong and think it's right,
Where people don't see, hear and watch,
They don't know how to feel and think but only how the system of the world has taught them to...
I see her in distance, I see her stupidity,
She walks fast away, pretending not to notice I'm around, and closes her squeaky car door slightly, it sounds like her hypocritical thinking...
Back on my balcony smoking my cigarette,
It starts to rain a little, the smell of earth after the first rain puts me in this intense love mood, it's strong, I need love... I feel soaked wet and lost...
It's been 17 days since we broke up,
It feels like the second day after New Year's Eve when Christmas and partying is over,
When all your friends, close friends, travel back to work and you left alone sober while the sun is setting,
Or a Sunday dark wet evening when you fucked up so bad,

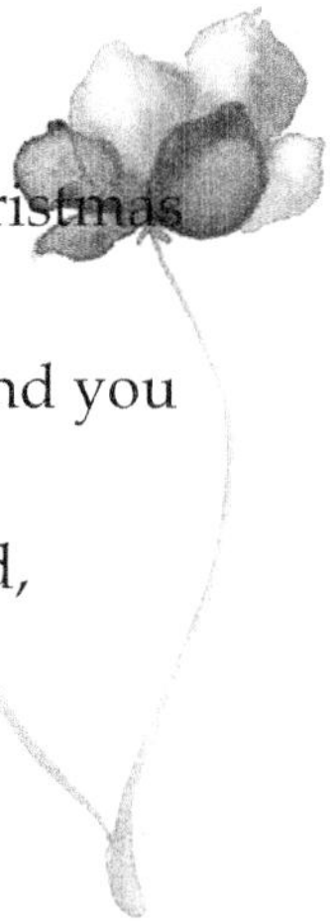

Or heroin come down...
Wintertime and back to work, addiction in my blood,
The deeper you love, the deeper the phobia, insecurity, and death feeling...
Love is made to make us suffer and separate, this building world is mean...
This place is not for me, I don't belong here and it's against my will to cope with it since it's a waste of time, boring and meaningless...
It always feels like I'm waiting at the airport for my plane...
I go for a walk to an abandoned Luna Park, a great mystery feeling,
I feel free but yet in solitary confinement through this love feeling, living in a depressing paradise...

THE DAY AFTER

to the world Outside, Isolation not a choice
He, a Man, anxiety drive his mind
Feeling, the none rejoice
Devastation, true reality find
Within the struggles unvoiced
Foggy solitude, he, chrysalis in a cocoon
Butterfly awaiting Wings to fly
He, in the present sleep in the gloom
Slavery of lace Rapture to Dry
Freedom, Wishing flutter in bloom
A lady, a Muse to come along his way
Fastened thoughts agree on Liberty
more than once, He, dreamy days
Born to the world, a Man, fruit tree
The nectar of Life sip Ablaze rays

Copyright Maria Elvira Fernandes Correia

SO ALONE

will you out there
just give a smile
just touch my hand
and stay awhile
look me deep
my heart doth weep
It dead, alone
so dark
and blown
so yearn for a link
what do I do now
to make it better for me and thou
hate me
alone and numb
not seen or heard
so want to live
do you hear
the unspoken word
the breathed out pain
is someone
out there

Copyright Mona Sharma

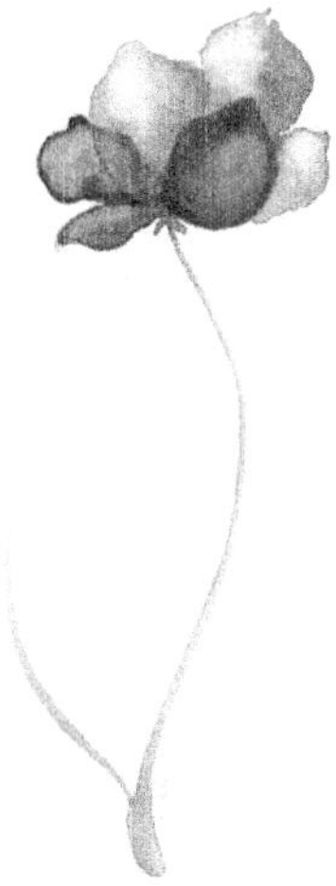

TAKE ME HOME

Wrinkled face.
Teary-eyed.. alone
Expecting no one.
Silence is deafening
Watching the world outside.
Home for the aged
His home for years and days to come
No family to call his own.
He closes his eyes
Trying to remember
The youth of his past.
But that was years and years ago
The youth is gone
What is left is a sick old man
Waiting for his time.
Oh, God !" What takes it so long?"
He uttered
"I am weary, lonely, and sad
Take me now to my rest."
Take me home.

Copyright Lucy Abellana Mendiola

WINE

I go to church to seek divine
To eat the bread and drink the wine
But Covid times have changed the plot
Now Father gets to drink the lot!
And when we say: 'Peace be with you'
If you shake hands the boys in blue
Might come and write you out a fine
And make you walk the thin blue line
Now hairy chins - I'm not a fan
But I wish I could hug my nan
They say there's not a walk so brisk
Can outweigh Covid-19's risk
So Nan just sits there in her chair
We used to take her everywhere
And I'm starting to think the nurse
Insisting Nan's locked up is worse
Then saving her from isolation
Freeing her from indignation
Yet she rocks there all alone
A life lived on a telephone
Her legs have seized up now they say
And soon she'll bid us all goodnight.

Copyright Jonny Paul

LOVE IN WAR WITH DISEASE

Life is misery.
How can we live without love?
Love had earlier wanted an end.
Its sweetness makes it impossible.
Yesterday was Human Immune Virus.
Love's best part was stopped.
We love without sex.
Lovers found a lasting solution.
Checking the partners.
Human Immune Virus was defeated.
Today it is a coronavirus.
Stopping love's initiative part.
We are bound to kiss.
Coming close is forbidden.
How can we love,
without coming close?
How can we date,
without coming close?
How can we whisper,
without coming close?
How can we kiss,
with the lips carrying a red cross?
How can we sex,
without touching each other?
We are isolated
like stars in the sky.
Bound for coming close.
Bound for traveling.
Bound to kiss.
Bound to date.
Does this not kill
more than a coronal virus?

DESERTED DAYS

Prolonged nights
Eager evenings
Miserable mornings...
may meet someone somewhere...
.own people embracing each other's well-being.
Tears n smile all along compacted
Connecting soul's
Alas!
The days are no more.
When bunches of sweetness ripen in hopes
of love swimming across the ages of youthful enchantment...
Never go the joy of pure positivity.
Praises as well as preludes
all have had their positions...
Ahh...
Will it be a reality to respond
Or it would be mere days of isolation....??
like never before......

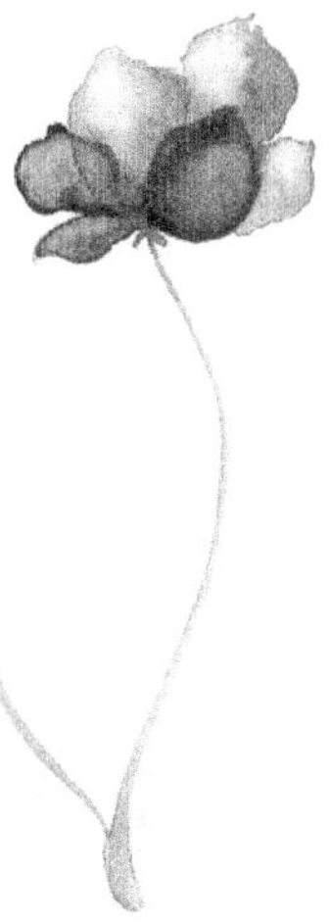

LOCKDOWN

Sickening - the cruel confused isolation of the weak
Sad, wasted, dead behind the eyes elderly people
Pleading for a touch
Are you not stunned, shocked appalled?
Are you not fighting this fear-ridden mantra?
Mindless mockery of basic human rights
I weep to see it
I am silenced by the clinical coldness
Swallowed the pill until my stomach retched
Let me wipe the brow and hold the withered hand of the fading, fragile, frightened woman
Who worked and bore a lifetime of sorrows
Who sacrificed and held lives together
Who grafted morn till eve to provide
Who touched, loved, held, washed, touched, comforted, gave when all giving was gone
I hang my head in shame.
I cannot look the machine in the eye
It cannot cry.

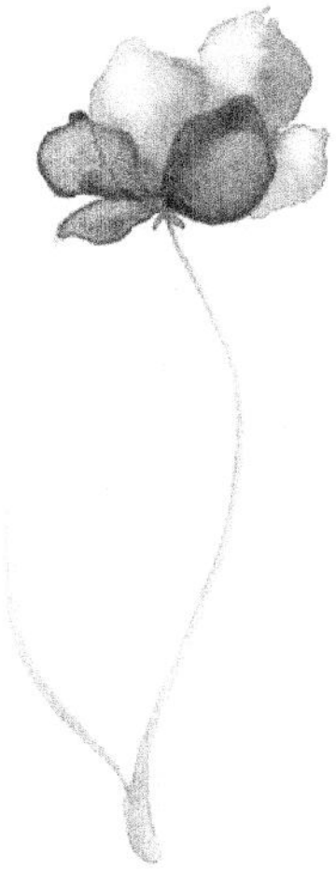

WHEN SADNESS OVERWHELMS ME

When sadness overwhelms me,
Tears washing out my weary eyes.
There's someone I'm so longing to see,
That the feeling of isolation is cold as ice.
The memories keep haunting,
To the point that I'm mesmerized.
Do you know the pain of losing?
What took you so long to realize?
You loved me, I loved you,
What's the point of letting go?
Leaving me behind without a clue,
For my wounds to heal by so slow.

ON BEING ALONE

My age is catching fast with me,
And my face is wearing a wizened look,
I'm looking at my future sitting alone,
Living in a state of isolation; my
Near and dear ones are not so far,
Yet nobody is turning his eyes at me;
I'm waiting for someone to come and hold
My hand and walk side by side
With me in the journey of life ahead;
I have kept my mind's window ajar,
And my heart's door is still not shut;
At my young age, I was full of
Zest for life, and took along
All my friends and relatives together on
The pathways of life full of thorns;
I cared for my old parents,
And helped anybody crying in distress,
Though I didn't realize even in bad
Dreams that with the advancing age and ennui,
Alone I will be left to lock horns;
But the circle of life moves mercilessly,
And takes a toll on nurtured hopes;
Being alone is largely predestined, and
We sulk and grouse as life marches
Ahead in unobliging mood and mechanically.

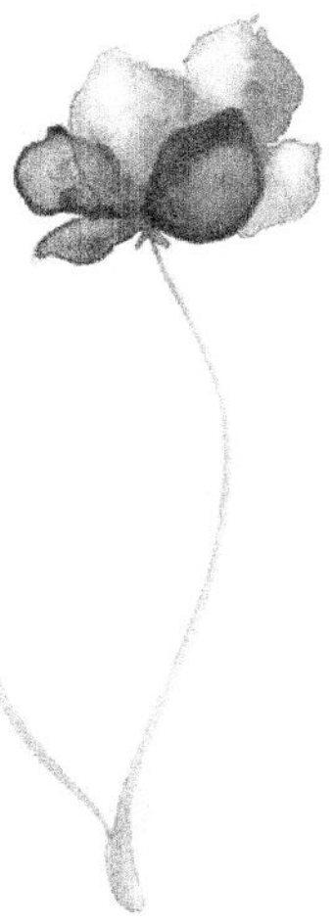

NOT ONLY A STATE OF BEING

also a state of mind
Solitary confinement can
make a happy man unkind
No one to confer with,
no smiles to be shared
Nobody to hug you and tell you that they care
Time moving in slow motion
As you isolate within
Your mind not thinking clearly
The depressive mode sets in
You must escape the torture
Open up that door
Escape from your confinement
Reach out for something more

Copyright Kat Singer

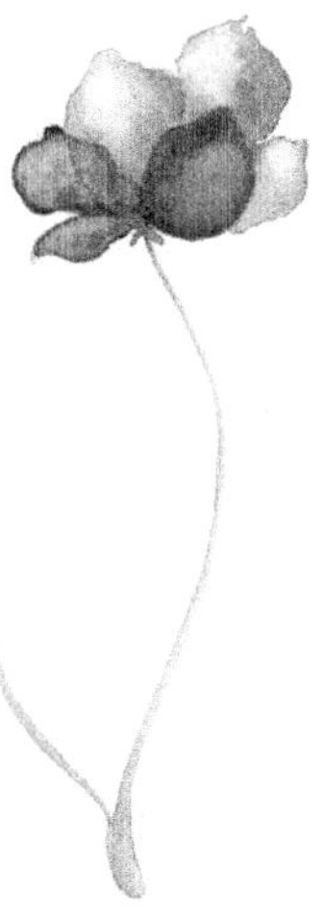

NO INDIVIDUAL CAN LIVE IN ISOLATION

No individual can live in isolation,
No matter how annoying life is,
Individuals all seek a companion.
Despite the drizzling of light everywhere,
I feel as if my mind finds nothing.
As if my times those passed by,
Forgot my existence.
I'm now at the shore of the sea trying to isolate the feet prints from the wetted sand.
Their tearful eyes sparkle saying not to separate them.
Bluewater flowing through shed white tears having a salty taste.
Invited the blue sky above to come down for the helpless moment.
Beautiful days passed away now isolated Oakwood from the soft mind.
It's painful isolating painful melodies from the dear heart.
On the last day of the calendar, don't pull out me from having my last breath because isolation is very painful.

Copyright Rajbanshi Manmohan

COVID IN THE CANE

The planet is in lockdown
And folk are gone insane
But there's nothing like a lockdown
With Covid in the cane
The mountains keep their splendor
The sunsets each night
With colors bursting through the sky
In red and orange light
The last shades of day flicker
And bright blue fades to dark
The stars come out and shimmer
A billion magic sparks
No misery to speak of here
No claustrophobic meltdown
Nobody living life in fear
No societal breakdown
As canefields spread like carpets
Where taipans hunt for rats
The wood glows in the firepit
And shadows dancing bats
We bath in crystal waters
When Sun is at her peak
Where dappled light shimmers
Off rainforest mountain creeks
It cleared the smog in China
When we thought nothing could
Is it wrong to say Corona
Might have done the world some good?

Copyright Jonny Paul

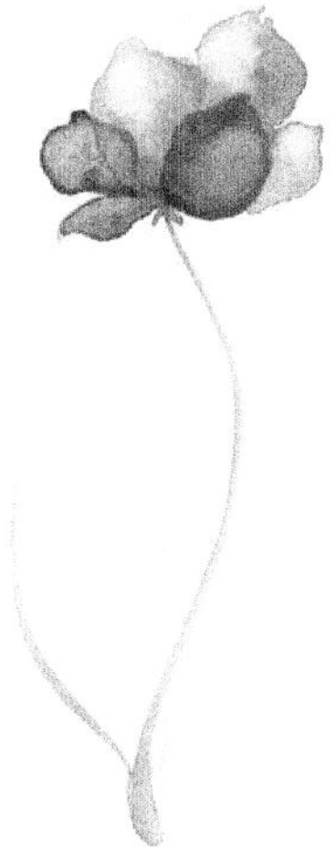

PAUPER

How can this social leper cope
Denied the olive branch of hope?
His pain triples at each social snub
Despised as the filthy city's grub.
Friends are vapid as winter cold's insipid
Where their lukewarm looks failing to bloom rapidly
Looking away when a needy hand stretches to beg
Why worry even about the scavenger's skinny leg?
Under the choking blanket of smog
Turning trash bins like a hungry dog
He scavenges from sun up to sundown
Lonely in the very busy streets of the town
Face gaunt, lined, haggard before it's time
He lives most meagrely without a dime
The affluent, social workers, haven't his time
God knows well he hasn't committed a crime
Shadow-like and grim, smudged in a fifth of street
Faster he waned than the shoes on his feet
To keep him warmer there was no fat
Skeletal look reeked of fate's cruel bite
Wind cuts through his clothes so thin and worn
His eyes' fading gleams show he'll soon be gone
His sky holds only the promise of storms
As his world empty and cold slowly grows
Was he not born to belong and be loved?
And in a tribe of social bonds be nurtured?
Loneliness will remain a vice in his heart
If this darkness covers his inner light
Love alone is a salve that'll soothe his night

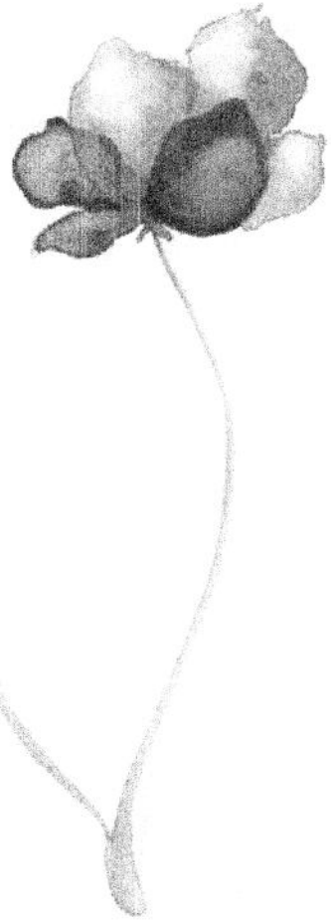

Copyright Ngam Emmanuel

FOR A BETTER TOMORROW

Let's isolate ourselves,
From those vibes,
That, just jibe.
Let's isolate ourselves,
From those thoughts,
That leaves one distraught.
Let's isolate ourselves,
From those negative words,
That, pierce like swords.
Let's isolate ourselves,
From the hate and hatred,
That may prove, ill-fated.
Let's isolate ourselves,
From every single deed,
That may lead us to greed.
Let's isolate ourselves,
From those tears and sorrow,
That hinders a better tomorrow.

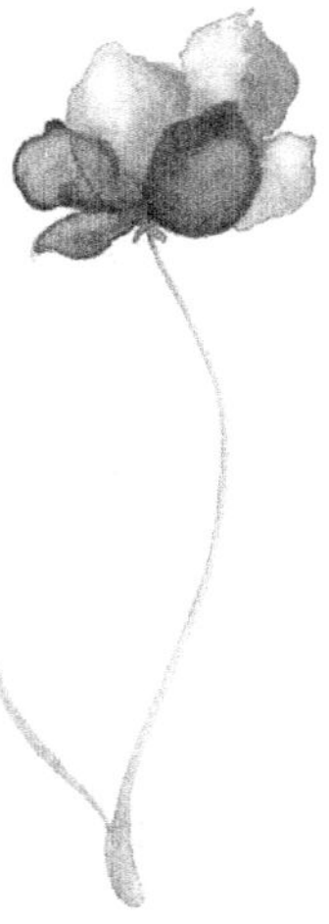

LIFE IS A JOURNEY

Where we find ourselves
alone and lonely someday.
We walk through all ups and downs, twists and turns of paths.
Sometimes we find a road full of roses,
A life full of hope, love, and happiness
Sometimes road full of thorns with obstacles, miseries, and heartbreaks.
Life becomes isolated and deserted,
No one to talk or share with.
When one becomes old and weak
They find that they are alone standing.
Whole life ran after name, fame, money
When near and dear ones left behind
Couldn't recall.
Just sitting near the windowpane
and trying to recall those happy days
Of togetherness.
Waiting and watching the dusk casting its shadows behind of passing days.
A feeling of living in borrowed time
No one to hug or care only memories
haunts of guilt and crimes.
Live a simple life with love and peace
Let your soul reach the tranquility and
Let your heart Kindle the light of hope and positivity to distressed
souls striving isolation just hug them and bring a smile
Let love knock every door of passing lane for miles.

SILENCE

I am here all alone,
No one is calling me on the phone,
I want someone close,
Because this feels like a curse,
I am surrounded by silence,
Everyone's ignoring me like I have no conscience,
No one seems to care,
People just stand and stare,
I look outside through the window,
My heart is filled with sorrow,
I am treated like I am dangerous,
My thoughts feel contagious,
I rarely enjoy the sunshine,
Everything is measured to me like medicine,
It's hell being in isolation,
It's a human beings worst situation,
It's like my prayers go unanswered,
I am afraid I won't be remembered,
I wish there was an escape,
It's not easy to cope,
This is an insane treatment,
Why do they take me for a human experiment?

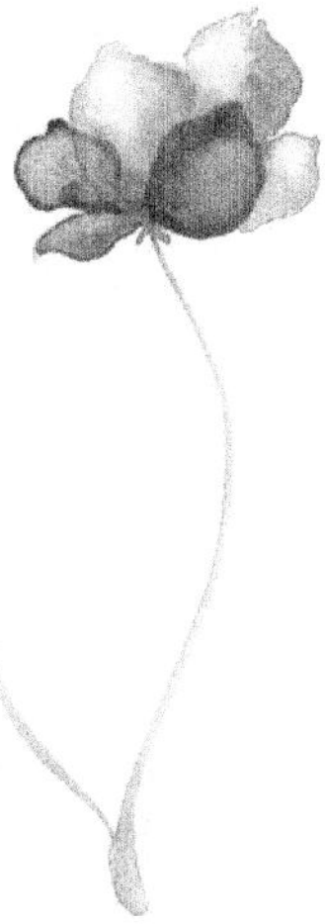

HUMANS CONCEIVED,

Born, in company
Isolation alien
To humanity
Craving intimacy
Primordial, innate
Denied relationships
Health deteriorates
Communication,
Reaffirms identity
Segregation damages
Emotional stability
Effects of separation
Well known
The Pandemic conveyed
Awareness to all homes
Psychologists warn of
Societal consequences,
Implications to well being,
And the Public purse

Copyright Margaret Karim

WHEN I WAS YOUNG

when I was young I never realized
the harsh reality of life
how to manage the internal conflict
of my pain & smiles
I was blinded by money& power
when I became mature& wise
jumped in a mad race with the crowd
never felt marooned even for a while
I never realized that one day I will
become week& fragile
will lose interest in things far which
I was once full of pride
friends& foes were lost one by one
like stars falling from the sky
kids to whom I nourished with my
blood, no more share my smile
In the twilight, the sun forget to bid me goodby
nightingale no more sings a song at night
moon rarely peep through the clouds
The rainy season comes&goes without noise
failed to awake my emotional desires
birds are chirping to make me smile
seeing my miserable plight
now I live with images of my past
feel jealous with the moonlit light
with fading colors of my blue sky
love has lost its original smiles
the sermon of Gita make me remind
alone you came to survive
alone you suffer to die
our relations are selfish& superficial

cracks are visible with my blue eyes
at fag end of my life I realize that my blind
love& expectations from near& dears
is the main reason for my pain& cry
in isolation, I am looking for peace of mind
searching bliss in the serenity of the night

Copyright Rattan Noori

IT WAS ISOLATION

It was isolation
But for me it was insulation
I was sort of staying away,
Sort of keeping away
From the merciless
And respectless
Virus
And in no way a minus,
From the misery
It carries in its history
And its history was not up too far
Like a star,
It's novel,
New, like some Novel,
But its effect was so debilitating
And devastating.
I went to hide from the unseen
To safeguard my being.
The long wait
That seemed too great,
The sameness
That almost ate up my plainness,
The one place
That nearly broke up my face,
Where some of the war I had to fight
In the battle that almost took my might.

1

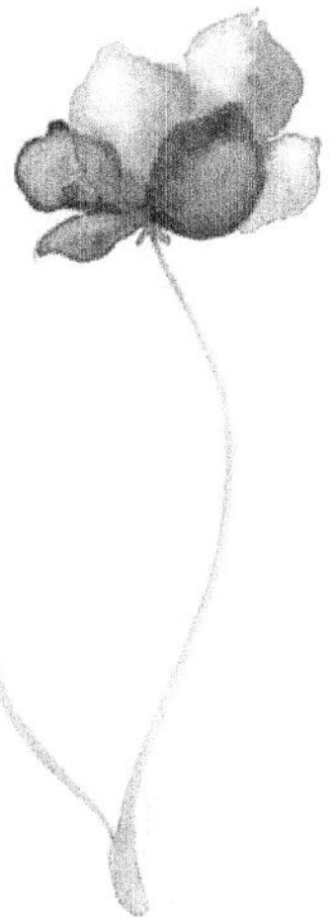

DISEASE OF THE YEAR

The emptiness of children, after a nice summer,
the emptiness of mothers, after waiting
for the children from abroad.
The horror of a new hard day,
covered in a variety of masks,
many of us are waiting for an answer
from the laboratory: positive or negative
Instilling fear in the bones,
forgetting for a moment your fears
and pain,
pain and fear grows more
for the fate of those closest to you,
dearest, youngest,
powerless get you most tired!
And someone hero? .. shouts naively
without respect for the other
I have no fear,
I don't have a mask, it's true, it's a lie. !!!! .....
Strange pains tighten the bones
and every vein of the nervous system.
You want to shout loud
Stupid ... ... what else?
Laughings, indecently, irony
and fear make him,
funny and interesting,?!
The days are coming, hard,
like black pearls around his neck,
like the heavy shackles of the long
China Wall.
The difference is, this wall you
do not want to see, feel, paint.

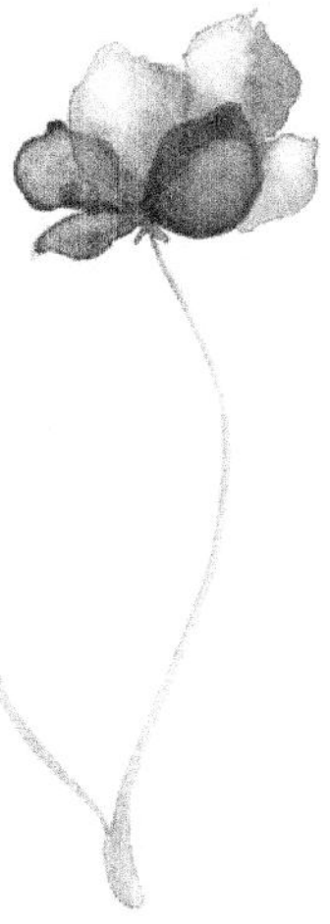

The sky is dark as the invisible
abyss deep, leaving traces
for fear of being infected,
crying over the lost fight
after a loved one.
Pain for months, you wish
to see loved ones
Covid 19 still exists and you wonder
Does it exist, you do not believe,
lie is.....
How long will you continue to,
until when?
Creating mistrust, spreading hatred
is our everyday life that lasts
without end ...

Copyright Sabaheta Eta Mersimi

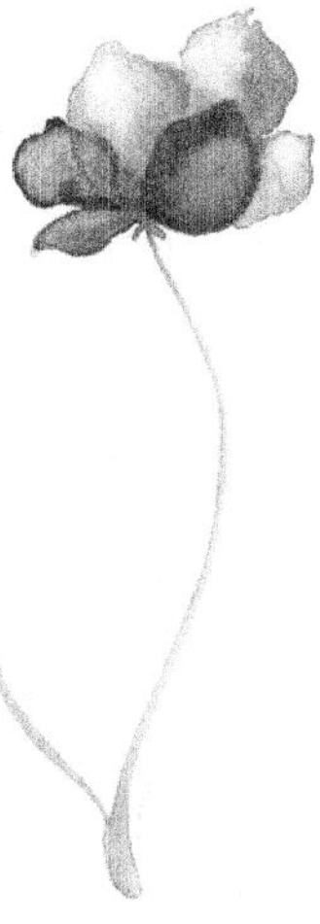

......FROST LANES...

Lost in echoes of thoughts
My heart at pause, soul frost
I pray for a day not to come
For in night Peace sweeps the harm
On my sleeves my face I hang
Am broken inside, peep and see the pain
When I smile, it hurts
I pretend to suit the walls
Unspoken words chained on my tongue
I once had a voice, now
Not even signs can awaken my neighbor
Can I talk to you
But two don't keep secrets
I wish to you
I would open up
Wrap up
And find me
But this isolation
Is sweet
It drives me

Copyright Taferi M. Simon

DEATHROW

The clock hanging on the wall,
His only companion in this world,
Chimes the twelfth note
In a strange melancholic tone.
He has survived another day.
Will he survive the next day?
On death row isolation is ominous,
Where you are told your life is a minus.
It has put many next in line to the gallows,
With no hope for tomorrow.
A Felon is on death row!
Drained of his wits, he heads to the gallows.
Isolation is not only for the Felon,
Nor is Deathrow made for him alone.
The Barber's wife condition worsened by the day;
Worse than others in the sickbay
For whose sake she was isolated,
But the Doctor's efforts seem belated.
Inch by inch, day by day
Draws her closer to her final day
Until on her death bed, she lay.
The heartbroken hides indoors to cry,
The Leppers flee into the caves to hide.
Lest he is sent to the prison cell,
The Debtor ignores his doorbell.
He has sold all there is to sell
To pay off some of his debt.
A Widow is in solitary confinement
Over her husband's entitlement...
Bit by bit these Folks drift towards deathrow
Where there is no tomorrow.

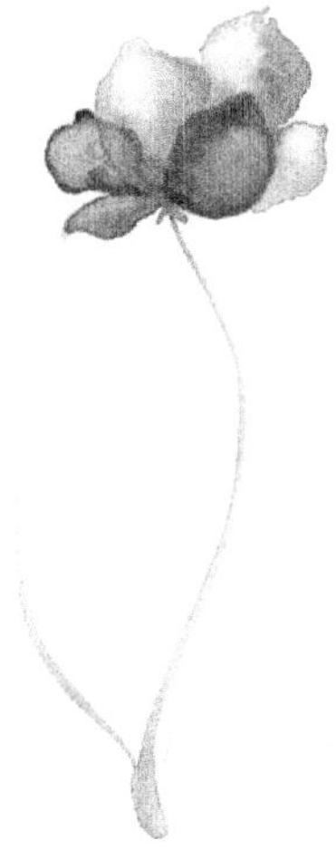

For so many seasons,
For so many reasons,
Many have suffered desolation.
More still languish in detention
In the guise of isolation,
Yet we look the other way
As we go on our way.

Copyright Samuel Oseyoma-Onoseri

ABANDONED

And I, shattered by my light
Who obliterated the past to make his future bright
Am I abandoned and thrown away only to lament?
Like a used napkin, once the beauty of a table and the whole ambiance
Now thrown to be taken by the rag pickers
I silently think, but yearning badly
Like the shed tail of a lizard, wiggling like a snake
Only wishes to get the soul of its life again
Grimy strains and aches seem to make soundless screams,
Silence creeps into my veins
Amongst the strangers of this new home
Obligated, I breathe for survival,
Being enveloped in a
deserted unknown-place,
My throbbing heart roasted, as a sun-burnt face.
Sanity lost in my tragedy
Words fail to express the deep-rooted gloom,
Heart still hopeful for that caring bloom.
Every incident of my replica's childhood, I have narrated
Now every corner of this home wants to meet you?
Will you come?

A SOLITAIRE

A solitaire diamond shining alone,
As if it is only making the king's crown thrive,
A pearl that is surviving alone in the shell,
As if nobody is ever going to touch,
A single wandering cloud,
Talking swiftly to the huge sky,
An unic orchids blooming freely,
Telling their tales of being clustered or dancing singly,
The midnight moon moving swiftly,
Spreading its breeze in divinity,
The shining bright sun,
Standing alone to spread the light,
An isolated caterpillar transforms in loneliness,
To a dynamic, beautiful butterfly,
Then, who says isolation is a curse?
When the mind is lost in useless thoughts,
When the world seems no more beautiful and divine,
Peculiar emptiness hover in the mind,
You forget to hold your ambitions high,
The battles are lost, before even being fought,
Unworthiness surrounding the days and nights,
Confusion becomes the only companion,
Rebelling within to prevent your true essence to shine the brightest,
Pause, let the self flourish the best,
Utilize, the "me-time" to the fullest,
Trust, in your vibes to the richest,
Never allow loneliness to make you the weakest,
Find the solace in the isolation,
To retreat the self with joy and abundance.

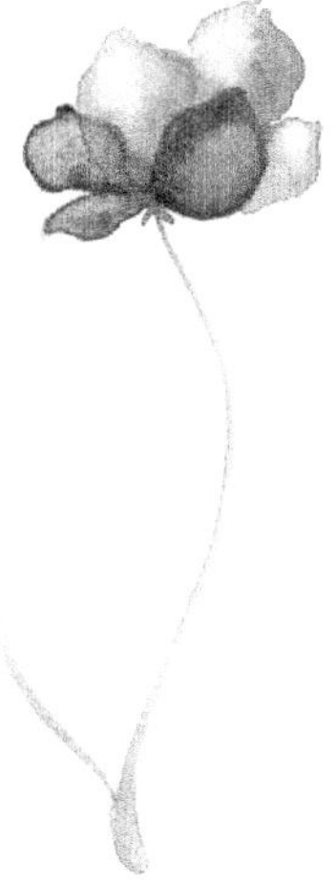

SAD TRUTH

In this fake world full of crowds
The old man lives alone, rarely he speaks aloud
His wrinkled skin, blurred vision
Make him remembered he has crossed so many seasons
I have been seeing him since childhood
In my childhood, he cut and collected wood
All-day and night he worked hard and honestly
To feed the members of his family
He lived in a small house near the meadow
Long trees surrounded it, they provided with a shadow
A cold breeze blew during summers
The silence broke with Brooke's murmurs
Every villager loved him for his benevolent nature
He exchanged a smile whenever he met with others
He had many children whom he sent to school and studied
Poverty never stopped him from making them educated
All of his children are now well established
But they, unfortunately, forgot about their past
The old man remains alone in his hut
He is never unhappy with them but blames his fate
His wife had already departed a few years ago
He is alone in the ocean like life's shore, without an inflated ego
Counting his moments to leave this earth
He knows very well now that he has no worth
Yes, this is the life he accepted
He is a good man, so never regretted
He knows that this is life
Amidst the struggles, we have to strife
Loneliness wraps us in old age
We have to live like a bird that is inside a cage
Blurred vision restrains us from seeing the colorful world
People seldom come to us to exchange words

The old man isn't the only one who is isolated at this age,
But it's a common scenario for all the people in this stage
Life is really mysterious, where people don't know about their destiny
People live alone within their crowded family

IN A CUL DE SAC

Life moved on with a velocity
Didn't give me time to think
There was no stopover,
I reached the finale in a wink.
Inside me, I'm a child but
Others treat me with respect,
I'm naughty, romantic, and coquettish
With this crowd, I don't connect.
I walked on unmindful
Of clouds and sunshine,
All of a sudden I'm sidetracked
While many people are inline
I don't find any change in me
Except for some certain wrinkles,
My lips retained their smile,
And eyes did not lose twinkle.
How come! I am so different now?
When did I become a senior?
I, still, partake in contests with a
Young heart as earlier.
Some friends of my age
Have gone to heavenly abode,
It's unfair that they have left
I am so lonely on life's road.
Where did I lose my way?
My mountain trek, my green valley
I was bang on a challenging path,
How did I land in a blind alley?
I cannot show anybody my
Helplessness or my pain,
So what if the horizon is cloudy

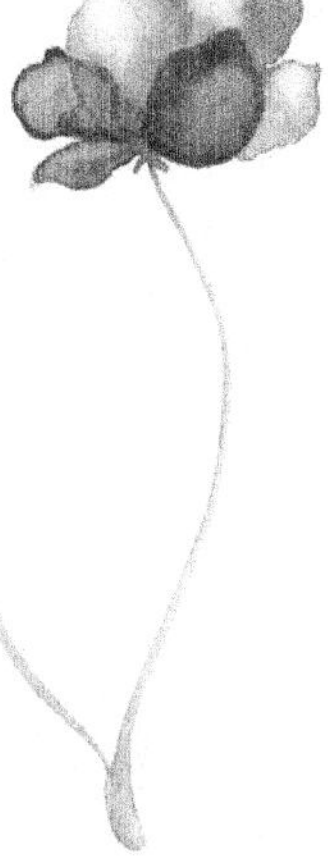

I must feign to enjoy the rain.
A superannuated person, cut off
From life's important quest,
Finds solace in memories,
Secure in heart's treasure chest

Copyright Sudha Dixit

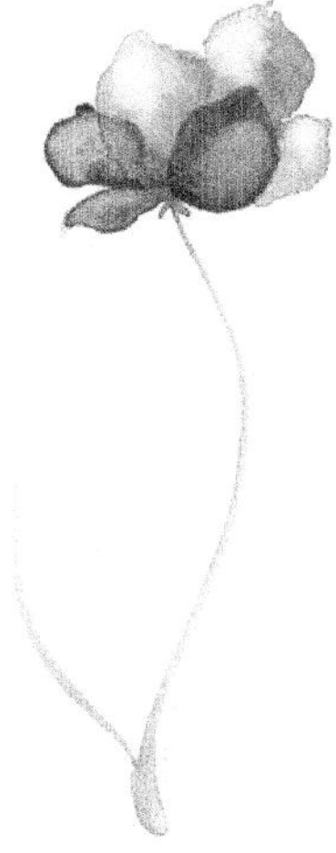

THE FEARS OF OLD AGE

Loneliness and isolation,
Are the greatest fears
Of people growing old,
They need someone sincere,
Someone with a heart of gold
To look after them.
Old age is never a problem,
When you live in a big family,
With children, grandchildren,
Brothers and sisters,
Aunts and uncles living together,
Under one roof.
But now in a nuclear family,
When children leave the nest,
You are all alone,
Your offspring faraway,
And you feel helpless
And how do you deal with loneliness?
How do you deal with the depressing darkness,
Which surrounds you?
Get some good books,
Find some good music,
Watch some movies fantastic,
Find some activity,
To keep away your anxiety,
The best gift you can give your loved ones,
Is being independent,
Living cheerfully,
And dying peacefully,
Without troubling anyone,

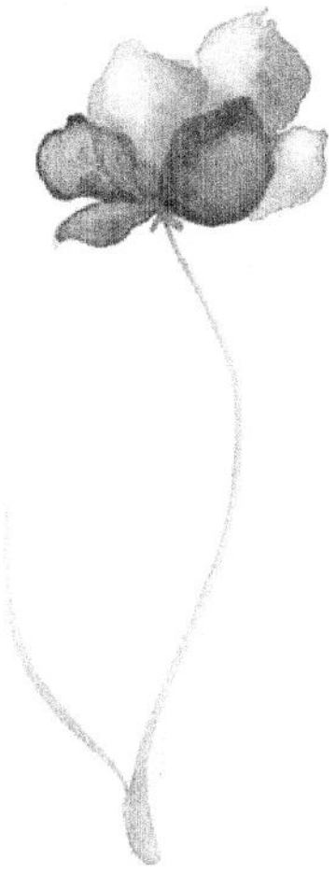

Going into the unknown future,
Courageously,
As if it is a wonderful adventure.

Copyright Vasudha Pansare

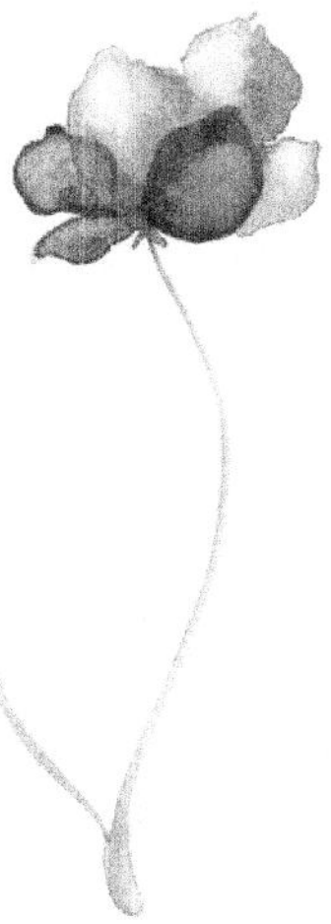

SOLITUDE

Solitude is a lady
With dual personality
Looked upon both with
Negativity and positivity
To some, it is hated
To others addictive
One can either feel free
Or can be a captive.
It is a place where most
Beautiful arts are a breed
Inventions, innovations
From its womb are birthed
Where maniacs' evil schemes
Are hatched, incubated
Scene of a gruesome crime
Carried out at its best.
Solitude sustains
The deepest loneliness
When your wounds and scratches
Throb and ache the most
Yet it's also when you taste
The sweetest ecstasies
In the loveliest illusion
You'll love to drown, get lost.
Mayhem and unrest
Go hand in hand with crowds
Solitude is a haven
Away from this menace
Yet crowds could be a cure
To most of life's malaise
Alone we could free all our tears

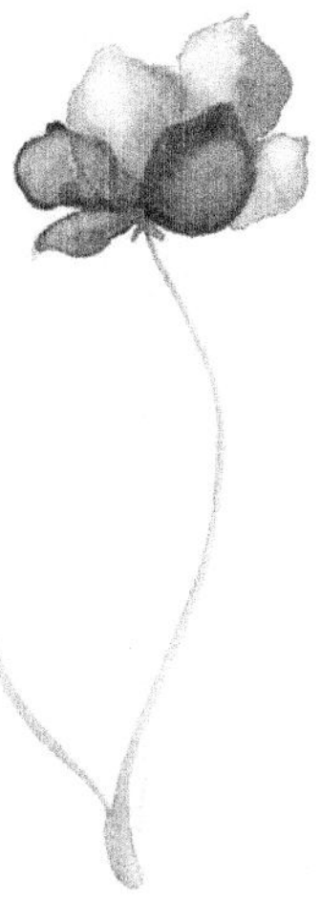

And so could sob out loud.
Man is no stranger
To the ways of solitude
Most of us were conceived
And were born all alone
It's only while alive
When we have a companion
But inside our own grave
We will not have a mate.

Copyright Myrna E. Tejada

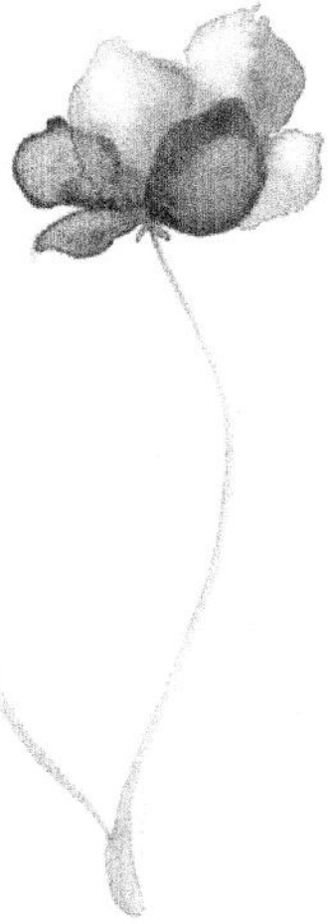

THE NIGHT SPILLS

The night spills pitch-black ink hastily,
The weary moon trudges up the sky,
All alone she has to accomplish her journey,
Despite the overwhelming darkness she has to try.
The breeze sings a sharp chilly song,
A lone bird waiting alone in her nest,
Her soft cheep conveys a need to belong,
Single life seems to be an onerous test.
A world of emptiness within the house,
A solitary soul, heartfelt of desolation,
Void echoing between the walls arouse melancholy,
A moment spans into eternity in isolation.

HIS LIFE WAS VOID

His life was void; aimlessly he wandered in quandary,
Was he a lonesome, or did he wrongly fix his boundary?
His eyes transfixed in vacant space, yearning for a flight
Yet, gripped in isolation were his days and the nights.
Seeking the bliss of 'Solitude' that evaded him
He buried deeper into social media's dark abyss;
Fighting his alter ego, isolated from one and all
He found solace in on-line chats, his greatest pitfall!
Isolation had crept deep, his life in existential obsolescence;
The fall came eons ago, in years of his adolescence,
Dragging through life, in pretense with family and friends
Would he be out of the woods, or would he feign ignorance?
Affected by low self-esteem perennially in stress
Aloofness in his life had caused all the distress.
Despite a lovely wife who was the love of his life,
He isolated himself in body and mind, entangled in strife.
So enveloped in a midlife crisis he sailed across the seas seven,
Venturing out on a solo trip in search of a peaceful haven;
On a remote island he was seeking, the bliss of solitude
But alas! It was not to be, loneliness overtook his certitude.
But fate had different plans as he began his lonely sojourn
From the pangs of deprivation, a yearning for love was born.
As the morning sun fell on his eyes, he saw a beautiful dame
She lay bare on the sand, beside a boat's wrecked frame!
As they spent some time together, cupid joined the session
Both embarked on a solo trip, gripped by veiled isolation!
Loving each other's company, they forgot their lasting woes
No rescue teams for them, was Pandemic their friend or foe?
A slew of events that followed saw the Pandemic wane
But the two were rid of isolation, their trips not in vain;
That morning a chopper on a rescue mission had so landed

And the damsel and her paramour were caught red-handed!
His isolation though was not by design but by sheer default
Alas! It was too late to recommence, his infidelity was at fault!
It was all his doing, for some unscrupulous recreation!
In the shadow of Pandemic, he found an unholy union!
As he returned from 'Isolation', he was glad to be back home
Strange are the ways of the world, his wife had left his home!
She had left for her destiny, and it would cost him, dear,
'Isolation' hounded him again, with bleeding hearts and tears!

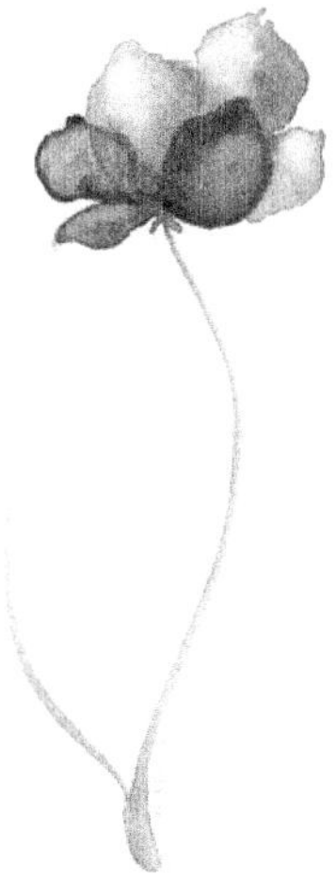

"OSTRACIZED"

Strange and new growing disease
hovering like a swarm of bees
freely crossing international boundaries with ease
creating havoc chaos and lockdown
Alas! in the 21st century.
She is fighting in her mask, gloves, and gears
taking care of those smitten by virus and fears
she continues to fight day and night, risking her life
suddenly she coughed to surpass pneumonia
combating for her own life.
In her war, she felt losing to contagion
isolation is the cure for the Pandemic
will there be a few to send her off
on her last journey.

LONE TWILIGHT

Winged Time moved so fast,
Snatching away precious moments,
When the innocent childhood went by,
When was the youth taken away?
Slipping like sand from the fingers,
Only the good bad memories linger,
Slowly the friends left me alone,
For who will love a sad old man?
Where are the children that I bore,
Made of my flesh and gore.
Like old Tithonus I stand to rot,
Waiting for angels to take me along.
Birds fly overhead in flocks,
Honeybees hum a chorus in tune,
Flowers bloom in blossoms bright,
Why am I the only one left alone,
While the twilight is almost gone?

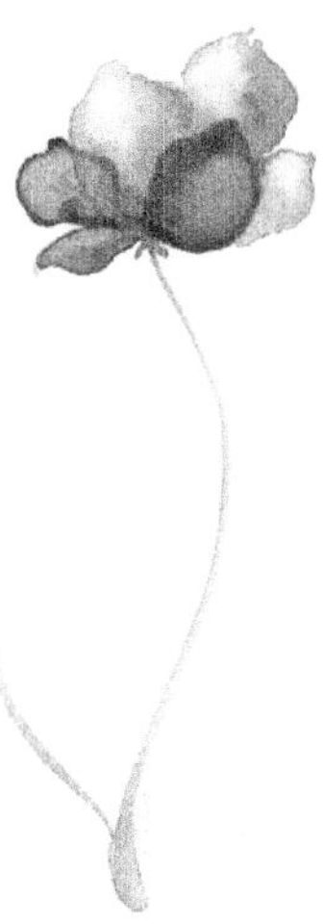

WITHIN ISOLATION

It's a lonely thought being in isolation
Although so sad within your mind much with action
Because the silence dictates loud to your notion
Silence reminds you to be in great devotion
Of something and somewhat is odd to emotion
A note that gets into you to say orison
Within the silence, God will hear you with your assertion
As you believe in God your prayer He can't shun
He will hear you loud and clear with that assumption
You'll not feel alone, your conscience will clear the burden
Upon your creed will get into your emotion
And to know yourself being in isolation

OLD AGE ISOLATION

Away from neighborhood
Away from a social gathering
He stays in isolation
Within four walls of a room.
Gone are those beautiful days
When he was young and strong
A nice family he stayed with
Also colleagues and gatherings.
After education children flew away
To far off places for livelihood
Life partner left for heaven
After a short illness soon.
Friends and neighbors hardly visit
Children never get time to come
He stays as an isolated one
Home has become a dungeon now.
Old and weak as he is
Unable to do all his works
Life has become a miserable
Helpless he has become now
Such are the lives of old people
Several places in this world
Now an ever-growing problem
Must be addressed in a civilized world.

THE LIVING FREE

The Unreal Man as earth incarnate,
evolving around the soul, bodied
and revolving around the Absolute ;
To be the Real Man
One innately thirsts to be resolute.
As a slave of situation, problem, idea ......
one is earthly ;
To be separated from them is heavenly.
Body and mind as whirlpools, ever-changing
Nevertheless, one listens to OHM humming.
Betwixt habits, bad and good, one is crucified,
But the good desires to be patiently nurtured.
Lives-long cleansed dirt make one a free human ;
But to be a soul, free,
Needs to have self-restraint as psycho design.
Fearlessness for limitlessness one has to cultivate ;
Narrowed finite individuality needs to be broad and finite.
I and my limit perennially do erode
with the aware mind or not;
The finite fire's spark for everybody secretly does wait.
Self -made wrongs need to be excavated
Creation as hell perception from earthly eyes needs to be removed.
The Living Free, Fearless and Perfect does have true isolation ;
One as a Unit Existence has pure self-realization.

Copyright by Dr. Amiya Rout

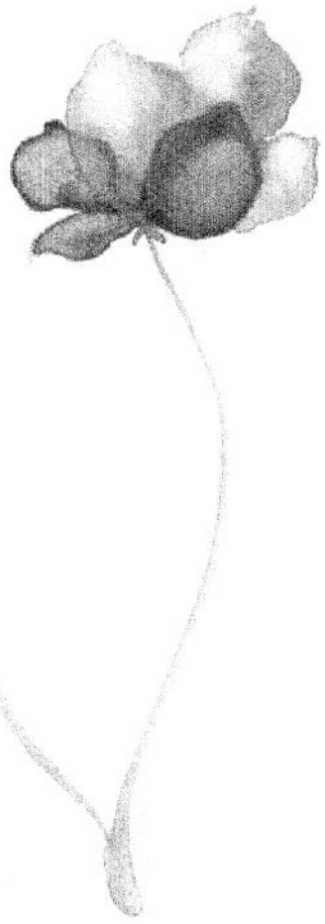

I FEEL PRESSURE IN MY CHEST,

I feel pressure in my chest,
I'm missing oxygen,
I miss the hug,
I miss the honest handshake,
I miss the crowd on public transportation,
carefree children in the park,
I miss everything
and most of all freedom.
I don't accept isolation,
I don't accept the cage,
because the window glass,
it cannot replace heaven.

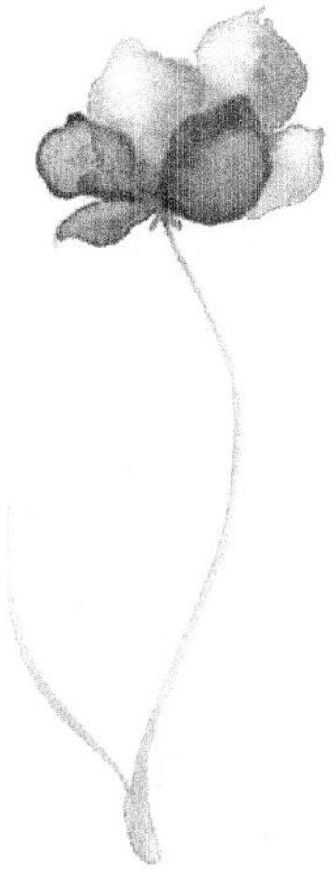

TRAPPED CARD LETTER

When I said, "I want silence"
I didn't mean to go away
I just needed time to be me
I never meant to scream
Pushed to the edge
I couldn't take the fall
Too risky for my kin
You closed your ears to me
Shielded yourself from my cautious words
You brought winter when I was at my darkest
With a fixed face, you kept my rays from you
You made me look dark when I offered the light
Embarrassment was the joke around me
I was never spared like world war two
You left your mark on me as if you would return
Closed yourself to me, all I had was false hope
I let you go every time I was hurt
But you never let me as if you cared
Showing compassion as I walked out
Making me the cause like I didn't care
I let your deeds slide
But mine was at my neck
Like forgiveness was extinct
"What changed?" you never told
Isn't garden a place of peace
So why does it hurt
Every time we pass by?
Is it me or is it you, I need time to think?
First day at work
My mind was in yesterday
With too much niceness

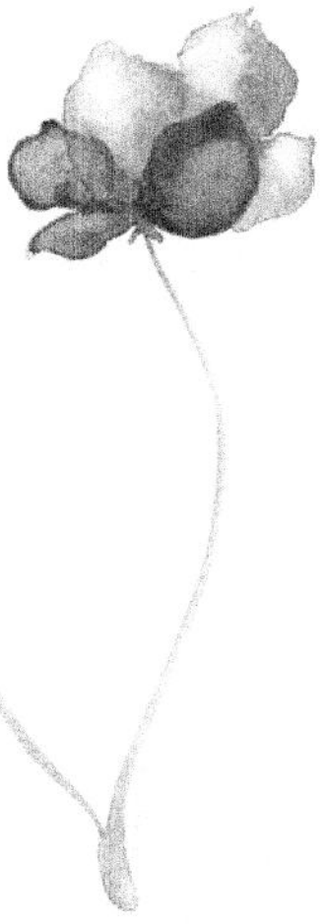

The noise triggered the mark
At home, no one could speak to me
Like a charity case, I was like the donation
No one asked why or wished to know.
And just like that, I was left alone.
I didn't ask for things to go this way
"Blue scars to turned against me."
Why did I not listen from the start?
In a way "I brought this to myself."

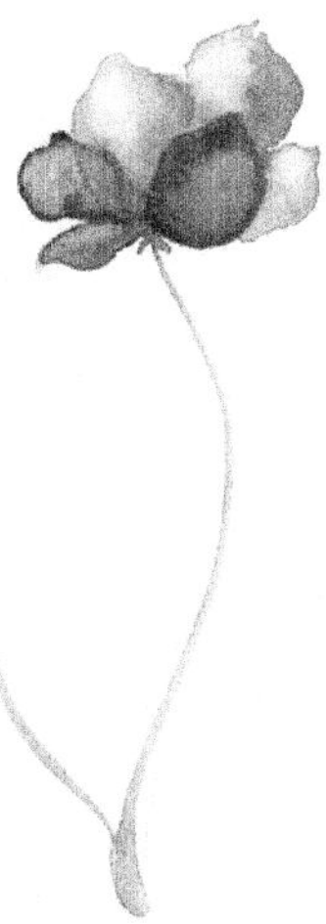

BEING ALONE IS INEVITABLE

I went to my room, I chose to be alone
I am a writer and sometimes find a need for seclusion
Can I write a better poem amidst conversing people?
Oh, it's a regret that I will lose my attention.
Isolation is not always good, it is an accepted opinion
No man is an island, a common adage
In life, one always needs a caring companion
Living alone by oneself is a curse draining one's emotion.
Love begets love, so with another one must get along
Love is not a word; it is a feeling quite strong
It is something shared by two loving persons
One can't possibly express it if he lives in isolation.
When I lost my husband, for a while I lived all alone
No one is with me to assist me at home
No one to hug me; no one to hold my hand when walking in the mall
For days and months, I cried in isolation but now I have moved on.

BEYOND ISOLATION

How ironical! Man is looking for life on Mars!
While back on Earth human history is in scars;
Humanity was ashamed as the man turned inhuman
In deep indignation discover the disdainful man
Jails and Prisons to silence men in Isolation!
The Cellular Jail in Andamans, a historical shame
A sordid reminder of atrocities inflicted with disdain
In solitary confinement men incarcerated for life
Freedom fighters consigned to the "black waters"
Voices were silenced and limbs locked in fetters.
Many were condemned to such misery and Isolation,
But some managed to steer through deeper desolation
Like Marco polo, the Explorer imprisoned in isolation,
'Description of the World', his memoirs were written
With prison-mate 'Rustichello' in collaboration!
Who can ever forget Mahatma Gandhi in prison?
Lost his dear wife, while in solitary isolation;
"My experiments with truth" was written in jail,
Showing us the right way to fight and not fail,
He won freedom for India, with health so frail!
Pandit Nehru wrote his book, "Discovery of India",
From the four walls of prison devoid of media,
Martin Luther King too was lodged in Alabama Jail
But like all great men, undeterred by his isolation,
He wrote of civil rights for the American nation!
We all might at some stage go into self-isolation
Perhaps due to lack of company or indignation;
Let us not lose time and precious moments then
But beat freckles and frowns and pick up the pen,
Creating 'Books and Anthologies', with determination.

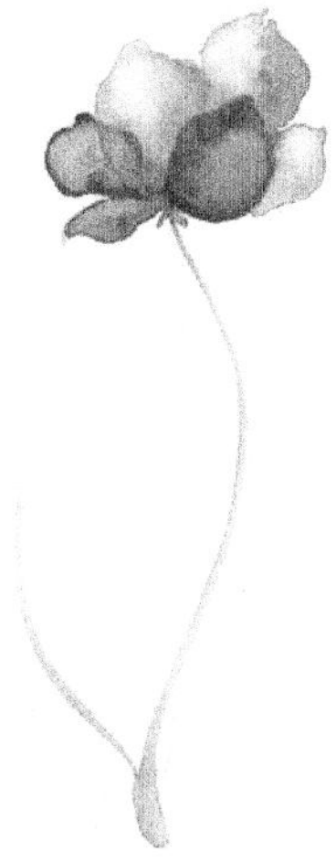

Copyright Jyotirmoy Ghosal

BLESSING IN DISGUISE

For some, isolation is a blessing in disguise
Enabling them to meet their own-self which is forgotten otherwise
For some isolation seems to be a curse
Finding their life so difficult, without having someone to nurse
Isolation to them, seem to be depressing
It leads them to a mental condition that is so suppressing
Blessed are those souls who are isolated and solivagant
It's in their deep meditation, such virtues are experienced
Those finding bliss in their solitude and isolation
Only experience Supreme's revelation
As absolute solace resides only in loneliness
Blissful moments are only then to experience
In the chaos of this life, one is all alone deep inside
Loneliness is one's company that accompanies one side by side
Wish all find solace in their isolation, wish all have peace
In this world of suffering may all live at ease

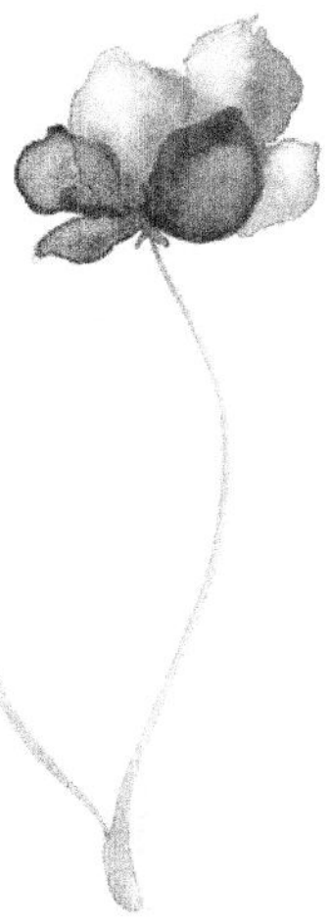

OLDEN AGE

Olden age, are golden days of life,
As good as a double-edged knife,
Some enjoy peace, some face strife,
Largely miss partners, especially their wives.
Morning time passes pretty quickly,
Noon challenges as sunshine brightly,
Evenings are reserved for the gang strictly,
The night times in isolation are prickly.
Friends are the key to survive each day,
Together they keep their worries at bay,
A few talented ones, continue to play,
Walking and talking they move away.
To maintain good health, they dwell together.
Years of togetherness makes them pals forever,
Being dependent on outsiders, they prefer never
Promising each other's companionship, they move over
Everyone understands it's tough to stay in isolation,
Being dependent, there will be a feeling of obligation,
Ailments in the company add to existing frustration,
Being in a friend's company, they prefer salvation.

ISOLATED IN ISOLATION

The inky onyx clouds hovered over his head,
Not a single soul to speak to as if all are dead,
As the pandemic hit the pervasive wide world all over,
He finds himself cocooned to his house, looking for a clover!
Every day the same routine, not a person to visit his home,
Entangled in the mundane routines and the stress level foams,
No newspaper to visit his door or the milk packets are thrown carelessly,
With an unshaven beard, he looks from the window listlessly!
Today will someone arrive with a trolley of fruits and vegetables?
What if there is a power cut or a thunderstorm that snaps the cables?
The air of uncertainty constantly nags his head and makes him nervous,
But being a man, he doesn't portray his tears lest they consider him callous!
With a bold persona, he carries on with his daily vagaries,
Tries hard to brush away the pains and agonizing memories,
Occasionally his son gives a call or a text from his friend,
To his drab world some times of happy moments they lend.
Time passes from creating food from the meager supplies,
Borrowing some moments, looking at the pictures of his granddaughter he sighs,
Some globules of tears lace his wrinkled eyes,
He tries to evade them by thinking they are just pretty lies!
In the spaces between his house from the bedroom, kitchen to the drawing-room,
Loneliness crawls at his walls and he cleans them with a broom,
Reminiscing good old days when disaster looms,
Somehow thinking of his bereaved wife, flowers bloom!
He gathers the dust-laden cobwebs formed over the walls,

Despair attaches to his body as he ruminates and recalls,
As the news blares on his television of the horrendous death crawls,
He is unsure as his head spins and he wonders what is going to befall?
Isolation has taken a toll on his health,
Craving to have a human look, he no longer needs wealth,
He is habituated to the sounds of silence and stealth,
Praying to God for the well-being gives him all the strength!
Years of rattles but now the conversation has reduced to naught,
His iridescent aura has deteriorated with silence fraught,
His crinkled face desires for a mate and an ardent company he sought,
But this pandemic, he realized the priorities that it brought!
Old age has unfurled a plethora of problems,
Webbed in the cataclysmic diseases, his frail heart shows the autumn,
Anybody listening to his wails and silent ramblings?
Fortunately, his son came and rescued him from his continuous fumbling!

Copyright Amrita Lahiri Bhattacharya

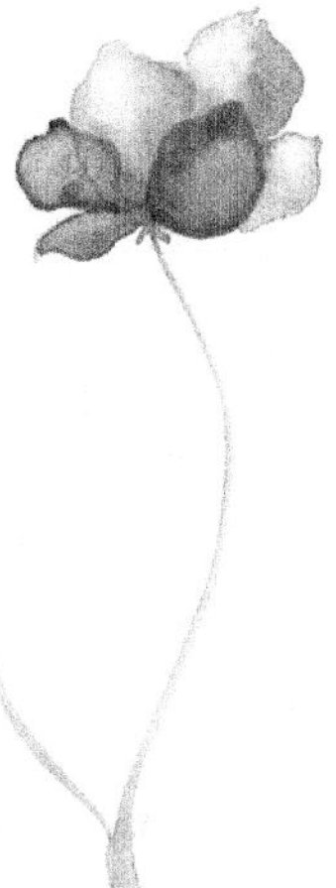

ENJOY OLD AGE WITH GRACE

Is old age a cage?
All scared of old age
Full Isolation, deprivation
Let's face it with courage.
It's time when the heart is young
The body gets wrinkle, high strung
How time slips, we want to age with grace
Welcome each day with a happy face.
In twilight years, in peace, want to live
I had some property in my name
Child forced me to sell property, playing games
Son, daughter-in-law enjoy life to the brim.
Son is a son till he brings a wife
Daughter a daughter all her life
Sit in a closed room in isolation
But her family enjoys my destroyed mental peace, my destruction.
Lost all contacts with friends
Have no money to spend
I want to travel, live, smile
All want me to cry, still, I find joy in small things of life.
My friends have departed to another side
With relatives, lost all touch, contact
Lose track of days and time
Try to hear music in the air, and the sun's chimes.
Staring at walls, pondering, I sit
Sweaters I love to knit
No one in the family likes to wear
All wear ready-made warm gear.
In old, sweet memories, I float, glorify
Stories Granddad's told us as a lullaby
Folk tales of the village across borders

Which I will not visit see in this life.
Sit enjoy, Isolation writing my book
Folk stories, as Granddad's told us as a bedtime story
For children to read enjoy, moral tales, across the country.

EMPTINESS

I find my self in an empty room,
Being locked and nowhere else to go.
When I looked around, and all I can see,
Is an incredible and empty space.
I realized, did anyone notice I am here?
Did anyone concern to think about me?
It's very hard dealing with the hurt,
I feel like no one's there during all my sorrow.
I have nothing left to lose, and nothing left to gain,
I fight through those days, with no one at my side.
All my days are terrible, dark, stormy, cold and grey,
Emptiness keeps growing so quickly as I slowly fade away.
If I broke down and lost all my control,
Would you come and save me from this empty room?
I have no courage left to go out in this sphere,
No helping hand to pull me to free myself out.
I am sad,
I am lonely,
I am irrational,
I am complicated.
For a while, I try so hard to fight away my doubts,
So far away, I assumed they are already gone.
But I think nothing lasts forever,
The pains, darkness, tears, always find their way,
To come and bring me to the empty side of myself,
That I am trying to fight to get over and free myself out.

I'VE YEARNED FOR YOU FOR SO LONG

Isolation
I've yearned for you for so long
For what seemed to be my whole life,
Many days I bore ground teeth
And fought my instincts to hide,
But life got in the way and forced my presence.
Never being truly happy,
And itching for what I couldn't have.
Now I find myself amid bliss
Yet I reflect on the past with envy
I look to the future with hope,
And stuck here alone
Amongst all the wishes I once had
Buried by my regrets.

ENJOYING THE GREYS

He glances at the grey clouds,
and feels their grief as soon,
the clouds will be empty.
The gentleman empathizes,
thanks to his grey hair of experience.
He is grateful to God
for bestowing him with a blessed, long life
and a good speed of grasping grey cells.
His wrinkled face has a grace of wisdom,
earned during many years of living …
But, of late, he feels isolated and aloof,
The veteran is happy under his home's roof.
He prefers to live alone, but he is not forlorn,
He talks when someone traverses to understand his verses.
He has a pact with solitude,
solitude is his accepted fact.
He does not shun human company,
at the same time, he is not desperate
to enjoy a social symphony.
This memory collector finds colors of nostalgia in black and white
photos and memories,
The practical person, in him, also loves a prism of present colors
and looks forward to future hues and shades.

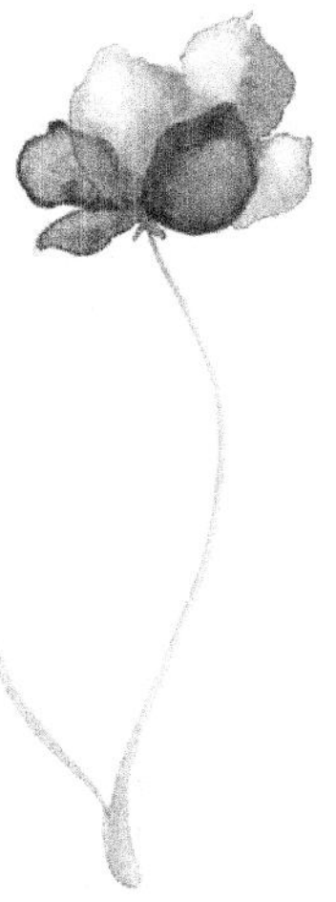

"UNTRODDEN ALLEY"

Everyone left him
broke all the ties
He was left alone
isolated and lone
His riches were his sole companions
What happened?
what caused all this?
It's the mistakes of the past
that brought him to the brim!
His children didn't like to see his face
his spouse too left him in a haze.
He was the person of peace
was provoked by some misdeeds
He wanted to pluck even the stars for his kids, but destiny had something else written.
After a bad night when he woke,
he felt as if it was a nightmare.
Nothing was left with him all vacated and clean.
He knew the way he wanted things
to happen was not in his hands.
HE is the master and he knows what and why he has planed
He never called them to be with him again,
He accepted his life as what came his way.
With no interest anymore in anything he lost all his deals,
now he was back to, from where he started with glee!
Still, his eyes are plopped on the alley
untrodden, unknown
With the hope that his loved ones will show up once more.
His weary eyes are still waiting for the dawn of his life
When everyone will forgive him for his mistakes and
He will once again be happy and fine.

ISLAND OF ISOLATION

Paucity of time smothers
Relationships, understanding,
Shipwrecked I stand marooned
On a lonely island.
Here, mornings and evenings
Weave a song of monotony,
Splashes of life break
On the shore of tedium.
The mainland entices,
Invites to humdrum
Yet, another loneliness bites
As each one is cocooned in a box of his own.
The lonesome island
Isolated, lies destitute
While the mainland moves
At a supersonic speed.
Old age stares forlornly
The ship of youth
Wrecked in the waves of time
Sighs in the despair of isolation.
Memories old, neatly arranged
In the albums of the past
Heightens the pain
Of being alone, companionless.
Will, there be a tsunami
That will flood the island
And become the vast ocean
Does that encircle it?
Or the paean of life
Sing on in solitude
And winter of life pass into

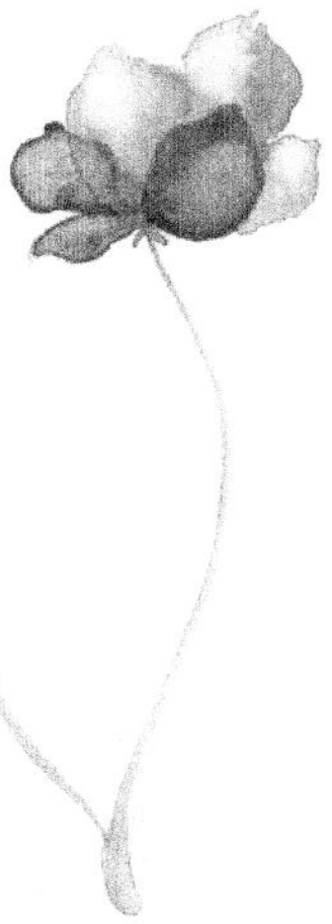

A quarantine of obscurity?
Or will the nightfall come in stealthily
Cloaked in detachment
Tuned to an elegy
Leading to the final retirement?

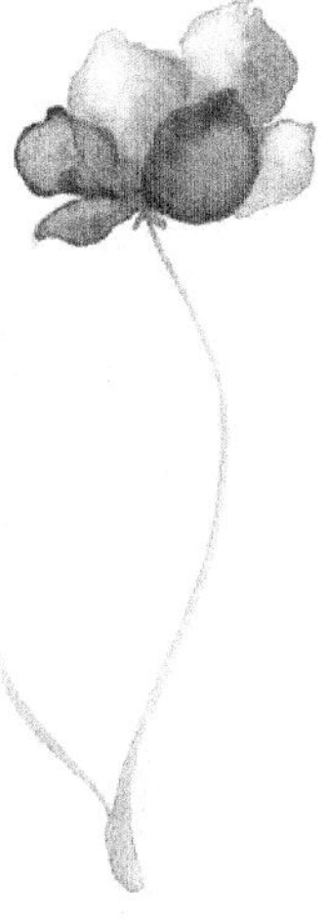

DYING ALONE

After the death of his wife.
His life turned upside down.
His children have settled abroad.
He isolated himself from people in near relations.
That made him feel more lonely and pathetic.
He denied confronting when anyone came to meet him.
His health deteriorated day by day.
He glimpsed outside from an apartment window.
Watched people struggling over the urgencies of life.
He missed his wife more and more as days passed by.
He didn't talk about his feelings with anyone.
With declining health,
He felt the loss of his independence.
No one to support him.
The home was a place for him,
Packed with memories of his beloved wife.
It was a huge part of his identity.
He feared losing people in his life.
His fears got bigger,
As they were not vocalized.
Companionship is much needed in older age.
His wife was her best companion.
After his retirement,
He spent most of his time with her.
They enjoyed listening to songs on the radio.
They cooked meals and played board games together.
By sharing, caring, laughing, and learning
They were aging happily.
But sudden demise of his wife,
Changed things in his life.
Wrapped in a prickly blanket of sadness,

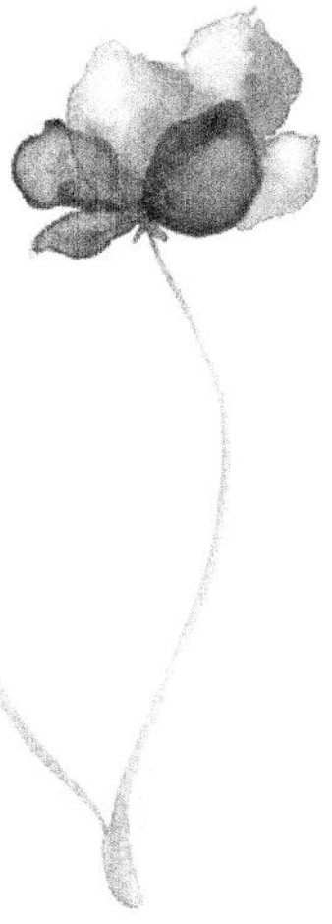

He thought all about his isolation.
He waited for the right time to die.
His last wish,
To see his children before he died.
Alas! he died without seeing them.
Dying alone was the saddest thing to think about.

Copyright Hema Mordani

ISOLATION: INUNDATED IN THY CAMARADERIE

And things start changing all of a sudden after the turmoil,
Existence a barren heath now, once life's fertile soil
People leave, memories weave
A web of images lost over time's trepidations
Waves of waning wistfulness pervade
Whirlpool of nebulous nostalgia
At the fag end of the day the temple bells ring
I sit back in seclusion watching the fading streaks of crimson in the west
Leaving behind the world to me after the day's fest
Isolation ignominy at times, a catastrophic curse desperado
Dejected in dolor I wait for the unknown to make its advent
To my tortuous silence, I give vituperative vent
I try to wake up my dormant illusions
I try to tear apart my tears of delusions
I wait for thy Light to arrive to deliver me from stagnation
Friends, kith, and kin I lost in transition
On a moonlit night, the Great Bear insight
The starry firmament smiling at my pitiable plight
Familiar voices reverberate in vibrant tones
Amphitheater of faces floating amidst tempests blown
The fairs, fests of unfathomable glee all gone by
The dejected host seated on the dining table now a bit shy
The guests used to arrive with greetings sweet
The assemblage inundated in enthusiastic meet
That used to be a long time back, probably years ago
When the mortal frame was agile, senility kept away from the show
I walk upon the bewildered paths of wilderness
Some say I shall die in harness
Whatever be the case after the race is run
Amidst the jovial joy gone and the present glum

I dwell in detrimental despair without a soul nigh
Loneliness is not solitude exclaims cognizance with a sigh
I had my days, I lost them all
The isolated self doesn't quite enthrall
I try to live with my album of assimilations
The occasional light seems to penetrate through the creaking doors and perforations
The inevitable hour approaches fast with conviction
I pack up and line up without the slightest dereliction
Of duty assigned to me by Providence supreme
To live, thrive, and die alone with esteem.

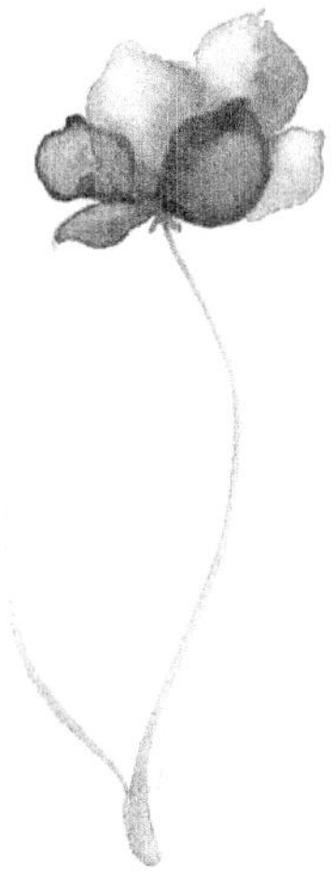

THE HOURS OF ISOLATION

The hours of Isolation are blissful
for some
Yet for many, the hour of isolation is a constant challenge
They constantly wish, to be united with their near and dear ones
Every hour of isolation drags
them further into a dark pit
Constant fear and emptiness,
only becomes their companions
Every hour, they dwell in constant
pain
They shed their tears in agony to
meet the dear ones
This isolation is a severe punishment
Nothing comes and nothing
goes out for an unknown fear
There is a terrible emptiness, surrounding them each hour
The seasons come and seasons
go, but those in isolation, are never exposed to these
It appears, like the hours of isolation have frozen the memories
The hollow, vacuum and destitute, are the only
gifts for those who have to live
in isolation?
They deserve to be united with
their loved ones
Oh, dear! don't confine such
free lives in caged isolation
Free the birds, free those who
live constantly in the fear of being
confined
Give them new hope, by freeing
them from the hours of isolation

This separation, this life in chains, is a sin if extended for many days.
Sing songs, embrace your dear ones, spend time with them regularly
Please watch out for they need
to live under the free sky regularly.

Copyright Aditi Lahiry

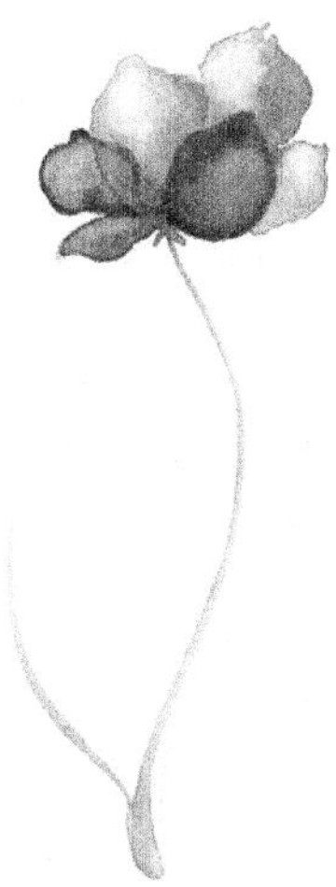

EVERYDAY AS I WAKE UP,

I look at my window,
To look up in the sky,
To watch the sunrise.
As my days go by,
Waiting for a new day,
To come & let me smile,
In my room that I have been lockdown.
What a world of mine.
What pity am I...
Being here,
Alone & just waiting for days to pass by.
Looking around,
How beautiful is my playground,
The birds that flying by,
The flowers that bloom nearby.
But now can't reach them by hand,
Can't be nearby them.
For I am here,
In my room alone & just looking by.
How I wish,
This will be done.
So I can be free again,
Like the birds flying up high.

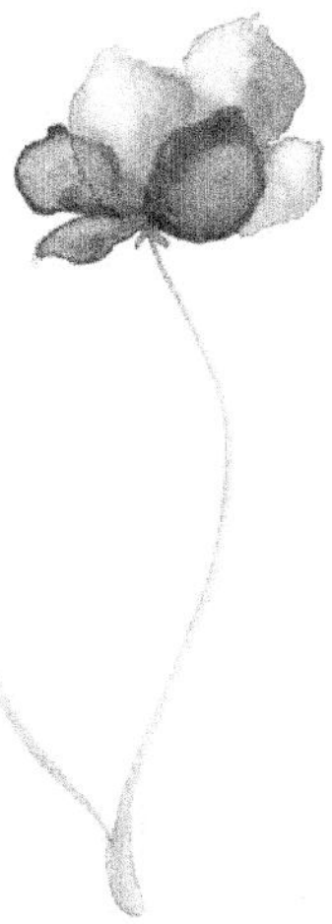

OLD AGE

Old age comes with many health issues,
Do not throw elders like used tissues.
You're at youth, enjoying whatever is 'cause,
they gave up their youth without a clause.
Appreciate them, spend time, and laugh
Include them, don't enjoy on their behalf.
Enjoyment doubles with togetherness,
children will also love elated happiness.
You're at the doorstep of old age,
your children will put you on the same page.
Make your today glorious, awaiting beautiful tomorrow.
no isolation, company of grandchildren, no sorrow.
The worst scenario in the home is that of isolation,
A person can die, before his time, given a situation.
Appreciation, applaud, laughter is the spice of a happy family.
With the elders of the family included in every celebration
mutually.
Don't let them sit alone, pondering,
'was I good in giving up my youth for you.'
Make them laugh, merry, enjoying
together having together the brew.

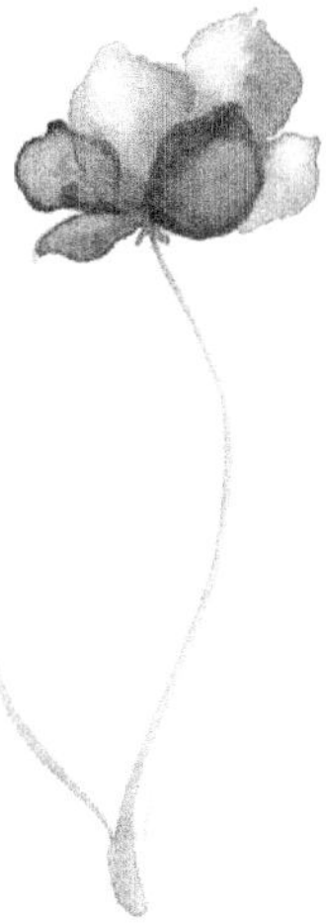

ISOLATION THOUGHTS

Many days I have been left behind.
The world has been cruel, not very kind.
My children have left, they're on their own.
Now I sit here at home all alone.
The winter's storm has made its bed.
So much snow I need a sled.
Oh long wintery nights, and early to bed.
Makes you face another sunrise, with such dread.
I thought my senior years would be full of joy.
Wow, I so wrong, boy, oh boy.
My heart and home now feels empty without my wife
The Covid 19 virus has taken her life
We had planned so many wonderful things to do
But when the pandemic surfaced I had to bid a fond adieu
My empty heart hurts so very much
My children and grandchildren don't even keep in touch
They say we'll text you and that's a laugh
They know I have no idea about that, they haven't even asked
Being in Isolation is a daunting thing
Well, some hope has arrived, it almost Spring.

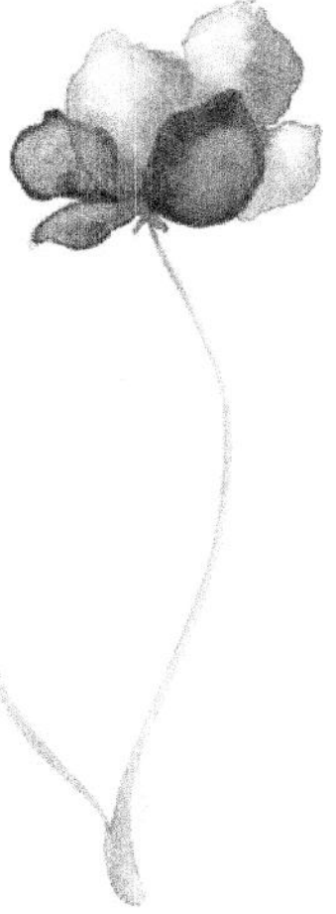

BEHIND CLOSED DOOR

Love is life in all aspects
If you miss love
You miss life's beautiful secret
Love is the most beautiful thing in this world
Like magic, it's full of surprises
But now comes the greatest violation of a person
Under the guise of love
Love is given within condition
I may be wrong with my conviction
But I'm sick and tired of this seclusion
My mind goes bleak and weary
Thoughts of doubt and fears
For those who are far away
It seems I'm in the middle of nowhere
Can't find ways to overcome fears
I started questioning my existence
If I can be there for their convenience
Make them feel more comfortable with my presence
And with all life's obstacles
Leave behind something tangible
With my final years,
Beautiful memories will remain
Even in their wildest dreams
Behind closed doors
I missed all the people I adore
Touching, holding, and smiling at each other
Jokes and laughter linger
Echoes gaily in the air
How long will I stay in loneliness
Is it forever, away from the others
Like a long hunt with no prey

Life turns into sadness and dismay
Counting days into years
With my eyes shedding tears

MANY FACETS OF SOLITUDE.

Not so courteous...
Like a guest not gracious.
Will not knock on your door...
Arrives uninvited from a mystical shore.
It will not see whether your tresses are still black
Or you have a silvery grey streak...
I have seen how a young bride used to sit in isolation near a window...
Sipping tea after tea gazing at her lonely shadow.
Waiting for her beloved, with the wind she hums
How sparrows become her chums...
How she waits for a first star to appear in the twilight skies.
How she counts stars till the next dawn rise.
And her spouse drapes in olive guards the border
In the silence of the night, the nightingale and the moon sobs for them together.
I have seen even amid the crowd
With kin and kith, it shows its clout.
In the cacophonies too, it exists.
It is all about a state of mind, one cannot resist.
If your beloved and dear ones are not homely.
With them, you can feel like an island lonely.
Both boon and bane, such an enigmatic...
For many it is charismatic.
Many cuddles loneliness for creative glows
Love to keep my distance from fake shows.
And in journey final, when we have to leave all other medallions
It shall walk beside us like a true companion.

Copyright Mousumee Baruah

I LIVE ALONE

I live alone at the shore of my longings.
With the trembling courage that sustains me to live with joy and optimism.
I was immersed in the silence within my soul
I have no friend but my sorrow.
But there's no tomorrow to offer me love and compassion.
I don't know where I belong, Neither do I know who belongs to me
So I write and try to remember there's still love in this world
I write about me
About the changing seasons of
Hello and goodbye.
Pain and sorrows of emptiness.
And memories that I hold onto.
Thanks! God is with me and HE is my only friend,
In this world and the next

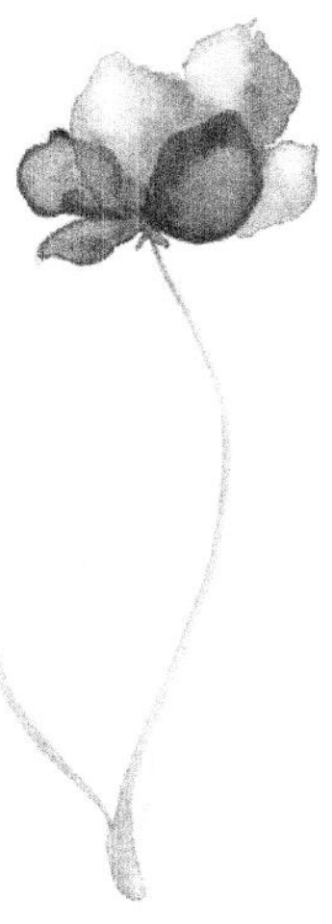

EARTH IS VAST AND BEAUTIFUL

Earth is vast and beautiful

With tweeting birds,

dancing butterflies

Green Meadows and above the blue sky,

Cheerful kids and creatures

But I'm isolated inside

He left me with all the dreams

Seized into the darkness

I'm alone with sadness

Passed decades

Copyright Faseela Mv

ALONE AND LONELY

Alone and lonely, not a soul to turn to
My twilight years spent just seeing through
The haze of a life filled with love and laughter
Those days of sunshine bringing cheer...
Now, old and irrelevant, my life spent
Senses too depriving me of their essence
Counting my days of solitude
Reminiscing the days of rectitude...
Cast aside as burdensome
Isolated from everyone
This room is my prison
My thoughts and emotions imprisoned...
Unable to express
Unwanted in excess
Life in distress
Feelings compressed Sentiments perplexed...
I gaze into the farther realms of nothingness
That is seemingly in stillness
Not a leaf stirs
Nor a butterfly flutters...
I gaze into the yonder heavens' of emptiness
My eyes panning the extent of the vastness
No fragrant whiff of flowers to cheer
Nor chirp or chatter of birds on trees near...
No one to sing a song for me
None to bring some pitter-patter spree
No giggles and babbles of folks around
Nor a kind word or a compassionate sound...
A vegetable I am, just living in my space
An old man in, ' ISOLATION', confined to his pace
No greetings or good wishes, or showers of surprise

Nor any sympathetic words of grace and joy...
Those companions and nostalgic colorful days
Sweet nothings and willy-nilly ways
Some romantic and carefree times to recall
Memories and memoirs fading into the walls...
Not many twilights left to see afterall
Waxing and waning evocations tall
Foggy perceptions and wobbly stroll
Time just hanging heavy waiting for the Heavens' call.

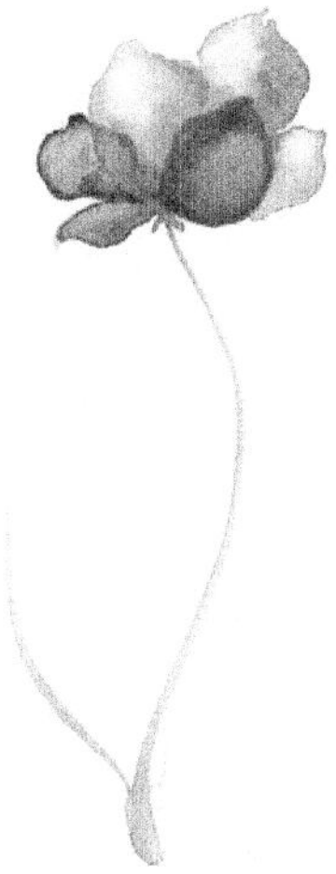

IT TAKES ONLY A REASON

Isolation
It takes only a reason
To come out of your comfort zone
To outshine or to deem
Decide whichever means
Everything can work out
When you pour your heart out
Every problem has a solution
If we carry out with proper calculation
If life has knocked you down
Stand up with more strength facing miseries that prolonged
Don't give up on anything
Chase your dreams and start living
It is ok to feel frustrated
It is ok to get distracted
Even when you feel dejected
Think again a reason why you started
Everything is hidden in you
Just take a look through
Give yourself some time alone
To figure out your inner voice
Not every time everything matters
Don't let your dreams shatter
If you can utilize sometime for yourself
You will be able to achieve your goals at any cost

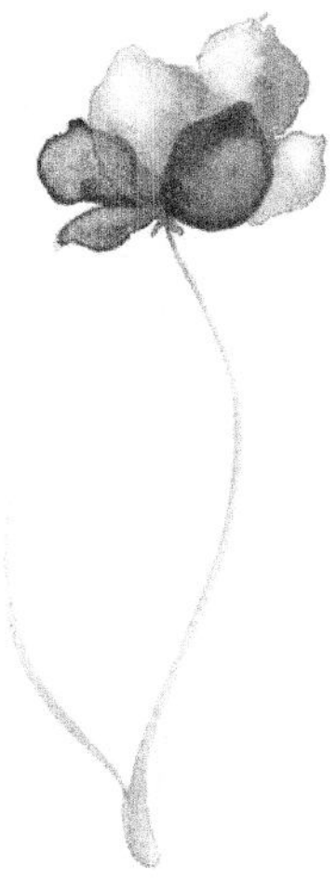

Copyright Alifya Kothari

RETIRED BUT NOT TIRED

Tired and retired are two important words
Pointers to old age, a different world
For so many years I worked, slogged
Life now must enjoy, fulfill desires for which I worked.
At the retirement party, all asked how I'll pass time
I smiled, told them to fulfill my dreams, which chime
On my children, never be a burden due to my health
Look after my health as health is wealth.
Keep me busy, take a wife on a trip
Before we become preys, caught in old age's grips
Know about my country, pursue my hobby
Instead of sitting and enjoy in the lobby.
There is no time to waste or do things in haste
Think before you speak, look before you leap
There is so much, to do, have up to date knowledge, supportive people to reach
I'll be in touch, my friends, now let's enjoy, the eats.
As he enjoyed the farewell party, he thought
One part of the journey is over
Now I'll take my wife on a trip to South and North
I booked tickets, for North.
We traveled to Hardware, Simla, Delhi Kashmir
Returned home, for rest, then visited South
Temples we visited, good food enjoyed
Brought for all handicrafts, gifts as souvenirs.
Six months we enjoyed holidays, journeys
Staying in home, for few days so bored
The wife looked, relaxed, fresh after the trip her face glowed
Sons daughters, married, settled, no longer needed a guide.
Time on wings flew I worked with environmental groups planted trees

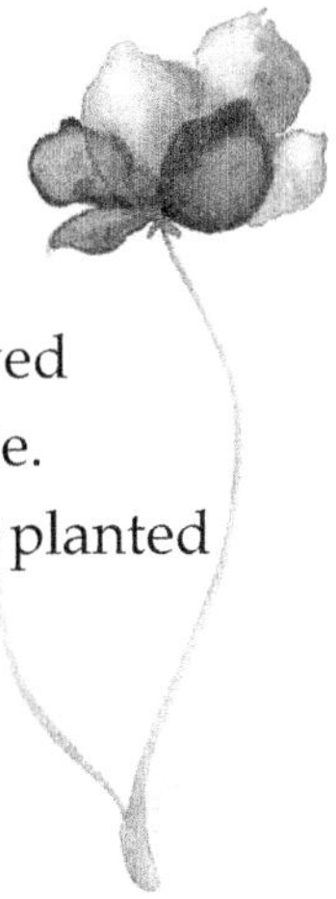

With young students time passed in glee
Wife passed to another side
My children no longer need a guide.
I don't interfere with anyone, I enjoy, survive
At festivals I invite, sons, daughter's family, give them gifts, great pleasure, I derive
Not dependent on them, not burden on them, I live in joy.
Young boys, girls, of my environment group, ideas we share enjoy.
They visit me we eat, I call grand-children we all eat, food together
I have money, good health which is a must in old age
Money is honey, sweetens old age makes people love you forever
Without money, an aged person feels, helpless and caged.

The last moments of living in hope
seeing every spark in the eyes of others,
in every sigh a fake smile and anyone's reaction.
Last movements and loss of breath,
for a new hour of existence
struggling with severe pain
breathing, sadness in the eyes
dearest
I still hope
maybe just a request
almighty God
to fulfill my last wishes,
to return my will_
my great love in
struggle with breathing,
last air force,
living for a new morning
, sunrise-sunset.
Love and hope keep
I make you stronger
still, live, just one more day!
And then ... you give up the fight,
You are not alone.!
The arrival of thousands of people
in a world of all colors, races, and religions,
fighting for life,
in the fight against "Kovid 19"
Everyone lives in fear and hope,
we are not alone!
A new challenge, a will, holds you back
so strong
It's not the end!
Another one is coming,
hundreds, thousands of new patients are coming,
All different a
all from Kovid 19

Someone is surrendering
with severe torment
without fighting for a new day,
They are dying slowly
losing last hope.
Quietly leaving a message
to all of you;
Stay, don't give up,
take care hope deep inside !!
Believe it!
I hope Nada lifts you,
helps you
in combat, it strengthens you
in temptations
until the end of life

Copyright Sabaheta Eta Mersimi

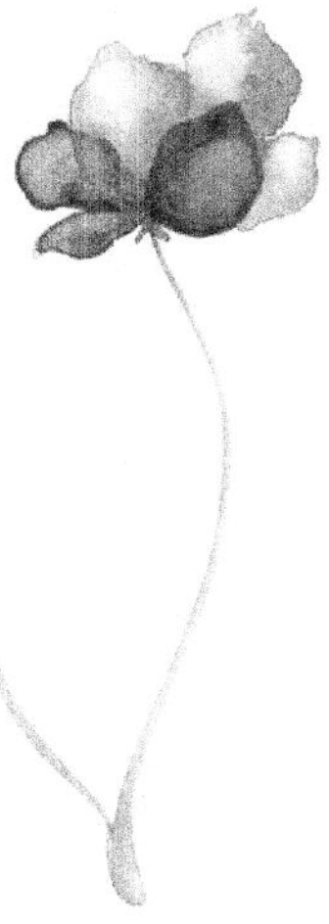

CHAPTER 4

MASKED

Quotes

Even at the rise and fall of the sun, being forced to have you tinted in between my nose

Copyright Chinagorom Samuel

"The Gods of Air --enchanting breath of life, inside window lair. Crying, awakening in the mere sunshine day."

Copyright Daniel Miltz

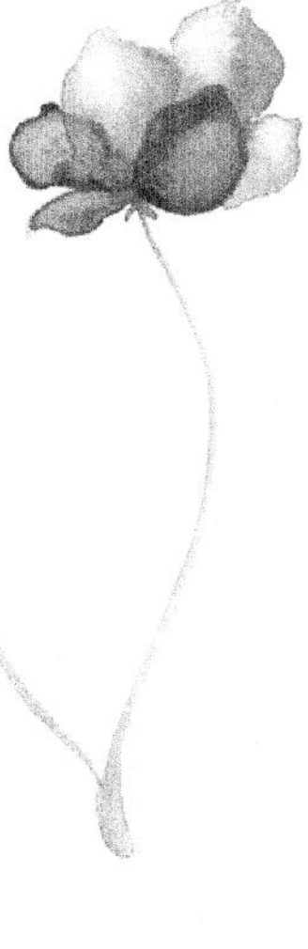

The world has been cloaked in fear

We must not venture far

Our touch is only through a glass

Many barriers to connection

I hope this all soon will pass

"The day by day, I adore you, saying, seeing you, never so beautiful."

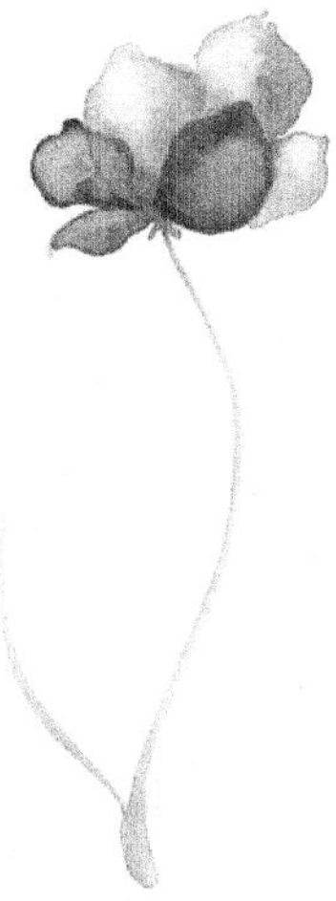

The earth tilted on her axis

Vanity masked by festering fear

A hungry invisible monster

Devouring humanity relentless

Rendering them breathless

Shattering their hope of normality

Copyright Vee Maistry

How invisible love sign seen

During the Corona pandemic scene

Awaiting for you O my dear sweet honey

On this unforgettable Valentine's □ just for love redeem.

Copyright Dr.Satish C.Srivastava

Contagion throughout the world

Limits human connection

Hide from the unknown but

Know my love penetrates

All obstacles to reach you

Copyright Vicki Hangren Hauler

Waiting at the window with my mask.

Getting rid of Corona is quite a task.

Looking after loved ones held dear.

The end of this pandemic is very near.

Copyright Ferguson Frances Lylia

Invisible fear covers whole azure.

Hope- the sanguine sun will give,

the ray of life to beat all dangers.

A spiritual connection to God-

for seeking the pristine golden abode.

Copyright Afrose Saad

Waiting to throw away the mask,

Waiting to go out into the sun,

Waiting to feel the breeze on my face.

Copyright Vasudha Pansare

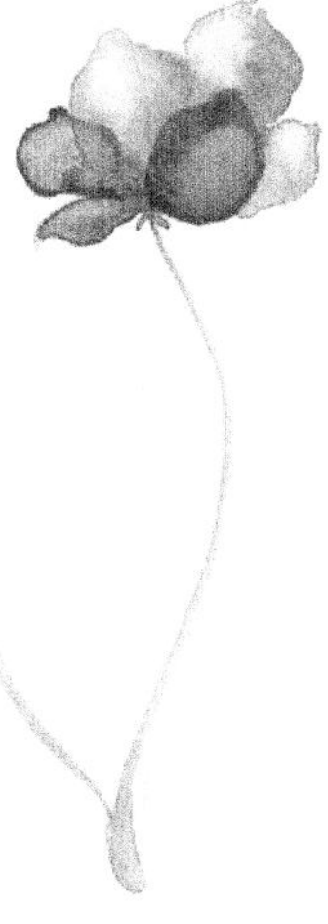

The vision is unclear and virtual,

The lacunae that underlay the future,

Amid storms and tempest,

A kin breakthrough that beams the glass,

Isolation my home.

Sun rays Host,

I am never alone.

Pandemic a matter of tone,

Silence comes.

Hoping the virus will vanish,

Hoping the vaccine will vanquish,

Hoping I can go out without fear,

Hoping for some joy and cheer.

Copyright Vasudha Pansare

Sun rays do not Shield Hope, each new morning
lights to the right beginning.

Copyright Maria Elvira Fernandes Correia

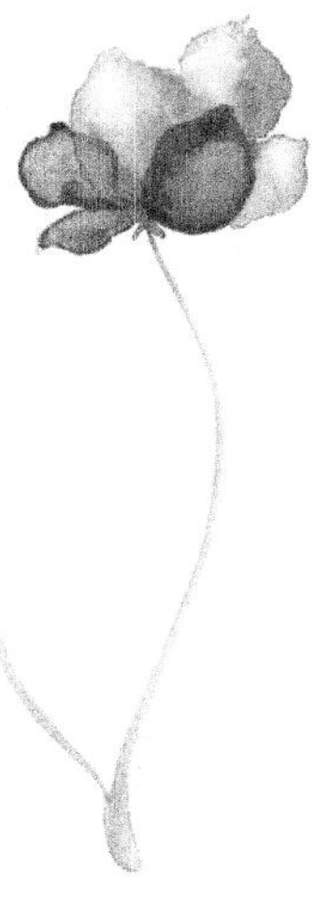

Mundohem me imagjinate te te prek,
nderkaq qe ti je larg, nderkaq
qe nuk me lejon kjo maske
e ky virus vrastar.

Copyright Ollga Farmacistja

The window of clearance of nowadays mayhem
still obscured, and the sweet smell of air still with
a virus, so to all keep safe for your health sake.

Copyright Ency Bearis

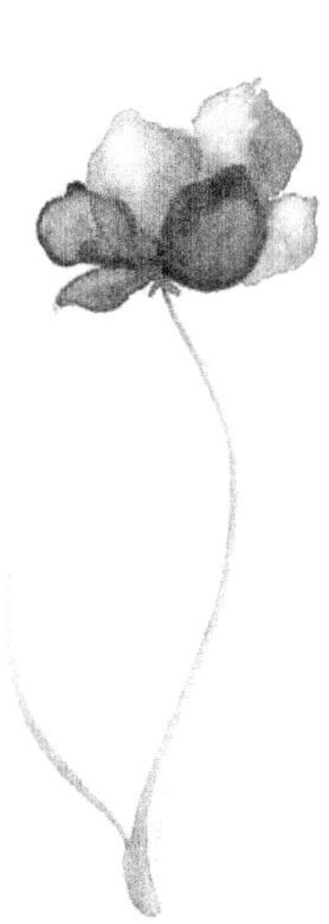

This vivacious gaze at the glass

Depicts how well the mask

Adorns the down part of the face

To halt the inhaling of unhealthy substances
including the corona virus

Skinuću crnu masku sa lica

Da bih mogla dohvati nebo

I vinuti se pod oblake k'o ptica

Da istražim porijeklo pandemije

I način da živimo zdravije.

Bota e gjitha u gjunjëzua

Një maskë e vendosur mbi buzët e tua

Cdo gjë e bukur u ndryshua

Kur do vijë ajo ditë vallë?

Jetën ta jetojmë si më pare

Copyright Silva Alisa Xhemo

No matter what the situation we have at the moment the sun still shines to give us some light that gives us the inspiration to hope for a new tomorrow.

Copyright Estelita Sagum

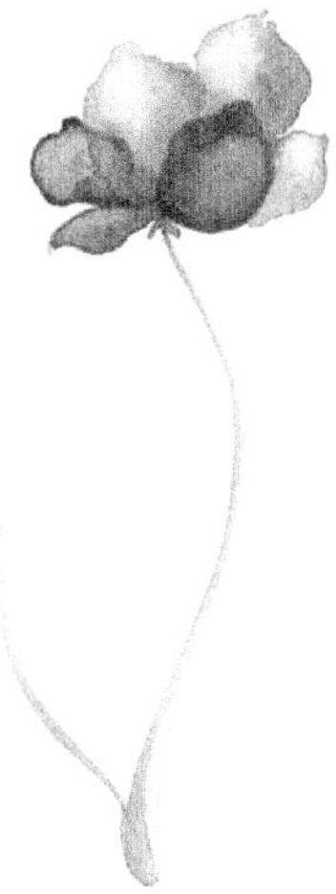

I may still keep the mask, lest I got contaminated
but I have to push the curtains and conjure the
beams of sun-carrying whisks of hope.

Copyright Sehma Helaa

As the sun rises and its rays penetrate window
blinds, so shall the hope for the end to covid 19
pandemics be realized!

Copyright Muhammad Aminu Hassan

Today is a chance to see the future so let every moment be the hope by taking care of yourself.

Copyright Daisie Fpartido Vergara

The darkness will end just like the day and tomorrow we will be facing the light.

Copyright Daisie Fpartido Vergara

Quarantine and social distancing are not separations after all;

As the sun rays touch us from a distance so as love binds us all as children of God.

Copyright Ellen Retoma

Just a deep breath,

Just a glimpse of sunrise,

Few more waiting

A new dawn is breaking

The world will be unmasked.

Copyright Ellen Retoma

A new day approaches

Beaming its hope that

One day we shall be

Unmasked to enjoy

The beauty of the world again

Copyright Sarah Ramphal

The unseen enemy keeps us away from our loved ones... Restricted to touch and be near to them.

But our love will keep us alive and hopeful to everything will turn out alright

Copyright Lucy Abellana Mendiola

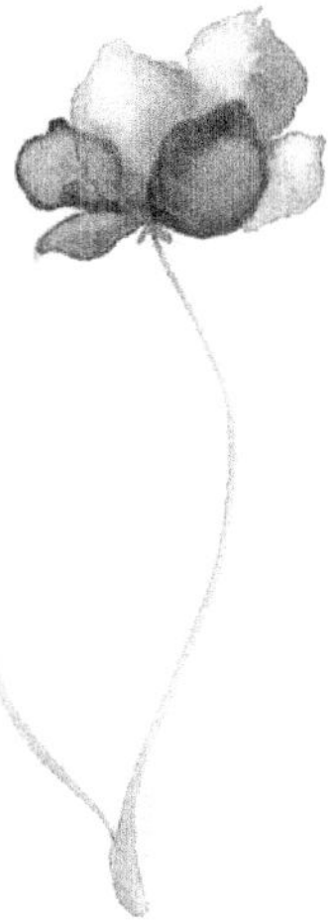

Mask protects the concealed hopes and fears,

but the light will be the guiding shield

against all odds.

Let the world feel the universal healings,

Love in action, faith in motion.....

Copyright Ninfa Vasquez Mateo

Present the world only your eyes

Let your soul from its window prance

Shielded noses, covered mouths

No more well-designed snoots, kissable pouts

Equality between swan and mouse.

Copyright Myrna Tejada

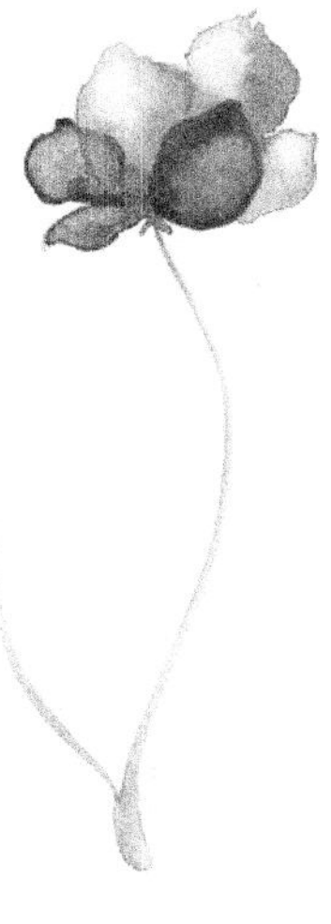

Some run and hide from the dark,

While others fail in the light.

Losing their souls through the day

And becoming zombies at night.

Some prepare for battle,

And line up just like cattle.

Others hide behind their mask,

And Prey that it won't last.

Feeding on each other's fear,

Unable to get to near.

Some run without looking

Towards their own personal doom's,

Whilst others die

All alone in their rooms.

So Prey, Prey, Prey

But remember

Viruses can't hear

And don't care

OK...

Copyright Phillip Gibson

The sun rays are beckoning

me to start a new day. A day full of hope and
positive vibes inspiring to walk through all odds
of life with a smile.

Copyright Aruna Bose

Here I'm standing in front of protective glass and
musk on my face but one can't stop from your
remembrance.

Copyright Rajbanshi Manmohan

We stay indoors like prisoners,

We are bored staring at the four corners,

We want freedom out of this quarantine,

Not even masks can prevent kissing this valentine.

We cannot touch except through the window glass,

This virus has made everything a mess,

Even without wearing a glove,

I feel the emotional message of your love.

Masked those feelings never to let know what behind it stays

The cavern of thoughts is treasured there safe.

Copyright Dr. Ekta kaur Sachdeva

As we showed our dependency on artificiality,

Mother Earth responded proportionally,

Caged us in our home's, with masks and sanitizers,

Exemplified, that to every action, there equal and opposite reaction.

Copyright Mrinalini Saurav Kakkar

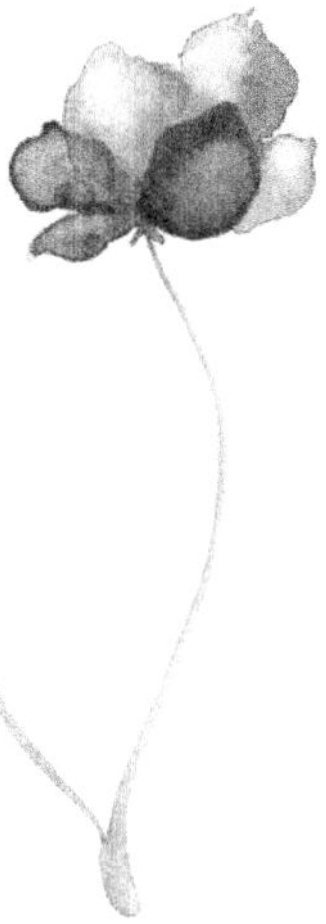

When hopes despair,

Clouds of fear hover,

Wait for the light to shine,

Don't seek outside,

It lies somewhere within,

All you need to trust your instincts.

Copyright Mrinalini Saurav Kakkar

This bright lighting kissing my window will melt my mask and get me out one day, for sure!

Copyright Deepa Vankudre

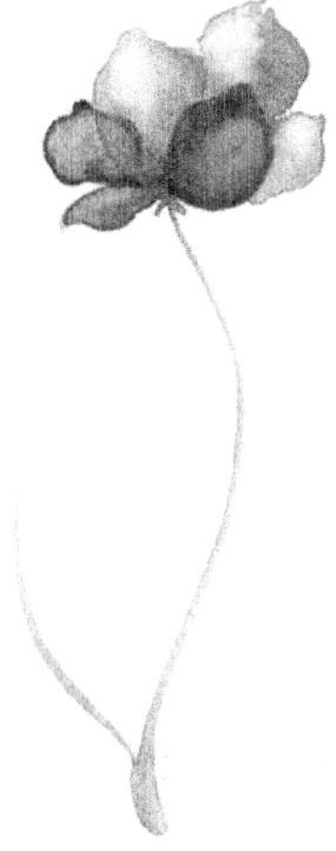

Touching the shimmering light

Hopes after seeing the dawn

Emptiness will be tomorrow's memory

Shielding with faith and love

Almighty God is healing the world.

Copyright Ninfa Vasquez Mateo

The atmosphere outside my home is obscure

But the end is always pure

Copyright Rrafika Rangwala

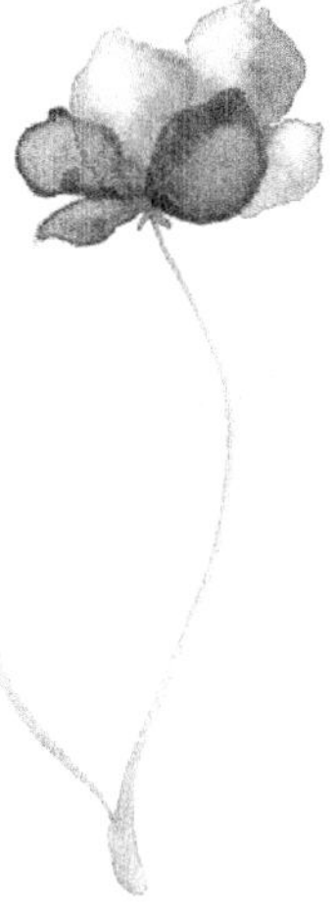

Waiting for you dear eagerly

My eyes expanding up to the horizon

But unable to get a glimpse of you

Many question marks on my sweet emotion.

Copyright Ashutosh Meher

Ephemeral

Serenading with muted soul-strings

That roasted orange fluffiness

Horizon quilt, an embrace

Trickling tale from the sliced breeze

Reflective eon

Ephemeral

Dews in trance

Opal

Mist

Copyright Jyoti Nair

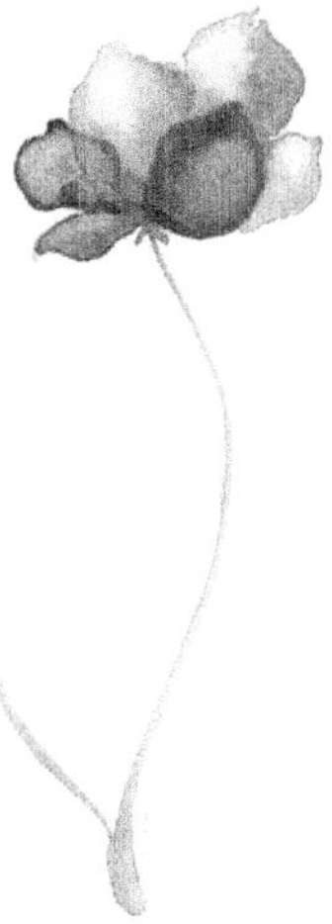

Covid forced us to stay apart

So cruel fate is, oh my darling dear

Still awaiting you with all heartfelt precautions

When life is divinity, whom we should fear ??

Copyright Ashutosh Meher

New Sun rises giving hopes to mankind,

end of despair happiness is just around the corner.

You've risen above all species, but don't forget to be kind.

Copyright Shikha Gupta

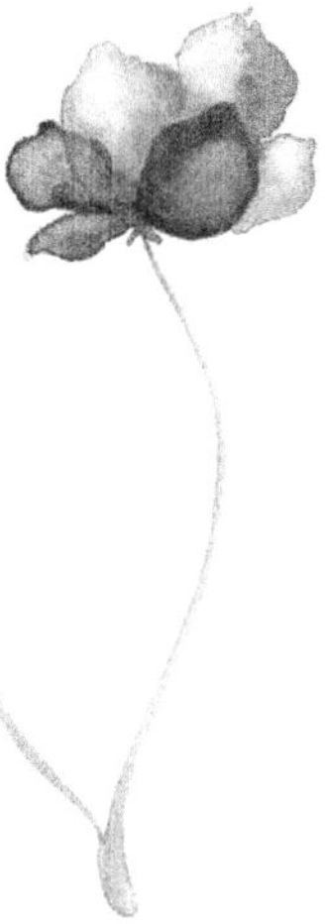

We are waiting for new dawn after months of suppression

We have survived so let us be thankful for his creation

Copyright Dr Harmeet Kaur Bhalla

The pandemic outside has taught a lesson that is forgotten otherwise that pure air and sunlight are the necessities that should be conserved for getting them to suffice.

Copyright Anu Gupta

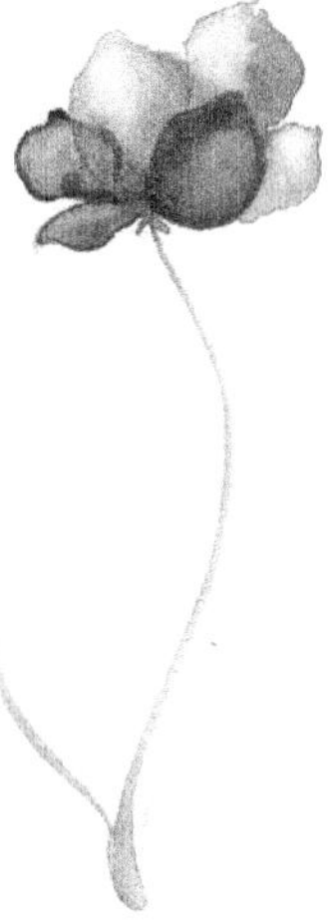

You feel like you are dying a thousand death today.

But what if a happy life is another death away.

Copyright Stephenite Orlando

Wears mask, longingly looks out of the glass cage barrier, if only she could fly, reach to souls, breaking this cage, help them fight Corona Viruses, dangerous, rage.

Copyright Vinod Singh.

Far away from family,
Taking care of patients quarantined
My love for my countrymen
Is much more than any Valentine.

Copyright Bhawna Himatsinghani

Wearing a mask and gloves is not suffice
To keep away from being infected
take care and maintain distance and wash hands!

Copyright Meenakshi Dwivedi

In a tumultuous, chaotic world that's ablaze, be like the sun and enrich with healing rays.

Copyright Meenakshi Dwivedi

God's bright, white light will make everything alright - have faith!

Copyright Meenakshi Dwivedi

The masked face is always a saviour. It solves life's major problems, gradually clearing the obscurity and preparing you to welcome the light.

Copyright Amrita Mallik

A woman always feels safe behind the mask, consciously averting misty scenes, and stealthily snatching some moments for herself.

Copyright Amrita Mallik

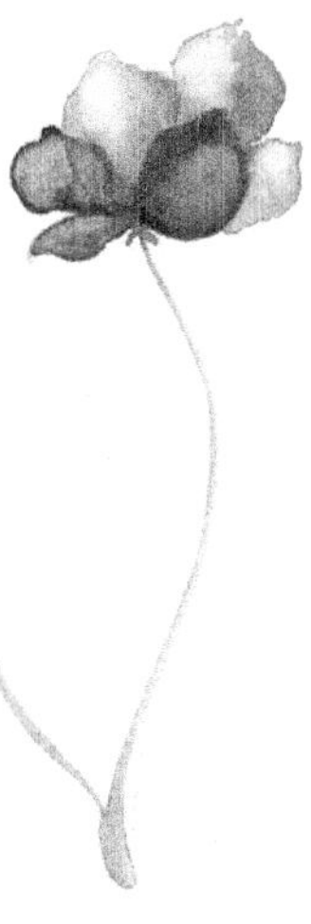

Under the mask, she masked her feelings for the return of her lover.

Copyright Amrita Lahiri Bhattacharya

The dawn commemorates the beginning of a new day bringing with it new hopes and aspirations.

Copyright Hema Mordani

Look to the window and let the light go to your heart. The sun is all.

Copyright Alexandra Oana Călin

Any virus can let you down if you have hope and love in your heart.

Copyright Alexandra Oana Călin

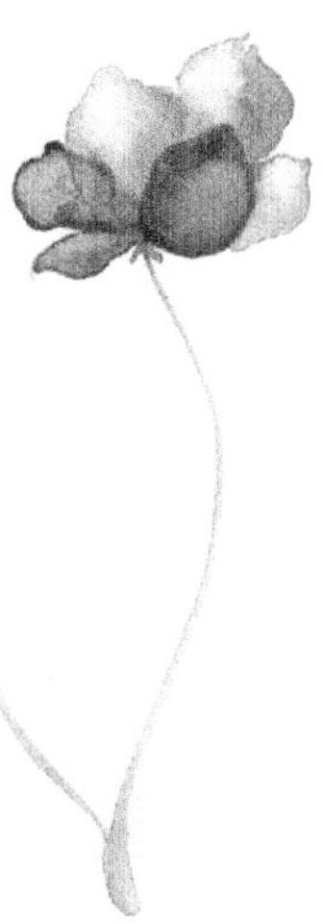

The pandemic has taught us to be compassionate with those who wear a mask as protection every day, people with cancer!

Copyright Amb. Maid Corbic

Different perceptions of living I recognized after being Quarantined

Copyright Alifya Kothari

I hope these golden rays bestows new beginnings in my life

Copyright Alifya Kothari

Entrapped to escape, masked to mitigate, praying for the pandemic to end, awaiting an answer to the agony, a panacea to a panic-stricken world.

Copyright Nandita De

Next time we meet O sun!

Hope this mask is gone

And world has recovered

From the dark dungeon of COVID.

Copyright Varsha Madhulika

A prisoner of my mind

A fugitive of some kind

From a monster in the wind

At this glass, I stay behind

Still, my breath is hard to find

But my eyes can see beyond

Copyright Denis Maira

With my present mask of deep understanding, I
wave my tumultuous past a permanent goodbye.

Copyright Babita Saraf Kejriwal

Wearing protective gear is

a must,

The latest fashion is wearing a mask,

But the mystical light of the Lord,

The ultimate salvation of

the world.

Copyright Ben-hur Sistoso

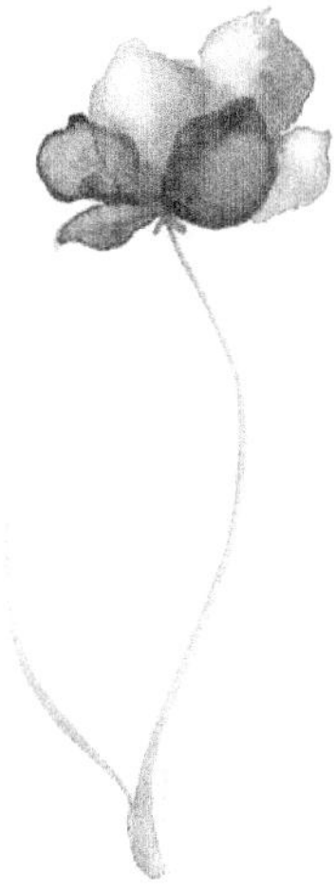

Close, yet distant;

When a heartbeat

Stands quarantined

With a love to touch,

But afraid; the social

Laws barricaded!

Copyright Victor Wesonga

Masks, hide all her painful smiles, but tears still flow down, missing her dears ones her lonely soul cries, holding out her hand in quarantine.

Copyright Vinod Singh

Trapped in our zone, hoping for hope yet to come.

Copyright John Carlo Miguel Perez

Sometimes deep evolution requires a temporary disguise, quite scary and heart throbbing, to fathom the way things are, life is - only to find a sun of newness hidden inside me.

Copyright Priti Dhopte

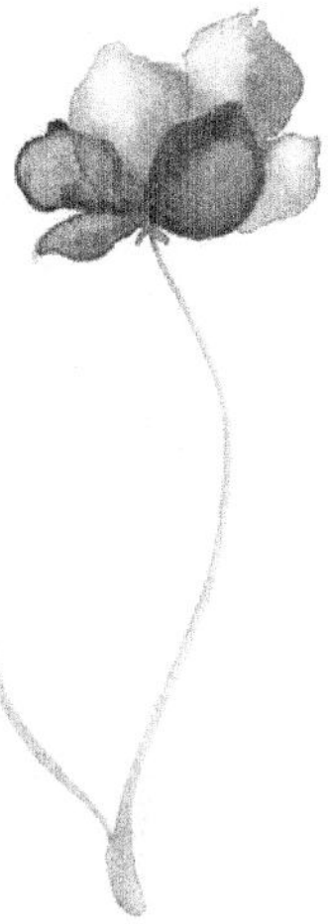

Every morning brings hope with newer rays
for people surviving a disturbed life

The glimmer of hope seen

A soul confined long

Soon to heave a sigh of relief outside
dithering to go masked or not.

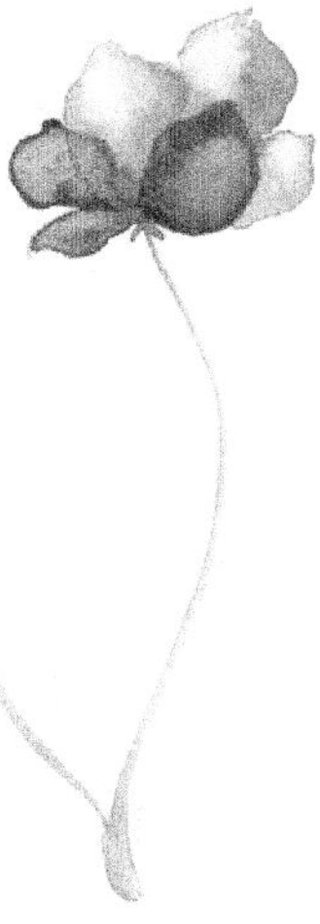

The pain of loneliness in quarantine days,
separation from family and the hollow gaze,
sad and broken self behind the mask,
accepting the new normal is not an easy task.

Copyright Swapna Das

Ray of hopes in the mind
to breath fresh air without a mask,
Ray of hopes in the eyes
to see green nature around,
humanity and love among people.

Copyright Veena Kumari

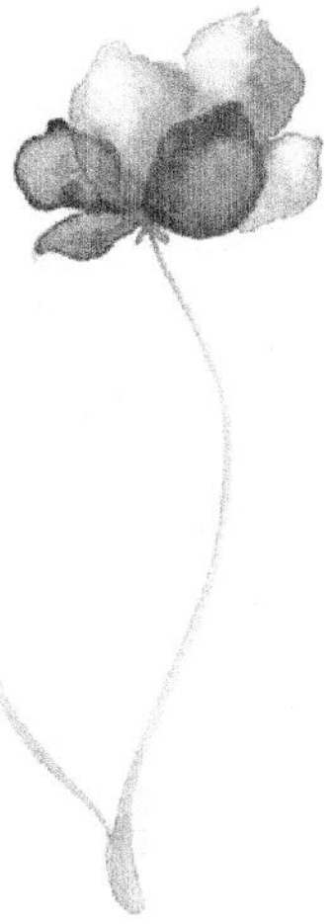

I'm accustomed to looking

Through the glass of the window,

Even before the pandemic, for

A glimpse of your passing shadow

Copyright Sudha Dixit

A few sun rays are filtering

Through my windowpane,

Let's talk of atmosphere and

Intense craving to fly again.

Copyright Sudha Dixit

The window is not the only barrier between us.

Donning a mask is now a must.

I hope my eyes convey how much I miss our idyllic dusks.

Copyright Leena Ritisha Auckel

A little sunrise in the early days brings in a reflection of beautiful glitters

Copyright Chosen Samuel

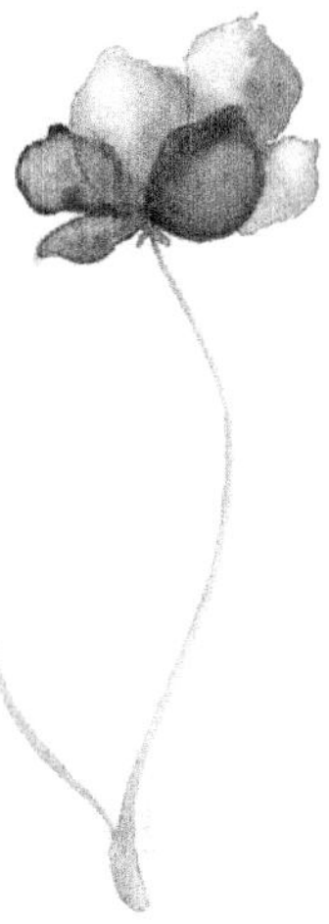

Through the one whole of the many pieces, there stands the sun - the hope and assurance of a new beginning.

Copyright Agu Samuel Chukwuemerie

Trapped in a parallel world created by adversity. Eyes convey powerlessness, despair, and sorrow, diluted by ever-present hope.

Copyright Margaret Karim

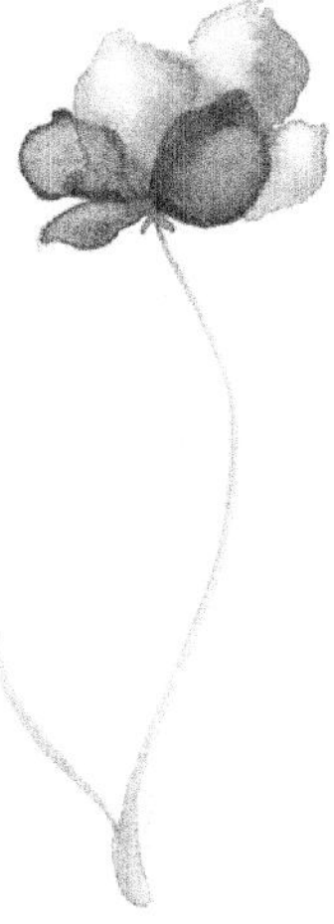

I am waiting for that sunrise that would bring a bloom to my paradise.....

Till then, let the fight to survive to go on, and

let's find our way back home.....

Use of the drug

to preserve eternity

is only at your risk.

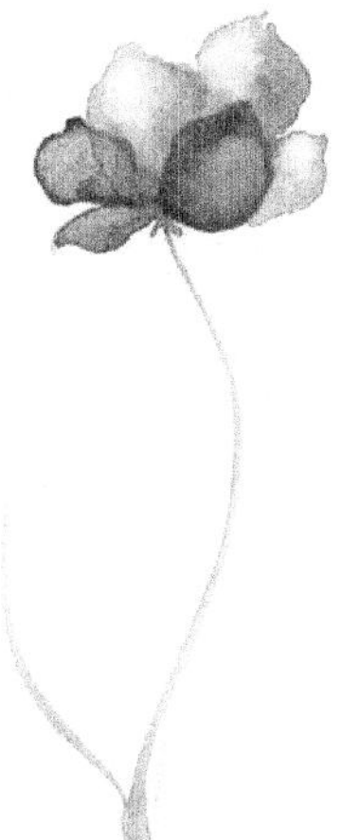

Laughter is in me because the cries created by loneliness,

I finally deafened myself with the vaccine.

Copyright Dijana Uherek Stevanovic,

As far as my eyes can see

nothing should limit the body

it has the ability and all capability

to help others with all humility.

Copyright Mildred De Joya Par

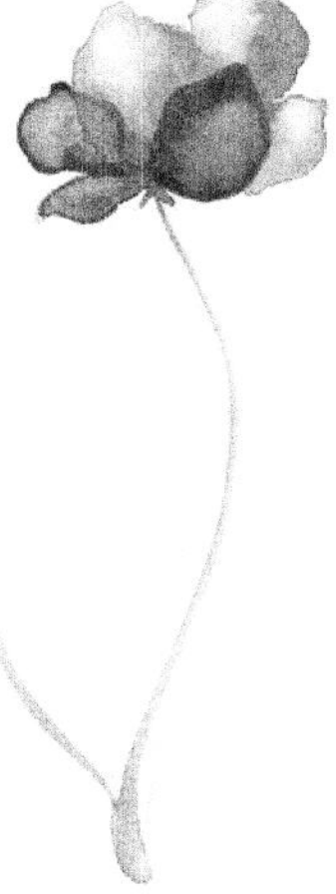

Mine is like Waiting for Godot that shall come into my haven. after the dusk. I gaze winkles, expectant, with faith for a sunny day to open my mask.

Copyright Narayan Maikap

Childhood was enjoyable for a ferocious mask;

But old age by an innocent one to avoid health risk.

Copyright Dr. Amiya Rout

Mask: a false appearance;

Mask: a means of self-surveillance.

Copyright Dr. Amiya Rout

Oh! beauty

To see the seagulls hopping on the twigs of light

Done cannot be through

My naked eye, blind, unaware

My stab of anguish ...

Bind in the windowpane

Copyright Erlinda G Tisado

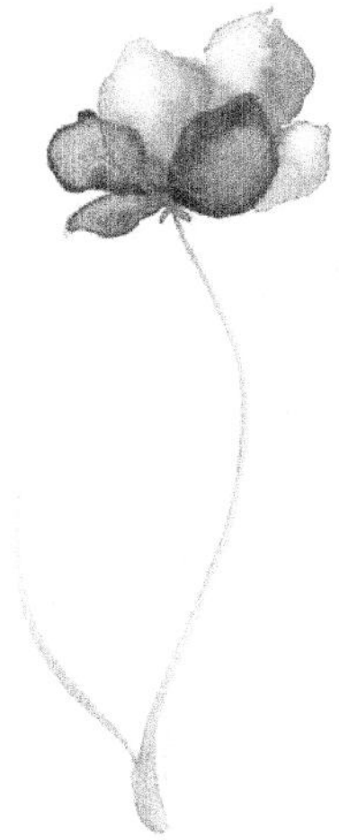

"Oh! my love.....

Unawares

Just a spiralizing thoughts

Anguish; tenderness

My gazed raked, scintillating

My blindness vigorously protesting

A riffle of panic towards silence

Gazing upon a dream

To see through "

Copyright Erlinda G Tisado

Old ways won't open new doors of life

Choose to move forward into a new normal.

Copyright Sudha Rani Pati

Accept the new normal of a life

Unmask your hopes and aspirations like the rising sun which radiates light after a night

Copyright Sudha Rani Pati

It's in the toughest moments that we find our true selves, in silence and solitude there's little room for anything else... we are all in this together.

Copyright Vee Barnes

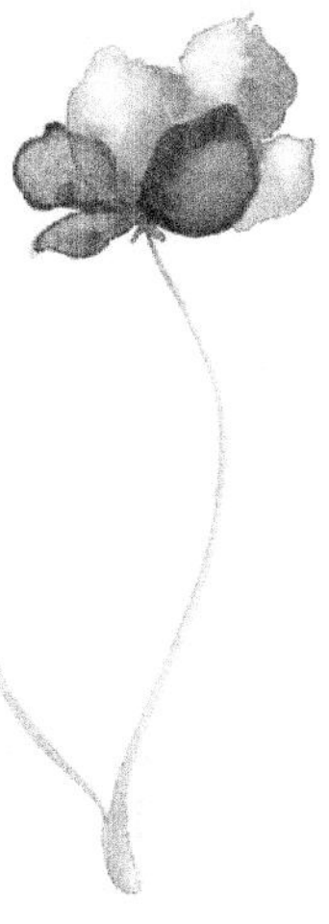

Divided not by walls but by love, we follow health protocols, considering every reason to ease a deadly situation

Copyright Ulma Taboada

Addiction recovery begins with a hope that can instantly fill up the emptiness inside. It's not an illness but staying true to yourself is a part of the battle.

Copyright Kanisha Shah

Addiction recovery for those who struggle in isolation is an ongoing process of growing and healing mentally, spiritually, emotionally, and physically.

Copyright Kanisha Shah

This sunlight kissing the window will melt my mask and let me out, for sure!

Copyright Deepa Vankudre

Printed in Great Britain
by Amazon

60357927R00237